T0157062

POOJAMMA

POOJAMMA

THE WOMAN WHO REDEFINED WOMANHOOD

M C RAJ

PARTRIDGE
A Penguin Company

Copyright © 2013 by M C Raj.

ISBN: Hardcover   978-1-4828-0103-3
            Softcover   978-1-4828-0102-6
            Ebook   978-1-4828-0101-9

All rights reserved. No part of this book may be used or reproduced by any means, graphic, electronic, or mechanical, including photocopying, recording, taping or by any information storage retrieval system without the written permission of the publisher except in the case of brief quotations embodied in critical articles and reviews.

Because of the dynamic nature of the Internet, any web addresses or links contained in this book may have changed since publication and may no longer be valid. The views expressed in this work are solely those of the author and do not necessarily reflect the views of the publisher, and the publisher hereby disclaims any responsibility for them.

Cover Picture by Preetam C Raj

Partridge books may be ordered through booksellers or by contacting:

Partridge India
Penguin Books India Pvt.Ltd
11, Community Centre, Panchsheel Park, New Delhi 110017
India
www.partridgepublishing.com
Phone: 000.800.10062.62

Dedicated To

Jyothi, The Indomitable Woman Power

CHAPTER ONE

'One would mistake it for a huge funeral procession of the President of any country. People were still jostling one another, as the procession kept moving. Leading the procession was a young attractive girl Kala. I followed closely behind her. While followers carried the body of Poojamma, Kala was carrying the legacy left behind by Poojamma. All her life Kala had followed her without arguing and dissenting. She almost worshiped Poojamma as her deity. So did all the people of that big district in Karnataka, India. That is how a frail looking young Pooja came to be named by her followers as Poojamma. The surging crowd bore living witness to the mind-blowing popularity that Poojamma enjoyed during her lifetime. She did not live to see that people would assemble in large numbers even after her death. She had seen many such processions when she lived. One public call to her followers was enough. People would assemble to have one more glimpse of their deity. But now she was following all of them, silently without being able to see the last bit of emotions they were pouring out for her. She advised all of them to become the subjects of their history and they did become. Now she was a mere object in their hands. A group of women were uncontrollably sobbing all along and were berating and beating their breasts in uncontainable agony. Another group of women were continuously singing the 'Sobana', a local form of mourning without being disturbed by everything that went on around them.'

Nina could not continue writing any further. Tears flew down her cheeks without any control. It took a long time for her to come back and sit to resume her writing. In the meantime she went and had a wash and a hot cup of coffee. But it was not enough to manifest her grief at the loss of

Poojamma whom she had almost come to worship along with the people of Karnataka.

It was one full year since she rushed to India to attend the funeral of Poojamma who led a tempestuous and eventful life. She took this long to gather herself into one piece of living flesh with a determination to write the story of Poojamma. Nina used to frequent India to meet Poojamma and spend days together in her house. Every time she returned to the US from Karnataka she used to be re-energized and would burst with boundless energy. But this time Nina came back with a heart that felt drained of all the resources of energy and was longing to be filled with energy. There were times when she felt that her heart had flown away with Poojamma in her last journey. She was groping all over her place.

Her coffee began to taste a bit salty. "Did I mix salt instead of sugar in my coffee?" she wondered and looked intently at the cup of coffee. The coffee laughed at her. It was when a drop of tears stood up out of the coffee that Nina realized that an overdose of tears had flown from her eyes to her cheek and found their way to the cup of coffee in front of her. She threw the coffee in the washbasin in the kitchen and opened the fridge. It was chill inside. Her hand withdrew from the fridge with a can of strong beer. Cold waves emanated from the fridge along with a heavy doze of melancholy that began to encircle her. On all such occasions she allowed alcohol to take a firm grip over her. Nina felt helpless at the loss of Poojamma though now it was more than a year. She was not alone. There was an ocean of depression that she saw in India after the disappearance of Poojamma.

Many men whom she encountered during the last visit for the anniversary of the death of Poojamma were swearing revenge. 'Is this what Poojamma would expect from you if she were alive?' Nina floored the men with just one simple question. She had the power of Poojamma filling every cell of her body. She could understand the anger that was welling up in those men. For the first time in their newfound life they tasted an irreconcilable defeat. After a year of the departure of Poojamma, Nina went back to her country with the faint happiness that she had prevented a possible chain of violence and mayhem among the followers of her most admired woman on earth.

Drowning herself with one more can of strong beer without realizing that in between the first and the second she had gulped down a few pegs of vodka, Nina slumped in the armchair. She still took courageous steps to wade through the ocean of depression that kept increasing its depth around her with the spirit that emanated from the beer cans.

Depressing memories rushed in wave after wave to have a sip from the can of Nina's beer. She was unable to brush aside the memory of the funeral she had witnessed a year back. She had asked for a special ticket to rush for the funeral of Poojamma. The flights were all full. But she went to the office of many airlines to squeeze herself in one of those open cubicles in the belly of the big bird. But the airlines turned her request down. 'Sorry madam, it is too late. We are too full.' Mechanized words from the fleshy lips of the airline staff. Just one of them had managed to extricate herself from the thralldom to machines. She suggested to Nina to give a try in Air India.

Nina was reluctant. But she had no other option either. The air in the US was always filled with harrowing stories of traumatic experiences passengers had with Air India. It was always the same about India. Just one bad experience was enough to fill the entire atmosphere with bad odor. Travelogues were filled with horrifying stories of US travelers to India. It was so easy to say and spread anything that one wanted about India. Indians in foreign countries succeeded to cloister themselves within their caste community and failed simultaneously to present a unified picture of Indians.

It did not take much time for the Americans to decipher the shallow depth of unity that existed among Indians. Many of them had imported their relatives into their countries from India and made them live there without mixing with other US dwellers. People were happy within their own caste community. They had enough customs and celebrations in their caste to keep them busy. They never felt any need for socializing as Americans did. They did not even care to learn English. Americans realized rather too soon that Indians were camouflaging their internal caste divisions with their occasional protest against discrimination. It was not necessary to divide Indians to govern. They were inherently divided. The British adage of 'divide and rule' seemed to have been borrowed from the caste divisions among Indians. In fact the British picked up many precious lessons of the Kautilyan principles of governance from India and only much later did the West see the rise of people like Machiavelli.

People in the office of Air India were more courteous than they normally were. The color of her skin did add much to the quotient of respect that she commanded. "Every Black wants to become a White ultimately" Nina vaguely remembered having read this from the book of Franz Fanon. The ultimate achievement in life for a Black is to become White. They listened with sympathy to all that Nina had to say of her predicament. The person in the counter excused herself saying all flights of Air India were fully booked. Her voice was not as convincing as she had heard in other airlines. Nina started pleading. It was of no use. Even as she was giving up the idea of making it for the funeral of Poojamma and took two steps back in slow motion, another officer came to the counter and asked what the matter was. An unknown radiance descended on Nina's face without her permission. It was as if the birds that had gone to sleep in darkness woke up to sing for brother Sun when he would arrive shortly. Nina had to go through the explanation exercise all over again. It was like a drill that she had to do when she was in school as a little girl. He listened to her till she completed and took aside the 'sitting' officer. Both of them came back and told her that they would accommodate her in the next flight. They took pains to inform her that they did it with much difficulty as an exception.

For a minute Nina stood there still gaping at both of them. The rays of the sun burst forth through clouds dissipating their resistance. The gush of vitamin from his rays energized the creatures beneath without any discrimination. Nina came back to life at the immediate possibility of jumping into Air and India to give a final farewell to Poojamma who had bidden her adieu to life itself.

Nina clearly recollected the speed with which she rushed back to her apartment, picked and packed a brief case ready to go. She left the high heels on her legs as they slipped out of her legs in her high speed. High heels and high speed did not go together. The inside of her suitcase was as disorganized as her room was. It was at sixes and sevens as usual. There was no one to seek order in the room except herself. It mattered very little then how the inside of the suitcase looked. She opened her passport to see that her multiple entry visa was still valid.

Nina's mind was least inclined to mind the commotion Indian passengers created in the plane. While waiting for the boarding announcement she was a bit amused at the number of passengers going to the counter to show their ticket and ask for explanations about the flight. The anxiety of flying long distance seemed to have overtaken them. The man at the desk was an exemplification of a woman's resilience. There was obvious excitement in the way some were howling at the top of their voice to their near and far ones to keep the luggage in the cabin above. Some of them already opened up packets of food that they had brought and began to share it among themselves. One Indian male had already occupied her seat. She saw stars at the roof of the plane and thought for a minute that she had no seat. That was the last thing she would want to do. She told the man that it was her seat. He vehemently argued that it was his seat. The airhostess rushed and looked at the boarding pass of both. She told the man that his seat was ten rows behind. He left without even a fake apology. Nina's lips stretched out a little in a reluctant smile despite the sorrow that surrounded her.

She was shocked a bit at the many seats that were lying vacant. As an airhostess went near, Nina asked her why there were so many vacant seats and the people in the Air India office told her that the flight was full. The airhostess explained with a broad smile that it was a Tuesday.

"Tuesday? What is the connection between the travel and Tuesday?" Nina asked in surprise. Normally she would have bottled up such surprises to let them loose in the presence of Poojamma. But now she was not alive to lap up her surprise-filled questions. The airhostess came in handy for Nina.

"Indians consider Tuesday as an inauspicious day, Madam. Many passengers cancel their flights in the last minute if it were possible for them to travel on another day." Said the airhostess.

"But I see many Indians in the flight today. Why are they traveling if Tuesday is an unlucky day?" Nina asked in her naiveté.

"Well not all Indians are like that. There are still some who cannot avoid the travel and you see them here. Many of them would have gone to a priest and paid him to say prayers that would ward off any evil on

Tuesday." The airhostess began to speak in her Indlish accent. Nina enjoyed it thoroughly. Nina shook her head a bit more violently than it was necessary to disapprove of such a thing.

The airhostess took serious note of the 'American' attitude of Nina's and she decided to hit back.

"Why are you shaking your head like that Mam? Look at the row of seats in this plane. There will not be 13th row. It is because you people do not like to sit on row 13. They do not make any plane with 13th row. All countries have one or other such superstitious beliefs Mam in spite of high level of education and claims of higher civilization." The airhostess seemed to be more erudite.

"Yes, you are right. I am sorry about that.' Nina said in profuse apology. 'Shut up you American bitch" was what Nina heard in her ears. She didn't want to acknowledge it to herself.

"That's ok Mam. It happens with all of us." The airhostess left to help the other passengers settle themselves well in their crammed up seats. Nina's eyes searched for the much needed sleep. But the noise in the plane did not allow them to find it. It was once again the same airhostess who came to Nina's rescue. The big bird had started roaring in the sky and was moving towards eternity. All the airhostesses got busy calming down the passengers with their choicest drinks. The same airhostess approached Nina with a big smile.

"What will you have Madam for your drink?" she was all politeness personified.

"Give me a glass of red wine please." One glass of wine followed another. Nina would have had ten if there were a chance. She wanted to drown all her sorrows in the wine glass. But it was not possible. Her eyes began to sing their song. Nina went into deep slumber and with that flew into a trance in her sleep.

"Mmmmma . . . ." 'The bellowing of a cow in the village was a normal sound in Guddahalli. But that day it was rhythmic as many cows followed suit one after another.'

'Guddahalli! It was unusually disturbed and full of commotion that day. There seemed to be a bizarre permeation of tension in the entire village. The air everywhere was quite tight. The trees stood still without shaking even one leaf. They were telling strange visitors that their hairs were standing up in tension by showing off their still leaves. Leaves stood still gazing at the empty space in the village. The cow wondered why her normally boisterous calf was lying low without even getting up to have a taste of her huge udder. Normally it was a naughty calf. Under the pretext of sucking milk from her mother he used to keep on playing with the udder in gay abandon. But not that day! That morning the rooster's voice had gone on a flat note as if its chest had got congested with phlegm. It sounded like the voice of a singer with a sore throat. They were least interested in chasing the hens into every nook and corner of the streets as they usually did. Men in their village used to be after their women as soon the sun went down and the cocks went after hens as soon as the sun began to put up his head. The rising and setting of the sun had a rhythm in organic life.'

'Deep suspense engulfed the entire village. Palpable tension visited every household indiscriminately. Men, women, children, no one seemed to be spared. It was the Day of Judgment. No one could even make a guess as to what the judgment would be. The village was sharply divided into two camps taking opposite positions. Everyone was in anticipation that his side would win by all means. There was also the tinge of suspicion in everyone that his side could lose out ultimately. The entire village was waiting for that moment when the judge would open his mouth to pronounce the words that would change the history of the village either way. Many were walking forward and backward without knowing why they moved back and forth in the same path . . .'

'Progress and regress were matters of personal choices, often without knowing the reason. Guddahalli was no exception. It was neither progressing nor regressing. It was a replica of most Indian villages that stagnated with age-old traditions followed just mechanically year after year. The village did not even have an inkling of the type of economic development that the rulers were croaking about. They did not have necessary education to read newspapers. There was the odd one who got educated but no one was interested to spend that extra money to buy newspaper. There were many other essential needs in their lives. It typified the way people had surrendered themselves to what was written on their forehead.' Kala had started her narration in style. It was prearranged that Kala would be the narrator.

It took only a few seconds for Nina to recognize the hidden potential of the girl who sat in front of her, ever ready to open up the sluicegates of heavy streams of information that she contained within herself. She was like the Krishna Raja Sagar dam in Mysore that was always pushing the sluicegates to open in order to gush forth. Unable to move forward there was heavy wobbling of the waters. Kala at last got one of the best opportunities to gush forth.

Coffee making was Kala's hobby. She had many hundreds of people visiting her home in a month. Making many variants of coffee, serving it to visitors and dishing out more variety of information to all of them, to each according to her needs, was her mission in life. Sipping her portion of the homemade filter coffee Nina provoked her further.

The aroma of Indian filter coffee emanating from the kitchen filled the hall of the house. Drinking coffee was only an additional joy. Kala was short and smart. She was exceptionally beautiful. Though she had the 'much in demand' fair skin in the village, she also had the features to become a Miss Universe on any day in the calendar. She had become strong in her resistance to the many lads who found her bulging breasts an added attraction. They were just beginning to grow and were not yet used to the touch of boys. She was deeply aware of it and her hand automatically went to take her slipping sari to cover them. She did it so frequently that even when the sari did not slip her hand often adjusted her sari to the top of her breasts. A new and growing awareness in her of something she cherished and treasured.

"Written on the forehead? Is something written on the forehead of all the people in Guddahalli?" Nina's naïve questions only raised an explosion of laughter in Kala. Nina admired the pearls inside her mouth arranged in a row by a master goldsmith. The village means a lot of space for everything. One could talk loud, laugh louder, cry and scream. For growing up girls like Kala laughing out loud was a way of telling young boys in the village that she was very much there and they had better take notice of her presence. The older and traditional women in the village would chide young dames precisely because they understood the intricacy of LoL. After all they had done the same when they were young.

It had become a habit in many. Whenever they had to laugh they did it loud without any inhibition. Nina was surprised. In her country only the compulsive elements would laugh loud without any reason. It was a way of taking out their suppressed anger and frustration. Even the person who laughs out loud would be embarrassed at the end of it all. Kala could not have such compulsions in life at that early age. She was just a budding teenager.

'Nothing is written in anybody's forehead. It is simply the belief in people that god has pre-determined everything in their lives and that they are helpless about everything. No amount of effort would do anyone any good, as only what god has written on the forehead will take place. You have to simply accept god's will and live your daily life. This blind acceptance of someone else's will is what is called 'writing on the forehead'. Laborers had to obey the dictates of the landlords, Dalits had to follow the dictates of the caste lords, women had to follow what men wished and desired, children had to obey parents etc. Things were written not only in the forehead but also in the scriptures. The educated quoted scriptures while the uneducated showed their forehead.' Kala now presented herself in a different mettle. She had suddenly exhibited a knowledge and maturity of thinking that was beyond her age.

Nina remembered how she was drilled into believing in the will of god as the ultimate guideline of her life. The will of god was the Christian way of enforcing the 'writing on the forehead. The Bible stood as the strongest embodiment of the writing on the forehead', she thought. Whenever there was an insurmountable problem in the family the head of the family would gather all members for prayers and demand that the family resigned itself to the will of god. Added to that was the Christian priest, who would solemnize the will of god in his official capacity as the agent of god.

—oo◀◯▶oo—

'All Poojamma's gift.' Kala understood the meaning of the look of surprise in Nina and solved the riddle before it was put to her. 'She has been training the village people for so many years. I supply coffee, tea and food to them. They invariably enter my ears. Repeated banging in my eardrums have drilled my mind and settled down there.' Kala said with a broad smile and a side-glance.

"Ok, ok! Tell me more about the tension in Guddahalli. You spoke of the Day of Judgment. What was the judgment about?" Nina kept alive the story line. She had come all the way from the United States to gather stories in India. She would not settle down for anything less than that.

'You cannot enter the Day of Judgment without traveling the journey of life of Guddahalli. It is a tiny village of only 40 houses in Karnataka. . . . .' Kala started as if she was waiting for Nina to open one of the sluicegates.

"Where in Karnataka?" the journalist in Nina propped up her character interrupting Kala.

'We are only two kilometers away from Guddahalli. The houses are constructed without much planning. You will not see many streets. Walls of houses are not separated from each other.' Kala had this nature of a fast moving train. If she was on track nothing could stop her except some red lights here and there. If there were no strong signals she would just keep marching ahead. When she happened to stop it was only for a while. She would resume from the same place that she left without minding the crisscrossing of interruptions.

"If it is only two kilometers away from here, I like to visit that village. I am from the US and I do not understand anything when you describe a village to me. Can you go with me to that village?" Nina began to feel easy with Kala.

'That is a good idea. When you are in the village you will find out about the Day of Judgment. But I cannot go with you. I have to prepare lunch for you. When you come back lunch will be ready. There she is.

Poojamma has come. Both of you can decide what to do now'. Kala was adept at handling situations of any type and good at passing the buck too.

Nina was not the type to get up when someone entered her place. She knew Poojamma for many years closely and had never raised her level in her presence. But she could not understand why she got up that day as soon as Poojamma entered the dining hall. It was so spontaneous that Nina herself wondered if she had gone weird all of a sudden.

"Sit, Sit. Sit Nina, why do you stand?" Poojamma was seeing stars at the change of air that had come about.

Nina realized that talking even for only a few minutes with Kala had instilled a new breath of humility into her. Now she began to breathe on her own. Respect for Poojamma seemed to be contagiously infecting the entire area and afflicting all those who ventured into it.

"You have really trained this girl very well. She speaks such good English. She is very confident of herself and has much information at her fingertips. Mmm . . . amazing!" Nina was all smiles as she remarked while simultaneously passing her glance at Kala.

"What did you tell her Kala? You are earning everybody's admiration. Good. I am proud of you my girl." She tapped at the back of Kala and turned to Nina. She could not help turning towards Nina as she was already on the edge to capture the time of Poojamma. Nina was nimble enough to capture both of them in her frame. There was also a flash of light from her camera.

"I was asking her if she would take me to the village. But she says that I must ask you. Can she take me to the village? I want to take a stroll around the village and gain a feel of the people and place. Kala explained to me about the village. But I am not sure if I have grasped even quarter of what she said. I have no idea of an Indian village." Kala had not yet put the frying pan on the stove but Nina was already frying her words like mustard seeds.

"Which village did you speak of Kala?" Poojamma doused the heat, as was her wont.

'I told her about Guddahalli. You have to go there today. Therefore, when she asked me about the people in our villages I began to tell her about the struggle that is going on there.' Kala's voice had lowered considerably in the presence of Poojamma. Now she was also wondering if she did the right thing in raking up the events of Guddahalli to Nina. Poojamma was adroit in reading the eyes of Kala. Often Kala spoke more with her eyes than with her lips though when she spoke words used to flow like the waters of river Kaveri.

—◦◦ἰϬἰ◦◦—

Kaveri had this mesmerizing effect on those who walked along her path or dared to crisscross her march forward. She was like a haughty peacock all along her path. She had every reason to be. The people of Karnataka had bloated her self-image by singing her praise on every possible occasion. In her turn she inflated the false pride of Kannadigas in every nook and corner of Karnataka.

She is a beautiful and young dame of humble origins. A native of Talakaveri she is claimed to be a precious possession of everyone in Karnataka. She becomes a bone of contention in her youthful fragrance. A mountain dwelling tribal girl of the Brahmagiri hill! She is very shy and often hides her true self till she blooms into a buoyant and attractive young girl who has come of age. She bids her time. Bombarded by the monsoon she gets wet all over and even gets engulfed in messy waters. From under the belly of the sky she slowly comes into her true form and begins her dance of life.

A vagabond that she is, she begins to move towards south in search of her boyfriends. In her drunken mood she oscillates towards the east and begins to jump downwards whenever she comes across a sloppy land. She is no ordinary tramp. When she is in her elements she can travel 765 kilometers at one go. But she stops here and there searching for her peers and boyfriends.

As she moves along in excitement she calls out to her girl friends: "Hey freakish Shimsha, romantic Hemavathi, bubbly Arkavathy, jaunty Honnuhole, perky Lakshmana Tirtha, cheery Kabini, vivacious Bhavani, sparkling Lokapavani, ebullient Noyyal and chirpy Amaravati, come and join my exuberance, you idiots. Don't you know that I am coming? Where have you gone and hidden yourselves. Bring your hands to me and let us all move together to search for our boys. That was enough. In fine anticipation they spring forth from their hiding and join together in a circle at a picnic spot Shivanasamudra and begin their community dance. People gather around them. They are forgetful of all those around them. In their gay abandon they jump down a valley of 320 feet without any fear of death. Death flees from them, as they are the embodiment of life and fill everyone with full life. When they see plain ground on their sides they make a march past so that all those on both sides could draw as much life as they would wish.

In her curiosity to see places she moves along with her friends to the neighboring Tamilnadu and begins to get the scent of her boyfriends. In her anticipated anxiety she traverses narrow by lanes and crooked paths at Hogenakkal. She calls out aloud to her boyfriends the doughty Palar, chivalrous Chenna and the brawny Thoppar inviting them to play and travel with her. Boys and girls together, blinded by their romantic exuberance are ready to move on and on. Men on the way are highly perturbed. They now decide to tie them up into a marriage of sorts in Mettur and channelize their uninhibited energy in different directions so that she may walk only according to their design of her course.

Stupendous energy! Angry at being tied down by arrogant humans she begins to break out into uncontrollable energy. Anyone who dares to touch her has to be ready to die an instantaneous death. Regretting her blind fury she channelizes her unlimited energy into illumination. But she extricates herself from the clutches of men though in subdued form and resumes her journey and moves till Tiruchy and Tanjoor. When she resumes her journey she discovers that her friends have already deserted her. Once again she becomes the humble but beautiful dame and loses her direction. She wanders into the paddy fields all over and splinters her personality. Left to herself and unable to hold alone she is highly depressed and in her helplessness merges into the Bay of Bengal at Poompuhar.

—oo•◄O►•oo—

"Oh, it is only two kilometers from here. I think Kala has to prepare lunch for us. Today the weather is good. It is now quite cloudy and not warm. I can take you by walk to the village. Do you mind walking? It will also give you a good bit of idea on the countryside of India." Poojamma was never as relaxed as she was that day. There was no tangible reason. She was a natural person. She was what her body made her. She never tried to put on an air of artificiality around her personality. People of that area had already stuffed her with their own adulations and plethora. Often it became too burdensome for her to bear the heavy halo. She was a woman who worked according to a system. Her time had to be highly organized. However, working among the poor and living in the village meant responding to situations that she did not anticipate. Though she had reconciled to this at the rational level her personality and the tinge of perfectionism that she had did not allow her to be completely at peace with herself. Without her own knowledge certain level of tension entered into her system.

The poor had a reason to do what they did. They had a rhythm of life of their own. They were never in a hurry to catch a train or a flight. The quagmire of poverty eternally tried to pull them into an unknown death trap. The clutches of India's caste system had spread its thorny tentacles all over their social and personal lives that they got themselves submerged into an irredeemable fatalism. The country had not even given them a sense of the need for education. Whatever they could earn in their lives could be done without big education. They had to save their skins and fatalism was the easy way available.

Poojamma had knocked the writing on their forehead so violently that many in the area began to lose the direction of their lives. Not many dared any more point to their forehead in her presence. Whenever tragedy of low and high intensity visited them they used to take the easy way of raising their fingers to their forehead and confirmed their faith in fatalism. Everything was written in their forehead ages before they were born. Hinduism had taught them the art of escaping into inaction and lethargy in utter helplessness. The priestly class thrived well on the ignorance and helplessness of the innocent masses. It busied itself by writing illegible writing on the forehead of the poor and ignorant. Poojamma rang the death knell of fatalism and pulled the people out of the quagmire of false beliefs that Hinduism had pushed them into. They began to see her as a symbol of their liberation. When they saw the symbol they began to embellish it according to their needs and convenience. Poor Poojamma!

"Oh, that is wonderful to hear. You are taking me to the village. What more do I need? Come let us go." Nina was ready for anything. Her travel to India was an adventure in any case. Now that she knew she was in safe hands she was ready to go to any extent. Many people in her country had advised her not to go to India. Travel advises in the internet had warned her that it was risky for a woman to go alone to India reminding her of the ever lurking dangers of rape and murder. It threatened women to be careful of the ravenous eyes of Indian men at the cleavages in their chest. But the most orchestrated threat was cheating and stealing. When her pears appreciated her impertinent courage to venture out all alone into India she chided them with her sarcastic charm. "As if our country is any better! Even here in the US women are raped if they happen to be alone and should we enumerate the number of thefts and violence that take place on women and children? We live in a false world yar. We are convincing ourselves that we live in a free country. Are we women really free in our country? We want the rest of the world to believe that America is the safest haven for all people of the world. But can we deny the fact that it is one of the most unsafe and violent places on earth? Anyone can take the gun and shoot many people for no reason at all. Even our children are shot dead in schools."

"But you don't have big breasts to show off in India. No harm will come to you." Her friends reminded her of the story in the US and in Europe of how men always looked at the breasts of White women. There were many funny stories doing the round in these countries about Indian men's prowling eyes on women's boobs. Nina bent down to have one more look at her breasts to make sure that they were big enough to make her proud. As her friends giggled touching their big tits Nina retorted. "As if our men in the US are not at all fond of our boobs! It is our double standard that we want White men to have a good look at our boobs and we even fill them with artificial stuff. But when Indian men look at us out of curiosity we create a big story against them. If we are so clean why do our women go about exposing more than half their boobs on the roads in India as they do here?" Nina's aggressive defense of Indian men used to floor her peers.

CHAPTER TWO

"Yes, let us start". Poojamma took her hand and led her out of the door. Soon they found themselves on the road. It was the national highway. They walked on the service road. The highway itself was a four-lane road with service roads on both sides. The highway was fenced all along with steel mesh so that animals might not go into the road and cause accidents.

"Out there in the US most people believe that India is very poor and people do not have enough to eat. But when you see roads such as this one, it is impossible to believe that India is really poor. This road was not here when I came last time. There is such a lot of change in a short period of time. This is as good as some of the roads that we have in the US. This even looks better." Nina started the outdoor conversation in style. Cars and trucks were whizzing their way past them without giving even a fraction of a thought to them. They were just walking without bothering about the speed that was at their doorstep. There was no hurry to cope with the vehicles.

"Yes, it is true. Here in India an inferiority complex generally invades and conditions our mindset, as we see the type of luxuries that are available in your country. We think that to develop is to become like your country. US is the role model for most Indians. Our rulers want India to develop as the US has developed. That is a sad story." Poojamma spoke now a bit dejectedly.

"Why do you say that? I know that the United States is not the best model of development and its inside is as stinking as many other poor nations of the world. But tell me why you do not want the American model of development." Nina now started provoking Poojamma. She wanted to take out as much as possible from her in order to puke them out in her book later.

"Yes. We had the Congress party ruling over India for a long time. People were quite romantic about Congress as it was that party that fought for the freedom of India. Since common people in India did not know that it was one Mr. Hume who started the Congress party it was easily possible to associate Congress with Gandhi. Anything that is associated with Gandhi sells not only in India but in the entire world."

Nina interrupted Poojamma at this point. "You seem to know a lot of history Poojamma. I did not imagine that there is so much of history hidden in you." She wanted to indulge in a bit of adulation. It was contagious in that area.

"Perhaps you have not yet accepted that fact that Indian women can be as intellectual if not more, as their men." Poojamma's slingshot hit Nina at her temple.

"I am sorry. Perhaps you are right. Racial prejudices may be. I am truly sorry". Nina was profusely apologetic.

"When people got disillusioned with the Congress party because of its internal division, the Congress party rode once again on the huge popularity of Indira Gandhi. Till now she is the greatest Stateswoman India has seen. However, she made a political hara-kiri by imposing emergency on an unassuming nation. When a sense of invincibility gets into your head you are most likely to dig your own grave." As Poojamma exposed her political acumen more and more, Nina began to get into her shell quietly. The process seemed to be proportional. The light from Poojamma shone on the eyes of Nina too sharply and she ran for cover.

"You are wondering why I am taking up the political history of India when we started talking about roads in India." Nina wondered seriously how Poojamma could read what was going on inside her head. But then she was not too surprised as it happened occasionally during her earlier visits too.

17

"Yes, that was going on in my mind and you found that out. How is it possible Poojamma?" Nina asked a question for which she knew the answer and Poojamma knew that Nina knew the answer.

"There is a direct connection between the road that you see and the politics that I speak of. Indira Gandhi began to open up the economy of India to global forces in an attempt to emulate the way the West and the US were developing. All parties that came after her followed her path though they created a different rhetoric. Now the BJP is in power and they have coined a new slogan to mesmerize the people."

"A slogan to mesmerize the people? Why do they need that? They should implement some programmes to mesmerize the people." Nina thought she had drawn out an idea from the heavens.

"Yes, that would be better. But no political party in India is interested to develop the people. They only want to create a grand illusion that they are developing the country. Therefore, BJP created the slogan "India Shining'. Now you see how India is shining." Poojamma was in her sarcastic best as she pointed out to the road. Nina had a look in the direction that Poojamma's hands pointed out. She was almost shocked. She saw a man grazing his two cows right in the middle of the road. The government had grown beautiful grass in the broad road divider. It had also planted flower plants. The grass in the road divider was tastier to the cows than the grass in the farm.

Nina laughed loud and asked, "But how did he manage to take the cows there? It is all fenced on both sides of the road."

Poojamma pointed out in the yonder at the fence. There it was cut big enough to allow the cow and the man to walk into the middle of the road. That was India shining.

Just then a group of people in rugged clothes, unkempt hair and rather dirty clothes stopped Poojamma. They were eight of them. All of them touched the feet of Poojamma and surrounded her. 'The buffaloes that you gave us have kept us alive today'. One of them said it so loud that the entire village must have heard it.

"Are all the buffaloes giving good milk? How much milk do you get?" Poojamma asked one of them while keeping her hands on their head as a gesture of blessing.

"We get enough milk for us. Children have milk every day. And we send two litres of milk to the milk dairy. The people in the dairy prefer our buffalo milk, as it is thick. They buy our milk first and only then do they buy cow milk" One of the ladies in the group spoke with pride.

"Okay, okay. I am very happy for you, especially that your children have milk to drink at home. She turned to Nina and introduced her to the entire gang of village people. Nina could not make head and tail out of what Poojamma spoke to them, except her name. She smiled with much difficulty in order to please the people." The artificiality was all too evident for Poojamma.

"Early in the morning one group of people from Guddahalli was in the house of Eeranna. There may be some problem when you go to the village. Very ungrateful people Poojamma! You have done so much for all of us. Yet when it comes to improving in life, they only want to follow their old traditions. But you do not worry Poojamma. You will succeed today. People will come round you and accept your decisions. The judgment will be in your favor." Vociferous affirmation of support and solidarity!

"Let him do what he wants. If people listen to him they will only go back into their abject poverty. You people know that only too well. I am sure they will realize the truth one day or other and come back. Let us see how they behave today and what the Judgment is going to be." Poojamma was quite clinical in her interactions with the people. She understood their emotions and gave in good measurement whatever was needed to satisfy their surging emotions. She also knew exactly how many words should be let out of her mouth when she spoke of the villain Eeranna who was the biggest politician and landlord in the area.

—◦◦]◦[◦◦—

Nina could not contain her curiosity any more. "What is happening? There seems to be a palpable tension as you meet people. Is it something related to the Day of Judgment that you mentioned?" Her intuition took the better of her and she did not hesitate to give verbal expression to it.

"Yes. There is tension all around. But first the women and men who met us informed me that their children are having milk at home everyday. This is because of the loan that I arranged for them with the local bank to buy buffalo. They have a little land and during monsoon they cultivate ragi. After harvesting they have the dry hay to feed the buffalo. The local bank came forward to give them loans to buy these animals. Am very happy that the children are better fed and that the women have some added income in their family kitty." Poojamma tried to assuage Nina's tension a bit.

"But what is the tension all about?" Nina was sharp on her journalistic pursuits. She would not compromise on that. The JCB, an efficient machine at any time! At the yonder it was doing its routine duty of digging out as much earth as was possible. There she was, digging out as much information as possible.

"You see that house there." Nina turned her eyes in the direction of where Poojamma's fingers pointed out. It was the biggest house in the entire region, a three floor building. It was painted with exotic colors and stood as a showpiece for all eyes to covet. There were the odd ones who cynically called it the eyesore of the region. They had a reason to say so. When probed further they would sarcastically assert that the house was built on blood money.

"Blood money? What is it?" Nina asked for the obvious. The answer was as clear as day and she knew it.

"Our people in the villages would say that the owner of the building sucks the blood of the poor and it is with such exploited money that he has built the house' Poojamma said without any show of emotions.

'Beautiful and big house for a village! Whose house it?" Nina's eyes were still on the house even as she raised the volume of her words.

Before Nina could wink her eyes she saw two elderly women falling fully flat at the feet of Poojamma. She bent down to touch the shoulders of the two women and raise them up to stand equal to her. It was an arduous task but not a Himalayan one. Poojamma was a short woman. All around the place there was dry air. Yet the eyes of both women were not wanting for water. They were flowing with tears.

"Is there any serious problem for them. Why did they fall on the ground like that? Their clothes are dirty." Nina extended her hand to shake off the dry sand that had managed to stick to their sari. They were excited and more water flowed from their eyes.

"No, no! There is no problem. They are simply on cloud nine at seeing us." Poojamma wanted to be inclusive. It was ineluctable for her. She would never exclude anyone even from the love that she received from others. It was a sort of compulsive inclusion that she had developed. "People in this region are an empowered lot now. You know the situation in which they lived a few years ago. You have seen them being frightened to the core in the presence of the landlord of this village. But today they walk proudly with their heads held high. Their poverty has not been removed completely. I have not been able to do that. But they have acquired a pride, a new self-confidence that does not come through money. Whenever they see me they are in transports of delight at the way their children enjoy a new freedom in the village." That makes way for their tears to flow even without their control. A free flow of tears!

"Yes, I can see the transformation that has taken place from the way Kala speaks and the way people are venerating you even on the roads. But how did you manage to do that, especially being a woman?" Nina was sharp on her target. She wanted the stuff for her forthcoming book on Poojamma and on India. That would make her hugely popular in her country. The highway work was going on still as they were walking slowly. The many JCBs that were at work were still scraping the ground and succeeded to accumulate a lot of material in their huge arms. Nina the JCB from the US!

"Have a little patience Nina. You will see it soon. Am taking you to Guddahalli where a big struggle is going on. I have to be there today. You will see for yourself how illiterate mass of people can still have their sense of pride as human beings despite religions shaping them as magnum ignoramus."

"Are we going to take part in the judgment today?" As Nina asked this in excitement Poojamma stopped for a while and looked at her intently. She wondered how Nina came to know about the Day of Judgment.

"Ha, tell me that. Kala opened her mouth a bit too early. I wanted to keep it as a surprise for you. Yes, today is the great Day of Judgment in Guddahalli. We shall soon be there to witness that." Poojamma spoke with fine anticipation without letting the entire suspense out all at once.

The two elderly women started walking with the duo back.

"You were going somewhere. Please go. Why are you following us now? Go and do your work. We are going to Guddahalli and will take some time to come back." Poojamma gently prodded the two elders not to feel obliged to follow her in any way.

"What bigger work do we have Poojamma than accompanying you? Our work can wait. But when shall we get another chance to walk with you? We also knew that today is the Day of Judgment in Guddahalli and we want to see what happens there. The Gollars there are already divided into two camps. You have done so much to that village. But half of them still want to go back to their old wretched ways and not listen to you at all. Kariyamma shed more tears as she said this.

"It is not the people of Guddahalli who are at fault, Poojamma. It is that son of a bitch, that son of a whore, that jackass who is dividing the people. You know our people are just idiots and Gollars are more idiotic than many of us." Shivamma picked up necessary courage to add a retorting spice to Kariyamma.

Poojamma did not do a word for word translation now. "This woman seems to be abusing someone. Whom is she abusing so much and why? She seems to be very angry with him. Who is the man?" Nina thought that a landmine of information was opening up for her asking.

"He is the invisible hand that controls the life of people in this entire region. You know India to some extent. We have the rule of law that should be implemented. But it is only the caste master of the village who will determine what law should become the rule of law. The people are slowly coming out of their stupor and it will take some more time for them to be free under the rule of the constitution of India." Poojamma now began to slowly manifest why she was a much-admired woman not only among the poor and the Dalits but also among people at large.

"Shall we be meeting this mystery man today?" Nina was in a hurry to gather dirt under her wings. Anything that would sell was good for her. She was ever ready to grab anything that came on her way. She was confident that later she would sit alone and sieve the chaff from the grain.

"No, not today! He will not come to Guddahalli today. He normally operates behind scenes. That is why I call him the invisible hand. He will appear only in public meetings and functions. And especially today he will not come." Poojamma began to unfold some mysteries to Nina.

"Why not? Why does he not appear? Today is the Day of Judgment, na?" Nina's curiosity knew no bounds.

'Because I am there! He will not come if I am there." Poojamma began to further unfurl some inner secrets of her political acumen.

"Is he afraid of you?" Nina the provocateur!

"No, he is not at all afraid of me. But when I am in the villages, people throng around me and will not give him much attention. That is something that he cannot stomach. I am a Dalit woman. He is a caste man. People giving me great respect in his presence is totally unacceptable to him." That was a bombshell for Nina. She could not grab the power of this bomb. She decided to explode it later.

"That is the house that people are referring to. It is the house of Eeranna. He is not only a landlord but is also a politician. He thinks that my presence and popularity in this region is his biggest threat. He gets frustrated often at the love and affection that people shower on me. Therefore, he leaves no stone unturned to dissuade people from coming to me and having discussions with me." Poojamma said without a modicum of frustration in her voice.

'Why, does he want to be the undisputed king of this region?' Nina had already picked up some nuances of Indian reality in her previous visits. Therefore, she interjected the conversation with some India specific remarks.

"None of us will have any problem with him being the undisputed king of this region. But it is his way that is problematic. He wants to use all sorts of short cuts to become rich and powerful at the cost of the people. If someone shows signs of independence he demolishes them ruthlessly. When we go back to my house I shall tell you in detail of his shenanigans. It is nauseating. Let us not spoil the day by talking much about him." Poojamma diverted Nina's attention and with that also changed the direction of their path.

—oo◦}◦{◦oo—

"Wah, there we have the shining India and here we have the gloomy India." Nina gave out a loud laughter that resembled the bellowing of the village buffalos. She was referring to the village road into which Poojamma led her. From the National Highway now it was a mud road that led to Guddahalli.

"Why is this road so bad? It is just attached to the national highway and takes only a little money to also make a good road to the village. Why can't the government just do it?" Nina started fuming. With her also the wind that blew rather angrily and raised all the dust in the mud road. Poojamma anticipated the raising of dust. But not Nina! Her face was covered with red mud in no time. Poojamma reached out to her with her sari and wiped her face of all the mud that stuck on her face. Nina could see her red face on the sari of Poojamma. The color of her face could not change, as she was simultaneously red with anger.

"Yes, I tried talking like this to the authorities. I myself have fallen several times on this road. When it rains it becomes a mass of slush all over and you cannot even put your foot anywhere. But the highway authority says that they have mandate and money only to lay highways and not village roads. Village roads come under the authority of State governments. And finally no one takes responsibility. The best thing bureaucrats have learned is to pass the buck on to another department." Poojamma was so engrossed with her education of Nina that she hardly noticed a group of her admirers who saw her from afar and rushed to welcome her to their village.

They had a garland ready for her and one of the women placed it on her neck. All the others clapped their hands. It was then that they were embarrassed that they did not have a spare one for the special guest who accompanied Poojamma. She spared them of half the embarrassment by removing her own garland and asking them to garland the White woman guest. It was quite sometime when they recovered from their stupor of being in the presence of a woman whose entire body was white beyond their imagination.

Whenever someone went from the village to the town the girls invariably asked them to buy them some face powder and vanishing cream. Being dark in complexion was a clear disadvantage in the village and so dames always tried to make themselves as white as possible. Village boys were fond of girls with fairer skin. It was enough that a girl only had fair skin. Their features mattered very little if only the color of their skin was a little whiter. Many young men would vie with one another and often fight among themselves to grab the attention of girls with fair skins. Added to this were TV advertisements that praised fair skins in order to sell their fair and lovely vanishing creams.

A woman with her entire body covered with fair skin. "How much vanishing cream she should be using. They are very rich people." Village people's simple assumptions manifested in silent thoughts. They had seen only pictures of deities painted so fair and white. The unimaginable demiurge from some foreign land had descended on their village. Poojamma was a great woman as she had many such divine friends. It was then that they turned their eyes towards Poojamma.

This was the other camp that opposed the ways of Eeranna. Poojamma was the cynosure of their newborn hope for a better future. They gathered the necessary courage to openly take stand against the crooked ways of their locally powerful political and caste leader.

"Oh, don't fall down. Walk carefully. Our roads are full of stones." Some men rushed to hold Nina as she stumbled upon a stone on the road. The road was full of stones at places. Nina struggled hard to walk. Poojamma wanted her to have that difficult experience and to understand the plight of the poor in rural India. Men were happy and were in seventh heaven that they were able to touch a woman with full white skin. They had an inexplicable glee on their faces. Other men who could not touch Nina cursed themselves for their bad luck.

Nina had never been touched in her life with hands that took her imaginations to crocodiles. She had only imagined that the outer skin of crocodiles would be very hard. These men had palms that were harder than some wooden pieces that she had handled. Their palms were hardened nuts. She felt hurt by their touch. She was in the grip that one of them had on her hand. She wriggled herself out as quickly as possible from those clutches of innocent love. Such love could be very painful at times in the hand.

Even as Nina recovered herself from a possible fall she noticed a small thatched hut that looked almost like a small cave and one feminine face peeping out to have a look at the visitors. Her head was covered with clothes. It looked as if she was protecting her ears from wind. Nina could easily make out that both the ears were fully covered. She pointed out the feminine face to Poojamma and asked: "What is that woman inside that small hut doing? She cannot even stand up there. Why is she there in the first place?" Her curiosity at some things Indian knew no bounds.

Poojamma pretended as if she was seeing the hut for the first time. She did not want Nina to notice that symbol of ignominy in the village. But Nina's voluptuous eyes left nothing to chance.

"Oh, that is a very bad custom that this particular caste people practice in this village. All their caste people all over Karnataka and many other States of India practice this. You have seen only the woman inside. But there must be a newborn baby along with that mother. I shall ask the women here to explain the custom to you. You will have a lot to write now." Poojamma smiled reluctantly at Nina.

She stopped for a while. Called the women around her and asked them to explain to Nina why the woman was inside the hut. Poojamma opened a great avenue for the journalistic explorations of Nina. She took out her pen and book to jot down the finer points that would possibly play with her memory later.

————∞❉∞————

It was Manjula who came forward to narrate to Nina the age-old custom of Guddahalli. She was a 'very' highly educated girl for that village, the only woman who picked up rare courage to board a crowded bus everyday to go to town and do her pre-university education. Usually girls gave up education at matriculation. Most of them failed in English and Mathematics. But Manjula managed to pass both subjects with narrow margins. When girls were able to pass all subjects and wanted to go to college their parents became the biggest stumbling blocks on their way to dreaming about their future.

"Ha, you speak English. That is surprising. You are the first person I have heard speaking in English in the village." Nina gleefully appreciated Manjula. "Are you from this village?"

"Yes, of course! I am from this village. All because of Poojamma! It was she who persuaded my parents to allow me to continue my studies in the town." Manjula was speaking in a mix of Kannada and English, which was locally called Kanglish. It was difficult for Nina to understand Kanglish as it was like a new language for her. But being used to different dialectics in different places she was able to put two and two together to make it five. Every now and then Poojamma intervened to insist that it was four. Manjula was extremely happy that she was able to show off her Kanglish in front of her village dames.

"But why would your parents object to your studies. You will get a good job and earn a lot of money if you study in the town and get a degree." Nina brought her intellectual foreplay to the fore.

"Our parents have more to worry about than our future and earning money. They think that if we go to town to study, boys of all castes would disturb us and that we may fall in love with one of them. They will accept anything in their life but not marrying us off to boys from another caste. The first thing they want to do is to get us married immediately after we finish our matriculation. Some parents do not even wait for that. They marry our girls off as soon as they attain puberty." Manjula was non-stop and was in a mood to talk.

The woman in the hut now put her body out to wish Poojamma. It was a comic relief for Nina. She was like a huge python trying to wriggle itself out of a small hole on a tree. Both Poojamma and Nina took a few steps forward towards the cavy hut. Others followed suit.

"Why is she kept in such miserable condition? Her clothes are dirty and unhygienic. Is it a sort of punishment that she is kept out of the village and is confined to this cave?" Nina was visibly angry. The journalist in her took a fast flight in a Dreamliner jet. The woman in her took over the space vacated by the journalist.

Poojamma looked up to Manjula to take over. She responded as if she had anticipated it.

"Blood madam, blood! It's a bloody mess here that is happening in our village. Any blood that comes from the body of a woman is considered to be pollution. In the name of religion and culture our women have been subjugated in inexplicable ways not only to men but also to caste system." Manjula was now giving free vent to her surging feminine feelings.

"What has blood to do with pollution?" Nina knew the answer but she simply wanted to provoke Manjula to speak further. She was simultaneously making an internal assessment of the level of education that Poojamma had done among the ordinary and simple masses of people.

"A woman giving birth to a child is considered to be polluting the village. Therefore, at the time of childbirth she is cast out of the village into this inhuman hut and fend for herself." Manjula continued with anger.

"You mean to say that she is not allowed to get any support and has to manage childbirth all by herself?" Now Nina was flabbergasted and was completely upset looking at the distressing look on the face of the woman in the hut.

"Only her mother is allowed to take food for her from home and assist her in childbirth. But for three months the new mother and child have to remain ostracized from the village. Do you have such cruel practices in your religion and culture?" Manjula reversed the question and answer pattern.

"We rejected such religion and culture long ago. Most people in our country do not have any religion. I cannot even think of such practices existing anywhere in the world in our times. This is simply obnoxious." Nina spoke like a possessed woman.

"Can I touch her?" Nina looked at Manjula intently expecting a negative reply. Poojamma also was curious to know how Manjula would handle Nina's query.

"Yes, you should touch her. But please do it quick. If anyone in the village saw you touching this woman or the child they will not allow you to enter the village. We shall surround you so that no one in the village will see you. Go ahead and break all these bloody customs of our caste. In any case you do not belong to our caste system and therefore, you are not bound to follow it." Manjula roared like an angry lioness.

Nina went forward, bent her body to 90 degrees and asked the woman to give the baby to her. Manjula told the woman with an aggressive tone to give the baby. She obliged. Poojamma followed suit and petted the baby for sometime.

"This is called 'soothaka' in our language. It means pollution. Now that you have touched the baby you have become polluted according to our belief. The mother and child have to remain in this bloody hut for three months in order to cleanse them of all pollution and only then can the family take them in their house." Manjula was like a beetle that had fallen accidentally on a frying pan.

"But this is atrocious. Can't you people do something about this? You are an educated girl and you must fight against such irrational customs." Nina started her preaching.

"Why do you think Poojamma is coming to our village today? We are going to take a decision about this goddamn practice. The village is assembling today to decide whether our women should be kept outside the village during the period of childbirth or whether they can be kept in their houses. This is a major decision that we are going to take today. Poojamma is our savior. She will not leave anything untouched. Today is our Day of Judgment." Manjula was jumping all over in the frying pan.

"Oh, is that the Day of Judgment that Kala was speaking about? So, you have brought me here with a purpose Poojamma?" Nina was all flowing with surprise.

"No, the Day of Judgment refers to something else. You will soon realize what it is . . . ." Even as Poojamma unfolded another mystery there was a loud roar on the path that they had taken. Nina jerked with a shock at the sudden uproar from the drums. A group of men and women danced all the way beating their drums and were hurrying up towards Poojamma. As they came near, the drums stopped and all of them touched her feet in veneration. The drums started their roar once again. Now the crowd started swelling on the path to Guddahalli. At the sound of the drums more people came out of their houses and started lining up to welcome Poojamma. There were the odd ones who looked the other way and Poojamma did not fail to notice the toughening of muscles on their faces.

"Who are these people? Why have they come with the drums? Is there a festival going on here?" Nina was like the summer shower that came unexpected with big drops of water.

Before Poojamma could reply to her, Nina noticed a group of three women sitting on the side of the road opposite Guddahalli and was watching all the fun. That they did not get up even to greet Poojamma surprised Nina. In the commotion of the drums and village streets peppered with people, she turned to Manjula and asked her why those women were sitting and gaping at all who passed by.

"Once again blood madam! This bloody blood determines the fate of our women." Manjula was ignited once again.

"But they do not have a hut and children with them. Where does the question of polluting blood arise here?" Nina began to show signs of irritating inquisitiveness.

Poojamma once again looked at Manjula expecting her to take positions as the official spokesperson that day. "All the three women here have their periods, madam. It is the custom in this caste that when women have menstrual periods they should come out of the village, as they are considered to be polluting the village. They can go into the village to do their normal chorus when their period stops." Manjula completed her narration in style being proud of her feminine identity despite the society's ascriptions on women.

"And all the men in the village will look at these women having periods? What sort of an ignominy is this? Why should men know at all that women have their periods? It is their private affair and you expose them to the entire village." The tempo of irritation began to increase.

"Yes, you are right. This is something that goes beyond human comprehension." Manjula supported Nina.

"Do you also sit like this during your days of period?" Poojamma smiled broadly as Nina asked Manjula. The other women did not understand the words of Nina but they got the meaning of the smile of Poojamma.

"I used to do this in the beginning stages of my puberty. But I have rebelled against it now."

"Are you the only one to have rebelled or are there other girls of your age who also rebel like you?" Nina became the journalist once again.

"How will anyone know that I have my periods on any given day? That is impossible for men in our village to know unless they do a physical search of me. I go about doing my regular studies and now my regular work." She was assertive.

"How about other girls in your village? They can also follow your example and rebel" Nina poked her.

"But the problem is that we, women have accepted male domination. We have internalized the paradigm that men have the right to determine our behavior. Moreover, this is a custom practiced not merely in our village. It is a common practice in all the villages of our caste . . . ." Before she could continue Nina interrupted her.

"So, this is a caste practice. Does each caste have its own rules and regulations? What will happen if you decide to take legal action against this type of practice? . . . ." Before Nina could complete Poojamma intervened.

"Nina, this is something that will require a long discussion. May be you can do this later in our place. Manjula, you may come over and have discussion with Nina after we complete the judgment today." Poojamma was heavily weighed down with the thought that time was running out and if she did not run out there would not be enough time for the judgment. Nina had a good look once again at the women who were sitting there as showpieces of 'women with periods' and she shook her head rather violently and followed Poojamma. All along the way she held her camera and was clicking photos of all possible things. The women were shy that they were being photographed in such a shabby fashion.

Poojamma now nudged Nina, took her aside and told her: "Listen Nina, everything is not as bad as it looks or you think. There is a positive dimension to this practice. In the beginning I too thought that it is an obnoxious practice. But then women of this village told me that their period is the only time when they are free from their men. At night when their children are asleep and women too are fast asleep their men slowly pinch them and pull their saris demanding sex. They do not care if the woman is ready for sex or not. All that they want is to quickly fix their cock into the cockpit of their women and release their compulsive energy into them. Once their business is over they go to sleep. But women are completely drained out of energy with the day's work and now their husbands do not allow them to have peaceful sleep at night. Staying out of their house for four days gives them the much-needed rest. Look at it this way and you will never want to change this custom." Nina opened her mouth in amazement of the intense wisdom that Poojamma possessed. It was not for nothing that people venerated her.

"Can I take photos of them or will they be offended?" Nina crosschecked with Manjula with her American sensitivity.

"All of us like to be photographed and then see our own photos to make sure that we look better than other women. Taking photos is a big event in the villages. Women wash their faces, apply face powder and cream and want to look bright in the photos. Husbands take wives and occasionally also children to studios in the city to take photos and that is a big family event. Nowadays of course, much of this has changed because of Poojamma. She brings in many people from different countries and all of them come here with cameras. Our women are now used to being photographed. However, taking photos will always mean washing faces, applying powder and standing up in particular positions." Manjula spoke a lot for every small question that Nina raised.

CHAPTER THREE

By then another group of men came from one of the streets in Guddahalli and surrounded Poojamma. There was perceptible fear on the face of Nina as to what was happening in the village. She did take care to watch the faces of Manjula and the people who accompanied them. Manjula was as normal as ever and did not show any sign of being perturbed at the onrush of men towards Poojamma. She would have been surprised if men did not rush to meet Poojamma.

It was then that Nina noticed that some women and all men who followed Poojamma did not now accompany her into the village. They waited outside the village at a distance and were discussing something among themselves. If Nina were not anxious about this change of scene she would not have been eligible to be a journalist. The men were still smiling and greeting Poojamma. That put the anxious Nina to rest.

That interlude enlivened her a bit and she pulled Manjula aside to ask why women and men who accompanied Poojamma stayed put outside the village instead of going along with them. Scene extraordinary, shrouded with mystery!

"Oh, did not Poojamma tell you? Today is our Day of Judgment. It is for this that Poojamma has come to our village today. These groups of people who have surrounded her are the loyal ones to the type of changes that she wants to bring about in our caste community. There is another group that is opposed to whatever change Poojamma wants to bring about and the type of rational awareness that she creates in this entire area." Manjula now slowly was transforming herself into a cauldron, a burning cauldron. Nina felt the heat in her voice and saw fire on her face.

"But tell me why are those people waiting there. They should go along with Poojamma into the village and defend her just in case there is an attack on her." Nina now gave voice to the shivering she had deep inside. The situation as she saw was threatening her inside.

"Oh, don't you worry about Poojamma. No one can touch her in this area and in the whole of India. She is like our goddess. People will worship her but not attack her. Even her enemies know the goodness that she is constructed of. It is only that idiot, Eeranna who is out to destroy her reputation and the admiration of people for her. But he will soon bite the dust. Don't worry." The oil in the big drum was now beginning to gather enough heat. Nina was waiting for the moment it would begin to boil.

Nina was on fire now. "But Manjula, you have not yet told me why those people from the neighboring village have stayed put outside the village. I am anxious to know that."

"That is the Day of Judgment that we are all speaking about. I took it for granted that you were informed of it. Sorry. Those people waiting outside our village are from the neighboring village where Poojamma lives. They are untouchables. According to our caste custom they should not be allowed even to enter the village where Gollars live. We are those bloody Gollars, you know!" Manjula fed a lot of firewood in excess.

"What? You do not allow people even to enter your village because they belong to another caste?" Nina became extremely inquisitive now. She knew already quite a bit about caste system and how it functions, much beyond any ordinary American knew. Back in the US she was an expert on caste system as she had first hand knowledge of it in some cases. She also added her own American flavor to the stories that she narrated and became a sort of heroine in her surroundings. But now she could hear aloud in her own ears empty gongs ringing and reminding her of the shallow depth she thought she had about caste system.

Just at that time the group of men who came to wish Poojamma took her away to one of the houses. She turned back to Manjula and asked her to take care of Nina till she returned. "Manjula, please see to it that she does not eat anything very spicy in the houses." A mild warning before any tremors could shake the ass of Nina. Both of them smiled at each other, as they knew why Poojamma had to ring that warning bell. In one of her previous visits Nina pretended to be very courageous and gobbled up food that village people had prepared. She had enough warning. But she wanted to be a feminine macho. Before they could reach home her stomach began to sing and dance like the rock music of Michael Jackson in his History Album. Nina felt like running to all corners of the world, nay of the universe. But she was bottled up in the vehicle. The driver understood her predicament as even he could hear the rock music in her stomach. He converted his car into a Ferrari and himself into a Michael Schumacher and was in Poojamma's place in no time. The first thing Nina did was to run to the toilet holding her ass with her hand. She was small built and there was no problem holding it.

When she came back it was too late. She had to be taken to hospital and was bedridden for a week. Both of them understood the secret meaning of their smile leaving Manjula to immerse herself in a mystery. But then she had other things to preoccupy herself with.

"Yes. It is tragic that these people are not allowed even to enter our village. Actually we also do not allow Brahmins to come for any of our functions and rituals. This is very special about us that only our caste does not take assistance from Brahmin priests for our religious ceremonies. All other caste people in Hinduism have to take the assistance of Brahmin priests. Even if it is not mandatory they call Brahmins for their functions for social prestige. But not our caste people!" Manjula was in a mood to talk, go on talking.

But Nina was made of a different stuff. She would not allow anything to bypass her. "Are you people anti-Brahmin then? I have heard that Dalits are anti-Brahmin. You do not allow Dalits as well as Brahmins in your village. You seem to be a strange caste".

"We are. We worship Krishna as our god. He is from our Gollar community. We are a cow-herding community. Krishna also belonged to our caste. Though he is from the lowest caste, Shudra, in the caste ladder the caste people made him a god in order to take us also into the Hindu fold. He actually gives the central teaching of Hinduism, the Bhagavad Gita and today we are very proud Hindus. Being from the Shudra caste our community has never allowed the Brahmins to have any dominance over us . . . ." Nina cut her short with one of her quick arrows.

"But why do you not allow the Dalits also into your villages if you are from the Shudra caste?"

"We allow other Dalits in our village. We do not allow only this particular caste people called the 'Madhigas'. They are the shoemakers. Actually these are the people who were cast out of the villages when the Aryans began to take over India. The people who came with Poojamma belong to the Madhiga caste. They are socially the lowest among Dalits. But what our community does not like in them is that they deal with dead bodies and shit. We consider them as dirty." Without her knowing Manjula proved that she was still a Gollar deep inside and that disturbed Nina quite a bit.

She kept still and quiet for some time. However, the journalist in her would not let her rest or sleep. "But as cowherds you must also be dealing with a lot of shit, I mean the shit of cows. Does that not pollute you?"

Manjula was flabbergasted at the sudden turning of the tables. Her self-pride was punctured a bit and she did not like it a bit. Her face changed. It became hard. Nina patted her own back for having challenged someone who considered herself to be superior to other human beings.

"No. No! In our religious view cow dung is holy and it purifies us from all pollution. In fact when we happen to touch Madhigas or when Madhigas from big positions come into our village we purify our village by applying a paste from cow dung.' Manjula knew that she was putting up a very weak defense on her lapse. 'I should have just acknowledged that I made a mistake." She thought.

"What have the Madhiga people to do with today's Day of Judgment? Everybody speaks of the Day of Judgment in your village. But no one has told me till now what is the judgment all about? Can you tell me what it is all about and why are the Madhiga people waiting outside your village?" Manjula was greatly relieved at the fact that Nina changed the topic. She wanted to do that too.

"Well, you know that Poojamma has been fighting against the practice of untouchability in our area and has succeeded to a great extent. She also took up the question of Gollars in our village not allowing the Madhigas into the village and educated our people about the evil consequences of caste discrimination among human beings. Though all our people like Poojamma, Eeranna of the neighboring village misguides some of our men. He is a big fellow and a politician, a crooked one at that. He wants caste system to continue as it is. He finds that it is hugely advantageous to him to keep village people divided on caste lines." Manjula recovered from her negative mood sooner than it was normal for her.

'Poojamma held several rounds of discussions in the village as part of her mission. She allowed them and often even provoked them to come out with their views for and against the prevailing practices of discrimination in the village. The village was sharply divided into two camps. It was not because of Poojamma's raising the issue of caste discrimination. They loved Poojamma and listened to her always. But some of them owed loyalty to Eeranna and that caused the birth of two camps in the village. She was deeply aware of this and was not in a hurry to change anything in her favor. She knew that one-day people would understand the core issue and would come around.'

"But what is the issue in your village? Is it simply the practice of untouchability or something else? You speak of the Day of Judgment without giving me a clue as what the judgment is all about." Nina was now beginning to get annoyed at the suspense.

"Ok, ok. Don't be angry with me now. The issue is the question of allowing the Madhigas into our village. Even Poojamma did not know this for a long time. She knows that Madhigas are treated very badly by the society and as the worst of untouchables. But she was shocked when she learned that Gollars do not allow Madhigas even in their village. Usually they are not allowed only to enter houses of caste people. But in Gollar villages they cannot even enter the village."

"Did she bring them into your village? What did she do?" Nina was sharp on point.

Manjula laughed a bit loud at the naiveté of Nina. "Poojamma never does anything like that. She never imposes her views on us. She makes people think a lot and come to their own decision about any issue. Ultimately it is our decisions and we become owners of our decisions. That ownership brings in a lot of responsibility on our part. This is what marks Poojamma different from other Dalit leaders and government officers. She is in the business of empowering us and not spoon-feeding us. She identified Madhiga masons to construct houses in our villages. But some of our people objected to Madhiga masons. That is when things began to heat up."

"So, you people objected to the Madhiga masons entering your village? What happened to the house construction? You would have lost the houses. I know Poojamma would never agree to such unabashed caste discrimination." Nina was quite incisive in her statement.

"You are wrong, madam. She would never make us losers because of our folly. She called for a meeting of the entire village and reasoned out with all the elders in the village that such caste discrimination is against humanity and against the law of the land." Manjula evenly matched Nina word for word, attitude for attitude, and aggression for aggression.

"Then why are you not having the houses yet? I do not see the houses in your village yet." Nina's reaction was quite two-fisted now.

"Our people agreed with the reasoning of Poojamma. To me it looked like a smooth running. Even Poojamma thought that our Golla fellows would easily allow the Madhiga masons to enter our village. But one strong follower of Eeranna had other ideas." Manjula continued.

"Poojamma, we respect you profoundly. You have been almost like a goddess to us. But our caste has some rules and regulations that we cannot easily violate. If we allow Madhigas to enter our village it would invite the wrath of our clan gods and our entire village will be punished. When that happens people will blame you." Rangappa picked up the courage to challenge Poojamma. He was armored with the weapons provided by

Eeranna. The spirit of Yellamma had already possessed him. She is fondly referred to as the goddess of liquor.

Poojamma did not take much time to understand who was talking from inside Rangappa. She knew immediately that he was remote controlled by Eeranna and played her game carefully. "Since I am the one who am asking you to change your tradition, your god should actually punish me and not you. I am ready to accept any type of punishment that your god may send to me. Many people have changed their traditions in many of our villages. All of you know that. But their gods did not punish them. It is not the work of gods. It is the work of some evil human beings that has kept you entrenched in enthralling traditions. Get educated and try to move with the rest of the world. Lay bare a progressive path of prosperity to your children. Your children are like my children and that is why I am struggling so much with you." Poojamma made an emotional appeal to all the people.

"What Poojamma says is the right thing. Why should you be punished for something good that you are doing to us Poojamma? If gods punish us for listening to your good advise for our well being, I am also ready to accept any punishment that may come from our gods." Malik picked up the courage to stand against many in the village. He never liked those who took camp position with Eeranna.

Women supported Malik unanimously. They did not take any camp position. They had only one camp and that was Poojamma's. They began to use some of their choicest epithets against their own husbands for joining Eeranna and for having brought divisions in the village. Men in Eeranna's camp began to feel the heat. There were whispers here and loud talking there among them. Poojamma allowed everything to happen in its own time. She waited in patience.

"No, we should not violate our village traditions. Our ancestors gave them to us and all our elders have seen to it till today that none of our traditions would be broken. Even many of our educated people have kept alive our traditions. We should not allow Madhigas to enter our village and invite the wrath of our gods. Caste has been given to us from ages by our religion. Today we cannot go against our religion for the sake of these bloody Madhigas." Rangappa poured out the anger of his master.

He was his master's voice. There were others who joined his chorus hiding their mouth with their palms so that Poojamma would not notice the movement of their lips.

"Do not use harsh words against the Madhiga people. Just as you are my people they are also my people. I shall not tolerate any abuse of any human being. Moreover, you must know that the law in India does not allow you to use such abusive language against the Madhiga people. You can be easily put in jail for this." Poojamma spoke in atypically angry voice and that flabbergasted even her followers and admirers.

"No Poojamma, he is an idiot that is why he is speaking like that. Please do not take him seriously. We shall tell him to behave. Hey, you mother fucker, don't you know what to speak? Is this the way to speak in front of our Mother?" Nagaraj, a disciple of Poojamma tried to save Rangappa's skin by his pretentious anger. Poojamma knew him well and rebuked him with her look.

"You fellows always abuse your mothers even when you want to scold each other. Stop abusing your mothers." Poojamma turned to Nagaraj and rebuked him with a smile.

Nagaraj ran and hid himself behind her being unable to look straight into her eyes. Poojamma had this very special quality of looking into people's eyes and many of them did not have the courage to reciprocate the same gesture. It implied a lot of courage. She had terrific eyes that could pierce into peoples' inner beings.

It was then that Puttamma stood up and began to speak. Gollars do not allow their women to speak in public. But over a period of a few months Poojamma had transformed the women and men. Now many women began to show their true grit to their men. "You fellows are speaking of ancestors and elders. Did you not remember our elder in our village? For everything we ask his opinion and abide by his pronouncements. Why did you not ask him about this? Let us ask our Gowdajja and abide by his decision on this issue. What do you say Poojamma?" There was an explicit pride on her face. She turned round and gave a stern look to all those present.

It was a twist no one expected. But that was the tradition of the village. Both the camps now began to see a huge advantage in making the old man speak up on their behalf. Each camp made its secret calculation. Rangappa saw a clear opportunity for his camp, as he knew that the old man would not violate the traditions of his caste. "Yes, yes, that is a very good thing. How come none of us thought of this? We always do this in our village. What do you say, all of you?" He tried to checkmate Poojamma and she knew it well.

"Yes, yes, we all agree. What say you all? Let us all abide by the opinion of our Gowdajja. His verdict will be final. No one should say anything after he gives his judgment." Malik spoke on behalf of the camp that owed loyalty to Poojamma. She was in a fix. But this was the custom of the village and she respected such mechanisms of internal governance by communities of people. Though she apprehended that the decision could put the village in reverse gear she agreed to it. This is how the Day of Judgment evolved.

———◦◦◦❮◦❯◦◦◦———

Poojamma knew Gowdajja well. He had a very soft corner for her. He was over 120 years. A very grand old man, almost worthy of being elevated to the position of ancestor! He was the head of the entire clan who settled down in Guddahalli. When Poojamma saw him for the first time she mistook him to be senile. That was the way he showed love to her. He behaved like a teenager with her. Poojamma remembered her romantic days with her boyfriend whom she could never marry. But romance was an integral part of her early life. She realized that the man was fully alert and was in his senses. It was simply that his youth had returned to him after a ripe age, as many of his teeth started sprouting all over again.

"Do you eat meat even now Ajja?" She asked him with all the affection that welled up in her being. She was a natural lover when it came to old men. Her boyfriend used to tease her on her love for old men. She showed mock anger at him and hugged him. But he was no more. Yama, the god of death plucked him away from her too prematurely.

"Yes, whenever they prepare meat they give me some pieces. I am unable to bite bone any more. But with my gums I still eat meat. Mudde (Ragi ball) and meat are my favorite." Saying this he laughed loud as if he had cracked the biggest joke of his life. People around began to speak a lot about his younger days and how even at 120 years he was still walking to the nearby village. Poojamma often took refuge in the soft corner that he provided for her in his heart. She had reserved a much bigger space for him in her dome of human respect. She would go to meet him first whenever she visited Guddahalli. But that day she decided not to visit him. She had developed political acumen over the few years she moved to the village. She would never go to Guddahalli without taking some sweets for him.

"Give this to Gowdajja." That day she handed over the packet of sweets to Nagaraj.

"Why, Poojamma? Come and meet him. He will be very happy to see you." Rangappa tried to be a bit too nice to her. But she knew that if she visited him that day Eeranna's camp would interpret that she was trying to influence Gowdajja towards a decision in her favor. She did not want to create any such impression, as she was very keen that people should take their own decisions.

"They fixed today as the Day of Judgment. This is what happened in our village to bring all of us to the Day of Judgment, madam." Manjula narrated the past events to Nina even as Poojamma was waiting for people to bring Gowdajja to the temple at the center of the village. It was there that the village people had decided to assemble on the Day of Judgment.

Even in that tense moment Nina took Poojamma aside under the pretext of answering nature's call in the wood. There she chided Poojamma for not having shared anything about her boyfriend. "Did you have a bad experience with your boyfriend? Is that why you are not marrying? Please tell me what happened." Nina tried to turn on some heat at the wrong time. That was her nature. She could never wait for any information. Everything had to be asked at once and everything should be said to her without any postponing. Poojamma was in no mood to narrate to her all the details of her first love. However, she did not want to disappoint Nina. She knew her well by then. If she did not share something Nina would find it difficult to take notes of the Day of Judgment.

"Yes, we were very close to each other. It was a time of inexplicable romance for both of us. We were sure that we were becoming life partners. But it did not last long . . ."

Nina could not allow Poojamma to complete. "Why? Did he find another girl? Did he ditch you badly? Did you have sex with him? What happened?" When rain started it always used to be a torrent in Nina's world.

"Yes we had everything that a man and a woman of that age had. I do not share the traditional moral views on relationships and sex. But just before we could fix a formal marriage function we discovered that he had cancer in his liver and that he would not live for more than a month. It was too late for anyone to do anything. We enjoyed each other's company till he lasted. I am happy that I had a chance to serve him at his side for the rest of his life. His family was too good to me. They allowed me to take care of him. He died on my lap." Poojamma wiped the few drops of tears that pierced through her eyelids much against her wish.

"Oh I am really very sorry to hear this. I am extremely sorry to have dug this up from your mouth at this untimely hour. Sorry Poojamma." Nina embraced her.

"There the people are waiting. Come let us rush, Nina. We shall speak about it at another suitable time. Come, let us go." Poojamma held her hands and led her back to the village. People of her camp were watching all this. They had come to see where Poojamma had disappeared all of a sudden.

CHAPTER FOUR

Both the camps got busier and busier everyday. It was a question of prestige for all of them. Both the groups headed straight to the house of Gowdajja. They sat in front of him on the floor, as he always sat on the floor in his house with a woolen blanket around his body. He covered his head with a woolen cap just as most people in Karnataka did. His inseparable companion, the walking stick at his side was gaping at them.

It is a funny sight for people from other States of India. People of Karnataka believe in keeping their head always warm and never let cold wind dictate anything to their head. Even in summer they would cover their head with woolen cap. The house of Gowdajja was dark inside. All of them were used to darkness in the house. They took only a few minutes to see people inside in light. Their eyes were trained for such sights. Gowdajja had a good hard look at all the people who had assembled. Like himself his face always remained unmoved. He had seen every up and down of life and nothing could shake him now. He intuitively knew that something serious was in the air. As was his wont he did not raise any question. He also knew that the camp followers of Eeranna were also sitting in front of him. Being an experienced clan leader he did not open his mouth first. He waited for the others to start explaining the purpose of their coming.

He had every right to be arrogant at the ripe old age of 120. No one had ever succeeded to live his life as buoyantly as he did or did anyone manage to live it as long as he did. That he was able to walk nearly two kilometers to the next village even now made him prouder. He was a living witness of all the ups and downs of the village that he nurtured assiduously.

Poojamma was a stormy entrant in the village. No one had ever dared to challenge the morons in that village as she did. He liked Poojamma immensely without ever knowing why he did that. But that was what welled up in him and he did not want to do any violence to himself at the fag end of his life. He gave full vent to the budding love in his heart. She was young enough to call his son as her grandfather. But he cared a hoot for anything when it came to liking Poojamma. The people of Guddahalli however knew that he did not think much about what he did. He just did everything as it appeared to him.

He was grossly disappointed with all the men in the village as they were reluctant to listen to him any more. They only considered him as a senile old man. They would pretend to love him and listen to him carefully. But when they went away from him would do exactly what they wanted to do and not what he told them as the leader of their clan. He was terribly piqued at the new reality that a few of them opted to listen to Eeranna who did not belong to their caste and had nothing to do with the morals that the village had adhered to. Eeranna was a crooked politician and landlord who believed only in cheating people and government for acquiring more money and land. He hated Eeranna for his selfish leadership. Gowdajja and Eeranna two contrasting study for Poojamma.

Unable to bear his stern look for long Nagaraj began to speak up. "Poojamma had come to talk to us." He said in a pious voice but loud enough to reach the hardened eardrums of the old man.

"Don't tell me lies. Poojamma would never leave the village without seeing me." Gowdajja was exuding confidence in himself, his hand simultaneously fondling his walking stick. There was an evident slighting in his voice. "She likes me more than she likes all of you fellows." The voice seemed to tell them.

"She had come to speak about the construction of the houses. We only told her that she should come another day and speak to you." Lingappa spoke a bit louder than Nagaraj.

"Why did you tell her that you mischievous fellows? She is like a goddess to us. You must wash her feet and lick it, you numbskulls." He was almost

46

reproving them for their folly. The walking stick was now standing up in his hand.

"You know the problem well Gowdajja. She has told us that we should allow the Madhiga fellows to construct our houses. Can we just allow anyone to break our cherished traditions just because she has found the money to construct houses for us free? We told her that you should have the final say on this issue." Malik now placed his agenda subtly to Gowdajja. He had a strong message to the old man.

"Yes, I know this issue. But why did she leave the village so soon without even meeting me? She never does that. What did you do to her you meatballs?" Gowdajja smelt a rat.

"It is because these fellows told her on her face that we cannot break our traditions." Lingappa was blaming the other camp in an attempt to gain the sympathies of the old man to his camp. He belonged to the camp of Nagaraj.

"Did she leave in a huff? Did you knuckleheads insult her in any way? Was she angry?" He was a bit furious at them.

"No, Gowdajja! Why will she be angry with us? You know Poojamma. She is never angry with us for anything. But some of us agreed to allow the Madhiga fellows to construct the houses and some of us did not want to break our ancestral traditions. Finally we said that you should be the judge. We shall go by whatever judgment you give on the matter. Now you have to give us a day on which you will give your judgment. Poojamma said she would come on the day that you fix and abide by your judgment." Malik tried to lure the old man into his camp position by being very nice to him.

"Did she say she would accept whatever judgment I give?" Gowdajja wanted to be doubly sure of Poojamma's position.

"Yes, yes. That is why she left without meeting you. We asked her to meet you and go but she said that if she met you today these fellows who listen to Eeranna would say that she influenced you this way or that. She wants you to give a judgment according to your wisdom without any other influence. That is why she left without meeting you." Nagaraj gave an elaborate explanation that brought a faint smile in the lips of the old man.

"That is why she is adored by us, you woodenheads. Does any politician do things this way? See how unselfish she is. She has love in her heart. You dum-dums, how will you know all that? Is there any love in your hearts? You fellows, you have your wives only to fuck them day in and day out. The only days that you leave your wives free are when they have their periods. That is why our clan leaders have made it compulsory that women in periods must get out of your houses and stay out of the village. Otherwise you motherfuckers will fuck your wives even on those difficult days. Anyway ask all the people in our village to come together on the next full moon day. I shall give my verdict." Gowdajja solemnized the informal meeting in his inimitable style. The stick in his hand went back to its orginal position. When he abused them no one would retort. If anyone dared by any quirk of fate, he would take the stick at his side and let it speak to him.

Both the groups were aghast that the old man did not give a clue on what his judgment would be. They were instead drenched in his abuses for having let Poojamma go. Was it a correct decision to have asked Poojamma to let the old man take the final call on the question of allowing Madhigas into the village? The question was like a sharp spear piercing their hearts. But no one had the courage to acknowledge it. They began to put up a brave front saying the old man's judgment would be in their favor.

Malik carried the news to Eeranna faithfully. He instructed Malik to bring all his followers from Guddahalli to his house for a discussion.

"You motherfuckers, why is it that you are giving up your caste? Don't you fellows have any bloody white stuff in your head? Some fucking lady comes from another country and you fellows go and lick her feet . . . ." Eeranna was furious at his group of followers in Guddahalli. Aggression was his way of putting his followers on the mat.

Simultaneously, Nagaraj called for a meeting of all loyalists of Poojamma. The meeting was in his house in Guddahalli itself. "We have followed the path shown to us by our Poojamma and you all have seen the progress that our village has made. Today is a different day. You all know that some of our brothers have decided to owe their loyalty to Eeranna. This is not good for us . . ."

". . . No Eeranna, it is not like that. If we oppose Poojamma we shall not get the benefit of all the schemes that she is bringing in from other countries and from the government. Only her true loyalists will bag all of them. Therefore, we pretend as if we are her followers. How can we leave you? You are our local leader. She is after all an outsider. We even do not know from which country she has come." Harish wanted to have the cake and eat it too. Eeranna gave him a stern look half believing what he said and half distrusting him. Harish knew the meaning of his look. But then he was used to it. He tucked his tail between his legs.

"Hey guys, this is not at all good for the future of our children. All of us know that this Eeranna is a snake oil salesman. Almost all of us have suffered in his hands at some time or other. If we do not fight him now even our children will be under his terrible fetters. Poojamma is a god sent gift to us. She is like our Krishna ever ready to take on the might of our enemy. Let us be loyal to her and be united in our fight against this scam artist Eeranna. It is a pity some of our brothers are very egotistical and have joined his camp. It is a bad omen for our village." Shiva blew his trumpet a bit loud. Nagaraj put his finger on his lips and asked him to speak a bit milder.

"Our Eeranna has told us several times that we should stand on our own legs and not trust anyone who comes from outside our area. She may do a lot of good things to our people. But who will spend so much money without a hidden purpose behind. This Poojamma is a bloody vampire. We do not know anything about her past. We do not know how many men she had slept with in her life. From the way she speaks is it not clear to us that she is a woman of loose character. Otherwise why would she speak against our caste system that god has given to us. Among us there is only one educated person and one who can do everything with the Chief Minister and that is our leader Eeranna. We should stand with him till the end." This was Manjanna who had come newly into the group. He had to prove himself in the group for greater acceptance.

"He does not even know that Eeranna has studied only until pre-university and that too he failed in the second year. This fellow is trying to get into the good books of Eeranna. We must cut him to size already now." Malik talked under his breath to his neighbor mingling his muttering with intermittent coughing so that no one heard his voice.

There was something else running in the mind of Eeranna. He had seen enough politics in his life. "This Manjanna may have been planted into my camp by the cronies of Poojamma." He thought. He cleared his throat and spoke. "All that Manjanna has spoken may be true. But he should guard his tongue when he speaks in a meeting. If such disrespectful words are carried to the opposite camp we may lose our respect." He wanted to put down Manjanna in the presence of Malik so that he would not lose his time-tested loyalists.

"Which of our leader educated us till now on all the things that Poojamma has educated us? She has opened our eyes. We were fully ignorant till she came. We should be ever grateful to her for enlightening our minds on many things about which we were not at all aware. Who else is there in our area that can speak to us on the affairs of the world as authoritatively as Poojamma? She has studied a lot. She reads English. The other day I saw her speaking to our District Collector in English. She can even speak to the Prime Minister and to foreigners in English. Poojamma is our leader. She is our goddess. We cannot find any weakness at all in her. Whatever may be the tradition that our caste handed over to us, we shall listen to her advice and follow her path. Only this way we can build a bright future for our children." Nagaraj tried to fix the followers of Poojamma firmly in her path. There was an unrecognized desire in him to be the undisputed leader of Guddahalli.

"Yes, yes. I fully agree with what our Nagaraj Anna has said just now. We shall simply follow the path shown to us by our Poojamma. She is our everything." Manjula dared to thrust her voice in a room filled with male voices. Everyone turned to her with surprise. But no one objected to her speaking. They knew well that she could attack them vituperatively if they dared to silence her. They also knew the type of influence she wielded with Poojamma. They approved of what she said with their loud silence. But everyone admired the genuine love Manjula had for this goddess.

"What shall we do if she contests elections one day? How can we predict her hidden intentions? Already now people are worshiping her as a goddess. She is becoming increasingly popular in the entire district. If she contests elections she will surely win. What shall our Eeranna do if that happens? How can we allow a non-local person to become our political leader?" Malik gave a new direction to the discussion in Eeranna's house. Sycophancy of the first order! He stirred up a hornet's nest. The leader now began to burn inside.

"If anything like that happened, we should see how she will live in our area? We respect people for what they do. But if they cross the Rubicon then they will face the consequences." Eeranna was gruff in his intervention. He was not used to speak much in front of his minions. He wanted to feel quite superior to all of them. He only pontificated when his brown-noses spoke among themselves to communicate to him. But he became very talkative when some political bigwigs met him. Then he had to prove to them the type of following he had in the area. Politics according to him required the capacity to convince bigger leaders of his power to capture votes.

"I think it will be good to inform the Member of the Legislative Assembly whom we got elected last time and through him get this bloody female out of our area. We can bring an allegation that she is a foreign agent and ask our MLA to speak to the Chief Minister and order her ouster from this District or from Karnataka itself. Our Eeranna should speak to our MLA as soon as possible." Manjanna spewed acrimony.

"She is like a Prime Minister for us. She can do anything for us. She has contacts in the UN and in many other countries. People from all countries listen to her voice. What more do we need? Eeranna and our MLAs get elected once in five years. When they need our votes they come to our houses and fall at our feet. But after elections they would not even recognize us. Let us not believe in these political goons. Poojamma is our last refuge in life." Manjula dared to continue her assertions taking the silence of the menfolk as a tacit approval of her forays.

"You think you are smarter than I am? It is all done already. When she organizes a function in our area next time you will see that no officer will attend the function. Our MLA will speak to the officers and ask them not to attend her functions." Eeranna now let the cat out of the bag. It was unusual of him to reveal to the village people what he did from his home. He was always suspicious of all of them. They could shift sides any time. Just as there are no permanent enemies in politics there are also no permanent friends. But as they say even an elephant slips sometime. It was a slip.

His confidante Malik was quick to understand the slip. He did not want the others to give much importance to what slipped out of the mouth of Eeranna. 'But come to the point now. Why are you fellows beating round the bush? We have come here to see to it that the old man will give his verdict in our favor. This Poojamma must realize that she cannot ride over our local leaders and change our much cherished customary practices as she liked.' He succeeded in accomplishing his mission. Eeranna was happy that someone among them had learned some politics from him.

"We need to be very cautious. All of us know well that Gowdajja has a soft corner for Poojamma. But some fellows in Eeranna's camp are his own grandsons. They can easily influence him. Therefore, some of us should meet Gowdajja secretly and convince him that these anachronistic customs should be changed if our village has to see serious development." Nagaraj brought his camp to order.

Both the camps met Gowdajja frequently to make sure that his verdict was in their favor. Manjanna even got some money from Eeranna to buy good mutton from the city and asked his wife to prepare a tasty meal for Gowdajja. His wife knew well what the palate of the old man welcomed. Manjanna was the grandson of Gowdajja. He listened to both the camps with extreme patience knowing also well that both the camps were in a lather to know the roiling in his mind.

Eeranna had been giving strict warning that his camp should stick together and be in the good books of the old man till he delivered his judgment in their favor. They should do nothing untoward to antagonize the old man. It was a matter of his prestige. He had also sent word through Manjanna that it was Eeranna's wish that the verdict was given against allowing the Madhigas inside the village.

———•◦▮◦•———

It was with much caution and angst that Nina walked the talk with Manjula. 'Just in case the old man gave his verdict in favor of tradition and opposed modernity! He could be swayed any time. Much depended on what he thought on the given day.' The thought let loose millions of butterflies flutter in her stomach.

'Hey, be careful! Watch your steps! Our village streets are not like the paved streets of your country. Look down and walk. Otherwise you will go back to your country without nails in any of your toes." Manjula said even as she was holding Nina in her extended arms. She could feel the breasts of Nina in her hands.

"Thanks much" Nina said as she regained her position.

"Sorry" Manjula apologized. She removed her hands from Nina's breasts as if she had touched fire.

"Oh, don't worry about it. Both of us have the safe stuff in front. The difference is only the shape." Nina said with a broad smile on her face. And rearranged her boobs in their proper place.

"How uninhibited these foreigners are! They speak so openly about everything. They are not shy of speaking about their body parts. There is no taboo." Manjula ruminated within herself about cultural contradictions.

"And what is this?" Nina spread out her inspecting eyes all around the building in front of her even as she stood straight.

"This is our temple. You know our elders have said that we should not live in a village without temples. Our community builds a temple in all our villages and all our houses are constructed around the temple." Manjula now began to show off her superior knowledge of religion.

"But why is it locked? What kind of god lives in this temple? When do you worship your god?" Nina began to rain a volley of questions. Manjula did not allow her to move fast forward with her questions.

"This is the temple of Krishna. Have you heard of Krishna?" Manjula reversed roles. She began to ask questions.

"Yes, I have heard that song from Colonial Cousins. Krishna Nee begane baro. Is it that Krishna?" Question for questioning and question for answering!

Manjula blinked in the air. She had heard the song and liked it but never heard of Colonial Cousins. She admired the knowledge of Nina's and was happy that she knew about Krishna. "Yes, Krishna is our god. He actually belongs to our Golla community. He was a cowherd boy as well as a cowboy."

"So you also have cowboys as your gods in your country?" Nina brought glimpses of her culture into a remote Golla village in India.

"Yes, yes. He was grazing cows in the field. You know we are a people who rear cows and graze them. Krishna was our ancient king. He also had many forays among young girls and played with them all the games that people play with women." Manjula now began to touch upon a bit of history that she knew. "Actually he was one of our ancient kings whom we revered. He fought valiantly against the invading Aryans. They did not have anything to do with cows. They stole cows from us and learned milk economy from us. In order that we may not hold copyright to cow economy they transformed the cow into a holy animal and made people to worship it. We stopped eating beef from then on. The Madhigas continued to eat beef not heeding to the holy discourses of Brahmins. After coopting our community into their fold they made us also hate the Madhigas since they still continued to eat the meat of the cow that we began to worship. The anger of our ancestors against Brahmins for appropriating our economy still remains and we have also acquired this new hatred for Madhigas from the Brahmins. From then on we have been fighting against Brahmins and that explains why till today we do not invite Brahmins in our villages."

"But your temple looks like a Hindu temple. Do you have your own religion or do you follow Hindu religion? It is all very confusing to me." Nina was aghast at all the information she received from different corners.

"It is a very intricate matter. The Aryans could not defeat Krishna, our king. Therefore, they decided to take him into their fold. This is one of the most intriguing techniques of Brahminism. When they cannot defeat someone physically they extend an olive branch to the same person and after taking him into their fold they make the person and his followers bite the dust. This is what they did to our great king Krishna." Manjula now began to manifest another scholarly dimension of her personality.

"Are you saying that Krishna lived sometime in history? Do you believe that he was a historical figure? I have heard that he is a mythical figure. Is he not the one who preached Baghavad Gita?" Nina tried to prove that she was not lagging far behind Manjula in her scholarly output.

"I don't know if Krishna lived and if he was a historical figure. All I know is that we had powerful kings who opposed the Aryans. That is history and not myth. Rama and Krishna may be figures taken out from mythological stories. But it is history that we had Golla kings who did not allow the Aryans to run over us as they wished. It is also history that ultimately the Aryans subsumed our kings into their way of thinking through their cunningness. They played our kings against the Madhigas and divided us. This is the same case with Valmiki and Vyasa." Manjula now began to educate Nina on Indian history.

"Who are these people that you mention now?" Nina's intellect could stretch itself only to some distance in India.

"Valmiki is an ancient sage of the Dalit people. It is said that he wrote Ramayana. Rama is the hero of this epic. The other epic of Hinduism is Mahabharata. Vyasa who is from a backward caste community is said to have written this epic. I don't know if you are aware that Brahmins were illiterate when they stepped into India. They had to depend on our learned people for writing their rules and regulations. In order to write their epics they depended on the Shudra and Dalits. Even in modern times when India wanted to write her new constitution they depended on the untouchable Ambekdar." Manjula made a powerful rendition of her erudition.

"It is all very complicated to me. Let us come back to Krishna. You said something about your king Krishna getting co-opted by Aryans. Can you explain that to me?" Nina pleaded innocence and played ignorance in an attempt to know more from Manjula.

"You mentioned Bhagavad Gita. It contains the central teaching of Hinduism and according to ancient myths our King Krishna is the one who preached it. He preached non-violence in the battle field . . ." Nina laughed to herself and Manjula laughed aloud. "Yes, both of us know why we laugh. Preaching non-violence in the battlefield! The irony of Hinduism! The same Krishna exhorted Arjun to kill all his relatives and teachers only because he was born in the warrior caste. The Aryans have made a mincemeat of our great king Krishna only because he was an indigenous king and they could do anything with him that they wanted to do." Even as Manjula's voice lowered a bit Nina could sense that she was emotional.

"Hey Manjula bring that Madam to the meeting. Gowdajja has started off for the meeting. He will be there in a few minutes." One of the girls shouted to Manjula. She was unable to bear the sight of Manjula speaking to Nina in English for such a long time. There were millions of worms crawling in her stomach.

There were simultaneous calls everywhere in the village. Each one was calling out to his neighbor saying that Gowdajja was going to the temple. The anxiety filled excitement spread through the entire village.

"Where is Poojamma? Go bring Poojamma also for the meeting. Gowdajja will ask for her as soon as he arrives." Manjula shouted in return. Then she turned to Nina and said. 'At last the judge will arrive now.'

"Oh, Gowdajja is the judge on the Day of Judgment? Where is Poojamma? Will she be there in the meeting?" Nina exposed her naiveté once again.

"Of course, yes. Do you think such an important event in the life of our village will pass without the presence of Poojamma? No one will agree to it." Manjula was very assertive.

Just as she concluded, Poojamma appeared in front of the village temple. People had already informed her that the historic judgment would be delivered in the premises of the village temple. The temple had a verandah as well as a courtyard. It could accommodate all the people of the village. In fact the plinth area of the temple was very small. It was only enough to have the deity and the village priest. People had to stand in the verandah at the time of worship and assemble there on other occasions to have their meetings. It was the only public space available to the village.

There was a group of men and women behind Poojamma. One did not need much brain to understand that they were her loyal followers. But one could also locate some men and women who actually belonged to the camp of Eeranna. They did not want to show their camp position to Poojamma. No one wanted to hurt her sentiments. There was another group of fence sitters between both the camps. They would oscillate to the side that was more vocal and perceived to be more powerful on any given day.

Behind Poojamma was another group, mostly of men. Amidst them was the slow motion of Gowdajja walking towards the temple, covered fully with a woolen blanket. His walking stick was also in slow motion with him. He did not like a bit the efforts of some overenthusiastic men who wanted to give a supporting hand to him. He was a man of his own. He did not look up to see the crowd. But one could notice that his eyes were eagerly probing the crowd for someone special. Even the most loyal fellow of Eeranna's camp knew that Gowdajja was looking out for Poojamma. His eyes had a raving for her presence. He put down his face as soon as he sighted Poojamma. He became very comfortable at the knowledge that she was there. All those who surrounded him were mostly followers of Eeranna. They wanted to make sure that nobody influenced Gowdajja against their position. There were also one or two from the loyalists of Poojamma. Village style spying!

"Sit, sit, sit! All of you sit. Don't make noise." The usual prelude to any meeting in the village! Often the request not to make noise became the biggest noise and disturbed the meeting. Poojamma brought her both hands together to greet Gowdajja. It was a beautiful synchronization of symphony between both of them. No lyrics, no notes and yet a celestial and hypnotizing music. They liked each other immensely. He was old enough to be her grandfather at the age of 120. Their eyes however were glowing with love of young romantics. All the people were gazing at both of them.

Nagaraj took the lead in welcoming both Gowdajja and Poojamma. He did not want to leave the initiative in the hands of Malik. "Hey, also welcome that madam from America." Malik shouted to Nagaraj regretting that he let go of the initiative in the meeting. His friends were passing the sternest looks ever for the faux pas. He was more worried about how Eeranna would chide him for not taking the initiative in such an important meeting. The frustration permeated his entire camp and it came out in the form of unwarranted smiles.

"Gowdajja, we have gathered here today to decide about a very significant issue that affects our village and our tradition. Some of us are of the view that our antiquated custom of not allowing the Madhiga people into our village should be changed. In these modern times all are human beings. Poojamma has also informed us that such a custom is against the constitution of our country and that it could invite legal punishment on us if we persist with this antediluvian custom. Our village needs to change with time. It is god's blessing that we have got Poojamma to educate us on our constitution and rights and to also fight for us . . ." Nagaraj was in a mood to give a public speech for more than an hour. He was however interrupted by Malik.

"That is what he says, Gowdajja. Though we have a constitution in India we Gollars have also our own customs and traditions. How can we give them up just for the sake of the constitution? From time immemorial we have been following our customary laws. It is Ambedkar who wrote the constitution and he wrote it in their favor. Some of us are of the strong view that Madhigas should not be allowed into any of our Golla villages." There was fire in the face of Malik.

"It is not only a question of allowing the Madhigas into our village. There are also related issues such as the way we treat our women." Nagaraj looked at Poojamma with pride while saying this. She had kept her vision low to the ground anticipating many such looks. Nagaraj continued, "Keeping our women in an inhuman hut at the time of delivery and casting out our women at the time of their menstrual periods have to be changed. Poojamma has clearly said that it is against the health of our women and against justice to our women. She has said very clearly that delivery and menstrual periods have nothing to do with uncleanliness and pollution. Times have changed and if we continue with these customs we shall not be respected well in the society. Our children have started going to big cities in order to pursue their studies and career. When others come to know that we still keep these antediluvian customs intact our children will become objects of their derision."

"Why are you raking up all sorts of cock and bull stories now? Come to the point." Manjanna was itching to have the final word from the horse's mouth.

"Okay, okay. Nagaraj, ask Gowdajja to give his verdict on the point in question. What does he say? Can the Madhigas be allowed into our village or not. We can discuss other issues later." Malik joined the chorus with Manjanna fully confident that the judgment would be in their favor.

"We have gathered here to listen to the final verdict of Gowdajja. This is what all of you decided. I am sure all of you have informed him sufficiently on the seriousness of the issue. Gowdajja, now it is up to you. People here are ready to abide by your final decision. Please give your verdict." Poojamma now stepped in to bring Gowdajja to the center stage.

Gowdajja looked up at Poojamma with his usually glowing eyes. It looked as if he did not know what to say. Poojamma looked at all the people assembled. She had a reproving look at both the camps. "Gowdajja, you know well that Guddahalli does not allow Madhiga people into your village. Now we have to construct some houses for the homeless people in this village. There are some masons from the Madhiga community and if you do not allow them into your village we shall have to find out other masons only for your village. When I told our people that it is going to be very difficult and that they should allow the Madhiga people into the village, some of them agree to it and some of them do not agree. Therefore, they decided that all of them would abide by the verdict that you give on this issue. Now please let us know your decision." Poojamma spoke very slowly so that Gowdajja could hear each and every word that she spoke. She was an expert in communication technology. It was not for nothing that she became a powerful public speaker with mesmerizing talks. However, what she spoke that day turned out to be a masterstroke.

Gowdajja's face became brighter still. There was clarity in his vision and face. He took his stick and kept it in an erect position. He held that stick like the kings of yore when they delivered any judgment. Everyone knew that Gowdajja was now ready to talk. Each one anticipated words from his mouth that would spill out like diamond.

Gowdajja cleared his throat. He gave a solemn look at all the people assembled there. He also made sure that all the families of Guddahalli were represented in the meeting that day. His look at both the camps was as dour as ever indicating nothing of what was to come from his mouth.

Then he opened his mouth and with him also many in the crowd without realizing that swarms of houseflies could enter their mouths without any difficulty. "There are only two castes in the world. One is the male caste and the other is the female caste." Nagaraj and his camp followers began to clap their hands and were about to dance. But Poojamma signaled to them to indicate that Gowdajja had not yet given his verdict and that he should be allowed to complete his sentence.

"Therefore, from now on Madhigas are allowed to come into our village like all human beings." The final verdict was out. Succinct and sweet!

There was euphoria in the entire village. Poojamma was happy beyond her expectations. It was her Day of Success. Nina knew instantaneously that the old man had given a verdict in favor of the Madhiga people. It was a Day of Victory for equality and humane spirit, she thought. She checked with Manjula the meaning of the words of Gowdajja and was elated at the way the Day of Judgment had changed into a Day of Celebration. She was very happy for Poojamma.

All the sunbirds that nestled their young ones in the trees around Guddahalli were in a mad rush to sip a stomach full of honey. The beetles made a maddeningly buzzing all around the village. They flew zigzag unmindful of knocking down one another. The goats and rams in the villages tied till then sent out full-throated bleating as if their time for freedom had dawned. Children started running around all over throwing sand in the wind and trying to get underneath before the sand could touch the ground. A merry sand bath indeed! The roosters chased all the hens to stand on them and croak to the world the dawn of a new human spirit. Women began to sing sobana in praise of Gowdajja who had turned their fortunes upside down by challenging a tradition that he had preached and followed.

The camp of Eeranna was downcast and dejected at their apparent defeat. They never anticipated that the old man would turn the tables on them in such a devastating fashion. They had left no stone unturned to convince the old man to subscribe to their ways. But he changed their fortunes in order to favor a woman whom they considered as alien to their culture and history.

Poojamma got up to hold the hands of Gowdajja and thanked him profusely for being so young in his outlook at the ripe old age of 120. Deep inside she wished a much longer life to him and appreciated him for being so revolutionary in his vision of the world. She held his hand and led back to his house. Nina followed both of them together with Manjula. There was food for all of them, served with a lot of food for thought. The walking stick kept its cool all along the path now.

—∞◦|◦|◦∞—

Even as they were having lunch with Gowdajja there was big celebration at the entrance of the village. Poojamma's followers rushed there to inform the Madhiga people in waiting of the good news that they could now enter Guddahalli without any caste discrimination. Poojamma and Nina bade farewell to Gowdajja and left. At the entrance they encountered the Madhiga people who had accompanied them.

"Why are these people not excited about the news? I thought they would have a big celebration. But they seem to be despondent about the decision. Are they not happy to enter your village?" Nina asked Manjula in her journalistic style.

"They may like to hear the news only from the mouth of Poojamma. Till then they may not like to celebrate." Manjula gave her wild guess as a reply to Nina.

Poojamma did not talk much. "We must take them into our village in procession Madam. Let the entire world know that we have made revolutionary changes today. I shall give a statement in the papers about our decision so that other Gollar villages may also follow suit." Nagaraj let out sentences like the monsoon rain. His words came in torrents and poured like streams of water from rooftops.

"Tomorrow morning we can start work here. At that time you may do whatever you like to do." Narasimha, the Madhiga leader from the neighboring village spoke in a heavy voice. The excitement of a historic change in their lives was totally missing in the group of Madhigas who accompanied Poojamma. All of them accompanied Poojamma back to her house. "Now on he will only eat mud. It will take sometime for him to put his hand on rice." Nagaraj shouted in sweet revenge as they approached the house of Eeranna. Poojamma reproved him in mock anger.

ChAPTER FIVE

The 'D' day arrived. Poojamma got ready to go to Guddahalli. Draped in a sky-blue sari with black border she looked gorgeous. She wanted to take the Madhiga people personally and lead them into the Golla village as a mark of the beginning of a new era in Indian rural life. Nina got ready with her camera and iPad. She wanted to record every letter and event of that day for her writing later in the day. She did not want to miss any excitement of the historic change in the village. Of all the American people, of all the journalists in the world she was the only one privileged to witness this historic change in a caste-ridden society. Poojamma was her new feminine icon of liberation. She had already made a huge write up about the events that passed the previous day. As both of them crossed the village they saw a big group of people awaiting Poojamma. Nina did not make any mistake. She knew they were Madhiga people who wanted to accompany Poojamma to Guddahalli.

As they reached the entrance to the village people welcomed her with the usual fanfare. Nagaraj was in leadership to welcome the Madhiga people into his village. "Come, come! Why are you people standing there at the entrance? Do you know that Gowdajja has pronounced his verdict that you can come into our village hereafter? Come in, you are our brothers and sisters, nobody will say anything to you."

Poojamma turned back with surprise on her face. She waited for some time. She was static. Surprise on her face turned into dismay. The Madhiga people were static. They would not take a step forward to enter Guddahalli. In sheer shock Poojamma walked back towards them. Nina realized that there was something amiss but did not dare to ask Poojamma as to what was happening. Poojamma's face conveyed millions of meaning. Nina was all at sea to choose one meaning in that ocean of meanings.

"Come inside the village and start your work. We have had many meetings with the Gollar community and it is after much struggle that we have made them agree to take you into their village. This is not an easy thing in India. You know it well. You know how all caste people treat you. This is a golden opportunity for our community to make self-assertion that we are a people like any other citizen in this country. What are you waiting for? Come and begin the work." Poojamma admonished and pleaded in her inimitable style.

"We shall come Poojamma. You proceed. We shall follow you. We have to speak with our friends here and come." Narasimha was the spokesman on behalf of the Madhiga people.

Poojamma took Nina and went into the village to oversee the construction of houses. Two houses were still gaping at all the people who were busy constructing the other houses. The Madhiga masons were supposed to start work in those two houses. Nina followed Poojamma wherever she went. She knew that not everything was okay that day. The air that filled Guddahalli was heavy. She could see Poojamma breathing heavy. Both of them walked as if a big rolling stone was tied to their neck. Intuitive knowledge, a heavy beast of burden! So it looked.

For a long time the Madhigas did not come to start work in the village. Poojamma was ruffled badly. She had no clue as to what was really happening. "Did Eeranna play any game at night with the people? They have never defied the decisions of the community. Why are they hesitating to enter the village?" Many such thoughts crisscrossed the typically busy mind of Poojamma's.

"Puke the truth out you bloody jackass. Tell Poojamma what happened." Even as Nagaraj was saying this many of his companions were showering a rain of blows on the fragile body of Ganganna. Nagaraj had carefully chosen only Madhigas to beat up Ganganna. He knew well that Ganganna could file a complaint against him any time under the Prevention of SC/ST Atrocities Act of 1989. This Act had stringent strictures against the abuse of Dalits by any other caste persons in India. Gollars are not classified among the Scheduled Caste or Scheduled Tribes.

Nina had studied this Act carefully during her previous visits to India. Poojamma had spoken to her extensively on this Act, as she herself had used the same to bring to books many dominant caste fellows who abused and beat up Dalits in the area. This had sent shivers in the spine of Eeranna and his followers.

"Don't beat him up. What is the matter? What did he do that you beat him up so ruthlessly. Ganganna, speak the truth. What did you do?" Thunder and rain subsided as soon as Poojamma opened her mouth. Nina too opened her mouth in awe. She was awestruck at the fact that Poojamma was not at all perturbed at the way Ganganna was being beaten up. She seemed to be used to such treatment among her followers.

—◦◦◦✸◦◦◦—

Ganganna was the clan leader among Dalits in the village where Poojamma lived. But clan leadership had lost its sheen among Dalits. Caste people had imposed a cumulative serfdom on them over many centuries that Dalits were never able to govern themselves as a people with their own systems of internal governance. They never were able to pick up courage to gather among themselves in their settlements. If they dared there would always be one or other agent of the caste landlord who would keenly observe what was happening among Dalits and inform the caste landlord in the village. The next day there would be collective battering of all Dalits in the village, sparing only those who owed open loyalty to the caste lords. Open loyalty had its own specific connotations. It meant that such Dalits should do free caste labor for all households of the dominant castes.

"Hey go and bring that bloody son of a bitch." Eeranna passed orders to his minions. He was terribly thrown off balance at the news that Gowdajja had passed judgment in support of Poojamma. This was the order of the day in the area. One had to be either for Eeranna or for Poojamma. There was no possibility of neutrality in the entire area. Eeranna had firmly developed the habit of looking at every word and action in the area through the jinxed prism of Poojamma that he possessed. He could not see anything away from Poojamma. In fact it is the centrality that he accorded to himself that colored the glasses that he was wearing. His self-centrism had jaundiced his vision irreparably. With his jaundiced eyes he did not see people as persons. He was able to see them only as votes. Each person was a vote and he had to gain that vote in order to saddle himself in positions of power during and after elections. The popularity of Poojamma was a major threat to him. She could wean away his potential votes at any time. Nay, there was a greater danger that he perceived. He was shivering in his pants often thinking that one day or other Poojamma herself could garner all votes in the area and contest elections against him. That would spell his political doom.

He was angry with the people of Guddahalli and with Gowdajja. The old man was too old for him to do any violence. If he did anything like that it would negatively impact his popularity graph.

"Which son of a bitch should we bring?" Rajanna asked for clarification. It was a habit with Eeranna. Whenever he wanted to deal with someone he would send word to the fellow in question and talk to him with his idiosyncrasy. It was a character. The fouler the language was the more command one had over ordinary people. Poojamma was changing such a culture in the area. No one dared to speak foul language in her presence except when one was uncontrollably angry about something.

"Let us teach a fitting lesson to these gulamas. Bring that fellow Ganganna. We shall give a piece of our mind to him. These bloody gulamas should know where they belong." Gulama is a slang they used for Dalits in the entire area. No caste person would address the Dalits with the minimum courtesy required of a human being. The word itself signified slavery. Gulama is a slave. The caste landlords addressed the Dalits directly as 'hey gulama'. Poojamma's presence in the area had started bringing about a radical transformation in the caste 'culture' of the area. She prevented the use of such language among her followers and created a collective awareness not only among Dalits but also among the other caste followers that all human beings needed to be treated and addressed with due respect. The minimum that was required was to address each one with his/her name. This was established over a period of time. With the caste fellows it took longer time and multiple strategies. The Dalits were emboldened to retort in the same way whenever someone abused them verbally. They took recourse to such retort only when they were in the company of other caste supporters.

Eeranna stood as a solid rock of resistance to any such human evolution. "Oh, big man! Hey you dunderheads, what do you think you are? You motherfuckers have no bloody shame to run after that bitchy woman. Do you know where she has come from? Do you know her mother tongue? Do you know what religion she belongs to? Do you know her real caste? Are you such assholes that you forget your own caste and listen to some bitches who have come to our areas?" He gave full vent to his bottled up anger. Others who were listening to him had a secret smile. They knew that here was a wounded tiger that was licking its wounds.

"Anna, what can I do? I am alone. All our people love this Poojamma. She is such a nice woman. All the people know well that she only means everything good to the poor. Why are you abusing her? Please let me know what I should do?" Ganganna was a bundle of nerves.

Eeranna knew him well. There were some strong points in all Dalits. If they were touched on those points it provided enormous strength to the caste landlords. He signaled to his assistants. They brought a glass of white liquid and handed it over to Ganganna. He hesitated to accept it.

"Take it and gulp it you bloody bum licker. You fellows, you give him company." Eeranna was not in a foul mood. It was his natural self. When he gave liquor to Dalits he would never give it with happiness. Liquor and abuse of Dalits were inseparable companions in his order of things. But no amount of abuse deterred Ganganna from gulping the full glass of liquor at one go.

"Anna, what you order with your legs, I shall do with my head." He shook his head rather violently. Yellamma had started blurting out through Ganganna. He was fully spirited in his assertion. Now Eeranna knew that his trick worked without much difficulty. He knew that indoctrination of the ignorant was the easiest when the spirit was at work.

"You unlettered pea brains, you do not know what is in store for you from that bloody woman. Today she is flowing with milk and honey. It is all because you are ignorant that your people are following her blindly.

Do you know who is behind her? Where does she get all the money to construct houses for you? Have you ever asked her from where she gets all the money?" A volley of questions was the best way of flooring an inebriated Ganganna. But in all such pep talks Eeranna would never dwell on any particular data. He would only indulge on generalities so that he might not be asked to prove any particular allegation.

"Anna, you are great. Our people are dunce and do not know anything. That is why that woman has free access into our houses. We are not only poor. We are also airheaded. You come to our area tomorrow and educate our fellows." Ganganna threw a time bomb at Eeranna without knowing what he was doing.

"What do you eat, you dipstick? Are you eating rice or are you swallowing clay? You are the leader of your clan. It is your duty to educate your chaps. Why should I come to your area to educate you? You go and tell your people all that I have told you today." Eeranna was infuriated.

"No, no! It is not like that. Please do not get angry with me oh lord. I shall educate my people on whatever you ask me to teach them. Tomorrow you will see what I shall do." Ganganna stretched out an olive branch.

"Our Hindu religion teaches us about caste. It is given to us by Krishna, the god of the Gollars. Today you see what this bloody woman has done. She has got hold of that old Gollar man and has brainwashed him against what his own god Krishna has given to the entire India. What are we without our caste, man? Finally one day this woman will convert you to Christianity." Eeranna began to be rancorous now. He had not yet taken his quota of spirit. His words were clear.

"Anna, please do not say that about Poojamma. We have talked to her for many days on this. She has promised us that she will never convert us to any other religion. All our people are convinced of this that she will not convert us." Ganganna lost hold of the scent of the spirit for a moment and made some sense in his response.

Eeranna laughed aloud and turned to his assistants. "Look at this motherfucker. He seems to believe that she will not convert the Madhiga rascals to Christianity. Wait and see what she will do. She will take your people to foreign countries and make you all Christians." Saying this he winked eyes to his followers. They faithfully brought another glass of liquor and handed it over to Ganganna. His lips opened wide. Normally when he smiled they used to open only half the distance. The spirit can work wonders. It stretched his lips beyond the reach of his face. He gulped the second glass of liquor without any inhibition. Eeranna was very happy. So was Ganganna for the free bounty that came on his way.

Giving the glass back Ganganna asked, "You tell me what I should do. I shall do it. You are our lord and protector. I shall do whatever you say." He had to repay the gift that he got.

"Hey, you fellows tell him what he should do in order to save his people from that bitch." Eeranna turned to his assistants.

"Call all the masons your Poojamma has identified for house construction in Guddahalli. Tell them that if they enter the village the gods of Gollars would strike at them. They would visit them with all sorts of diseases and afflictions. Do not tell them not to go for work. Only tell them that their wives and children would have to pay a heavy price if ever they dared to enter the village of the Gollars. All the afflictions would fall on their children. You also be careful. Their gods are horrible gods. They would punish all Madhigas and not only those who enter the Gollar village." The instructions were pre-ordained by Eeranna. He made it look as if he had nothing to do with such instructions.

"This fellow has told all the Madhiga people that the gods of Gollars would strike at them if they entered Guddahalli. Now the Madhigas are refusing to take up work in the village. We have struggled so much to bring about some changes in the lives of our people and this fellow has spoiled everything for two glasses of arrack, Poojamma. If he had asked would we not have given him some money?' Saying this Nagaraj gave two more blows to Ganganna. He stood there as a sacrificial lamb. 'As long as that ninny Eeranna is alive in our area he will never allow our people to become rational and come up in life. He wants to keep all the poor in this area under his bondage." Nagaraj summed up the collective frustration of all those who were present there.

"What is happening here, Poojamma? Why are they raining blows on this poor man? Is he not part of your Movement?' Nina's face had become pale and almost white by then. She was frightened at the way Ganganna was being beaten up and at Poojamma not trying to prevent it. 'Who is this Poojamma? What is her true personality? People adore her as a saint, almost as a goddess and here she is allowing her followers to beat up a poor man." She ruminated within her.

That night Nina was rolling on her bed left and right. Many of her perceptions about Poojamma seemed to have come to naught. Not being aware of the political intricacies of the area she had imagined Poojamma to be a saint in the Christian order. This was exactly what Poojamma had given up. She did not want to be a saint. Instead she had decided to be a liberator of her people. It meant tackling of issues with a firm grip while simultaneously being extremely sensitive to the sentiments of people. That needed a fine balance. It was like walking on a rope at 150 meters above the ground. Viewers could not understand the actual difficulty of a ropewalker. They however, enjoyed the show. The personality of Poojamma was unfathomable for Nina. She could not grapple with the complexity of a person who was grappling with the issues of poverty, untouchability, exploitation and oppression.

Poojamma took pains to explain to Nina the fine art of building up a people for the future. Any selfless dedication required a rationality packed judgment on the future needs of the people. This would require harsh treatment of some persons at times. There could not be a universal soft-pedaling of all people alike. Each one had to be measured for what he was worth and strategies had to be worked out based on scientific assessment of the person concerned. Nina could not grasp all the intricacies of the strategies that Poojamma used. But she understood that Poojamma was a rare combination of the spiritual, the mystic and the political being.

In Nina's perception the dreaded night brought a nightmare of the entire struggle of Poojamma coming to naught because one man sold himself to the enemy camp. "Don't worry about the beating up. This is sometimes necessary to bring some sense into our people. A few blows are necessary to wake them up from their slumber. Otherwise they think they can get away with anything that they do. We have to be kind but our kindness has to be mixed occasionally with some bitter pills." Poojamma was casual in her legitimization during dinner. Nina could perceive the pain deep inside of Poojamma.

"So all your efforts have gone in vain! You struggled so much to bring about this change in society but when the rice was boiling the pot seems to have broken. What will you do now?" Nina continued her nightmare in the breakfast table. That was typical of the journalist and writer that she was.

"Success and failures are part and parcel of any endeavor at social transformation. But our people do not give up that easily. We shall find another way to teach a lesson to that political animal Eeranna. If we do not succeed in this he will gain a strong upper hand in the affairs of this area. That will spell disaster to the future of our children." The paleness in the face of Nina dissipated totally by the time Poojamma completed her sentences. Poojamma did notice that her face had regained the red complexion that kept reappearing on Nina's face. Nina's perplexity turned into admiration of the womanpower of Poojamma. 'Wow, what determination this woman has! It is not for nothing that people worship her.' Nina tried hard to contain her exclamation within herself.

———◦◦◦)◉(◦◦◦———

"Call all the Madhiga households for a meeting this evening" Poojamma got into her elements when she started giving instructions to Nagaraj.

"Yes Madam, where shall we have the meeting?" Nagaraj was the only exception in the entire area. He always addressed Poojamma as Madam unlike all others who called her Poojamma. Her real name was only Pooja. But people added 'Amma' to her name as a mark of their great respect for her. In the course of time her name became Poojamma. No one ever called her Pooja except when she went to the passport office.

"Let us have the meeting in the Dalit area of the village. Invite also the Lingayats, the Nayaks and Vokkaligas of the area. Let people of all castes assemble in the Madhiga area and we shall resolve this issue once and for all." Nina saw the true extension of Poojamma's hidden personality now. She was not any more the soft-spoken saint that Nina had generally seen her to be. She was now the avatar of Kali, the woman goddess of fire and brimstone, about whom Nina had read quite a bit. People usually put out their tongue for eating and speaking. Kali put out her tongue a few yards when she was angry and wanted to swallow the enemy wholesale. There was fire in the face of Poojamma. She was not ready to take any failure lying down.

"She seems to have the great capacity to turn every threat into an opportunity for her people." Nina thought aloud but did not allow words to flow from her mouth.

"Yes, did you say something Nina? I thought you said something." Poojamma turned to Nina suddenly and enquired.

"No, no! I did not say anything. Please go ahead with your instructions. I am just admiring your multifaceted personality." Nina managed the situation well. But deep inside she was wondering about the hidden potentials of Poojamma. "How did she hear what I was thinking? Can she read my mind? Or did I think a bit louder than necessary?" She was a mixed bundle of questions. Nay, she was a bundle of mixed questions.

"Can I also come for the meeting this evening?" Nina played her game very cautiously. She saw a very powerful woman in front of her and began to shrink in front of her.

"Of course, yes. If you like to come you are most welcome. I shall call Manjula so that you will have someone to translate for you. I shall be very busy talking to the people this evening." Poojamma was very concerned even in the most controversial situations. That made her a very special person.

Came evening. All people had their dinner and assembled in front of the village temple under the neem tree. No one in the Dalit area had a house large enough to provide a sitting place for the crowd. People had planted a neem tree in front of the temple years ago. Now it had grown big with a personality of its own. During day it gave shade and cool to the people and at night gave shelter to many birds.

It was a special night, as people from all neighboring villages had come. It was Poojamma's singular achievement that people belonging to all castes assembled in the Dalit area of the village. This was something unthinkable before she entered into the lives of the people in that area. Dalits had pooled their money to prepare tea for all the VIP guests who had come. All other caste people were VIPs for Dalits. Poojamma and Nina were given a warm welcome with the traditional garland. But after receiving the garland Nina started moving around with her camera. She noticed that there were some people who were not part of the gathering. They seemed to be only curious about her color and dress and her half naked legs.

"They are agents of Eeranna. He sensed that there would be some discussions about him in todays meeting. Therefore, he has sent some of his agents as observers. This is the usual thing he does in all our meetings. He has a wide network of informers in the entire area. Be careful with them. They are all drunk. That is the wage of sin that he pays to his agents." Manjula gave a briefing to Nina in between her escapades.

"What you have done is just outright betrayal of all that we stood for till now. After Poojamma came to our villages many of us have given up our ignorant practices and have become educated and clever. We are respected everywhere because of the knowledge that we have gained. Some people in this area reap rich benefits from our ignorance. They want to keep us in eternal darkness. When we are ignorant they can do anything they want. Poojamma struggled so much with the people of Guddahalli and made them agree to take you into their village. I am completely shocked to learn that you people have refused to enter the village. It is a direct insult not only to Poojamma but also to people like Nagaraj." Chikkanna, a dominant caste Lingayat leader gave a strong introduction to the meeting. He was very direct and had no habit of beating round the bush.

"We have lost our land to the landlords of this area. After losing our land we end up becoming daily wage earners in our own land that we have lost to the landlords. You know whom I am talking about. He has grabbed not only all the government land in this area but also small little landholdings that we had. Last evening he called our Ganganna to his house, gave him drinks and instructed him to misguide you. That is why you people have refused to enter Guddahalli village. Do you think what you have done is the right thing? Will this help your future generations?" Lingappa, another dominant caste Vokkaliga was a step above Chikkanna.

"What evidence do you have to say that Ganganna had drinks last evening and was instructed?" Shiva dared to challenge Lingappa. There was a big commotion in the crowd as soon as he began to speak. He was one of the people standing outside of the gathering.

Nina went running to Manjula to find out what the commotion was all about. Manjula explained to her that the man who spoke up was a known agent of Eeranna and people were highly agitated that he dared to speak in their meeting. "He is fully drunk. I am sure Eeranna has inundated his throat and sent him here to create trouble. He does this often." Manjula also added her own interpretation.

"Oh, he is such a bad man. I really admire the courage of Poojamma." Nina added her own spice to the evening's turbulence.

"Bring the photo of Ambedkar from your house." Poojamma ordered the wife of Ganganna. The woman rushed to her house, which was only five houses away from the temple. She came back with a photo of Mother Earth.

Everyone assembled there shouted: "Bring the photo of Ambedkar. Did you not hear what Poojamma said?"

"We do not have Ambedkar's photo in our house. We have only Mother Earth's photo. This is what we worship everyday. We have no one else to go. This is what we learned in our Dalit Panchayat." The woman said boldly without any hesitation.

"Oh, what is Poojamma going to do with that photo of Mother Earth?" Nina asked Manjula.

"Have some patience. Wait and see. Only Poojamma knows why she does what she does." Manjula gently pressed Nina's hand and asked her to be patient.

"Now Ganganna, you come forward and swear on Mother Earth in front of all the people assembled here that you were not given drinks last evening. Also swear that you did not tell your people not to enter Guddahalli village.' She held the hands of Ganganna and pulled him firmly to the photo to swear.

Ganganna was in an inextricable dilemma. If he swore falsely his own people would not respect him. All of them knew that it was under the influence of liquor that he instructed some of the village Dalits not to enter Guddahalli. He also had the fear that if he swore falsely Mother Earth would punish him. If he refused to swear then all the people from other villages would know that he was guilty of something. Added to his woes was the pre-eminent presence of Poojamma. Being bereft of the strength of the spirit Ganganna became a melting pot. He fell at the feet of Poojamma crying aloud and shedding tears confessing to his mistake. He promised aloud that he would never repeat the mistake again in his life. He also appealed to all Dalits not to do what he did the previous evening.

Followers of Eeranna were grossly disappointed. Some of them rushed to inform him of what was happening among Dalits. Frustration and anger started permeating the entire body of Eeranna. His mind started scheming in sheer exasperation. That he could not do what he wanted to do against Poojamma struck him off balance. He took up his phone and took an appointment with the MLA, the Member of the Legislative Assembly to meet him next morning.

"In this case tomorrow all of you will go to Guddahalli under the leadership of Chikkanna and enter the village formally without any fear of any god. You are doing something very good for the future of your children. Gods, if ever they existed for the poor, should be happy about what you are doing. If any god punishes you for this good thing that you are doing such a god cannot be a good god. If there is a god who is angry with you because you love your children we do not need that type of god. Do you want to worship a god who wants you to be slaves of caste system all your life? In spite of all this if gods want to punish you let all their punishment fall on me and consume me." She ended her conclusion with a solemn stirring of emotions. People were squirming in their bodies.

"No, no Poojamma! We shall reject such gods." The crowd shouted in unison.

"Okay, that is good. I am glad that you see light in your life and are determined to build a bright future for your children. You must always think of this. What is it that you want to leave behind for your children? Do you want to leave behind the slavery to which you have been subjected? Do you want to leave the indignity that you have suffered at the hands of the caste forces? Do you want to leave the illiteracy and ignorance that you were plunged into? Do you want to leave to your children the poverty that you have experienced in your life? Leave behind something that your children can remember you with pride and honor." The spontaneous clap of the people rent the air and pierced through the ears of Eeranna.

"This is the genius that Poojamma is. See how she has given the responsibility to the people. She has asked a Lingayat leader to lead the Dalits into the Gollar village. She is an organic genius." Manjula was giving a running commentary to Nina of what was happening.

"What do you mean by organic genius?" Nina pinched Manjula's bum a little.

"You know that Poojamma has done something that ordinary human beings cannot do. But she is not a schemer. She does not pre-plan all this. It comes naturally to her. She just does things as they occur to her. And they happen to be genius of plans. That is what I call organic genius. If you ask Poojamma where she gets all these bright ideas she would retort and say that she draws them from the cosmos." Manjula was in her elements in all the excitement of the evening.

"Wow, you are a genius now. And what type of genius are you?" Nina pinched her bum again.

Manjula tapped rather hard on her back. She got up and said, "Come let us go for dinner."

⸺•◦❂◦•⸺

"Madam, what shall I offer you for dinner, vegetarian or non-vegetarian?" The airhostess tapped at the shoulder of Nina. She woke up with a jerk. She rubbed her eyes, looked at the airhostess. "Oh I slept well I think. I dreamt as if a friend of mine tapped at my back and here you are."

"Yes, I saw you in deep slumber and did not want to disturb you. But I was wondering if I should leave you to sleep and go hungry. Sorry I woke you up. But please have some dinner. What shall I offer you?" The airhostess was very friendly.

"Give me some more red wine and chicken." Nina rushed to the toilet and came back fresh. But sadness was written all over her face. Those were days she spent with Poojamma and now it was a journey to bid her eternal farewell. "Oh big bird, why are you not moving fast forward? You make such big noise. Your loud noise does not match with your speed. Go fast bird, please go fast." She pleaded aloud silently with the plane.

CHAPTER SIX

'Hello Madam, you cannot understand it just like that. It has a history. Poojamma did not earn all the love and affection of the people in one day. She worked hard among the people and went through many tests, sometimes tests of fire.' Kala now began to mean serious business. Nina was sitting in front of her for real. This time it was without their beloved Poojamma.

'You are intriguing me Kala. You seem to be taking me into many lanes and by-lanes. Why don't you do a straight narration? The last time I met her was when she led the Madhiga people into Guddahalli. Now all of us have given a totally unexpected farewell. Please tell me what really happened to Poojamma from the time I left?' Nina began to exhibit a bit of impatience.

'Well, well you saw yourself the type of outpouring of affection that was there yesterday during the funeral of Poojamma. It is not just a journalistic narration for us. It is an outpouring of our hearts. Poojamma is not just an extraordinary woman for the people of this area. She is our goddess. You understand her death as departure. We understand her death as her re-incarnation into our lives. Yes, we are sad but we are also happy that she now belongs to all of us in a way that we deserve to have her.' Kala was speaking as if she was possessed.

Nina knew her during her previous visits as a quiet girl who was busy in the kitchen. She was an excellent cook. She had dropped out of school after her matriculation as she had failed in English and Mathematics. She had no inclination to continue her studies. She was even able to hoodwink Poojamma into not going to school. But Poojamma had trained her in spoken English. She was now able to manage any guest from any country on her own. Over a period of only a few years she not only mastered spoken English but also developed the capacity to elucidate the many rural issues with all their nuances to international guests who came to visit Poojamma. Nina saw a completely transformed Kala.

'Tell me Kala more about what happened after I left Poojamma last time. It is many years since I came here. Poojamma and I have been writing to each other several times. But Poojamma had very little time to write long letters. I knew that she went through many difficulties . . .' Nina wanted to continue her search. But Kala cut her path.

'Poojamma had not only difficulties. She also had many success stories. It is tragic that her enemies have felled her. But that is also a true statement of the level of success that we people have tasted under her inspiration and leadership. She has not left a vacuum. You saw that yesterday. She has left behind many people with knowledge and courage. We shall continue to build communities of dignity and equality . . .'

Now it was Nina's turn to cut her short. 'But Kala can we pick up the missing links. I am hearing things only in bits and pieces. Can you make me understand what transpired and led to the ultimate elimination of Poojamma.'

Kala was filled with emotions. It was only a day since they gave a solemn burial to their great mother. Like most people in the area Kala was in dire need of speaking out. She had to take out all the bottled up sorrow. It was unlimited. People in all the surrounding villages were talking to one another. The entire area turned into a place of collective mourning. Some among them were swearing revenge. But Kala had to look after all those who kept coming to the place. It was there that Poojamma was buried. Kala had many assistants to make coffee and tea for all those who came in streams. Many people came twice, thrice or even four times. They did not know what else to do. Pall of gloom descended all over.

'For you it is very hard to listen to the story of Poojamma in its complexity. Just imagine that this one woman had to go through all these lanes and by lanes of life in the villages in actual life. Have patience madam. Why are you in a hurry? I have to tell you the truth in all its complexity. But don't worry. I shall be as simple as possible.'

Kala continued: 'most people in every village chose to change the regressive traditions of the village and through that change they were ready to build a better future for their children. This was the consequence of a long process of education that Poojamma had done in this area. Others in the same villages thought that any move towards changing age-old traditions was a regression. People had to either love her or hate her. Nobody could be indifferent to her. She went to village after village, called the people together and had long discussions with them and gave discourses when necessary. She began to disturb the minds of the people and started hitting hard at the systems and structures of society, all of them. Those whom she discussed with and those who heard about the discussions were equally disturbed.'

'That means there were some people whom Pooja did not discuss with. They only heard about the discussions. Was Pooja not calling them for discussions or were they not coming?' Nina the provocateur!

'What madam, you know Poojamma so well and yet you do not know this simple thing about her. Poojamma went only to the poor and not to the rich. She would go to the rich only if they invited her. That is why all the poor people love her so much.' There was obvious sarcasm in Kala's voice.

'I know she worked among the poor people. But never knew that she chose to go only to the poor and not to the rich. That is discriminatory, I thought . . .'

'That is not discriminatory. That is the preferential option that I have made for the poor. It is not that I hate the rich people. But I definitely disagree with the way they make riches and shall never give the impression to the poor that I am friendly also with the rich.' Kala reminded Nina of what Poojamma had told her directly when she was alive. Nina admired Kala's stupendous memory power. Nina was not lagging too far behind. She recollected what Kala had told her on an earlier occasion when Nina raised the question of Kala's study with Poojamma.

'I do not want to study at all madam. Why do you want to trouble Poojamma about this? What is the great point of my studying more than high school? First of all my father cannot afford my studies in a college. I shall have to go to far off village to study. I am good looking and have a fair skin. All sorts of dudes will try to come behind me with their deep love for me. Do you think they will ever allow me to study? If I complete my studies in spite of this, my father will find a groom for me among our relatives who may not have even studied as much as I have done. That will be an additional problem. He will feel low and will start ill-treating me. Am I going to become an officer for the rest of my life? This is not at all possible. I must only aspire for what my father can afford . . . .'

Nina interrupted her. 'But now you have a job. You are earning a salary from Poojamma. You could do the same elsewhere if you studied well.'

'You will not understand all these madam. What I earn is not enough for the liquor that my father consumes everyday. We work just to live madam. If I question my father about his drinking habit he will threaten me with marriage. I am with Poojamma only to drag on my marriage as much as possible. I cannot escape that noose of becoming the wife of a villager who has no aim in life. He has to have sex, I have to have sex with him whether I like it or not and produce children for him and also work for his parents and children. I am happy that I spend my time happily here with Poojamma. Please do not spoil it.'

Nina could not help admiring Kala for her earthly wisdom and determination. Poojamma advised Nina not to try this with Kala, as she herself failed in that mission. Nina remembered this in the presence of Kala and wiped the few drops of tears from Kala's eyes.

There was a huge gathering again in the evening. People from different villages, rich and poor of all castes and religions assembled to pay their respect once again to Poojamma. Nagaraj made a moving speech about Poojamma. He did not have much time to talk to people at the time of Poojamma's burial. He did not have the energy either. They knew that Poojamma lived a very risky life. Intelligence reports of the police department clearly indicated an impending danger to her life. Nagaraj narrated to the people what happened two weeks before the 'final strike' on Poojamma.

'The Superintendent of Police had sent word to Poojamma to meet him in his office. Five of us accompanied her the next day to the SP's office. He wanted only Poojamma inside. But Poojamma insisted that there should be at least two people with her. After much persuasion the SP agreed to her demand. Chikkanna and I went into his office with our Poojamma. The SP told her that they had received information that some people might attack her any time. Her life was in serious danger. The government was ready to give her protection.'

'What does police protection for me imply?' Poojamma asked the SP.

'There will be two policemen who will accompany you wherever you go. They will be always with you till we are reasonably confident that the threats on you have disappeared.' The SP gave his official version of protection.

'Two policemen with me always! See how many of my people have accompanied me today! Five of them! There are hundreds of them to guard me. I have lived my life for my people. They will protect me sir.' Poojamma was strong but apologetic.

'Strictly speaking you are not obliged to take the protection that we offer. But I am sure you realize how important you are for your people. Any danger to your life will bring a bad name to the police department and ultimately also to the government. It is our duty to protect you.' The SP insisted.

'Thank you very much. But I am happy with the protection that my people give me. If something happens that they cannot resist, then let it happen. I am not afraid of death. Even if two policemen accompany me always my enemies can strike at any time they want. I shall only take the protection that my people can offer. I am ready to give you in writing that I do not accept your offer of protection. This will save a lot of embarrassment for you and for the government. Kindly accept my apologies. I am sorry to turn down your kind offer. I hope you will understand.' Saying this Poojamma got up from her seat.

The SP stood up and folded his hand. 'Please take care madam. You are in a very serious situation.' He turned to the men and said, 'you people take care of your Poojamma. Be with her always.'

'We brought Poojamma with the confidence that we would protect her always. But now we have lost a precious treasure of our lives. Instead of speaking much about Poojamma it is time that we carry forward the mission that she has left for us. She has shown us the way to build a brighter future for our children and now let us take a pledge that we shall follow in her footsteps for many generations to come.' He extended his hands in front and made an oath of loyalty and determination. The people who assembled there repeated the words after him. It was a very solemn ceremony. Nina stood there in complete silence. Tears rolled down her cheeks. She did not try to control them. Seeing her cry in silence the other women in the crowd started crying aloud. Some of them simultaneously muttered undecipherable words of affection and love.

'As a sign of our pledge to walk the path shown by our Poojamma let us all set up her photo in our homes and everyday remind ourselves of our solemn promise today. All of you put up a photo of our Poojamma in your houses and also spread this message to all neighboring villages. Let this become a strong movement and let all excluded people and poor know that there is a strong message of liberation in the death of our Poojamma. Let her death and her memory unite all the poor of the world.' Nagaraj was exceptionally clear and focused in that moment of sorrow.

Nina and Kala started the next day in deep silence with two cups of coffee. Kala remembered that Nina was waiting to hear all that transpired in the area since she left the last time. She slowly started her narration. It was a journey backward for both of them.

—◦◦❈◦◦—

'It is becoming too much here in our area. That bitchy woman is mesmerizing the people here and is weaning them away from our party. All are following her blindly. If it goes on like this soon we shall lose our vote bank. Next time it will become very difficult for us to garner votes. We must do something on a war footing.' Eeranna knocked at the door of the house of Dinesh MLA and as soon as he opened the door the floodgates of complaints against Poojamma opened without any difficulty.

The MLA closed his nose with his fingers. Eeranna was seeing stars. But he also had a pinch of the bad smell that emanated from the adjacent river. It was not Kaveri. All the sewerage water of the city merged together at one point and ran in the river. Occasionally foul smell emanated from that river affecting normal life of residents along the banks of the black river. For a minute Eeranna thought that Dinesh closed his nose to indicate that the bad odor was from his mouth.

'What is she doing. Tell me that. Do you think anyone can take away votes from our party by doing good things to People? You are such a fool, man. It is not by good deeds that we get votes. Don't you know how you get votes election after election? We shall teach her a lesson. But tell me first what she is doing in our area.' Dinesh was a cool headed politician who did not manifest signs of early disturbance.

'She is not doing just one thing. She is leading people into ignorance. She is destroying our religion and caste. Her latest is the entry of Madhigas into the Gollar village. In Guddahalli she has got the old man Gowdajja agree to allow the entry of Madhigas into their village. They have also decided not to cast out their women at the time of delivery. We have our caste system. Who is she to change all this?' Eeranna was pouring out his anger. Adjacent to Dinersh's house there was a huge pipe that was vomiting out the gutter water into the black river.

'If she is succeeding so much in my constituency, what are you doing? It means that you are not doing your work properly. Otherwise why would people follow her? In any case I shall speak to the Rural Development Minister and initiate a scheme to construct good buildings in all the Gollar villages for their women to stay at the time of delivery. The good buildings that we shall construct will preserve the custom and also will attract people towards us. We shall get the Gollar votes in the next elections showing this as our poll plank.' He was in a mood to shower a volley of questions and give many answers. But Eeranna cut him short.

'Yes, yes! You give me some money at the time of elections and then you are busy making money in Bangalore. You must come to the constituency sometime and see what is really happening here. She is bringing money from foreign countries and is pouring that in our constituency. She is an agent of foreign countries. People get a lot of money and benefits from her and they will definitely follow her. You must stop this at the earliest.' Eeranna was now more convincing than in his earlier statements.

'Oh, you did not tell me till now that the situation is so serious. If this is the case she will dent our vote bank seriously in the next elections. Okay, now what shall we do? We must stop the influence of foreign women in our constituency.' Dinesh began to manifest some signs of jitters.

'You come and meet the people directly. I shall organize a public meeting and you speak to the people and convince them that our party will do better things for this people than this lady nightingale. You announce to the people that the government has already approved your proposal for a new scheme for the development of Gollars in Karnataka. This will in effect keep the Gollars separate from other castes.' Eeranna was quite oratorical in his conversation with his boss.

Together both of them fixed a date for a public meeting. But they did not expect that Poojamma and her followers would organize a gala opening function of the houses that they constructed in that area. They had invited the District Collector to formally open the houses. The District Collector agreed gladly to go for the function. It was scheduled for an evening when all the people of the area would be able to assemble at Guddahalli village. The MLA and Eeranna thought that more than having a public meeting it would be more necessary to disrupt the function organized by the poor people of the area. If the function was stopped, they thought, it would create an impression among the people that they could not live peacefully by going against the whims and fancies of the MLA and his local agent Eeranna.

The District Collector had just entered his office. The telephone kept ringing. He lifted the phone.

'Hmm, Hey Collector, I heard that you are going for the inauguration of the houses constructed by that bloody bitch Poojamma. Is it true?' Dinesh was brazenly impolite to the highest authority in the District.

'Yes, I have agreed to go. They are very good people and are doing yeomen service to the poor. I know Madam Poojamma personally. She is a saint and is admired and loved by the people of your constituency.' The Collector laid bare some truths before the MLA. It did not take long for him to realize that he was throwing pearls in front of a political pig.

'I don't care about her goodness and saintliness. I care about my votes. Can I lose my constituency for the sake of a bloody saint who is misguiding the people of my constituency? This country needs political leaders and not saints. You should not go for the function.' He now became nasty to the Collector. The brewing conflict between politicians and bureaucrats!

'But in your own interest will it not be good that you also join me in the function? You will become popular among the people and will get more votes. If you antagonize Madam Poojamma you will definitely lose your votes in the next elections.' The Collector dug a deep hole in the den of a pernicious bandicoot. He proved in no time that he was an able administrator and not a politician.

'Who the bloody hell are you to tell me about my constituency? You are a harebrained officer appointed by a ditz government. I am the leader. I know how to get votes from the people at the time of elections. Are you here to teach me how I should get votes? What the fuck! You just do your fucking job and get your salary. I shall manage my voters.' Now it was the MLA's mouth that smelled foul. The Collector could smell it in the phone. He was furious now. He wanted to give it back to the MLA.

'I am the Collector here and you have no right to tell me what functions I should attend and what I should not. It is my right to decide. You are after all an elected member. If you are defeated in the next elections you will have to tuck your bloody wagging tail between your legs and salute all the officers. But I am permanent till I retire. Do not cross my line Mr. MLA' the officer was quite business like.

'If you attend the function next week you will see how powerful I am. You may be a powerful officer. But you should know that if I speak to the Chief Minister you will be shunted out to a remote dry district and when you do not have water even to drink you will know who is more powerful. You will soon know whom you are playing with officer. Go and play with your wife tonight. Do not play with fire.' The MLA stung and hung up the phone.

—∞◖◗∞—

Poojamma received the news only half an hour before the function that the Collector would not attend the function that evening. All the people had assembled for the function with great expectation. But they were informed that Eeranna had succeeded to prevent the Collector from attending the function. After some enquiry they also found out that it was the MLA who actually prevented the Collector.

'But we shall see how the Collector will not come for the function today. Now it is a question of an all out war. What does this motherfucker think of himself? Hey, people come, let us all go to the Collector's office and we shall block him from leaving his office this evening if he does not come for our function.' Even before Chikkanna finished his emotional appeal people were on the main road and got into whatever vehicle passed by the highway. Those who reached early waited at the roadside for the others to arrive so that they could all go together into the office of the Collector.

'What is the big commotion outside?' The Collector did not expect hundreds of people in front of his office. He did not anticipate that type of unity among the poor in his District. He rushed outside the office. But there was no space for him to move anywhere out of his door. People had surrounded his office. For the first time in his life he realized that his power was confined to the four walls of his office. He remembered what he heard often during his training in Missouri, "If only people rose in their power . . ."

'How can you promise to come for our function and decide not to come at the last minute? You should come for the function today. Thousands of people are waiting for you to inaugurate the houses. We have constructed the houses with our sweat and blood. You cannot disrespect us.' It was

Nagaraj who picked up the raw power of speech in front of the biggest authority in the District. There was a time when he was unable to speak even to Poojamma. He would cover his mouth with his hand whenever he had to speak to her. Poojamma transformed him from an utterly shy guy to one of the most vociferous fellows in the area.

'I have too much of work today. I shall speak to Poojamma over phone and explain to her my inability to come for the function. I am sorry. Kindly go back and let Poojamma open the houses. She is much bigger than I am. All of you love her more than anyone. She is the right person to do that.' The Collector tried to pacify the people without realizing their potential and their transformation.

'We know how important Poojamma is to us without you reminding us of that. You promised to come for our function. Whatever may be the work that you have, you can do that tomorrow. We do not allow anyone to insult our Poojamma. You have done that today. Do not try to mislead us by your sugarcoated words. You come for the function now with us. If you do not come, you will not go to your residence this evening. You will have to spend the entire night in your office. Hey people let us all sit here till the Collector tells us that he is ready to go with us.' Chikkanna took turn to show that the poor did not depend on just one individual leader. As soon as he said this Nagaraj shouted, 'Down down, MLA Dinesh down!' The people repeated it after him with more power.

The Collector realized that if the news of the people shouting condemnation of the MLA in his premises reached Dinesh, it would spell more trouble for him with the government. Before things went out of control he called his officers and asked them to organize a few vehicles. He asked a few officers to accompany him to Guddahalli. Now he was prepared for any threat from the MLA. As he got into the vehicle he was frightened at the sight of two from the group getting into his vehicle without any inhibition. Even officers working with him rarely dared to travel with him in the same vehicle.

'If I do not go with you the vehicle may take you somewhere else. Who knows you will not divert the vehicle on the way and escape. You cheated us once and we shall not allow anyone to cheat us once again.' As Chikkanna said this, the Collector was irritated. But after a few minutes of cooling his heels inside his air-conditioned car he realized that Poojamma had empowered ordinary village people in an unprecedented manner. He also realized that she had done more efficiently what he was supposed to do. He recollected the lessons he learned during his Indian Administrative Service training in Missouri that the job of a Collector was not only administration but empowering the people to be good citizens of the country. What the government failed to do, here was a frail woman who did it extraordinarily. He began to converse with Chikkanna in a relaxed manner and collected all the necessary information for his speech at the inaugural.

It was a long procession with the Collector at the center and Poojamma accompanying him. It was in a way very good that the Collector decided not to come for the function. Now there were many other officers whom they did not invite. Prominent among them was the SP whom the Collector called up in his wireless indicating that the agents of the MLA could create unnecessary trouble. A double boon from the MLA! The entire area was briskly active. All over the area there was a big talk about many officers attending the inauguration function. People began to see Poojamma not only as a woman of good heart but also as someone who had powers beyond their expectations.

'You have filled this entire area with so much of vibrancy madam. This is just unimaginable, the way people love you and the way you command their love and admiration. Tell me the secret behind this power, madam. I shall also try to do this wherever I go.' The Collector was like a pack of washing powder getting into all the clothes in a machine.

'I have no secret medicines for the ills that people suffer. They have power inside. I only trigger what lies deep within them. I do not administer anything to them. They have it in themselves. What you have witnessed today, the power that you experienced is all theirs.' Poojamma was an embodiment of utter humility and serenity.

'What great thing did you do today? That asshole Collector came with his officers and attended the function. I have lost so much of prestige here. You should have told me that you would not speak to the Collector and prevent him from coming. I would have taken some hundred people and forestalled his coming. You live in the city and so it is easy for you to ignore people like me. When elections come we have to slog it out for you. Now you have to face the people here during the next elections. They already know that you have no power. They think that this bloody bitch Pooja has more power than any of us . . . .' Eeranna was like small pieces of pappad in a frying pan. Dancing in a boiling cauldron!

'Hey Eeranna, I spoke to that bloody Collector and asked him not to attend the function. I even threatened him with transfer if he attended the function. Now let me teach him a lesson that he cannot forget for the rest of his life. So do not worry. You organize a public meeting soon and I shall come and speak to the people. Find a reason for some bloody function. But bring more people than the crowd that attended the house inauguration function.' Dinesh now got into his action fearing that it was already quite late for him.

Kala continued her narration of what happened on the day of the political meeting. 'Eeranna was very active on the streets. His mind was constantly roiling on the level of success he should achieve in comparison to what Poojamma achieved. Small minds, big efforts! He made a visit to all the villages and also sent his cronies several times to the villages. He wanted to make sure that hundreds of people turned up for the meeting. Much of his political fortune depended on the number of people he was able to mobilize. Number meant votes for Dinesh. Number meant success for Eeranna. Only if he saw a large number of people Dinesh would continue with Eeranna as his agent and appoint his friends in party positions. It also meant that Eeranna could go on cheating the poor and grabbing their land. Not only land grabbing but also pocketing a certain percentage of all government budget meant for development schemes. They were meant for the welfare of the poor. But he would threaten the officers and the village level elected members till they gave him a percentage of money. This in turn gave them the audacity to also siphon of a good chunk of development money for themselves. Added to this was the fleecing of the poor by both intermittently. But one of the worst things that he did was to have established a sort of parallel governance in the villages on caste norms brazenly ignoring the Constitution of India. Law and order much depended on what Eeranna decided and not on what the law books said. Through Dinesh he would make sure that only officers belonging to his caste were posted in his area, especially in the police stations. He would file false complaints against those who were inimical to them and threaten them with dire consequences.'

'After the arrival of Poojamma the poor in the area found a great relief from their difficulties and were slowly coming out of the clutches of Eeranna. Poojamma established friendly relationship with higher-level officers of the State and sent out strong messages to local officers that if law were not implemented they would be punished. Police in general were frightened of antagonizing her, as their promotions would be affected. However, there were many officers who also admired the way Poojamma brought about radical transformation in the mindset of the poor. That made things easier for them in implementing law.'

"Police officers, your duty is to implement the Constitution. That is the mandate given to you. Please act according to the law of the land without fear or favor. If anybody threatens you because you are honest and implement the law of the country, let me know." She would then turn to the people and say, "My people, you should provide protection to our officers when they need help." 'Poojamma would thunder in public meetings attended by the officers of different departments. It used to send shivers in the spines of Eeranna's followers.'

'That day was Eeranna's day. People from different villages started arriving for the meeting. They had voted for Dinesh at the behest of Eeranna. They needed a local benefactor and protector. Before Poojamma arrived on the scene he was the only one on whom people could depend. If they did whatever he expected of them he would support them. That invariably brought incessant fights and quarrels in the villages. If people were not fighting among themselves Eeranna would instigate his followers to spread rumors and divide people.'

'But if all people obeyed him why would he divide the people?' This was a big doubt in Nina. Kala was now able to explain everything to her.

'If people were not divided and did not fight among themselves they would unite to fight against him. This would in turn diminish his income level. When people fought among themselves he played the Good Samaritan on the one hand and sucked money from the people.

If he wanted more money he would send one fighting party to the police station and complain to the police. The police would resolve the case after threatening the people a lot. Fearing arrests people would run to Eeranna for rescue. It was his trap into which they walked easily. He would make them pay through their nose. Police would operate in connivance with him. Before Poojamma descended on the scene people also went to politicians belonging to the opposition party. They voted for different candidates and would generally go to them for help. This allegiance to one or other party and candidate always kept people divided. It was Poojamma who educated them on the need for being united if they had to have less trouble in their life.'

"You may vote for any party of your choice. This is your democratic right. But after voting and the announcement of results do not keep grudge against your own people. The politicians reap a rich harvest through your disunity. As long as you are divided among yourselves you are only allowing politicians of different parties to dance over your woe. If you are united and convert your number into votes, politicians will come running to you. They need your votes. Without your votes they cannot win. When they come for your votes you lay your conditions and demands before them. They have to fulfill your demands in order to get your votes. Be united my people at the time of elections. You may have a lot of differences among you. But at the time of elections set aside the differences and come together in order to vote as one force. Just imagine the power of your number. Take any village in our area. You, as poor, are the largest people. The rich are only a few. Politicians buy your votes and later only support the rich and landlord. Wake up my people. If you can convert your number into votes you will become an unassailable power. Instead of running after politicians for benefits you can make politicians run after you if you convert your number into votes. Dividing you is the mantra of politicians. Make your unity as your mantra." Poojamma's courage found no bounds.

'Though people saw the rationality of Poojamma some could not give up their old loyalty to Eeranna and to the MLA. After all the MLA had actual power. He had government on his side. They assembled to greet the MLA and to show to him that they voted for him. Many of them brought their petitions to present to the MLA.'

'Eeranna took the mike to welcome the MLA and all the officers who had come. It was customary that when the MLA visited an area, officers had to accompany him if he demanded. Eeranna touched upon the core issue already in his welcome speech.'

"Our Dinesh Anna has been fighting for development of this constituency. I have seen him several times not eating and sleeping enough. He is moving around all the time in order to bring many welfare schemes for this constituency. After he was elected by you people he has transformed this constituency like never before. You have good roads in your village. He has even brought a steel factory and some of your young people have found jobs. I have been giving him regular information on your needs and our Dinesh Anna has been doing all that I have told him. As long as he is for us no one can do any harm to us. He is godsend for us. For his commitment to the poor he should be given one or other ministry in the government. I hope the Chief Minister will soon make him a minister in his cabinet." 'There was loud clapping of hands. He was egged on to speak more with all the emotions that he saw among the people. Dinesh liked the minister part in his speech.'

He continued his welcome. "Of late we have some people coming into the constituency of our Dinesh Anna. They are foreign agents who will one day convert people to Christianity. All of us here in this country are Hindus and no one can convert us to a foreign religion. We are born as Hindus and we shall die as Hindus. It is with foreign money that they are building houses. Our government has enough money to build houses for all Indian citizens. I want to inform all the people that if anyone tries to convert the poor to Christianity they will face severe consequences . . ."

'At this stage many people in the crowd started shouting. They asked him to confine himself only to his welcome speech and not speak about others unnecessarily. One of them even climbed the stage and grabbed the mike from the hands of Eeranna. But there was timely intervention from police to avoid any untoward incident. The MLA showed signs to Eeranna not to overdo things already at the beginning. Eeranna was embarrassed beyond tolerable limits. The audacity of the followers of Poojamma stunned him. He concluded his speech hurriedly and sat down.'

'The moment people had waited for arrived slowly. No one expected Eeranna to cross the boundaries of basic decency already at the beginning of the meeting. It dampened the spirit of the followers of Dinesh to a great extent. He had to set right the damage done by his crony. He started thanking Eeranna and his friends for organizing such a big function in his honor. After customary greetings of all those who were sitting on stage Dinesh appreciated the people who turned up for the meeting.'

"You are my relatives and friends. It is because of you that I have become MLA. It is a boon that you have given me. As Eeranna mentioned in his speech, I have been working hard to develop this constituency. I have got many millions of rupees approved for the development of this constituency. You have seen the roads. You know that they were in pathetic conditions when you elected me. Potholes filled all roads in this constituency. The previous MLA had only big potbelly. I have made concrete roads in all the streets of Harijan colonies" . . . 'He was interrupted once again at this stage by a woman among the audience.'

"Sir, please do not call us Harijans. Gandhi gave us this derogatory name but now even the Government of India has banned the use of this name for us." 'She said this and sat down. No one expected this interruption. Eeranna got up and shouted along with his close aids asking the woman to sit down and not speak in between. Eeranna took hold of another mike and asked the audience not to interrupt the speech of the MLA.'

"But you are Harijans, no? Gandhi gave you this name to call you as children of god. What other name should I use for you, lady?" 'Dinesh was drenched in total embarrassment. He was a bundle of nerves. There was no way he could stop the drooping of his ignorance.'

'She got up again and said.' "Sir, Gandhi gave us the name Harijan to tell Hindus of this country that we are bastard children, that we do not know the names of our fathers. That is why he called us children of god. We shall not accept any god as our father, sir. All of us are born of good parents. You may kindly call us Dalits or Adi Jan." She made her point once again and sat down. Some policemen giggled among themselves. They were happy that a woman picked up the courage to expose the ignorance of the MLA. They remembered the times when he used to insult them in public in front of people. Now they were happy that a Dalit woman dared to challenge the MLA in front of all people. They thanked Poojamma in their heart who was the cause of this new resurgence in the area. Many others stood up to shout aloud more than the Dalit woman. But police walked into the crowd and asked them to keep quiet. Eeranna whispered in the ears of Dinesh that they were all followers of Poojamma. He was keen on saving his skin.

'Dinesh asked the police to control the audience and continued his speech. "I have spoken to the Chief Minister and got a promise from him to allocate 50 million rupees for the development of this constituency. All the villages in my constituency will have drinking water. I have many plans for developing all villages in this constituency. If I have to do this it is important that I continue to be MLA also in the next term. I am sure all of you will vote for me and re-elect me next time too. But I understand that there are some people who are misguiding you and are indulging in conversion to Christianity. I shall not tolerate such foreign people in my constituency. You should teach such people a lesson by not joining them and by asking them to go back to their country."

"You go back from here. Where have you come from? You do not belong to this village? Go back, Dinesh. Go back". Some unknown voice from the crowd shouted aloud. Everyone in the crowd was looking all over to locate the origin of the voice. But even the person who shouted was looking around and therefore, nobody made out who the person really was.'

Dinesh was totally embarrassed. He waited for a few seconds to see if the culprit would be located in the crowd. He continued his speech in a hurry. "Do not follow anyone else. I know that Eeranna is helping you people. He is a very good man. If you have any difficulty you can always approach him. He will inform me of your needs and difficulties. I request all officers present here to take special care of all needs of the people in this constituency."

"After the last election this is the first time you have come here. It is three years since you visited us. You came to ask for our votes and we are seeing you only now. You ask us to go to Eeranna to redress our problems. What if he is the problem for us? He is grabbing all government land and is registering them in his name. He pockets all development money that comes to our area. He instigates some people and beats up the poor people and police are supporting him. It will be good if you ask your agents to behave properly." As Ravi was speaking boldly to the MLA from the audience, Eeranna winked eyes to the police inspector. That was enough. A group of policemen rushed to Ravi and thrashed him ruthlessly in front of all the people. They dragged him to the police station. Some people rushed to the aid of Ravi and physically prevented the policemen from beating him up. They were also thrashed in return.'

'The meeting ended in a fiasco. Dinesh knew well what he should do in such circumstances. He went first to the house of Eeranna. There were angry outbursts against Poojamma from some of his cronies. Dinesh calmed them all. He realized that the strategy to deal with Poojamma had to change. Problems were much more deep rooted than he anticipated and he found that Eeranna was incapable of dealing with her efficiently. He decided to take on Poojamma. After having some coffee and snacks he rushed to the police station with all his followers running behind him. That was their job. In the police station Dinesh scolded the policemen for being rude to a poor Ravi. He admonished Ravi not to behave tough in such uncultured manner in public meetings. He asked the Inspector to release him immediately and not to register any cases against Ravi. Followers of Poojamma had assembled in the police station demanding the immediate release of Ravi. They argued with the inspector vehemently what crime Ravi had committed. 'Is asking questions to an elected representative legally wrong?' The inspector was astounded by such questions. Fortunately Dinesh rescued him. People knew well that the inspector was an admirer of Poojamma but he had to please the MLA on an occasion like this. Eeranna and his followers huddled themselves up in his house and rued seriously over the misfiring of their strategies. "We should teach this woman a fitting lesson Anna" was the collective flare of Eeranna's followers.

Nina was in continuous admiration of the narrative capacity of Kala. She had transformed herself completely into a towering personality from the time she saw her last. Then she was just a little girt who was learning small little things from Poojamma. Now that she had disappeared from the scene Kala seemed to be slipping her feet into the shoes of Poojamma without much ado.

CHAPTER SEVEN

Poojamma's followers took Ravi to her house from the police station and narrated all that took place in the public meeting. Poojamma questioned them on the propriety of questioning Dinesh in a public meeting in front of his followers. They were still angry about the way both Dinesh and Eeranna spoke in the meeting.

"What right did they have to speak the way they did?"

"What difference do you make if you also behave in the same way?"

"How can they let loose policemen on Ravi?"

"If anyone questions me in our public meetings will you keep quiet?"

'Poojamma insisted that norms of propriety were same for all. They could not use different standards to different people. After having educated them a little on public behavior she turned to Ravi and enquired about the seriousness of the beating up. Ravi informed her that it was mostly a fake beating up. The inspector apparently instructed his assistants not to use full force of police methods on Ravi. But that did not abate in any way the anger of Poojamma's followers.'

"If you have any balls, come to our village once again, you Dinesh. Last time we gave our votes to you but next time you will get our shit for sure. For such a long time you plunged the poor of this area in ignorance and you capitalized on it. We elected you to positions of power. Now you have decided to trample on our dignity and unity. You are unable to stomach the fact that we are becoming more and more aware of our rights. If you have any problem with this, go and knock your head against the stonewalls of your house. We know the big house that you have constructed after you became MLA. We want to know what happened to all the millions of rupees that you got approved from the Government. You ass licker, you son of a bitch, if you have any guts come and show us the truth about the wealth you have made after you became MLA. We shall organize a meeting for you. If you are born to one father come again and address us in public. If you do not come to our village we shall find you out wherever you are. We know all the houses of your stepnis (mistresses)." Chikkanna was like thunder, wind and rain; all in one in a public meeting. They organized the meeting strategically at the side of the highway so that even those who passed by could hear them. Vehicles on the road screeched to a halt, drivers and cleaners got out of their trucks and listened to the polemics with glee. Cars slowed down but took up speed again without stopping. The operator of the sound system increased volume so that Eeranna could hear all the speeches sitting in his house.

'Chikkanna was like that. He was a semiliterate guy. However, like most village people he proved that literacy matters very little when it came to the question of intelligence and wisdom. He was clear in his thinking. After coming in contact with Poojamma he imbibed some new values in his life. But he was a sort of care a damn guy who would take on anybody on anything. He was able to use his mind as much as he used his hands and legs. Often people did not agree with his logic but having him in their groups was a mark of strength for them. That he liked Poojamma to fight against the landlords of the area was a great capital for the unity of the poor. He belonged to the dominant caste but was poor economically and did not care about whose house he entered and with whom he ate. Thus he was an epitome of the caste unity that Poojamma often spoke of. He would allow any caste persons in his house and offer them food. After the death of Poojamma he took up frontline leadership in the Movement for changing caste practices and establishing equality of all people. He led the movement with his own example and with his speeches.'

Nina was looking at Kala with the greatest admiration that was possible for her. Nobody's looks could deter Kala from going on with her narration.

'This was the great success of Poojamma that though she worked primarily for the transformation of caste system and fought against untouchability practices and empowerment of Dalit people, she brought together in this movement people belonging to different castes. She was able even to rope in dominant caste people to speak against their own caste people. You know Nagaraj and Manjula of Guddahalli. They are not Dalits. I am not a Dalit strictly speaking. My entire family is a follower of Poojamma.'

'One of the first things Dinesh did after his ignominious exit from our village is to have transferred the Collector. He left the district within half a day as soon as the new Collector came to take charge. However, he did a good thing in his anger against the MLA. He gave a good picture of Poojamma to the new Collector and told him of the difficulty he had with Dinesh because he attended the function organized by the followers of Poojamma. The next day of his taking charge as Collector, Rajasekhar sent his official car to fetch Poojamma. As the Collector's car reached her house, one of the officers who alighted from the car invited her to accompany him to Collector's place. But Poojamma refused to go with the officer. She told him that she had her own car and that she would meet the Collector immediately. She asked the officer to go first and told him that she would follow him. He had no other go.'

'While going he already informed the new Collector of the encounter he had with Poojamma. Rajasekhar was happy that he was going to meet a woman of substance. Any other person would have jumped into the car of the Collector considering it as a big prestige. Rajasekhar understood why the MLA was very antagonistic towards Poojamma.'

"Welcome Madam! I am very happy to meet you. I am Rajasekhar. I have heard from several people even before coming here about the great work you are doing among the Dalits. However, I like especially your approach of involving caste people in bringing about equality in society. It is something that generally Dalits do not attempt to do. They do not have much credibility among their own people. How will caste people accept them? Moreover it also requires special skills to make dominant caste fellows to work for the welfare of Dalits."

"Thank you for inviting me to meet you and for sending your car. It clearly shows that you are well disposed toward such organizations and movements. Are you by any chance a Dalit?" Poojamma pulled him straight to the point.

"No, no! I am not a Dalit. But I have worked among the tribal people in Jharkhand and I know what it means to work for justice and equality. Being a woman it must be much more difficult for you in this male dominant society. Whatever help you need from me in this great work please let me know. I shall do whatever I can." The Collector was one of the humblest persons that Poojamma had met in Government circles. "Please meet my colleague Mr. Santosh. He is the special Collector for Development in this district. He will be of much help to you. Whatever development work you want to take up for your people you can always approach him for even financial help." Santosh folded his hands in reverential respect for Poojamma. She returned the compliments.

"It is wonderful to meet such exceptional men of good will in the government system. I am very happy to have met you and will come back to you for any type of assistance that our people may need. May I take leave of you now?" Poojamma was admired for her simplicity mixed with high level of professionalism. "It is not for nothing that she is so successful in her work" Santosh thought to himself.

"I am not as good as you are in professional dealings Mr. Santosh. I deal with situations that can never be anticipated and professionalism does not always bring about the best fruits in favor of the poor. I have to throw away my professional approach at times and be just disorganized with the people." Santosh was taken aback completely at the way Poojamma read his mind.

"Please sit for some more time. Tea is coming. Have a cup of tea with us. We are privileged to have you with us." They shared tea and some more pleasantries before Poojamma bade farewell to both the officers and left.

'News of the Collector sending his vehicle to fetch Poojamma spread like wildfire in the entire area. Followers of Poojamma were excited beyond control and shared the news with whomsoever they met, friends and foes alike. 'It is not a big deal. Why are you people making such big news about it? After all I only went to meet the Collector. He is come for doing good things for us.' Poojamma advised her followers to keep calm both in times of difficulties and at times of great success.'

'News reached the ears of Eeranna and he was burning inside. He just threw the teacup that he was holding in his hands when Manjanna informed him of what he heard. 'What is this idiotic MLA doing? Instead of bringing a bureaucrat who will help us he has brought someone who is supporting our enemy' he fumed and frothed. He lifted his phone and informed Dinesh about what happened as soon as the new Collector arrived. Dinesh was sweating on the other side of the phone. His throat was making a creaking noise. He seemed to have lost his voice. 'I told the Chief Minister to send a man who will support me. Many MLAs told me that Rajasekhar is a good man and supports our Chief Minister. I did not know that he is inimical to us. It must be the work of the previous Collector. He must have prejudiced him against us. But don't worry. Any officer has to function under my guidance in my constituency. You come tomorrow. We shall go and meet him in his office.' Dinesh got to the task of damage control.'

'That evening the Collector's car was in the house of Poojamma once again. This time it was at dusk. Most people in the surrounding villages had already taken refuge under the protective wings of goddess Yellamma. This goddess was a euphemistic reference to alcohol. Some would loiter in the streets of the village trying to grab all attention of bystanders. Others would quietly retire to their home not desiring to disturb their children. It was a necessary prelude for many to have good sex with their wives later in the night. Most wives even wanted their husbands to drink moderately so that they could have a prolonged sex with their husbands. Often men overdid it. They would have a peg or two extra and puke out their semen prematurely disappointing their wives grossly. They would have to wake them up once again in the middle of night to have another round to be satisfied with their husbands.'

'Globalization had its inevitable sidekicks in the lives of rural masses. Before its arrival, women had to go to sleep without removing their saris. Underneath their saris was their skirt. It used to be heavy. Husbands had a horrid time lifting sari and skirt together and finally when they managed, their cock had to reach beyond the thick sari and skirt that folded as a lump in their abdominal region. Added to this was the fear of children who were sleeping in the same room in darkness. If they woke up suddenly for drinking water everything would be spoiled. It would be a big show of xxx for their kids. After the arrival of globalization villages slowly got used to something called 'nightie'. There were different types of nighties. Women started wearing them even during day. They used to have a spare one for night. This second nightie would be light and wearing a skirt inside was not a compulsory need. Clever ones among women also bought the type of nightie with either an opening where it mattered or with buttons till the knee. Grown up girls in the families knew the tricks of their mothers and would giggle among themselves as they prepared to go to sleep.

It mattered very little for men. They wore only one type of half nickers before and after the arrival of globalization. Even when they sat in public meetings their balls would protrude in different shines and colors. Some even would show of their cocks with pulled-back foreskin. Women would listen to the public speeches but would cast frequent glance at such men and removed their sight at the earliest in order not to be detected. They needed enough fodder for their gossip in the village pond when they went to wash clothes together. Talking only of their husbands was boring. Talking of the size and shape of other men's balls and cocks often added a lot of spice to their gossip.

Just before reaching the house of Poojamma Santosh was stopped at the village by a drunken man who stood at the center of the road. Being dark outside Santosh got out of the car and picked up a conversation with the man.

Santosh chose his time carefully. He did not want to be seen much by village people and become an object of political gossip. It was almost like a visit in stealth. Poojamma thought that it was Rajasekhar. Seeing Santosh she was pleasantly surprised. She went out to welcome him and took him home inside. Santosh had carefully taken his wife too. He enquired about Poojamma's personal antecedents a bit without giving an impression that he was peeping too much into her private life. Santosh's wife liked Poojamma at the very first sight. She walked into the kitchen behind Poojamma and helped her to make some tea. Kala tried to avoid it. But she knew that if Poojamma went into the kitchen it was with some special preference and would not insist on her making coffee or tea. She knew the significance of that personal touch to some people.

Sipping of tea added a lot of taste as Santosh's wife had already confessed in the kitchen that both of them were Dalits. Poojamma knew it was exceptional courage on her part to reveal her Dalit identity that fast. Generally Dalit bureaucrats were inhibited to reveal their Dalit identity. They knew that they got into high positions precisely because they were Dalits with affirmative action of the government. But they were also afraid of the stigma that could harm their future because of their identity. Now Poojamma understood why Santosh had rushed to visit her. Identity had many positive faces. The officer perhaps also needed someone to lean on, someone whom he could see as his own for support and solidarity.

—◦◦◦|◦|◦◦◦—

The Collector's office wore a festive look next day. It was his first working day after he assumed office. He took a day to stay back at home. It was to get all possible background information about the District that he stayed at home. He called all officers of different departments, especially the police intelligence and gathered a correct picture of situations and different actors of the District that he had to administer. There was a procession of wellwishers with garland in their hands to welcome the Collector. Dinesh and Eeranna went together with a few other party workers. They barged into the front lines without caring for others who waited in the Que. His supporters pushed aside some saying that the MLA wanted to meet the Collector. Dinesh garlanded the Collector and told him that he was happy to have Rajasekhar as the new Collector. He took a dig at the previous Collector as very partisan and non-cooperative. He said that he transferred him within a day and recommended to the Chief Minister that Rajasekhar should be brought to the District as the new Collector. Rajasekhar just smiled and accepted the garland. Dinesh was disappointed that there was no exuberance on the face of the Collector on hearing the news of his power. He introduced Eeranna as his trusted captain. Eeranna extended his hand for a shake but the Collector did not reciprocate. It was a strong message. Dinesh pretended not to have seen the slight and requested Rajasekhar to extend all support and help to Eeranna.

Rajasekhar was an enigma for Dinesh. He would not say anything in response to whatever he heard. He had a standing in the State irrespective of politicians. He had established a niche for himself in the administrative sector of the State as a very efficient officer. All politicians including the Chief Minister held him in high esteem. Politicians themselves did not respect officers who obliged politicians easily. Such officers had a price fixed by politicians. But efficient officers like Rajasekhar could not be easily bought. Dinesh requested him to lend an ear to Eeranna. Rajasekhar asked them to sit and talk. He informed his officers at the door not to allow other visitors for sometime. He gave due respect to Dinesh who was an elected member.

'Sir, I want to inform you of a big dangerous thing that is happening in our District. Since you are new we already want to inform you of this. We have no other intentions of casting aspersion on anyone's character. But there is a woman called Poojamma. She is indulging in conversion work by misguiding people. She gets a lot of money from other countries. Unless she is sent out of the district soon we shall have problems in administration as more and more people will start following her and her religion.' Eeranna now began to slowly unfold his true colors also to the Collector.

'It seems you had invited her to meet you already on the first day. That is why we are here to tell you that she is a very dangerous customer for the government. The other day we had a public meeting in which she had sent her followers and created a lot of problem. They did not allow our meeting to proceed till police intervened and took them away. I had to plead with the police not to arrest them. Here is my written request to you to send her out of the District. Let her go anywhere else and do her conversion work. But in my constituency I will not allow even a single person to be converted. Please pass an order asking the police to send her out of the district. This is my humble request to you. Sorry to have brought this issue already on the first day of your assuming office. But this is a very serious issue.' It was Dinesh who spoke now. He wanted to convince Rajasekhar of the need to cleanse the district of subversive forces such as Poojamma.

Rajasekhar's face became hard. The smile on his face disappeared. He said that converting people to other religions making use of their poverty was a serious issue and he would do all he could to stop such type of conversions. "However, I need strong evidence that she has converted people to Christianity as you allege. If there are no evidences the case will not stand in any court. I am sure Poojamma will go to court seeking justice if I pass such an order. If courts do not have enough evidence they will pass strictures against me. I cannot take such risks. Therefore, what I suggest is that you provide me some statistics. Bring me some data on how many Christians were living in this district before Poojamma came here and the population of Christians now in the district. You also must provide some evidence that if there is any increase in Christian population in the district it is because of the work of Poojamma and not by mere population increase. The day you give me such statistics I shall pass orders to Poojamma to leave the district. What do you say?" The Collector made strong sense in his response to Dinesh.

Dinesh and Eeranna could not make out whether the Collector was speaking on their behalf or on behalf of Poojamma. They simply agreed to go and meet him another day with enough statistics and data. Going out of the office of the Collector they looked at each other and all their assistants were looking at their faces alternatively.

'The Collector called up Poojamma that evening over phone and informed her of what was happening. He was not supposed to do that nor was he required to do that. But he was a man of good heart and had a lot of space for Dalits and Adivasis in his heart. From intelligence reports in police records he knew that Poojamma did not believe in Christianity though she was born in that religion. She had given up all religions and even gods. The Collector had information that she was almost an atheist. Santosh also called her up a little later and assured her of all support in her work.'

Kala checked with Nina if she saw Santosh and his wife at the funeral of Poojamma. They came, participated in the funeral procession and left as soon as the funeral was over. They did not wait to speak to all the people assembled that day. Nina learned that there were many officers in the funeral of Poojamma but did not make a show of their presence.

⟶◦◦•◉•◦◦⟵

'Dinesh and Eeranna were not able to fully digest the happiness of their achievement of having transferred the Collector. They could not swallow it and they could not spit it out. The new one was not as supportive of them as they expected. They even nurtured a doubt that in the course of time he might support Poojamma. The indications were already there. They decided to take up the matter at higher levels. Dinesh took Eeranna to the State Secretariat and to the Home Ministry. They had learned their lessons from Rajasekhar. If they took up the issue of conversion the Home Ministry might also ask the same question and might demand statistical proof. They would then not be able to provide even a single case of conversion. Therefore, they changed tactics with the Home Ministry.'

Nina kept on admiring the narrative ability of Kala with so much of data and memory of events and people. Kala kept on making coffee while talking and sat with Nina to talk. She was tireless and on this score was a replica of Poojamma. Kala continued.

'Dinesh and Eeranna left for Delhi to meet the Home Minister of the Central Government. Eeranna had his first travel by air. He was more excited about his travel. All his sense of defeat at the hands of a woman disappeared into thin air at a height of 33,000 feet and at a speed of 870 kilometers per hour. When the big bird took off it was like two buckets of tamarind water poured all at once in his stomach. Both of them were in white attire and Eeranna bought a pair of white slippers for this special trip to Delhi. He had seen many MLAs and big politicians wearing white slippers. He wanted to feel like them. Traveling in plane raised his feelings above all his relatives and friends in his village. None of them could even dream of touching a plane. Most of them did not see a plane except when they strayed into their village high above the sky. Then it looked even smaller than the eagle that they saw in their village. Those who sighted a plane first would point their fingers in the direction of the plane that they saw. Others would take a few seconds to spot the plane.'

'The village was full of gossip and proud proclamations about Dinesh taking Eeranna to Delhi in plane. At the teashop in the village people belonging to both the camps talked among themselves as they sipped their tea. Followers of Poojamma took the upper hand in praise of their leaders.

They shouted aloud that Eeranna was going for the first time in plane and that too only to Delhi. Much worse was the fact that it was Dinesh who took him. But their Poojamma went to even foreign countries whenever she wanted.'

'It was too late to go to any offices in Delhi when they reached the Capital city of India. Dinesh hired a taxi and took Eeranna to a hotel in Karol Bagh. The area was full of hotels of all sizes and shades. There were many agents standing on roadside accosting the taxis to go to their hotels. Business was brisk. There was heavy competition and equal congestion. It was a good lesson for Eeranna that while agents were in high competition none of them fought with each other. When a customer decided to alight in front of a hotel on the invitation of one tout others smiled and wished him well. In his village there would be an immediate fisticuff.'

'Dinesh took a room for himself and asked Eeranna to stay separately in another room. "He is our MLA and needs his privacy. I am only his agent. How can I expect to stay in the same room with him?" he thought. Dinesh asked him to have his bath and said that at 9 in the evening they would go out for dinner. Ecranna agreed to it and switched on the TV in his room. He searched all channels for something sexy. Except for the Fashion TV there was no other channel that showed any explicit sex. "Is it for this that I came all the way to Delhi?" He thought and lay down in his cot watching TV.'

'At six in the evening there was a knock at the door of Eeranna's room. He opened the door and saw Dinesh standing there. The MLA invited him to his room. Ecranna dressed up and followed him. In Dinesh's room there were some liquor bottles kept ready. Dinesh asked him whether he wanted whisky or brandy. Eeranna was used largely to country arrack in his village. Now it was Delhi and he deserved a more sophisticated drink. Dinesh was sipping his whisky mixed with soda and ice. Eeranna could not understand how anyone could have a drink so slow. He was used to gulping a full glass of arrack at one go. Sometimes the smell of the spirit struck on his nose so violently that he had to close his nose and gulp the content of the glass. He used to keep spicy pickles ready to ward off the taste of arrack from his tongue. Dinesh informed him that 'high society's' way of drinking was different and that Eeranna should get used to it. By the time Dinesh had completed one glass of whisky Eeranna had guzzled down three glasses of brandy. He was laughing at the way Dinesh was having his whisky. By the third glass his laughter had become more voluminous and his words had become more 'biblical'. He was in his abusive best.'

'Dinesh enjoyed the drunken behavior of his ward. He also admired the amazing capacity of his minion to abuse people. He had no inhibition in abusing Poojamma. When the spirit was high ethos went down proportionally. That was the rule of politics at Dinesh's level. By the third glass of whisky Dinesh also had climbed the ladder quite high and in his elation he forced a fourth glass of brandy on Eeranna. Now both of them started a new camaraderie of using singular number in their addressing each other. Yellamma started her play on Dinesh. He began to blabber about sex now. Eeranna became more than eager to hear, as the same Yellamma also had entered his body without any inhibition. Dinesh took him to Thailand where he had his sexapades.'

'But Kala, how did you know what happened to Dinesh in Thailand? Did he narrate it to anyone whom you know?' Nina provided some comic interlude.

'Wait Nina! Have some patience! Before I can explain the nitti-gritties of knowing the how and the why listen to this very interesting scene in Thailand. I shall come back to your question later. In his drunken mood Dinesh started his narration to Eeranna in the following manner.'

"Two of us decided to visit Thailand as we heard that it was a land of tourism and that it offered easy sex to tourists." Dinesh started the story. But Eeranna immediately interrupted him. As soon as he heard the word sex his cock also stood up in attention to listen to the story.

"Did you also take your wife with you?" He asked

"Hey idiot! Will any sensible man take his wife to a place where sex tourism was thriving? We went precisely because we wanted to have some extra kicks, man." Dinesh let the spirit wander around freely. The spirit had filled the entire room and all who were in it. Eeranna was convincing himself that the ways of politicians were unfathomable and that he was still a bacha, a child in politics. He also advised himself that he had to grow like Dinesh.

Kala summed up the events that took place in Thailand in order not to keep Nina in suspense for long. She knew that Nina would not listen to the entire story with keen interest if she did not get her answer first. It was one day in her house that her father shared with his friend in an inebriated state. He thought that his children had already gone to sleep and that only his wife was awake with him. But Kala was wide-awake with closed eyes and fully opened ears. While narrating the chain of events she did not forget to add her own spice. It was natural and inexorable.

'Both of them checked into an ordinary hotel in Bangkok. Within half an hour of their taking a room in the hotel there was a mild knock at the door of Dinesh's room. The man at the door had a set of albums. As soon as he started showing the albums Dinesh understood what it was all about. He rushed to the next door and called his companion. The man was a pimp. He showed the photos of many Thai girls and explained to them different rates that depended on the complexion and beauty of the selected girls, their age and the duration for which they would hire the girls. They asked the pimp if the girls were safe. He insisted that they were all medically tested and certified girls and took some papers from another bag to show to them.'

'Dinesh's friend took him aside and told him that rates in the hotels were exorbitant and that they should take girls outside in the evenings. Dinesh asked him if girls were so cheap in Thailand. His friend informed him that he would see for himself how cheap Thai girls were.'

"Oh, I have been in Thailand several time. It is horrible for women there! Women there are in ghettos." Nina added more spice to the story. Kala continued.

'Both of them set out in a Thai tuk-tuk in the evening. Dinesh's friend hired a guide. He took them first to a brothel. Dinesh was initially shocked at what he saw in the brothel. He had visited the Red Light area of Bombay once in stealth. There were many pimps on the road pleading with customers to go into their building. They were all-persuasive and had photos of many girls. But this brothel was different. Girls were kept in cages made of steel mesh. Three or four of them were in the same cage. They hardly had place to sit. All them had decked themselves up with colors on their face, thick lipsticks and funny hairstyle. Though it was nauseating to see women in that condition Dinesh had certain small hangouts that urged him differently and urged him to look beyond the feminine values that his mother had taught. The dress of the girls showing off their boobs was an added provocation. In any case he had thrown most of those values to the wind already in India. Now it mattered very little in a foreign country. His friend told him that it was a very cheap place and there could be a danger of having sex with those girls even if they used condoms. The guide showed them the condoms he had brought for them already when they alighted from the 'tuk-tuk'.

'They hurried out of that place and asked the guide to take them to some other place. The guide checked with them if they liked to have dinner first. He told them in plain terms that if they were in the right place they would never have time and inclination for food. They saw sense in what he said though Dinesh was in a dead hurry to satiate his hunger beneath his stomach. The guide took them to a restaurant. Dinesh asked the guide why it was decorated with color lights. "If a restaurant is decorated with color lights outside it means that there will be special girls along with food." The guide laughed sarcastically at Dinesh's innocent ignorance about his motherland.

"Kala, you are a landmine of information. I have also read a lot about Thailand's tourism industry. But the way you explain things stuns me. You are simply marvelous." Nina added interludes here and there.

'Please reserve all your compliments to the end. After I complete all my narration you can flatter me as much as you want.' Kala replied and resumed her narrative mission.

'There was loud music that penetrated the eardrums of the Indians. Since these eardrums were not made in Taiwan or in China they were unable to bear the quivering sound of music. There was only some Thai food available. All the food looked like Chinese food for them. With the help of the guide they ordered for some food. As they were eating there was intermittent announcement in Thai language about something. The guide explained to them in broken English that the owner of the restaurant was inviting more customers with the announcement that some famous Thai girls would come soon. As they were finishing food there was a limousine that stopped at the entrance to the restaurant and all people inside started clapping their hands. There was a very well dressed woman who got down from the Benz car accompanied by two men. She looked almost like the queen of Thailand in the way she had decorated herself with all sorts of creams and colors. Her dress was not only glowing but was also flowing behind her. She was looking beautiful. She was taken to a room in the restaurant and all eyes were set on her.'

'After a few minutes the 'queen' bee came out of the room with a few other girls and now the orchestra took over from the music decks. They were wearing long gown but it was open all the way to show their slim and polished legs ending with much bigger thighs. Dinesh was already whining inside. He wanted to grab one of the girls and hold her tight. His desire came true in a few minutes. The girls went round and sat on the laps of customers and put their arms around them. Some customers grabbed their chance to plant a kiss on the cheeks of the till then unknown girls. Love went abegging to lust. The restaurant was filled with the smell of lust, unrestricted libido. The queen bee was standing on a slightly raised stage for all to see. Even while playing with the girls many stuck their eyes keenly on the queen bee. Dinesh also welcomed the girl to come to him. He opened his legs in anticipation of something beyond kissing. But the girls had come with strict instructions from their queen. They sat on the laps of customers only two minutes and then they moved on to other craving customers.'

'When the girls had completed their task and as they were moving towards the queen bee the boys in the restaurants moved in to all the customers who lapped up the girls and collected money. Dinesh did not know that he had to pay money. He let his hands probe his pockets. Probing by now had become a sort of habit with him. But his companion told him not to worry. He had paid for both. It was a moment of hyper excitement and the MLA would do anything for anyone who excited him at the right places.'

'Both of them finished their meal hurriedly thinking that they had to move on to another place to have their full release of energy. But then the music became loud and the owner of the restaurant began to announce something very exciting in Thai language. Many customers started clapping their hands and the most unexpected thing happened for Dinesh and his companion. The queen bee just pulled the string that had kept her gown together. Just as she did that she also removed the sleeves and the entire gown fell down. There she was fully naked standing in front of all the men craving with lustful eyes. Millennia of years, lust never dies down! Dinesh's excitement was uncontrollable. He had forced his wife to become naked quite a few times but this was something divine. But then it just lasted only for half a minute and then the owner of the restaurant took the gown and robed her again. Dinesh wished it lasted for an eternity. But then it was a free bonus for the customers by the owner. The show was wound up and the queen bee left in her Benz limousine.'

Women, the eternal object of men's insatiable sexual desires! Their personality defined and redefined constantly by the lust of men!

'After re-charging their batteries both the MLAs were ready to charge. The guide took them to a street in Bangkok that was known as the live sex street. He warned both of them that it was the last junction in their tour of the city. He also informed them that he would not go inside the place instead wait outside for them and that they would have to dish out quite a bit of money. The entrance to the hall was narrow and quite long. The path was splashed with many hefty and ruffian hoodlums who were prepared for any eventuality. All sorts of men went there. Both of them were surprised to see the hall filled with white men. Some of them finished their business quickly and went out quietly but there were also many other men who, after a few rounds of drinks felt they were on top of the world and behaved as if they were the owners of the joint. Dinesh had a look all around and became quite cautious. But at the end of the tunnel like entrance he saw a stage of moderate size with bright lighting focused heavily on the stage at the center. The stage was well protected with wire mesh. Inside the mesh, on the stage were many girls dancing. Dinesh's cock already tried to have a full look at the entire scene through his pants. It was a natural outburst as the girls at the center were fully naked and were dancing.'

'An attendant greeted them and showed some empty table for two. He asked them to go, sit and enjoy. As they were walking towards their table both the MLAs saw many men and women cuddling up. The girls were completely naked and the men were playing with their bodies without any inhibition of the presence of other men. When all men were doing the same what was the need for inhibitions? Some men took their girls towards a door and there was a woman who greeted them and led them into small cubicles. It was not difficult for Dinesh to guess what they did inside those pigeonholes. Some were coming back with their girls again into the hall. The girl who came with them left them and other girls took over from them.'

'The two MLAs ordered for some beer and something to munch as they were in full excitement all over. As they started sipping their beer two young girls came to their table and sat next to them. Their seats were not single chairs but small benches designed to accommodate two persons. The girls were not naked. They had white cloth around their body. The white cloth was transparent. Both the MLAs could have hazy vision of the body of the girls and that was enough to trigger a floodgate in them. But they preserved their energies for better time that evening. The girls asked them if they could sip some beer from their glasses. They welcomed it anticipating hyper excitement. It was there for the asking.'

'Both the MLAs now were like bulls in a China shop. It was easy for them to pull down the white cloth beneath the boobs of the girls. They allowed that with a broad smile. Both men started playing with the bodies of the girls freely. Each of them forgot the other and remembered only himself. Nothing else existed for them. They did not want anything else to exist. The elected members of people began to shape better ideas and removed the entire cloth from the body of their girls. The freedom of the girls shocked them. Even their own wives were never free with them. They always were shy when clothes disappeared from their bodies.'

'Dinesh was waiting for his companion to give him the signal to go to the cubicle. But the man was as busy as ever with the body of his girl. He seemed to have better capacity for prolongation than Dinesh. Like everybody else they also took the girls to the cubicle. There was no honey and no moon anywhere but they imagined a honeymoon. As they came out with the girls and took their seats the woman who pushed them into the cubicle slapped a bill on their table. The entire amount in the bill was in Baht, the Thailand money. The guide had told them everything carefully about money. Both of them changed their Indian rupees into Baht before they set out that evening with the guide. They cared a damn about how much it cost them.'

'All the money they carried to Thailand was robbed from the tax-money of the poor people. It was the development fund meant for the poor in their constituencies. But they had no qualms about robbing the poor. They were no Robin Hoods to rob the rich and give it to the poor. They were after all raw politicians who knew only to rob the poor in order to become rich. They had more drinks, real hot drinks. The two girls whom they fucked took leave of them. They waited for tips. But the MLAs pretended as if they did not understand anything. The girls left in a huff. Two other girls replaced them. Both the MLAs were very happy that they had fresh grounds to play. The women now were much younger than the previous girls. The owner of the bar had planned it well. The first set of women had to be a bit more mature to deal with ravaging men. Once they had let out their forceful energy he sent young dames so that men would not be too devastating with them. The girls were less than 15 years. The MLAs realized that they were having girl children in their families. But their lust blinded them. Both of them had raised the issue of child prostitution in their Legislative Assembly several times. They were fighting tooth and nail against the government on the question of girl children of Devadasi women. But now the girls were naked in front of them. All that they had spoken earlier vaporized in the air.'

'Even as they started playing with the bodies of the children a woman attender demanded money for the previous girls. The bill was obviously highly exaggerated. Instead of two bottles of Thai beer that they consumed the bills mentioned six bottles. Both the MLAs stood up protesting against the bill. It was enough they stood up and shouted at the attender. They were immediately surrounded by a group of thugs who were like roaring lions ready to shred their robust bodies into hundreds of unidentifiable meat fibers. They remembered the many times they threw their mikes on the Speaker of the house. They were ready to beat up any one in Assembly. They also functioned as the henchmen of the President of their party. But now it was a different story. They were surrounded by men Friday. They suddenly realized even while drowning that they were in a foreign land and could not muster enough forces to fight. They sat down without giving even a semblance of fight and parted with money.

Nothing was less worth for the type of returns they had with naked girls in fair skin.'

'It took a while for them to resume their foreplay. The girls helped them to gulp a few pegs of whisky fast. They were keen on their business. If the men finished with them fast two other girls would take turn and that would bulge the pocket of the owner of the place. Still they were struggling to get out of the defeat they suffered. Being politicians they were prepared for defeat any time. But when it looked them on the face it was difficult, as defeat was the most hated thing among politicians. The girls tried their best to bring the men back to fast movements. But they did not have adequate experience. Things were quite slow. After sometime things were beyond their control for both MLAs. They paid their huge bills and left the place craving for more of such Thai women. All women on the roads now looked naked to them. Body scan was an art that these men mastered.'

'When you men look at our back and say, "what an ass" we women look at your face and say "what an ass". Some women liberation organization had pasted this poster on the walls and the MLAs did not fail to read it. It was a donkey life for the MLAs and a direct insult on donkeys.

CHAPTER EIGHT

'But Kala, how do you know all the intricacies of drinking and sex? You explain these to me so well. Have you ever drunk in your life? Unless you have drunk sometime you cannot explain things in such fine detail.' Nina wanted to provoke Kala a bit and also to break the monotony of her narration. Some comic interludes were not out of place. Before she could ask the next part of the question Kala started.

'Oh, one of my close relatives worked with Eeranna for sometime. They were close to each other. But later during one election campaign they fell out as Eeranna pocketed all the money given by Dinesh without sharing with the people who worked with him. After his break off my relative started frequenting our house in order to have drinks with my father. When both of them were drunk many truths tumbled out from the mouth of my relative. I learned not only truths but also the way these men puked out truths when their spirits were high. They had very little control over themselves the moment Yellamma the goddess of liquor entered their body. Poor men believe they are very strong. But we women know how weak they are. All that we have to do is to wash them with a bit of liquor and incite them with a bit sex. We can achieve whatever we want. This is their strength.' Kala exhibited maturity beyond her age.

'And you speak so freely about sex. You are not even married and being a village girl you must be very shy. This is what I have imagined about Indian village dames.' This time Nina was genuinely perplexed as a woman and did not apply any of her journalistic techniques.

'You are from America. Therefore, I took the freedom to speak to you freely about sex. I am sorry. I think you Americans not only speak freely about sex but also have free sex. But you also have a misunderstanding about our village dames. We have no inhibitions to talk about sex among ourselves. In fact when we gather as girls, sex occupies more of our gossip time. We speak about every village man and the way each behaves. Many of our men keep showing their balls and bats through the half nicker that they wear and sit in public places. What other entertainments do we have in our village life? We are not allowed to speak to boys in public. We are not allowed to go with them anywhere. We are not allowed to go to town for a movie unless at least one of our parents accompanies us. Gossiping about sex is our pastime. We enjoy speaking about our men, especially those who are so careless about their sexual organs.' Kala was forthright in her confession.

'No, no don't be sorry. You are right about Americans and thank you for correcting my prejudices about Indian village dames. You women seem to be much stronger and liberated than your men.' Nina was apologetic in her assertions and gave necessary tonic to Kala to continue her narration.

———◆———

Kala continued. She was angry with Eeranna to the core and Nina could see her face being filled with anger and remorse.

'It was time to eat after a heavy drink and Dinesh's entire narration of their jolly good time in Thailand. Eeranna sent out an immediate request to be taken once to Thailand. There was no reply yet from Dinesh. The MLA in him was used to slow execution of others' requests and people's applications. Both of them took a taxi and went out to a restaurant to have Hyderabad biryani in Delhi. They ordered for mutton Biryani and also a mutton dish. Dinesh knew well that Delhi restaurants prepared very good mutton dish. Except for the fact that occasionally they also served spoiled mutton that resulted in food poisoning. The josh of having a good meal urged both of them to raise a toast. They ordered for a peg of whisky and brandy respectively. Half of the spirit that Eeranna had raised went down fast when he saw the bill. It was slightly more than the annual earnings of many of his relatives in the village. But that day was special and there was no time to feel guilty about anything. It was a day worthy of celebration, especially after having travelled for the first time to Delhi and first time in plane. His spirit was in high heavens.'

"Hey man, what are you doing? Behave yourself. There are many rich people here who may be watching you." Dinesh was bit annoyed with Eeranna. He was often touching his pants between his legs and was pressing at the place where his cock rested. Nay, he had to force it to rest, as it was quite restless. He still dwelt on the narrations of explicit experiences that Dinesh narrated in a drunken mood.

"What can I do Anna, it is all because of you. You had such wonderful things to do in Thailand. Can we not have something like that in Delhi?' Eeranna had gained the courage to speak himself out strongly backed by the power of spirit.

'Oh, is that your problem? Come let us go,' Dinesh got up from his seat, asked for the bills, paid them in quick rapidity and pulled Eeranna to almost storm out of the restaurant. He took a taxi and went straight to a street that was decorated with red lights all over. Eeranna guessed it right that he was going to have a feast. He was introduced to a different lifestyle of politics. He thought it was an essential ingredient of being a successful politician. Dinesh did the entire negotiation. The pimps seemed to have been used to men with white dresses and white slippers. They represented a class that frequented their place.'

'Both of them were led into two different rooms. Dinesh was an expert in the art of extramarital sex. Eeranna was just initiated into this finer political art. Sex and politics! Very familiar bedfellows! When both of them came out they were sweating like hell. There was no air-conditioned room there. Everything in there was hot.

'How did you like it? Was the girl cooperative?' Dinesh asked Eeranna with a sarcastic smile.

'Oh, the bitch was very rude. She wanted everything to be over in two minutes. I told her that we paid money. She said that there were many other men who also paid money and were waiting outside. But it was good for a first time. The only problem was that I could not shoo away the thought of my wife all the time.' Eeranna said as if he was in a confessional in some catholic church. Dinesh the High Priest of a decadent political order!'

'It was like that for me too when I went to Thailand. But now I got used to it. In fact, it is now difficult for me to have normal sex with my wife. After sometime it will be the other way round. When you have sex with your wife it will be the thought of many other women that will haunt you.' Eeranna admired the expertise of his mentor who was taking over slowly everything that mattered and did not matter in his life.'

———◦◦❂◦◦———

'Both of them set out for their business the next day. Dinesh had got an appointment with the Home Secretary in Delhi. Being Member of the Legislative Assembly it was rather easy to get an appointment with such high profile person. He had to make use of the power of the Chief Minister to get that appointment. It was difficult to get up early for both. The hangover from the heavy drink and the lethargy from their sexapade had pulled down energy level to a great extent. They had to rush, as they were expected to be in the office of the Home Secretary 20 minutes before time in order to go through regular security check up.'

"Hey, he is our MLA and you are checking him also. Leave him. He is a big man." Eeranna shouted at the security person.

'Dinesh pinched his hand hard and talked to the security apologetically. The security turned to Eeranna with a stern face and told him, "For you he may be your MLA. Here he is just an ordinary citizen and our machines will tell us who he really is. Our machines do not look at people as big and small. You keep your MLA's greatness to yourself. Come and stand here."

'Eeranna did not understand a word of it as the man spoke in Hindi and Eeranna did not know Hindi at all. He was the only one in the village to go till graduation. There were a few others who managed to study till Pre-university course. But Eeranna was a more enterprising fellow and wanted to have the experience of being a college student in order to be the only person to be educated that well. He always saw to it that he owned more land than others in the village, he had more power in the village than anyone else, and he had more contacts than others. If anyone tried to do something he would always do something bigger. He wanted to be one above others in everything possible.'

'Most students in the town hardly studied. So was Eeranna. It was below his status to spend much time at home on studies. He had better preoccupations than studying. In the college he had many other business than attending classes. He had the uncanny knack of gathering youngsters around him. However, he saw to it that his friends bought a lot of snacks and drinks for him with their own money. Only on very rare occasions would he spend some money from his pocket. Building relationship had to have a utility value. Nay, everything in life had to have a final end that was advantageous to him. He could not see the world beyond his own interest. His friends thus saw him often walking through narrow by lanes and sullied gullies of life.'

'He also gathered a group of young men around him who would generally sit only outside the class and tease all the girls and some innocent boys. It was his pastime. He never bothered about the feelings of others. It was their business to deal with their feelings and not his. When people asked him how he would pass exams without studying he would very boastingly say that only fools would study. He had other ways of passing in exams. He had by then learned from seniors of his kind that it was possible to bribe evaluators and get pass marks. This was an open secret known to all not only in the college but also in the city.'

"What? Do students bribe evaluators in exams and get pass marks? Is this possible in India? I could never imagine this. Does this really happen in India?" Nina interjected Kala rather nervously and violently.

'This is possible only in India, Nina. What do you think of my country? Everything that is not possible in law is possible in India. Children of many politicians and business people pass their exams simply by bribing. That is why we say "Mera Bharat Mahan". It means my India is great. Don't you think India is great?' Kala was derisive at the way things were being done in India. Nina just shook her head in disbelief. Kala continued.

'The honest ones studied hard to either pass in subjects or to score high marks. But when they came to know that some thugs got through in exams through power of money or through power of 'power' their hope in the future of their country dwindled like a wildfire that had to subdue itself to a cold shower from the sky.'

'The University had a rule that all students had to have at least 75% attendance in classes in order to qualify to write exams. When he did not have enough attendance, especially in classes where men were teachers, he would go with a group of friends and force them to increase his attendance threatening them with dire consequences if they did not oblige. But his threats did not work with Arif Khan, a frail looking conscienscious teacher in the college. Eeranna had become notorious in the circle of lecturers and professors. Some lady lecturers were in tears when they complained to the principal on the hassles Eeranna created during their class. The principal only advised lecturers to adjust and go. He had no guts to take disciplinary action against Eeranna. He knew the political clout of Eeranna's.'

'Sir he is a very good student sir. His father had some health problems and he had to look after him in the hospital. That is why his attendance is fallen short of 75%. Please do something and give him 75% attendance.' Eeranna's friends were willing accomplices in the creation of a make-believe world.

'Rule is rule. I cannot change records to suit any student. You go and ask the principal to change records if you can. Don't try all these tricks with me. If I do this to him today there will be many more students the next day asking for the same benefit. What can I do?' Arif protested with certain amount of authority.

The tone of the students now changed and leadership also changed hands. Eeranna took over directly. "What rule are you talking about? Is everything in the college done according to rules? Is everything in the country done according to rules? Only those who break rules become big in our country. Shut your bloody gob and give me attendance."

"You may go to hell with all your bullshit about the country. I care a damn. I follow the rules of the college and will follow only the rules of the University. If you are so keen, go and change the rules of the University and I shall follow those rules. The Government is paying me for preserving rules and not for breaking them." Arif wanted to instill some sense in his wards.

"It is only because you are following rules that you are like this Arif. Look at your shirt and look at our dress. We are wearing branded items and you are still wearing only dress stitched by our local tailor Ahmed. You will never improve in your life, you Paki. Find some ways and means of giving good standard of life to your two children. Be smart Arif and don't be an archaic idiot like your counterparts in Pakistan. Give me 75% attendance and you will save yourself." Eeranna's language now changed to singular address of his teacher and assumed intimidating tones.

"Hey, you are a student in this college and you should know your limits. Don't think you can achieve anything by bullying me. You may have your ways of coming up in life. But that is not what I teach my children and students. Get the hell out of here you bloody asshole." Arif Khan shouted at the top of his voice and some students and teachers gathered there hearing the brouhaha. Eeranna and his friends decided not to create a scene in the college. They had many other ways of teaching lessons to their teachers.

'The next day newspapers carried sensational news about the attack on a lecturer of the government college in the city. There were some news about lethargy and indiscipline among lecturers that led to a sorry state of affairs in the field of education. There were other newspapers that analyzed the growing hoodlum among students. Some reporters dug the personal life of Eeranna and found nothing to substantiate the news that he was the culprit behind the attack on Arif. Since Arif was a Muslim professor, newspapers also decried his personal arrogance and almost condemned him for what had happened. Muslim community in the city took out a protest and presented a memorandum to the Collector. There were many hundreds of such memoranda in the office of the Collector gaping at every officer who took charge there.'

'Arif was admitted in hospital with serious injuries on his head and shoulders. He was attacked with lethal weapons unawares and fell flat on the ground unconscious. Some bystanders took him to hospital and informed his family. They informed the Mosque and his relatives and rushed to hospital. After hearing his name doctors in the hospital were very slow in giving him treatment. Though he was bleeding profusely doctors refused to touch him till police came and told them to go ahead with treatment.'

'Many lecturers and professors rushed to the hospital with their principal. On their return they began to torment the Principal left and right for his inaction on many such incidents earlier. They realized that it could happen to any one of them at any time. That almost forced the principal to swing into action. He called up the Superintendent of Police and requested him to take serious action. The SP was a no nonsense man along with the Collector. Eeranna was arrested. But much before his arrest he had gone to the MLA and presented his case. The MLA scolded him in the beginning. But after knowing that he was from his own constituency and that too from a village where he needed one of his henchmen, he became sympathetic. He had nurtured a secret hope that one day Eeranna could become his trump card. He could make use of him to threaten voters and agents of opposition parties.'

'He called up the SP first and told him that Eeranna was innocent and that no legal action should be initiated against him. The basis of his call was that Eeranna was already invited by the local police station for an enquiry on the incident. It was then that jittery started setting in the camp of Eeranna. But the SP told the MLA clearly that his department was looking into the matter and that law would take its own course without fear or favor. Dinesh understood that he stood against a mountain of integrity in the SP. He called up the Collector who in turn called up the SP. The SP advised the Collector not to smear himself with mud in this case as there was clear evidence that the poor lecturer was attacked by a group of his own students in the government college. The Collector then called up the MLA and told him that the ball was in the court of the SP and that he could nothing to change the nature of the SP.'

The infuriated and power drunk MLA immediately dialled the Home Minister of the State and told him that both top-level bureaucrats in the District were useless and they should be transferred forthwith. He requested him to quash the case without filing any First Information Report. The Home Minister informed him quietly that the FIR was already registered and there was no way out. The only thing that he could do was to ask Eeranna to surrender and escape 'police treatment'.'

'It then became a question of prestige for Dinesh. "I am MLA here and you are treating me like shit. I cannot tolerate this any more. I shall take up the matter with the Chief Minster if you cannot help. After all, the lecturer is a Muslim and you fellows want to support him. Let me see how many votes our party will get in the next election by supporting Muslims. Our party will definitely lose Hindu votes because of you."

The anger of Dinesh made political sense to the Home Minister, especially after what he said about Hindu votes. Dinesh was quick to perceive the change of attitude in the Home Minister and suggested that he could ask the local police inspector to file a 'B' report, which would nullify the FIR. The Home Minister agreed to it and hung the phone. The SP was an upright man. He refused to budge in even to the suggestion of the Home Minister. He put his foot down very firmly. He said his primary duty was to implement law of the land and not anybody's whims and fancies. Next day he got his marching orders. Eeranna was spared the blushes of cooling his heels in jail for a few days.'

—∘∘❦∘∘—

"Sir there is a very serious problem in my constituency." Sitting in front of Home Secretary, Dinesh opened his stinking box of calumny. "There is a foreign woman in my constituency and she is harming our people by converting them to Christianity. But that is not what we have come here for. Everyone has the right to convert to any religion that he chooses. We have come to inform you of something more sinister. She is in league with Naxalites and Maoists."

"Are there Naxalites in your district?" There was a mark of palpable surprise on the face of the Home Secretary.

"What sir, you are Home Secretary and you should know this before we do. See, this is how our local intelligence officers work. They go to her and she gives them good stuff to eat. They go back and write good reports about her." Dinesh was sowing poison. So it sounded from the way he spoke.

"I know you are speaking of a woman. But who is this woman? You have not even said her name to me." The officer brought him down to earth.

"Here, this man lives in the same village. Her name is Poojamma. She is mesmerizing people in my constituency with all sorts of programmes for Dalits from funds she receives from abroad. Why should she work only for development of Dalits? Are not the other poor human beings? She is misusing money by indulging in conversion work. But more than that whenever this man, Eeranna and our people try to question her on why she supports only Dalits they are attacked violently. She has a good support from Naxalites." Dinesh was back in his best game of ploughing on concrete floors.

"How can you say that she has good support from Naxalites? Our records do not say that. Can you tell me how you know of this?" The officer did not like any bullshitting on his table.

"We know for sure that Naxalite leaders from neighboring Andhra border visit her regularly and have discussions with her at night. She even prepares good meals and serves them. All people in my constituency know this, sir. It is a surprise that your intelligence people do not know this. You should take some stringent action against this woman, sir. I humbly request you to do something soon." He said this and looked at Eeranna with pride. Eeranna was blinking like dimming lights in a serial set. He did not understand head and tail of what Dinesh said in his broken English. Language of foreigners! Sounded sweetest when broken and spoken.

"Okay, you can go in peace. I shall speak to officers in Tumkur and take necessary action. It is a serious matter. We do not take light anyone who develops such underground contacts. If what you say is true the law of the land will take its own course." He stood up with a broad smile, shook hands with both of them and led them to the door.

'Eeranna was happy that the officer stood up and shook hands with him along with his MLA. Dinesh said that the officer was a good man because he walked them up to the door of his office. He did not realize that the officer wanted to get rid of the troublesome guys.'

'Both of them went back with their hearts filled with much hope that finally some action would be taken against their sworn enemy Poojamma.'

—◦◦❦◦◦—

'When they were away Ganganna informed Poojamma that Dinesh had taken Eeranna to Delhi to meet some big officers. She could immediately make out that they had gone to give complaints against her to the Home Ministry. She called all her leaders together and placed the card on the table in front of them. It took sometime for them to get out of the initial shock. Anything to do with Delhi was a serious matter of concern in their thinking. What would happen to all the efforts of Poojamma if the Central Government came down heavily on her? But all of them pledged their unflinching loyalty to her. Some of them were genuinely ready to face any eventuality. Some of them were deeply frightened inside but said many things loudly in support of Poojamma only to hide their fear. Poojamma was a master planner. She understood the weaknesses and strengths of her followers and their leaders. Therefore, she did not place all her hopes on the words that came out in the meeting. There was a basket that she was holding close to her chest. Inside that basket were many eggs that were invisible to other visitors.'

'Officers from Delhi made a visit to Poojamma's place. She was sufficiently warned in advance by local officers of the same department. That is how Poojamma's fragrance worked. Without scheming anything many things worked in her favor. She was not completely in dark about the impending visit. They themselves wrote a mail to her saying that she should be present on the days that they visited her. They kept two days for the visit. From the way the mail was formulated it looked that it was a matter of serious concern. It was a game. Sometimes you win and sometimes your opponent wins. Poojamma was prepared for both as always.'

"Was Poojamma in any sort of trouble?" Nina could not wait for Kala to describe the entire episode.

'Who, Poojamma? Do you know Poojamma only this much?' Kala teased her and laughed loud. In the next moment she became serious and continued her story telling.

'The officers came as they said. Poojamma asked some of her confidante to keep a low profile. They waited at a distance. After a cup of tea a 'big' officer among them asked Poojamma, whether they were sitting in her residence or whether it was the office of some political party? Poojamma's hair stood up. She asked the officer why he was asking such a question. Taken aback the officer pulled down his peacock feathers and said it was because he saw photos of many political leaders at the entrance. Poojamma laughed loud and said which party he suspected that she belonged to. There were photos of all leaders. She said that all of them were Dalit leaders and she respected them. There was no political color in any of their photos. The officers were bowled over by the way she sprinkled her words with a good blend of liberty.'

'The officers were quite stiff despite the ever-cooling tender coconuts served to them after a while. It was a ploy by followers of Poojamma to go in and find out what really was taking place. Tender coconuts with hard shells! She knew the ways of her followers and approved of them with a secret smile, which only they could see and understand. They had carefully avoided the local intelligence officers. They had a chat with Poojamma for about half an hour and the senior officer among them got up to say goodbye to Poojamma. She was totally surprised. That is a gross understatement. She was shocked. She asked them why they were in such a big hurry when they had indicated that they would need two full days.'

"Madam, conducting enquiries is our regular business. We can make out a person and her character already in the beginning of our conversation. We prolong our stay only if we feel the need to substantiate our initial findings and if we have a need to collect evidences. In your case we have no need of collecting any evidence against you. We received some complaints against you and it was mandatory that we visited you. Now we are also confirmed that ordinary human beings cannot do the type of work that you do. We belong to the government and we cannot do the type of service that you do to this country and her people. The government knows only to help the rich and the powerful. The best we can do to the poor is not to put a spoke on the good work that you are doing. If you have any difficulty please remember that our local officers will always help you. We shall talk to them. We consider it as a blessing of god that we are able to meet you in person. All the best Madam! May you live long to continue your yeomen service to these downtrodden people." Saying this they took leave of Poojamma. She was not only free of tension but was elated at what happened that day. As soon as the officers left all our leaders gathered around Poojamma. Seeing her broad smile they understood that there was nothing to worry about the future from the government. After all, the government was also sensitive to the needs of the poor.'

'I was dancing all the way at what transpired that day. In the beginning of their visit I was cursing that son of a bitch Eeranna for having brought so much of difficulty to our Poojamma. But finally I realized that at every step of their grueling life there is always something good that happens for poor people and for Poojamma.' Kala finished one part of her narration. But she was not at all in a mood to stop at anything. Nina saw it clearly. She let her speak as much as she wanted to. Otherwise she would break into many pieces at the departure of her beloved Poojamma. She was letting out a lot of steam. Nina gathered all of them in her paper.

—◦◦◦◦⬥◦◦◦—

'The information came very handy for Poojamma. Chikkanna divulged to her that there was very exciting news. When she asked him what the rousing news was he said that Eeranna's wife had left him and had gone away to her mother's house. There seemed to be insurmountable strain in their relationship. This was a common thing in village life. Men always looked down upon women as their objects, often as their sexual toys. Women were very happy to be so. But more and more men took anti-advantage of their wives' generosity towards them and destroyed the feminine meaning of sex. They went to their husbands' home with much hope of living a life of fulfillment both in mind and in body. But they realized that their bodies were totally lacerated at the sexual altar of their bloody husbands and their mind had no semblance of their personality traits. Some women accepted this as their 'writing on the forehead' and resigned to their fate. For other women it became unbearable and they left to their parental home only to teach a lesson to their wayward husbands. Men had to go and plead with her parents and make a compromise with her in order to take her back. If she were not there he would have to rub his cock only against a wall or press it hard against the ground. Even this he had to do often in empty stomach or after consuming unsavory food on pavement restaurants.'

"I thought it was a bad news and you are so excited about it Chikkanna. You should learn to be more polite even with your enemies, especially when they suffer in their lives." Poojamma would always bring some values. Often it happened to be most unexpected.

"He should also think like that when he troubles you Poojamma. If only he had one hundredth of your goodness all our villages would have flourished by now. Let that bloody asshole suffer. Only then will he know what pain of women is." Chikkanna gave free vent to his stuffed up feelings of anger and remorse.

"Just because he is not civilized enough and behaves in an unacceptable way should you also be like him? Then how will the world improve and how will there be peace in society? If we knew only to take revenge the entire world would plunge itself in a pool of blood." Poojamma would always have the last laugh in any such argumentation.

"If only you knew the reason for his wife going away, you would not speak like this Poojamma. He is not at all a man. I really wonder if he has his balls in the right place." Chikkanna took some liberty. Poojamma was quite used to the use of such liberal epithets.

"Hey, what happened to you today? You seem to be in your evening mood already in the morning. Did Yellamma bless you already in the morning?" 'Poojamma pulled his legs with broad smile. By then I handed over the teacup that I prepared while listening to the entire conversation. My heart was a ball of mixed emotions.'

"Did you not really hear the news, Poojamma? Everyone is speaking everywhere about the recent visit of Eeranna to Delhi. How come it did not reach your ears? I thought you already knew this." He still kept her in some sort of a mystifying suspense.

—◦❃◦—

'After coming back from Delhi, Eeranna was drunk together with his friends one evening. When the spirit took deep roots he began to puke out all that he heard from Dinesh on his sexapade in Thailand. His friends enjoyed every bit of it in a drunken mood. Eeranna had provided enough fodder for them to munch when they got back home. But when the spirit got diluted next day Eeranna realized that the news about the MLA had spread like wildfire in the constituency. Next day was an extremely difficult one for Eeranna. News had not yet reached the ears of Dinesh. But his wife was gathering the dirt of his upchuck of the previous evening. She had developed some strong doubts about her husband. Unable to keep anything within herself she began to pull him by his collar next morning.'

"So, if this is the type of man you are associating with, then you must have also done something similar in Delhi when you went with him." It looked like a gentle breeze when it started.

"I have lived with you so many years. Do you doubt me now? Why should I go to other women when you are there? He took me to such a place in Delhi but I did not do anything there." The fellow proved what type of a lummox he was. His wife knew every nook and corner of his personality and his stupidity threw much light on hidden corners, which his wife could see instantaneously.

"Go and look at your face in the mirror. You look as if some devil has slapped you on the face. What are you trying to hide from me? You cannot tell one lie well and when you tell a lie you cannot hold on to it. Tell me, did you or did you not go to a brothel in Delhi?" She seemed to mean serious business. He was taken aback by the sheer strength of her questioning.

"I told you that I went to that place with the MLA but I did not go inside. I waited outside for his return. I did not do anything against you darling." He went near her pretending to embrace her. But she pushed him aside rather violently. The gentle breeze was now gathering storm slowly.

'Realizing that he would not acknowledge the truth of his misadventures with other women she took the phone and dialed the number of the MLA. Realizing danger he pulled the receiver from her hand violently and slapped her left and right repeatedly. He did not realize her physical strength. He had only touched her body all over and had felt her softness everywhere. But he did not realize that there was a hardcore personality beneath the softness of the woman. She had been too kind to him. Not any more. From his violent reaction she understood clearly that he was guilty. She slapped him back and kicked on his balls with her folded knee saying that he should not go to any other woman thereafter. Since she had her sari on she could not thrust her legs as fast as she wanted. He ducked and saved his cock by instinct. It was too much of an insult for him though it took place in front of his 14 years old son. He ran to the next room and came back with a dagger in his hand and threatened to finish her off. His wife also ran out and brought a thick club to clobber him. Already being angry and seeing his father with a dagger the boy ran to him and held the knife in his hand and pushed Eeranna hard aside. He fell back losing his fine balance. But in the entire melee the knife tasted the blood of the young lad. His mother threw the club in her hand and rushed to her son's rescue seeing blood oozing from his palm. She took a cloth and tied the wound. Eeranna also got up and apologized to his son profusely bleeding son. The boy pushed him away once again and took off with his mother grabbing whatever few clothes that they could gather. They headed off to the village bus stand leaving Eeranna alone to fend for himself. He tried to prevent them but was also aware of the shame it would create if affairs went public. He sat on a chair feeling helpless in front of the savage strength of his wife and son. He unnecessarily provoked a sleeping tigress and her cub inside his own home.'

'News spread to all over the village. The village hid nothing from anybody. It had an undersigned transparency that did not discriminate anyone from its openness. Privacy as cherished and valued in the city did not have much place in a village life. When husbands beat up their wives the main recourse of wives to teach their husbands a lesson is to run out of their homes and beat their breasts while wailing loudly. The entire village would hear her wailing and would rush out of their homes. Some daring ones would run to her and hold her so that their husbands did not dare any more touch her. Menfolk would go to him publicly rebuking him for being so unmanly. He would give all sorts of excuses for beating up his wife. But they would further rebuke him. They would then turn to the wife and ask her to forgive him and be nice to him. In the meantime she would have already announced to all women of the way he behaved with her at night. Women would laugh thinking of how similar men were and push her into her house.'

CHAPTER NINE

The lamb entered the lion's den unsuspectingly. The den was filled with filthy stink. A starved lion prowling for a prey!

"Yes, what do you want?" 'Eeranna asked the question with a tough face. But his eagle eyes were body scanning the shape and size of Pramila. She looked fair and rather beautiful. She was not a stunning beauty but could beat Aishwarya anytime in a contest. The only difference was that her skin was not madly addicted to cosmetic creams available in the market for the asking. She was naturally beautiful. TVs were full of ads propagating the idea that being dark in complexion was a curse of god for girls. Boys had decided for themselves that girls whom they wanted to marry had to be proud owners of fair skin. Otherwise they would become ineligible to be worthy of their black skin. Nay, it was precisely because they were teased of their black skin that they craved for fair skinned girls as their companions. Once married, they would become suspicious of their wives for being very beautiful and would start ill-treating them. Poojamma had to counsel many young couples for such marital problems and take a tough stand with boys and heal their mindset.'

'Village dames were the worse victims of such ads in TV. Being poor at home they craved for the attention that girls were getting from handsome boys in TV serials and thought that their real life could be as romantic as they saw of reel life in the idiot box. They wanted to dress and decorate themselves like the dames in TV ads.'

'However, Pramila was a woman made of a different stuff altogether. She was a natural beauty and realized that she did not need all the gel

133

and cream to make herself more beautiful. As swift as she was, the very looks of Eeranna took the sheen out of her. She became pale and pathetic as soon as he raised his hoarse voice. Her psyche had been conditioned already by what she read about Dinesh in newspapers. She equated Eeranna with Dinesh as soon as she was face to face with him alone. The entire scene that she read came to her as a flash in a pan.'

⁘

'Who is this Parimala whom you are introducing now? Is she in any way related to Poojamma? I have not known her till now.' Nina was fluttering in a hurry.

'Just have some patience Nina. You will see the connection for youself.' Kala soothed her impatient journalist.

'Ramani had asked the government for a transfer to another city where her husband had been posted. He worked in public works department and she worked in revenue department. Usually the government is quite lenient with couples that wanted to be in the same place. But it was not as easy as it looked on the surface. The second one, wife or husband who sought transfer had to have right type of contact plus right type of bank balance to succeed in efforts of transfer. A workable contact would be the MLA either of the constituency in which one worked or of the constituency to which one sought transfer. Ramani went to Dinesh for help to get her transferred to the District where her husband was posted. She was of middle age and was ordinarily beautiful. But then lust had no age bar.'

'Dinesh was looking more at Ramani and less at the written petition that she gave him. He pretended as if he was reading the petition while actually he was scanning her body. She had full-blown boobs and he was already imagining how it would be to fondle both in one hand. He was in the Travellers' Bungalow of the government when Ramani met him.'

"Okay I shall give you a letter of recommendation. But it will not work here, with the present District Collector. Since you want to go to another District I have to get permission from Revenue Minister. It will cost you something. Are you ready for that?' He asked her looking at her from top to bottom. It was a devouring look of a starving lion. As she was wearing a sari with a low-cut blouse her contrasting skin from the bottom of her breast to her navel was visible. His eyes were fixed on her bare skin.'

"How much will it cost, sir?" She asked innocently.

"It will be good that we speak about it in private. Come with me." 'Saying this he got up and went near her and put his hand around her back in the visible area of her body. He slowly rubbed his hand to the end of her bra and the clips that kept them together. She realized that he was up to some mischief. But she did not object to his probing her bra clips. She needed his help and was not sure if it was done intentionally or was done on purpose. She walked a bit fast in order to avoid his touch. He was now sure that he had an easy prey and led it to his den.'

'As soon as she entered the room behind him he turned back and bolted the door from inside. Now she was sure that he was encircling her into a vicious circle. She noticed a spider in one corner of the room weaving fast a web around a fly that had fallen into its net inadvertently. Her eyes were fixed on the spider for sometime.'

"Wow, Kala what a comparison, ya. You could be a world-class literary figure. I have been watching the way you present things to me. Your imagination just fascinates me. Come on, go ahead my little darling." Nina gave full marks to Kala for her narrative style.

"What are you doing sir? Why do you bolt the door from inside? I am frightened." 'She allowed him to start weaving his web. He had to only splash the liquid around and make her immovable in his net. The indications were clear.'

"Nothing, nothing! Why are you afraid of me? Am I some sort of a monster? I only want to protect you. There are all sorts of people here and if someone sees you they will spread bad stories about you and me. You need my help and I told you that it would cost you something. You need to cooperate with me if you want to get a transfer. Many women do that besides also paying some money. I do not need all the money. I have to pay the Minister some money to get your transfer. I am a good man. I do not ask you to give your body to the Minister. You don't have to meet him at all. But it will be good that you cooperate with me if you want your transfer. If you refuse to cooperate I will see to it that both of you will never work in the same place for the rest of your life." While saying this he released the clip at her back and her boobs tumbled a bit inside the cup of her bra. That created a mild tremor of emotions in her. Without her permission her nipples began to wake up. It was repulsive in her mind, as she was not used to the touch of another man in that place except her husband and her children who used to suck milk from there. Now she was frightened beyond her power. In no time his hands traveled through her sari like lightning and measured the size of her boobs. The touch exhilarated him into a tizzy. She resisted mildly and that was a clear indication that she was willing to allow him to go further. Her resistance lacked power and was more like an invitation. The thought of transfer overtook her resistance.'

'By the time she could resist substantially buttons in her blouse were open and her bra had been already thrown on bed. Her sari had half deserted her.'

"Sir, please leave me. I am like your sister. I have never done this before with any other man." She gave exactly the type of resistance that he anticipated. He became bolder.

"I shall not do any harm to you. Allow me to fuck you without any resistance. That is the best way for your promotion." 'Saying this he disrobed her swiftly and completely. He had not seen even his wife so plain. She made him understand that she was a willing victim, as she was fully wet where it mattered. For a minute she thought that he gave up, as he removed his hand from her. It was the final gasp of breath that the poor victim had in the net of the spider. Her eyes were half closed. He took her to bed and pushed her to lie down. She was lost.'

"Sir, you will give me transfer for sure, na?" 'She asked him while she readjusted her sari and blouse to look as if nothing had happened inside the room.'

'Dinesh was a clever politician. If he had sex with any woman officer the next thing he did was to transfer her from the district. However, there were some women who willingly had sex with him and wanted to have more of him. After getting their promise of secrecy he would invite them whenever he wanted their company and shower them with latitude for their corrupt ways. He had become quite notorious in the State for his wayward ways. Many elected members in the Legislative Assembly welcomed him into their brotherhood.'

'Ramani met Poojamma just before leaving for her new destination to join her husband. She revealed everything she did with Dinesh in order to get her transfer. Poojamma wanted to take the phone immediately and inform the Superintendent of Police. However, it flashed on her that the family of Ramani could be completely destroyed if the news came out and reached her husband. Some truths need not be revealed only because they are truths. Hiding truths is not the same as telling a lie. Strategic hiding of the truth! The discerning spirit of Poojamma's slowed down her search for truth. A family was saved from perishing.'

"Kala, you are literally making me wet by your narration. You have reached to a height where your age cannot take you. Simply marvelous, my girl."

"Oh, I am sorry Nina. I did not mean to do it to you. I just described events to you as Poojamma once narrated to me and added a lot of spice to the story. I think I have age on my side to do that." This was Kala in reply.

"Don't be sorry. Just be yourself! Getting wet is my problem and I shall deal with it. I only wish Poojamma were here to hear your style of narration." As Nina said this both of them became silent for a while and sipped their coffee silently.

———⚬❉⚬———

Becoming aware that Nina would not stay with her for long Kala was almost in a hurry to complete her narration. She resumed.

'All that Pramila had heard about Dinesh came and played an orchestra as she was in front of Eeranna. "Will he grab me and play with me violently?" 'She could not help the recurrence of this thought. In the meantime Eeranna had come to know of the incident from the horse's mouth itself in one of the evening forays. He dared to walk in the footsteps of his master. After all he had his ambitions in life. Certain things had to fall in harmonic symphony to achieve success. High society had its rules of its successful path. Politics had its specific rules of success. He did not want to miss the bus.

"Sir I have applied for a clerical post in the government. They have called me for interview. This is a lifetime chance for me. If our MLA calls up the interviewing officers and puts a word to them about me, my selection will be done rather easily. I do not know the MLA and I am afraid to go to him directly. Manjanna told me that you are a good man and that you help people by recommending to the MLA. Please speak to the MLA on my behalf and ask him to do what is needed. I am ready to give the MLA whatever money he wants in order to do this favor. Manjanna told me not to speak of money with you. But if there is a fixed fee for you too please let me know. I do not mind paying you, as this is a job that will fetch good returns." Pramila mustered all the courage that lay hidden in her all that while and poured the words without any interruption.

'Now Eeranna became a bit relaxed from his stiff-necked position. "No, no! I do not want any money but the MLA may expect something. He is known to be corrupt. I am not like him. We shall speak about it later. Do you have a copy of the letter that the government sent you asking you to attend the interview?" He mellowed down quite a bit in his tone. Pramila became a bit more at ease.

"Sorry sir! Today I have brought only copy of the application that I sent to the government. I forgot to bring it." She probed her vanity bag thoroughly. Women security at the airports would have taken training from her for frisking innocent women as if they were thieves and terrorists. But she came up with empty hands just as the airport security. "Sir, I shall bring it to you tomorrow by all means."

"Oh, it does not matter. I shall speak to the MLA and give him all details about you. He will help you. He is a very good man though a bit corrupt. People like you should join us and work for our party. We need votes. You are very attractive and people will vote for you if you speak to them with your sweet voice." Eeranna thought that Pramila was like many other women who would become easy prey for adulations men heaped on them. He just started an age-old male practice.

"No sir, I am sorry. I am not interested at all in politics. Moreover, my parents and brothers need my support. I have to work and earn some money for them." Pramila now picked up a bit more volume in her voice and became sweeter in Eeranna's ears.

He was looking around to see if there were other people waiting for him. There was none. "You can make a lot of money in politics if you have the right aptitude. Look at me. I am the son of a village farmer. But today I have become the richest person in this area through politics. It is enough you work for the party and make the right connections with bigwigs. You can make money and look after your family. In addition to that you can also live like a queen." He tried to convince her.

"No Sir! I am sorry. Politics is not my cup of tea. I have no inclination at all. I shall just be a government servant. Please help me." 'Saying this she went a bit near him and handed over the paper touching his hand. It was a soft touch. A high voltage touch from a beautiful young woman! Eeranna had starved for quite some time now since his wife left him in a huff.'

'Sensing that she was a broad-minded girl Eeranna pulled her to him and embraced her in a flash. He was surprised that she did not resist him much. As he began to probe her body a bit more she only pretended to resist him, as it was normal for a girl. If she did not resist at least a little the man would take her to be a loose character. She put up a façade of resistance.'

"Sir, let us go inside. Some people may see us here and it will be very bad for your reputation." 'She held his hand and took him inside his house. A boon from the sky! Ramba and Urvasi in one body. The divine enticer had entered his house uninvited. He was ready for the kill. Pramila allowed him to disrobe her and hold her tight to his body. As he touched her bra to remove it she pulled his hands out and led it to her panties. He touched her panties and was about to pull it down.'

"Sir, it is that time of the month for me. I am very sorry. I shall come again after three or four days. By then you would have spoken to the MLA. Please do not bring your wife home till then. Be ready for me when I come. Today I am extremely sorry Sir. It is a difficult time for any woman, you know. Moreover I have horrible stomach pain at the time of my periods." Saying this she put on all her clothes back.

'Eeranna was highly disappointed. But he was happy that Pramila had agreed to go back to him. He awaited a big festival. "But how did you know that my wife is not here?" The thought crossed his mind in the form of words.

"What sir, the entire area is full of the juicy news of the fight you had with your wife. I have heard that you are quite liberal with women and that is why you had problem with your wife. People in this village even say that you go to prostitutes. Don't worry sir. I do not believe all such cock and bull stories. Some women are very narrow-minded. They do not know the nature of men and their needs. I shall come again sir.' She said with a broad smile and left.

Her angelic face, her swift movement, her sweet voice, everything in her fascinated Eeranna. He stood still and watched her back as she walked back in style. The movement of her ass stirred up something in his front. It was a complete circle. An ass at the back and an ass in front! "A perfect jackass" Pramila muttered the words to herself as she left.

"Anna, did you have a look at TV6? Your entire history is reeled out there." Manjanna called up Eeranna with conflicting emotions.

"Why, you idiot? What is going on in TV6 about me? They did not come to me at all and how could they show something about me? Have you already drowned yourself in Yellamma's ocean?" Eeranna was irritated with Manjanna.

"Just tune in TV6 and see what is going on there. Even you would not have seen this much of your history." 'The sarcasm in Manjanna's voice was not lost to Eeranna. He rushed to tune in the TV. The first scene that he saw tore him apart into many pieces. It was the scene of his disrobing Pramila. The TV showed it as a regular piece and repeated the same in slow motion several times. Men and women had chance of watching porno in their homes. This was a good compensation since they could not watch porn films at home. In some houses, parents asked children to go and eat in order to divert their attention. They saw Pramila standing there only with her bra and panties on. It was then that Eeranna put his hand on her bra and she removed his hand. He did not realize then the aversion with which she had brushed his hand aside. In slow motion it was more than evident. While removing his hand the TV clearly showed a black small instrument sticking to her bra. Only the tip of the instrument could be seen. Many who watched Pramila and Eeranna on TV were focused on the size of her boobs and waited in expectation of Eeranna removing the remaining pieces of clothes from her body. That was the climax that they waited for. But the TV marked the black stuff in the bra with red ink and showed that again and again with the hope that viewers would understand it as a bug.'

'Right in front of them Pramila was seated as a well-clothed woman. She narrated the entire drama that she enacted to expose Eeranna. It was a stink operation that she conducted. She wanted to show to the world the true character of politicians. She said that Eeranna was only the tip of the iceberg in the whole gamut of corruption and sex. "Many innocent lives are lost everyday in the world because of games politicians played in the lives of women. There are many big whales behind Eeranna. The media should expose them one by one. But I hope this operation will sufficiently warn all politicians and make them behave in future."

'Eeranna was fuming and frothing at what he saw. He called up his wife's home frantically to check if she was watching it.' "Yes, yes, we are all watching your big sex drama. How many more women do you want you bloody idiot? Is not my mother good enough for you? She has been so faithful to you and has been your slave ever since she married you. But you bloody . . ." His son hung the phone without speaking further.

The next one was Manjanna. He was in his vituperative best as soon as Eeranna picked up phone. "You have done it well Anna. But I am surprised that you have left the job half-done. You have done all that one should not do in our area. On top of that you have allowed that woman

141

to take a video of all that you did with her. I never thought you are such a low level creature. That Poojamma is a divine intervention in the life of the poor. All of us knew it. But only for the sake of our friendship we distanced ourselves from her and worked against her at your behest. Now you see where you have brought us. Will we be respected even by our own wives and children in our house?' Manjanna was a small little violent storm.

"But that bitch told me that you sent her to me, man. Who is she? Tell me where she is from? I shall kill you. Soooo this is all your game. You sent a bloody bitch to my house and also inform the TV about it, eh? I shall go immediately and butcher the bitch.' Eeranna brought out froth from his mouth.

"What? Now do you want to get me involved in this murky affair of yours. Do you know the meaning of friendship? Do not play such games with me. I shall have to teach you a lesson. Till now I had great respect for you. But now what you say is crossing beyond your limits. I shall not tolerate this. I do not know who the girl is and where she comes from. You should have checked this before you made an attempt to lick her bloody cunt." Manjanna turned an unusual abuser of his most admired friend.

"But why this stink operation? There are big crocodiles in politics. You have left out all of them and have taken a small time politician for your operation. Can you explain to us the rationale for your choice of Eeranna." The TV anchor asked Pramila.

"As I told you earlier, he is the tip of an iceberg. If you touch him you will know all people who are behind him and who are like him. It is the duty of the government to order an inquiry into this affair of Eeranna's and his political boss Dinesh and get into the entire truth. There are many women and girls who are being enticed by this duo and their future is thrown to wolves."

"Hey Manjanna, who is this bloody dimwitted girl? Do you have any idea? It is the future of our party that is at stake. At one stroke she has cut at the roots of our party. We cannot win the next elections if this is spread in our constituency. We shall not let her go free. She will have to pay a heavy price for this." Eeranna's tongue wagged much faster than his tail.

"Honestly Anna, I do not know this girl at all. You do something about this to control the damage. Do not precipitate matters. That is what you can do now." Manjanna showed why he could not climb up the political ladder.

'News reached Dinesh and he did not want Eeranna to get the upper hand over him. He called up TV6 and got into serious business straightaway. "How much do you want to get me into a live interview tomorrow at the same time that you telecasted today's news?"

"Ordinarily we charge Rs.20,000 for an interview. But yesterday we did not charge anything at all, as it is sensational news. If you want to counter that news you have to give us ten times more." 'A deal was struck between Dinesh and TV6. A team from TV6 went to Dinesh's house to take an interview of him. Eeranna was present there in his best clothes. Money was ready in a small briefcase.'

"It is all the work of that foreign woman Poojamma. She has been converting people to Christianity and has very close collaboration with Naxalites. She is doing all this because she wants to contest against our Dinesh Anna in the next elections. She has come from some other place and she wants to become the leader of our people here. How can we allow this? She knows well that we are educating the people against her tricks and conversion efforts. She is not only angry with our Dinesh Anna but also wants to spoil his reputation so that she may contest next election in his constituency and defeat him. But this is very silly way of playing politics." Eeranna was like the firefly banging itself repeatedly against domes that cover bright light of the night.

"But what have you to say about the video that Pramila has produced? She has provided indisputable evidence against you. It is also widely believed that your Dinesh Anna does similar things as you do. She is ready to bring many women to the TV to prove her allegations." The TV anchor wanted to create a sensation despite the deal. He also wanted to create an impression among viewers that there was a genuine telecast and did not want to give an inkling of the deal behind the screen.

"These are days of modern communication with internet and computers. You have seen how people morph scenes artificially. I do not know this girl at all. She never came to meet me. Ask any of my followers if they know this girl. She has been hired by that bloody woman Poojamma to somehow spoil the name of our Dinesh Anna and me. That is her aim in view of the next elections. She must be a woman of loose character. But this Poojamma does not know how popular our Dinesh Anna is. People may like her. It is all because of the money she brings from foreign countries but they will not vote for her in elections. She is desperate. That is why she is taking recourse to these unethical and cheap methods. We shall soon expose this girl, if she exists at all and bring her to this studio to tell people that all that you have telecast yesterday was a hoax." Eeranna had prepared his defense well.

"But Pramila has given us this CD with your picture in it. Can you deny that it is not you? Please have one more look at this." The TV played it once again. That was their way of getting mileage out of everything possible.

'This time it was Dinesh who intervened. "Even I can produce many such CDs. This is an engineered CD for the purpose of maligning my name. People should not believe in such morphed CDs." Both of them got up from the interview even before the anchor could formally conclude.

—∘∘◦|◦|◦∘∘—

"So he himself agrees that he knows how to produce morphed CDs. What bloody liars these are." 'Chikkanna, Nagaraj and a few others were watching the TV show along with Poojamma and Pramila. All of them knew Pramila as the master artist who accomplished an almost impossible Operation. They admired the scoop that she did without ever being noticed by Eeranna. None of his cronies had the guts to enter Poojamma's place and find out for themselves if Pramila was stationed there.'

'Pramila was educated by Poojamma in the city of Bangalore. Her parents died early in her life. Her father was a drug addict and washed his intestine everyday several times with the 'spirit of Yellamma'. It was a special boon of Yellamma that she took her devotees soon to her. But no one in his family had ever seen peace in their lives. Everyday she would possess him and he would dance at home not allowing his wife either to eat or to feed her only child Pramila. He considered Pramila as the biggest impediment to his having sex with his wife whenever he wanted. Fortunately for both of them, he embraced the lap of Yellamma rather too soon and what was left of his wife was only Tuberculosis. She too kicked the bucket immediately after his death leaving Pramila in the lurch. One of her neighbors had given a room for a young man from the village. He found a job in Bangalore and needed a place to stay. It was he who informed his neighbor about Poojamma. She suggested that the child should be educated in Bangalore itself. She contacted some sisters in Bangalore who ran a famous school and they readily agreed to accept Pramila. They had a hope that they would convert Pramila one day and get her into their congregation as a religious nun.'

'Poojamma suspected the intentions of the sisters and sufficiently warned Pramila tenderly of the impending danger. When some sisters tried their religious tricks with Pramila she spoke to them with a broad smile and silenced them with her diplomatic words that she would think of it after completing her studies. Sisters were much too disappointed with the frugality of her words. But with Poojamma she was very generous with her words. She had long discussions with her on issues that pertained to the affairs of the world and her life. When she came to know that Eeranna and Dinesh were creating innumerable problems for Poojamma she decided to teach them a lesson and coaxed her to agree to her plans of stink operation.' Fishing in troubled waters, an art well-known to sisters.

"But Kala, where is Pramila now. We do not hear much about her. Even Poojamma did not tell me about this girl. What happened to her?" Nina was all at sea at this unexpected turn of narration.

"Did you not notice that there was a big officer who came to place a wreath on the body of Poojamma? Many policemen with black uniform surrounded her when she came. Did you also notice that she was the only VIP who stood there for long and cried? No other officer cried though they were quite downcast." It was not much difficult for Kala to remind

Nina of the obvious. Everyone in the crowd noticed her and was followed by all the followers of Poojamma when she left.

"Yes, I remember the scene very clearly. But then, I thought that she was one of the big officers whom Poojamma knew well. I did not have any inkling that she was Pramila. Where is she now? Can I meet her?" Nina's personality threw itself up.

"Yes, you can meet her with a prior appointment. She is a very big diplomat now in the German Embassy in Iraq. She became a German citizen and is hailed as a genius of a person. She is very bold and courageous and volunteered to be German Ambassador during the Iraq war. She was one of the strongly dissenting voices in Germany about the war and the killing of Saddam Hussein. Though the German government did not like her outspoken nature they liked her courage to stand by what she said and also substantiate her position. That made the German government to take a very cautious approach to their collaboration with American government on the question of its war against Iraq." Kala was flying all over in flying colors.

"Oh, is it this Pramila? But she has a German surname. I could never connect her to Poojamma." Nina stated the explicit.

"Of course you could not. Pramila married a German diplomat and has his name as her surname. They are now heading many policy decision-making bodies in German government. It was a sheer luck that she was allowed to fly to India for the funeral of Poojamma. The Indian government had to downplay her visit, as it was private but was more than willing to provide tight security to her. This is the contribution of Poojamma to the world." Kala broke down at this point and cried loud inconsolably. Nina allowed her to cry as long as she wanted.

—∘∘⦿∘∘—

It took some time for Kala to resume. But Nina exceptionally waited for Kala to come to her own.

'Chikkanna and Nagaraj spread the news of stink operation in all villages and adulated Poojamma for her political acumen. They were proud that they had a person who could stand in their favor up to any political shenanigan that Dinesh designed.'

When Eeranna's followers came to know what really transpired they began to walk in the streets downcast. Many of them went to Poojamma and begged her pardon. She was always very generous with her forgiveness and accepted them into her fold. But the duo of Chikkanna and Nagaraj made life hell for such new converts and would tell Poojamma that such people should be put into a test of fire. If they came out unscathed they could be trusted.

'But Kala, did Poojamma have to go through so much of trouble in her life? I did not know that the situation was so serious when occasionally she used to mention over phone that there were difficulties from politicians. But the way you have kept a track of all these events is amazing. You should now sit down and begin to write down all these.' Nina said in all seriousness.

'These were not really difficulties for Poojamma. She considered such things as fun in life and that is how she treated all of them. She was utterly light hearted about what we considered as mountainous troubles. We used to be worried but she would go about smiling and cracking jokes as usual. What other work do I have Nina Madam except to remember all that happens to us and to the people in this area? As for writing, why have you come all the way from America and why do you spend so many days with us? You are a writer and it is your job to write about Poojamma. I am a housekeeper and it is my job to look after people like you when you come here.' Kala banged Nina right on her head.

"The stink operation however, is something that I never imagined of Poojamma. Was she such a type of person even if what she did was right? I have never known her like that. Many things may be right. But there are some things that some people can never do. I thought Poojamma was not cut out for such type of operations." Nina began to challenge Kala a bit mildly.

'All of us gave credit to Poojamma for the stink operation. But only I know that it was not Poojamma's decision. I was a witness to a serious argumentation between Poojamma and her daughter Pramila. She was beyond herself with grief when she learned of the difficulties that Dinesh and co created for Poojamma. She moved quietly into the village and gathered all personal details of the duo. Poojamma came to know of the operation only when Pramila had already handed over a copy of the video to TV6 and played it to Poojamma. She was in controlled anger. She did not agree with the way Pramila executed the operation. But Pramila did not care. "I shall do anything in my power to save you from these hawks, ma. You may disagree with me or throw me out. But my conscience is clear. I shall never tolerate any ill treatment of my mother at anybody's hands." She was just an uncontrollable tempest.'

'I understand now the genesis and end of the operation. I think Pramila was right in her own way. So Poojamma has two daughters then?' There was a look of surprise in Kala's face.

'Impossible Nina! You are badly mistaken. Pramila is the daughter of Poojamma and I am only her follower. No one can grab the place Pramila has in the life of our Amma. Pramila is a genius par excellence, a worthy daughter for a fitting mother.' There were tears once again in the already wet eyes of Kala.

—◦◦◦❈◦◦◦—

'Dinesh met the Chief Minister and through him called up the Home Minister in Delhi. The Chief Minister was informed in no uncertain terms that according to investigations of Home Ministry officers they found no substance in the allegation of Naxalite connections. It was a concocted story on the part of the politician Dinesh and so the Chief Minister should rest in peace about Poojamma. The Home Minister even advised the Chief Minister of his responsibility to support an exceptional person like Poojamma instead of casting aspersions on her character. The Chief Minister evaded a direct reply to Dinesh. He promised to write to the District Collector to take action against her and send her off.'

'Dinesh and Eeranna went back to spread the news far and wide that Poojamma's days in the district were already counted and that she would flee from the district soon. Their followers began to tease members of her group whenever they spotted them alone and asked them what they would do once they lost their beacon of hope. When this was repeated again and again even her followers became spooky. Chikkanna gathered all of them together with Nagaraj and took them to Poojamma one morning. They took up the matter with her and asked her what they must do next if what they heard became true. She advised them strongly that they should carry on the mission of helping and uniting the poor irrespective of what happened to her.'

"What will you do if I happen to die today? It can happen to anybody . . ."

'Manjula interrupted her before she completed her sentence. "Poojamma, please do not even think of death. You should live for thousand years at least, for the sake of all of us, poor people. If you did not come to this place just imagine what would have happened to all of us in this entire district. We would have had to wait for another thousand years to come to where we have come in such a short time." She was crying while saying this.'

'Poojamma walked towards her and lifted her up. She embraced her. "Manjula, you make me feel so proud. My life has come a full circle because of you. You have made me realize that I have achieved what an ordinary human being cannot achieve in one's lifetime. What more do I need? In saying that I should live for another thousand years you have shown that I am not needed any more for you. You people have come to a level where you do not any more need a person like me. You have made a strong assertion that you have become a people of your own. If Dinesh succeeds in his design it may be nature's message for all of us that you have to face the ups and downs of your life on your own strength." Poojamma embraced her and held her close to her heart for a long time. All the others were waiting in complete silence for the two grips to loosen themselves. The eyes of men were filled with tears.'

When that happened, Nagaraj added a little more spice. "You are right Poojamma in what you have said. Manjula has summed up our feelings and culture beautifully. I wanted to say the same thing. But she has said it even more powerfully than how I would have done. We are not worried about your death anytime Poojamma. If you die we shall bury you amidst us and you will live among us forever. Your body will belong to the earth, which we touch, venerate and walk over. We are not thinking of what you are going to do to us and to our children any more Poojamma. What we need is your presence among us. You came from Bangalore. But you have become part of us, part of this part of the earth. You have become our mother. This is a relationship and we want to enjoy this relationship as long as you live. We shall never allow anyone to separate you from us, to take you away from us. No one on this earth has the right to separate us. You will be with us as long as you live." Saying this in an emotional way Nagaraj went around, gathered some firewood. Everyone wondered what he was up to. He came back and put all the firewood at the center. He lit it up and invited everyone present there to swear on fire that they would even give their life to safeguard the presence of Poojamma among them. All of them stretched forth their hands over the fire, felt the heat of fire and swore to safeguard the eternal relationship that they had with Poojamma. Even tons of tears from the eyes of Poojamma and many in the gathering could not douse the fire. It kept burning and lit many hearts on fire.'

"Just beautiful" Nina concluded Kala's narration temporarily.

'The Collector was not moving anything according to the expectations of Dinesh. The croaking of Eeranna began to sound quite stale in the entire area. Both of them cooked up their next plot to oust Poojamma from the district. They organized a big protest march in Tumkur town. In preparation of the protest they published pamphlets. They had enumerated all the evil things that the 'foreign' woman Poojamma did to the poor of the district. There were no bridles to their imagination, evil at that. Eeranna sent all his minions to distribute the pamphlets in all the surrounding villages and in the city. He got more money from Dinesh and spent only one fourth of the money. It was customary for him to pocket public money.'

'The duo held a press conference a day prior to the protest march. The media was more than happy to give publicity to the MLA and his crony clown. They cared a damn about truth. All that they wanted was sensationalism in order to increase the sale of their newspapers. The Fourth Estate was dismantling its four legs beneath their seat one after another through its avarice for money and wealth. The city was agog with easy gossip about Poojamma. They only needed some free fodder. Some munched it and some others ground it. The press conference addressed by Dinesh and Eeranna had its expected results and impact in Poojamma's camp. They had not yet developed necessary crocodile skin in the game of politics. They were so used to speaking truth and straightforward ways that when people behaved crookedly and uttered untold lies it became difficult to deal with. They were two worlds apart. But the paradox of both the worlds had to be lived. Both were in one world.'

'Followers of Poojamma poured out their frustration without any inhibition and asked for her permission to 'teach' a lesson to the infidels. They wanted to make it the last stage of their battle. They gathered all their forces and were ready for any consequences provided Poojamma agreed to their itching and urge to take up a fight. The fighter cocks were in the forefront of the visualized battle.'

"Did Poojamma agree to them taking up to violence? I know that Poojamma did not live by dogmatic positions. But she shunned violence of any kind." Nina intercepted the narration of Kala. She was like a spacecraft that keeps rotating the orbit to complete its explorative mission.

'You don't know Poojamma enough. Do you think she would simply ask them to go and fight with those political thugs? Poojamma was always keen on empowering our people at every chance that came on her way. She told them pointblank that if they had any guts to fight they should have gone and fought with whomever they wanted to fight. They were asking for permission only because they did not want to fight. If Poojamma gave them permission to fight they would invariably blame her when something went wrong. They were making Poojamma their scapegoat subconsciously for their inability. They made use of this inability to prove to Poojamma a non-existent loyalty. She challenged them to go and take up a physical fight if they wanted. The message was crystal clear that they should be responsible for all the consequences of their decision.' Kala was unstoppable.

"Amazing, Kala! But tell me how you know and remember all this. Did Poojamma explain all this to you?" Nina was curious.

'Ayyo! I am such a small girl for Poojamma. She did not have time to explain the meaning of all her actions to everybody. But when some people came from abroad and enquired her of the difficulties that she faced this topic came up and she explained to them the nuances of her strategies of empowerment. I used to listen to every word from the mouth of Poojamma even as I was preparing coffee and tea for guests. Every word from the mouth of Poojamma was a pearl of wisdom and I did not want to scatter it in the gutter.' Kala was mature beyond her age and she knew it by the open-mouthed look of Nina.

'Only a few days before the planned protest march, Dinesh went to Chief Minister and applied enormous pressure on him to transfer the Collector. He said that their party would lose one seat if the Collector were allowed to continue in the District. That seemed to settle the issue for Dinesh. The Chief Minister yielded to his pressure out of the political compulsion of not losing even one seat in the next election. It was a shock to many in the District that the Collector was transferred without any allegation of corruption or mismanagement. The news sent unbearable shock waves among followers of Poojamma. Eeranna warned his followers not to make big news of the transfer, as that would send wrong signals to other officers in the district. If they took officers lightly the same officers could play some tricks on the day of election and ensure the defeat of Dinesh.'

'The procession against Poojamma was organized on a grand scale. There were big banners in significant places of the city with photos of Dinesh and Eeranna occupying prominent space. It looked like a virtual preparation for the next election. Newspapers had predicted that there would be law and order problem because of high turnout of the followers of Dinesh. Police department had made elaborate security arrangements in order to prevent any untoward incidents. That there would be a huge turnout in the rally became a talk in the camp of Poojamma. Chikkanna and Nagaraj were the only exceptions. They told Poojamma that there would be a rally but it would be the waterloo of Dinesh. Poojamma smiled to herself knowing well that her strategy of empowerment began to bear fruit sooner than she expected.'

"You have number as your biggest resource. You do not have land. You do not have money. You cannot trade and make money. If you want to build a bright future for your children you must build it on resources that you own. What is the biggest resource in your hands?" She would thunder and then ask in a lowered voice. When one or other in the crowd said that they had only their body she would immediately latch on to that person.'

'Pointing out her finger to him she would ask: "Yes, your body is the biggest resource for you people. You are a very clever man." She would take the slightest opportunity to appreciate her audience and that led to an increase of her followers.'

'Her speech then would be shifted to a conversational mode. "Yes, tell me. What can your body do? How can you make your body the biggest resource? Think a little more deeply." She would cajole and coax them to reflect.'

'Surprisingly it was one of the young men in the audience who spontaneously blurted out, "We labor with our body and get money". The young lad was not even looking at Poojamma while saying this.'

"You young man, stand up. Let all the people here have a good look at you. See what type of cleverness and sharp intellect we have in our communities. This young boy knows what is the big resource that we have as poor. It is our body. We have the energy for labor in our body. All of us are laborers. If you can come together as laborers, what a strength that will be! If you can come together as Dalits, what a strength that will be! It is not enough that we are educated. It is not enough that we are united. Much of our labor goes free to landlords and to industrialists. We must convert our numbers and identity as votes. Out vote is the only resource that we can sell and make money. You do not have to acquire capital to have this resource. It is the cheapest capital in the world. By the mere fact that you are citizens of this country you become owners of this capital. Politicians know this fact much more than you know. They know that this is a very big capital that you have and therefore, they do everything possible to make a huge profit out of your capital. Your capital increases when you bring all your votes together. It becomes a very unproductive resource when you stand alone and cast your vote. It becomes the future of your children if you stand together and vote as a people. That is the reason why politicians are keen on dividing you at times of elections. Our disunity and weakness are their biggest strength. Therefore, convert your number into votes and no one can shake your future."

'Chikkanna and Nagaraj remembered the message very clearly. They went into villages and began to speak to key people in each village asking them to dissuade followers of Poojamma not to go for the political rally of Dinesh. They also walked into houses of those who voted for Dinesh but were not followers of Eeranna and spoke to them of the futility of supporting this rally of Dinesh. It was organized only to make Eeranna win in next Zilla Panchayat elections. Most of them agreed that Dinesh was making a serious mistake in attacking Poojamma listening to canards of Eeranna.'

'News that morning was highly disappointing. The camp of Eeranna began to wear melancholic faces. Their eyes were fixed at the other end of every road looking out for individuals. Every person who walked on the road seemed to be coming for the rally. But somewhere on the way the persons would turn towards shops. Some vehicles came rushing with high pitched and full throttled slogan shouting. Eeranna's face began to light up. But as soon as the vehicles went past him his face became pale. There were hardly ten people inside vehicles that could carry 70 people. After waiting for more than two hours from the fixed time they decided to start the procession with hardly 500 people attending. Dinesh's face was like the bottom of a kettle. He did not smile at anyone.'

'Chikkanna called up Poojamma and informed her that the function of Dinesh was a big flop. People did not buy their arguments and their false propaganda backfired on them.'

'The 500 people that assembled however, made a big show of strength on the streets. They danced on the road as the procession progressed. As they reached the office of the new Collector some policemen rushed to him to inform him. The Collector was not happy of the thin crowd. He went down quite reluctantly to receive the memorandum. Dinesh made a long speech before handing over the written memorandum. The Collector made a fool of himself in his acceptance speech. He said that he had heard many such allegations about Poojamma and would take necessary action against her after verifying facts. The crowd had just waited for this from the Collector. It danced and went haywire in a drunken mood.'

'Nagaraj and Chikkanna became panicky once again and called up Poojamma. She said that it was inappropriate on the part of the Collector to have made such a statement in public. She called up the previous Collector and informed him about what transpired that day. He asked her not to worry about anything. He meant business. Next day the Collector got a transfer order to an insignificant department. He tried his best to get his transfer order cancelled but could not succeed. He left the district with much shame.'

"The frog destroys itself through its mouth." 'Chikkanna said it aloud to all the people who assembled at Poojamma's place that evening. He referred to the frogs that begin to croak when it rains and betray their presence to snakes that are ever alert to catch them. People always associated the frogs falling prey to snakes with their croaking.'

CHAPTER TEN

'It was like any normal day. All were busy with the regular chores of work. Poojamma was busy talking to someone over phone. Suddenly there was a wailing outside the house. Some women were calling out to Poojamma to see them. All of us rushed out leaving everything in our hands as they were. Poojamma walked out to see what the commotion was all about. What we saw outside shook us out of shape. Women had brought about a dozen men from Guddahalli. Those men were oozing with blood. One of them was seriously wounded and blood was just flowing out of his head. Women were shouting and crying so loud that we could not make out what really happened. Men were too shocked to speak anything. Poojamma asked us to give all of them some water. She called me separately and asked me to make some tea for all of them. She called out to Manjula who had accompanied the wounded group and enquired from her what had really happened.' Kala started narration of the next link in the chain of events that took place.

"I am sure it was a fight among the followers of Poojamma and Eeranna." Nina made a correct guess. Though she was from another country she was used to report many such events and it was not difficult for her to guess events. She even sort of anticipated this.

'Nagaraj came running after a few minutes. He had gone to the neighboring village to resolve a dispute and someone informed him that there was a big fight in his village and that Manjula had taken all of them to Poojamma's place. It was amazing to see Poojamma swirling like a whirlwind to manage the deep crisis. She asked Manjula to immediately provide some first aid with the box that was kept always ready in her house. She called Nagaraj and asked him to inform Chikkanna to rush to the scene. She took the phone and informed the local police inspector that something serious had happened and called for police ambulance. Before the ambulance arrived Poojamma started stitching pieces together of all that happed at Guddahalli.' Kala was a very efficient and interesting narrator. This was one of the qualities she imbibed from Poojamma without being formally trained to be a narrator.

'It was early morning. Men in Guddahalli had just woken up and had assembled in the teashop for their early morning gossip and tea. They welcomed the group of people from the neighboring village. Though they were sworn followers of Eeranna they offered them some tea wondering to themselves why they had gone to their village that early in the morning. It was quite unusual. One of them said that there was no special reason for their going there. All of them sat in the benches of the teashop. It had a thatched extension under which more people could sit and have some snacks and tea. As one of them was serving tea a fellow from the neighboring village touched the elbow of the fellow serving tea. Naturally tea spilt on another guy. That was all that they waited for.'

'He got up and served his fist of fury. Others from Guddahalli rushed to the rescue of their comrade. There was an immediate fisticuff between both groups abusing one another simultaneously. There was a difference however. The people of Guddahalli were not prepared for such an eventuality. Guys from the neighboring village executed a previously designed plan. They pulled out strong sticks used in the roof of the thatched extension and started serving blows on men of Guddahalli. One blow fell straight in the middle of the head of one of them and he fell flat. But the others kicked him and served one more blow to his head. While two others went to his rescue the clubs from the hands of the fellows tasted their blood too. Two of them rushed madly to the house of Manjanna and brought some sickles. They began to leash the sickles blindly on all guys from Guddahalli. Both men and women rushed from their homes with sticks, brooms and sickles. Seeing that the entire village was charging at them the men from the other village took to their heels. They were chased but could not be reached. Each one disappeared in different directions. People of Guddahalli had other primary preoccupations. They had to look after their fallen comrades. Manjanna was not in the village. The drama was enacted to perfection.'

A few drops of tea spilt inadvertently were the reason for the stream of blood. 'Poojamma called up the SP and the new Collector. Both of them advised her to file a police complaint immediately. The SP called up the station inspector and instructed him to administer justice without fear or favor. Seeing the police ambulance rushing the wounded to hospital and hearing their loud blowing of horns all the way Eeranna got into his act. He called up Dinesh and asked him to do something to rescue his followers. Dinesh called up the inspector and told him not to arrest the culprits. The inspector told him to go to hell. The SP had directly instructed him to take stringent action against the culprits. Dinesh had other ideas, political ideas. He called up the Home Minister of the State and threatened him with 'votes' and one less seat for the party in the next elections. The Home minister's PA called up the inspector and instructed him not to arrest any of the culprits.'

'But how can they do this? Poojamma had formally filed a complaint and the police had to file First Information Report. This is the law of your land. Did they not follow it?' Nina was aghast. Desperation was written all over her face.

'I am sure Poojamma has told you how law functions in India. It is often compared to a donkey. Whoever manages to pull it in his direction will succeed. FIR was filed. But Home Minister asked the inspector not to arrest the accused so that they might have time to apply for bail from courts. They surrendered to the court and got bail. Then police would make what is called 'B' report, which almost closed the case. You can do this if you have either influence or money or caste, often all of them together.' Kala was not only a narrator but also an expert in interpreting situations in India to foreigners. Kala continued her narration.

—oo❧oo—

'Two days after that Poojamma did something that she normally does not do. After getting the people of Guddahalli discharged from hospital she went to the residence of the MLA, Dinesh. She had taken with her Nagaraj and Chikkanna. The MLA was in his casual dress with a dhoti and a banyan. Poojamma wondered if he was lazy or he had no work to do. But he cared a damn about what others thought of him. He sat on an easy chair with one leg folded and raised up and the other leg landing downward. There was no doubt that he was bent on insulting his visitors. Poojamma greeted him. He did not return it. Instead he turned to Nagaraj and Chikkanna and asked them what the matter was. They began to explain that Eeranna's cronies had attacked the people in Guddahalli. Half way through he turned to Poojamma and said:

"Ask your people to behave properly. They must know how to respect local leaders. You teach them good manners instead of teaching them to rebel against elected leaders. You people will come for some time and you will vanish. But we people will be always with them." He started his exhortation in his political style.

Poojamma was not in the habit of taking anything lying down. "You are elected only for five years and you spend such a lot of money to get elected. On the other hand, people love me and I do not ask for their votes. I spend money on them for their welfare. Do not punish our village people in your anger against me . . ."

Dinesh would not allow her to complete any of her sentences. "Do you know how many times people will elect me? Even if they do not elect me I have the power to help them anytime. Do you know anything about politics? You stop your conversion work here in my constituency. Go back to your country of origin". Dinesh began firing on all cylinders.

"But Mr. Dinesh, please listen. First of all take back your word about my country. The constitution of India clearly says that all of us are Indians and all states belong to the territory of India. Secondly I am not here to convert people to any religion. And I do convert people's heart to lead a dignified and decent life. That is why I have come here to meet you . . ."

Dinesh bellowed loud in an effort to laugh. "So now you are trying to convert me too. I have seen many people like you, woman. I am a politician and we have our own rules and law. We are lawmakers and you dare to speak to me about law. People have elected me and I know what is good for people. Who are you to tell me what I should do and how I should behave? Hey, you fellows, tell your madam to behave properly with elected members." He turned to Nagaraj and Chikkanna with antagonism written all over his face.

"Our madam is behaving well. Only you are not behaving as you should behave with a woman. What mistake have we committed against you that you should support this violence against our people? Are we not members of your constituency? If you, as elected member can support violence against people living in your constituency what right do you have to make law on our behalf?" Chikkanna picked up the cudgels against Dinesh. He was shocked.

Lowering his voice a little he said to both of them: "So you people have grown to this extent of talking on my face? Good for you guys. We shall meet again. I shall come to your village. When you need some support from me next time you will see my power. Now you go." Dinesh's frustration flowed without any boundaries.

Poojamma began to speak to him again. "Mr. Dinesh, we came to your house believing that you have been misled by your followers. But now I am wondering who is misleading whom. We came here to tell you clearly that we are not against you. We have a lot of other things to do. We do not want to work against you or against your followers. But they are crossing our paths often. Please ask your followers to stop their evil ways. If you also behave in such arrogant ways, it may become difficult for you in the next elections . . ."

Dinesh charged like a 200 pounds bull without horns on Poojamma. "You bloody woman, have you come here all the way to teach me about politics. Do you think you know better how to capture votes at the time of elections? You keep all your warnings with some idiotic politician. Not with me! I know how to get votes from these silly fellows at the time of elections. We politicians have invented many ways for many occasions. Do you think you can threaten me with next elections? You bloody get out of here and out of my sight. Let me see whether you will make it difficult for me in the next elections. You will see soon what I can do as a politician. Get the hell out of here."

'Nagaraj and Chikkanna signaled to Poojamma that it was not expedient to talk to the son of a bitch any more. Poojamma realized that they were wise in advising her already before starting, not to meet this fellow. As they walked out slowly they could see Dinesh's brother sharpening a sickle in the compound. It was a clear signal from the politician that he would be ready to go to any extent to get Poojamma out of his way. Both the men with her realized that it was a clear humiliation that Dinesh wanted to mete out to Poojamma at his residence.'

"I can see the sharp contrast, Kala. Poor people in these villages are so open to welcome guests and treat them to a meal in their homes. Their hospitality is a mark of their uniqueness. Dinesh who claims to represent them has nothing to do with their culture. If he stands in contradiction to their culture, how can he truly represent them?" Nina blurted out with a lot of pain in her heart. Kala offered her a soothing cup of hot coffee. She too shared the cup of woe.

———∞◉∞———

Nina asked Kala permission to take a simple walk all by herself. It was a bit too much for her, the difficulties, the oppression, the insults and the violence. How could human beings behave like this? Can they not make life a little better for all? One could make life a pleasant experience too. Why do people make a hell of it? Why all this dominance and violence? Power can be used in two ways. For construction and for destruction! Why is it that most people have to struggle in this world to construct their lives? Stray thoughts of a weird journalist from the US! She had a heart full of kindness. It made her gel well with Poojamma. She felt a significant part of her personality had departed from her. The death of Poojamma! An irreparable damage to many!

Nina was downcast and sober when they resumed. "Finally how did Poojamma manage to tame this evil man?" The anger in Nina gladdened the heart of Kala. She was energized to start all over again from where she had left.

'That day Poojamma understood well that the urge by her followers to give tit for tat would not work in the long run. One needed to know politics to checkmate a politician. Dinesh was a seasoned politician. Her followers were not even politically sensitive. All that they knew was to confront anyone who stood against their interest. A little sense of the system within which politicians operated would have served them much better. Unfortunately this was not the case. Poojamma understood her followers well and therefore, she designed a different strategy to face the onslaught of Dinesh and his crony Eeranna . . .'

'That evening Poojamma called together one leader from each village and placed before them the agenda of next local body elections. All of them unanimously shouted that they should put up their candidates in every local body and defeat all candidates put up by Eeranna.' Kala was cool without any tinge of excitement about this political strategy proposed by the followers of Poojamma.

"How many of you can win in elections? Even if all our people vote for you do you have the number to win against the candidates of Dinesh?" Poojamma's question sent chill waves in the nerves of the assembled leaders.

"That is the crux of the matter Poojamma. We have organized the people strongly. But till now we did not concentrate on counting votes. We have been too good to our people. We have shown them the path of development but not yet the path of power. We have always separated power from development. Dinesh was right when he said . . . ." Nagaraj was about to reveal to the entire gathering what transpired a few days back with Dinesh. But Poojamma put her fingers on her mouth showing that he should shut his gob. He understood the message and shut his gob on both ends.'

"We know how to talk Poojamma, but not really play politics. Speaking limitlessly is our biggest capital. You taught us to speak in public. Now you have to teach us to move beyond mere talking and play active politics." Chikkanna chipped in with his small harping.

"I am not a politician to teach politics. How will I initiate you into politics." Poojamma wondered aloud.

"There is nothing that you cannot do Poojamma. When you came to our place and started interacting with us this is what all of us thought, that you were a very simple woman who knew nothing about the world. We used to tease your way of speaking and walking among ourselves after you left us. But one by one you mastered every art that is to do with our life and you made us the architects of our life. Till now we have seen many leaders. All of them used us to the hilt and when their purpose was served they spat us out like sheer waste. You are the only one who has empowered us to develop the capacity to deal with the complexities of our life. I am very confident that you will lead us also into politics successfully. If not in this election we shall definitely contest in the next one and win. In coming elections it will be our victory if we only manage to defeat all the candidates put up by the bloody rascal Eeranna". Chikkanna became quite emotional as he went on building his premises.

"Let us stop talking about me and focus on you people, Chikkanna. We need to work out strategies of translating our empowerment into productive consequence in the lives of our people. So what do you think is the best way for us to make our presence felt in the next election to local bodies as an organized lot?" Poojamma began to make a lot of sense in her talk, business sense at that.

'Poojamma took a stock of all those leaders who wanted to contest in elections. She told them clearly that even if they did not win it was a great opportunity for them to expand their organizational sphere during the campaign. They should also establish contacts with new people in all villages and become leaders beyond the borders of their own villages.' Kala took over the narration in multiple ways. The master artist!

"Did anyone win and teach Eeranna a lesson?" Nina jumped the strategies a few steps too early.

'Before that you need to know a few missing links. Poojamma also realized within herself that if she failed to teach a substantial lesson to Eeranna, Dinesh would continue his dance of death unabated. She called Nagaraj and Chikkanna separately and worked out a secret strategy with them. Their plan was that they should not field any candidate in the village of Eeranna where also Poojamma lived. He would field a strong candidate in his village and it would be a question of his personal prestige. If the candidate of Poojamma's won it would further accentuate conflict in the region. She was not sure if the poor would be able to withstand the combined political strength of Dinesh and Eeranna. If their candidate were defeated it would demoralize the poor no ends. Therefore, they decided that they should not put up their candidate against Eeranna's candidate. Instead they would support another strong candidate of the opposition party who was courageous enough to take on Eeranna. They also decided that Nagaraj and Chikkanna would go to all houses in the evenings and talk individually to all voters canvassing for the candidate of the opposition party.'

'Wow, wow! What brilliant politics. Poojamma was an exceptional woman. I knew that she was clever. But I never knew that she could have such political acumen. What a woman!' Nina became rather emotional while saying this and could not stop streams of silent tears from her eyes. Kala held her tight and both of them cried for some time in each other's arms.

'So who succeeded finally?' Nina asked after a few minutes of crying.

'Both Chikkanna and Nagaraj found out to their surprise that they did not have much canvassing to do. Many people were already quite disillusioned with Eeranna. Now they were very angry with him for the way both Dinesh and he harassed Poojamma. Even those who were known supporters of Eeranna felt that a woman like Poojamma should not have been put into so much of trouble. To their great advantage, Eeranna himself spread happily in all villages the insults that Dinesh handed out to Poojamma. He did not realize that it would boomerang on him. They were able to sharply distinguish between political rivalry and personal rivalry. Poojamma did not have political rivalry with anyone. Whatever they did against Poojamma was interpreted only as personal rivalry. They did not want to be part of any effort against the person of such a great woman as Poojamma who did everything she could for the empowerment of the poor.' Kala was super in her narration. Nina sat still admiring the young girl's maturity of perception.

—◦◦❧◦◦—

'When results were announced it sent shock waves in the entire area and also in the citadels of power. For the first time in his life Eeranna was biting dust in his own soil. He never imagined that people would vote against his handpicked candidates in such large numbers as to taste defeat. Even in the height of earlier oppositions from political opponents he could make it with a wafer thin margin of victory. But this defeat was indigestible, as it had come from a woman in the first place. Added to his woe was the fact the Poojamma was not a local politician. She had nothing to do with politics of his kind and he never imagined that he would be defeated.' Kala was now a political narrator earning more and more applause from Nina.

'Eeranna rushed to his political guru for solace. Dinesh advised him to be careful with everyone. One really does not know which snake lives in which bush. Never underestimate the capacity of your enemy is the first lesson in politics, he told Eeranna. He sent him back with a bottle of brandy and told him to take care of next elections at the higher level in which he was contesting.'

'What was that election and was it Eeranna or Dinesh who contested?' Nina could not control her curiosity and her urge for more information.

'It is called the Zilla Panchayat election. It is two steps above village level local body election. It covers many more number of villages and powers of the elected candidate are also much higher. It was Eeranna who contested that election as the constituency was much smaller than the Legislative Assembly constituency of Dinesh.' Kala got visibly interested in narrating the way political events unfolded in the life of Poojamma.

'Eeranna was quite down with defeat of his candidate. There was melancholy in his camp. He had to give them a lot of drinks and money to lift their spirits up. He was now ready to do anything to keep them smiling. They too tried their best to put up an artificial smile in front of him. Eeranna knew very well that brickbats were common for every politician and that as a politician he had to set aside his sense of dignity and shamelessness in his dealings with citizens . . .'

Nina cut her short. 'But Kala how, tell me how you can be so philosophical in your explanations at this young age?'

Unmindful of her adulations and pretending not to hear them Kala continued. She knew well that Nina knew the answer and did not take pains to explain every known answer. 'Eeranna started preparing for elections much in advance in all seriousness. He organized dinner meetings for all his friends and for people whom he thought would join him if coaxed or coerced a bit. He awaited the list of contestants to be announced from different parties to fix his direct rival in elections. It was Anand. Third in the list of contestants was Prakash who was also a familiar face and a popular figure in the area. Within a few days it became evident that it was a tripartite contest though there were a few 'also ran' type of contestants . . .'

'. . . Eeranna called all these 'also ran' types and easily negotiated with them to become silent campaigners without offering any semblance of competition to him.'

'Poojamma's place was like a beehive. Vehicles and people were swarming her place. Almost all the media representatives and reporters asked for even five minutes appointment with her. "What is your role in this totally unexpected defeat of Eeranna? The entire world knows the battle between you and Eeranna in this area. What did you do to ensure his defeat?" Questions became stereotyped after sometime. Every reporter asked the same question. Poojamma became tired of denying any such far-fetched imagination. Her denial also became stereotyped. "I am a very simple person. I have dedicated my life for the service of the poor and have no political ambition. Please do not increase my troubles by asking such questions. If Eeranna and Dinesh read your reports they will only become angrier. Kindly leave me out of this politicking. Please leave me alone and ask any questions only about my work and not about elections."

'But Poojamma's political acumen became sharper and sharper with passage of time. She pulled off an extraordinary scoop towards the end of the campaign, only when there were two days for polling. She went to Bangalore for some work. But her face was radiant when she returned. I asked her what it was that made her so happy. She refused to divulge anything. She simply dismissed my query by saying that it must have been my surmise and that she was happy as usual. When all leaders of her camp were quite anxious about the results of the poll Poojamma sprang a surprise on everyone by not being disturbed at all. They were all swimming in highly stormy waters and here she was sailing in a boat undisturbed, with her back to the waters and her front to the sky. All of them tried to surmise as to what the secret was for the defeat of Eeranna.

They became gradually suspicious that Poojamma pulled off something that paved the way for his defeat.'

'Do you not know what Poojamma did to bring about the defeat of Eeranna? Why do you want to kill me by prolonging the suspense like this? Please tell me what she did that lead to the defeat.' Nina was almost on her knees pleading with Kala to be quick in her revelations.

'For a long time no one knew what led to the defeat of Eeranna. Even now not many people in this area know the truth of his defeat. Only some of us know it. There were some close relatives of Poojamma's who had come to spend a few days with her. During one of the light hearted conversations they enquired about her strength and the way she overcame her difficulties. It was then that Poojamma revealed to them that she had asked Prakash to meet her in Bangalore. She had to do a lot of convincing act. Finally he agreed to play a passive role and on the last two days of polling campaign inform all his supporters to vote for Anand. Thus she put two popular candidates against one Eeranna and brought all the votes of two opposition candidates together against him. Prakash became a poor third in the best interest of the poor in the area and in the bargain he also became a close confidante of Poojamma's. It stood him in good stead. Not even Anand knew this secret understanding between Poojamma and Prakash. This is called a political scoop.' Kala concluded for the time being and both of them went for another cup of hot coffee.

—••◦❖◦••—

A little break did a lot to bring together their scattered attention and recharge their batteries. Nina took a leisurely walk among the trees. As she touched the trees they began to laugh and dance welcoming her. They knew the sadness that had enveloped her. They were exuberant that their Poojamma was now closer to them without previous preoccupations. She sucked her nourishment from their roots and lived as one among them. Now that Nina was walking amidst them they danced in joy of welcoming one of the closest friends of Poojamma's. On her return Nina made it a point to tell the trees that she would go back to them after listening to the story of Poojamma. She touched them and caressed them as she walked past them. They were very happy. Kala waited for Nina's return from the small walk and both sat together again.

'There was gloom all over the political circles of Dinesh at the defeat of one of his trusted agents. Political parties were even angry with Dinesh for having failed to get one seat for their party that they were sure of. Needless to say that Eeranna was on the way to become a persona non-grata. Anyone who made a loss to the party in terms of seats was not easily acceptable in the party. Dinesh's political romance with Eeranna began to slump. Angry inside, Eeranna's diatribe against Poojamma also dwindled drastically as he knew for sure that she had done something to ensure his defeat. Prakash's frequency to her place added further fuel to his burning doubt. But then he did not fail to read the writing on the wall. People did not simply appreciate the way he and Dinesh decried a good woman.'

'What was the reaction of Dinesh to Poojamma after this? Did he also become apprehensive or did he continue to rely on Eeranna?' Nina became politically alert.

'Dinesh was actually busy preparing for the next election to the Legislative Assembly where his own fate was at stake. All three elections came one after another. He could easily dismiss the defeat of Eeranna in party circles as a temporary setback and that things would be rectified soon. Deep within he was concerned about his political future. If he did not win the seat it would re-write his political status.' Kala manifested maturity much beyond her age. In the United States she would be easily elected as Governor of one or other State for the type of political acumen that she manifested.

'Against the advise of some of his companions in the Legislative Assembly to discard the services of Eeranna, Dinesh appointed him as his election agent. Eeranna argued vehemently with him that in politics ups and down were normal just as it was in sports and that one should be prepared for defeat. He convinced Dinesh that he would bounce back to prominence by making him get elected to the Legislative Assembly of the State as MLA. He pledged that he would work much harder, go to each and everyone in the constituency and convince all voters of the need for casting their votes for Dinesh and his party. It was not so much because he was convinced of Eeranna's capacity to mobilize votes but because he did not have another agent of that caliber that Dinesh appointed him as his agent. He was clearly aware that if he appointed another agent,

Eeranna would turn against him and that would put his winning chances in serious jeopardy . . .'

'But how did you know the thinking of Dinesh? How are you sure that this was the thinking of Dinesh?' Nina wanted to make sure that perspectives were placed right in her understanding.

'We had planted Ganganna in the camp of Eeranna as soon as Poojamma heard that Dinesh appointed him as his election agent. All these were the analysis of Eeranna himself about his own appointment. We learned much politics from our enemies.' The 'we' in Kala's narration grabbed the attention of Nina. Now she was able to make out why Kala was so passionate about every detail of her narration. She had become a sort of owner of the processes that Poojamma initiated.

'So Poojamma was really very political in her approach? I did not know this. I only saw her as a saint and far removed from politics and power games.' Nina now started provoking Kala a bit more to draw the best out of her.

'Whatever you may call her Poojamma was the epitome of love for her people. When you say she was far removed from power you must also qualify your statement. She was in the business of empowerment and it means power. Her people had to become powerful. How could she be removed from politics? Her engagement with the caste and political forces in favor of the poor was deeply political . . .'

'Stop, stop, stop! Sorry for what I said. I did not realize that she has prepared a philosopher to speak in her place. Kala, I do not feel that I miss Poojamma in explaining things to me. You have got into her shoes perfectly. OMG, is this the same girl who was shy even to speak to guests when I came last time? Amazing developments here!' Nina was filled with admiration not only for the visible but also for the invisible.

'Though being a defeated candidate at the Zilla Panchayat elections did not augur well for Eeranna and for Dinesh, people welcomed both of them when they went to ask for votes. Nagaraj and Chikkanna had instructed people not to show any animosity to both of them. They had clearly told them to show all respect. However, being seasoned politicians both of them suspected that voters could have other ideas about Dinesh's candidature. They decided that it was time to use other methods of gaining votes. They invited the police inspector without the knowledge of the SP for a dinner and served him foreign Scotch whisky. Every officer longs for this 'foreign' stuff. This is a mania in the government circles. They cannot afford to have costly drinks with their meager salary. Therefore, they always look out for an easy prey that would spend money for their drinks and sumptuous meal.' Kala took Nina into all gullies and by-lanes of the past.

Nina liked every bit of this travel. She did not mind the little prick of a thorn here and a piercing of gravel there. She was more focused on the cumulative effect of this journey with Kala, which was enriching and enlivening. 'But is the police inspector in your country such a powerful person at the time of elections? Can he influence voters in favor of a particular candidate? In our country policemen are not involved in elections at all.'

'Yes, I have heard this many times from Poojamma. She used to narrate this in many meetings and trainings. She used to visit some countries of Europe at the time of their elections. Once it so happened that she witnessed voting and then had a meeting with some of the contesting candidates. She asked them why she did not see even a single policeman during the polling of votes. They blinked at one another. After a bit of silence one woman raised her voice a bit and asked Poojamma, "Police? What is the connection between police and election? Police is different and elections are different".

'It seems Poojamma laughed loud at this and said, "Oh, I am totally and pleasantly surprised. In my country we need not only police but also army in order to have peaceful polling."

Kala replied to the question of Nina. 'Then Dinesh and Eeranna gave a drink and food party to the police inspector not because they wanted him to help gain more votes but because they wanted to ensure his silence, his calculated indifference. They would transport a lot of country made liquor and also high quality liquor and that the police inspector should look the other way. He should not book any cases against them as the law of the land did not allow such transportation of liquor.'

'Is this possible? Is law and order so bad in your country? Do even police violate law and order in such blatant manner?' Nina asked with considerable pain.

'In our country, governance works more by violation of law than by its implementation. Those who belong to particular castes have more power than the Constitution. People belonging to particular political parties have more power than elected members. It can be said that the singular contribution of Poojamma is that she has made the rule of law work in favor of the poor and Dalits in this area. This is not true of India. But it is true of Poojamma. She herself has never risen above law. She has also not allowed many to rise above law.' Nina saw now clearly that Poojamma had left her replica in Kala.

'In our country and in Europe we have drinks every day with our meals. Therefore, it is just impossible for me to grasp that people can be bought with the provision of liquor. But what happens in our countries is that people are highly introverted and fall prey to false promises. We Americans only think of our own interests at the time of electing our President. In fact most of us in America know very little about the rest of the world. We just do not care. I think it is mainly because of the filthy wealth that we have. No one wants to even bother how our government brings so much of wealth into our country. In a way that is similar to what your politicians do at the time of elections. Something is given everywhere in return for anticipated votes. Forward purchasing of votes, I think.' Nina became melancholic while reflecting loudly with Kala. Comparisons were inevitable.

—oo◖◗oo—

'Poojamma, that idiot has come asking for you. Please hide yourself in your bedroom. We shall tell him that you are gone to Bangalore.' Kala and another girl rushed to Poojamma's room to inform her.

'Whom are you speaking of? Why should I hide? Who can do anything to me? If someone does something to me it will be for the good of our people. But tell me who is the person who has come.' Poojamma protested to the young girls who were trying to decide for her on certain important issues.

'He, Poojamma that asshole, that son of a bitch, Dinesh has come. He wants to meet you and talk to you. We have told him that you were planning to go to Bangalore and did not see you going. We came here as if to check if you are here or if you have already left. You be here. We shall tell him that you have already left for Bangalore.' Kala poured out her unmitigated anger and played her brand of politics.

'Oh, at last he has come here. I thought he would come here one day. But I did not think that he would come so fast. Has he come alone or are there other people with him?' Poojamma enquired of the girls.

'Has he the courage to face you alone Poojamma? He has come with a big group of people. How will he come here alone?' It was Kala once again who shot her mouth.

'Has Eeranna also come?' Poojamma wanted to make sure that he did not come and Kala informed her that he was not seen anywhere in the campus.

'Okay, both of you go and prepare some tea. Get some biscuits ready and serve them. Should we inform Chikkanna and Nagaraj? No let me meet them first and if there is any need we shall call them.' She asked the question and gave the answer too.

'Why Poojamma, why do you want us to serve tea and biscuits to these bum-lickers? They have given you so much of trouble. We do not even know why in the first place they have come today and you want to treat them as your royal guests.' The girls protested vehemently.

'See girls! Do just as I say. Even our worst enemies, when they come into our campus in order to see us, are our guests. It is our culture to treat our guests with respect. What they are today and what they did to us yesterday is none of our business when they knock at our door. Go bring them and make them sit in the hall. I shall come in a minute. Both of you go and prepare tea immediately.' She got into her organizing mode and did it very fast.

"Namaste, Madam! Nice to see you in your house! These are my followers and we have all come to see you and pay our respect to you." It was

Dinesh who spoke as Poojamma entered the hall and greeted them with folded hands. He immediately called for the garlands and asked one of the women who accompanied him to garland her. Poojamma accepted the garland with due respect and asked all of them to sit comfortably. The memory that it was the same fellow who asked her to get out of his house when she went to meet him flashed like a lightning across the left side of her head. She also sat in one of the sofas as others began to take their seats.

"Madam . . . ." Even as Dinesh started Poojamma cut him short.

"You have come for the first time to my house. Please have some tea and biscuit and then we can talk. Are you in a hurry Mr. Dinesh?" She asked with all the politeness that a normally civilized person could muster at the most controversial time of one's life. The girls had already brought tea and biscuit. All of them took their share of refreshments kept in front of them. One of them was still standing in one corner of the hall. Poojamma asked him why he was standing when all were seated. "In this house all are equal and all are human beings". It was Kala who put a spoke in the moving wheel of Poojamma. She smiled. Dinesh wondered in himself that such a young girl spoke of equality of all and admired Poojamma for the way she had trained her followers. No wonder that she had a strong group of loyalists.

Chikkanna and Nagaraj entered the hall together as if it was just by accident that they came there. Poojamma looked at Kala. There were a million questions in that look. Kala did not want to look into those eagle eyes and pretended to be looking after the guests. Poojamma asked both of them to sit and have some tea. They obliged.

After the girls cleared the table she turned to Dinesh. "Yes, please tell me now. Why have you come? Is there something that we need to discuss or that I need to do for you?" She asked as if she was the elected member of the Legislative Assembly. Indeed she was a step above that, as she ensured that Dinesh was defeated in elections to the Legislative Assembly and that he even lost his deposit. Dinesh was like a toothless lion in his cage. The election results spelt disaster in his life. He did not expect to be defeated in the first place. But when he had to brush aside a lot of sand from his moustache he realized that he had lost his moustache. He lost his deposit.

It was a double blow to his self-pride. Now he was sitting in front of the woman who was the architect of his defeat. He never imagined meeting her in his life. He was keen on banishing her from his sight forever. But fate had its own plan.

Poojamma knew that he was a defeated hero. In her view he was one of the worst villains she had ever met. The defeat seemed to have mellowed him down quite a bit. Was he humbled? Yes, without any doubt! Or was he pretending to have become humble? Only he knew. Poojamma did not want to make any wild guess. But the way he had come with many of his cohorts at least indicated that he did not want to let go of his old glamour. Anger was written large on his face. That he was trying to put up a façade of good will did not escape the notice of Poojamma. She had anticipated more trouble from him after she ensured his defeat in elections to the Legislative Assembly. She did not expect him to turn up at her door that fast. Chikkanna and Nagaraj were ever ready to pounce on him the moment he said anything offensive of her. Dinesh did not fail to cast his glance every now and then at the two who stood alert.

Having taken the time to come to terms with himself, Dinesh cleared his throat a bit and started. "I am sorry Madam for whatever my followers and I have done to you. I was completely misinformed by many of my followers, especially that useless fellow in this village, Eeranna. Now I have come to know of the all the good work you are doing to the poor of this constituency. It was wrong on my part to have given you some troubles. But now I am happy that your services are recognized well. Hereafter we shall be good friends. I have come today to seek your good will and friendship. On my part I shall support you 100% on all that you do for people of this district." Saying this he turned to his followers and said: "Hey, you fellows, hereafter you should support Madam in all that she does. We have wasted our precious time till now listening to that fellow Eeranna. Now you take advise from Madam and do your work."

He turned towards Chikkanna and Nagaraj. "How are you two and how are all your friends? How is Gowdajja? You have chosen the best part. To be with Madam is a great privilege. That fellow misguided me. Otherwise I would have supported Madam and all of you. Now let us all join hands and work together."

When Chikkanna cleared his throat to speak Poojamma was literally seeing stars wondering if he was going to stir up a hornet's nest. "You are doing Sun worship when the Sun has already set in the West. We tried our best to convince your disciple Eeranna not to antagonize madam. How many times did we not tell him that we are not against anyone? Madam had always told us that we should not work against anyone. Anger against others should not guide our actions. It is only our inner being that should guide all our actions. We have grown up with Madam that way. But why did we have to suffer so much for being good to people? Now let us leave all that. I only want to know what guarantee we have that Eeranna or you will not create any further trouble for our Madam." Chikkanna meant business, serious business at that. Saying this he took a chair with legitimate pride and sat equal to Dinesh.

Dinesh wanted to retort in his political way. But he realized that he was in the wrong place to do that. "You do not worry about me any more. Believe me I am with you people 100%. About Eeranna I shall tell him strictly not to come your way any more." Saying this he got up to go. He did not want to sit as equal to a minion. Poojamma did not want to hold him back too long in her place. She was not convinced about his confession of support. He had to be studied for some more time. But she smiled broadly and folded her hands to bid them a fair farewell. She stood there at the door till he and his followers left her place. For the last time at the main door, Dinesh turned again towards her and greeted her with folded hands.

"What else can he do Poojamma? Has he any other option in his political career except supporting you? He may think that he is a lion. But only we know that you have tamed the lion in his den. He knows well that he cannot survive in politics in this area if he antagonizes you. But beware of politicians. The moment they find you are weak somewhere they will strike you hard at that spot. They never forget their defeat and will keep vengeance till their deathbed.' Nagaraj gave a clear warning to Poojamma. His friend Chikkanna nodded his head vigorously in approval.

It was a mature and collective strategy worked out by Poojamma and her followers to downplay the enormous victory they gained in the defeat of Dinesh. They did everything they could to ensure his defeat. Actually people of that constituency did much more than what followers of Poojamma did. They began to discuss among themselves about whom they should elect. The issue of Dinesh and Eeranna combining together against the only good thing in the constituency, that was Poojamma became a much-discussed one among them. There was palpable anger even in the ordinary voter in that constituency. Even those who were not in any way associated with Poojamma were angry. Dinesh came to know of this change of mood in the constituency and in his frustration he made the biggest blunder. He pumped in more money and more liquor into all villages. The voters too had become alert and were warned sufficiently in advance by the followers of Poojamma on such a consequence. They pulled their shutters down in an exceptional way. The writing on the wall and on the forehead of Dinesh was there for all to read. Even the illiterate could read that. Poojamma and her followers had decided to let the defeat of Dinesh pass as a non-event so that the same voters did not turn against their Movement. For the first time in his life Dinesh dug his own grave and did not push anyone else into it. He fell in the grave that he dug for himself. Natural justice!

CHAPTER ELEVEN

That evening Poojamma sat alone in a mood of self-reflection. She was like a lonely boat that traversed different pushes and pulls of a vast ocean. She could feel that for the first time there was a feeling of energy drain setting in her. The coming of Dinesh brought with him quite a bit of depression. This was not the first time that she went through this experience of low energy, or even negative energy. Her place was open to all kinds of people. When some people came and left her place she would go dancing all the places. She would sing and feel like being in the seventh heavens. But when some other people came she would immediately feel the permeation of a negative energy and would feel as if she was diving into the limbo. Even scorpions, spiders and snakes would start appearing in the place quite unexpectedly. It was beyond her rational explanation. She could not deny it and she could not simply accept it either.

Dinesh's coming that day seemed to have left a heavy load of negative energy all over the place. She took a quite walk but was restless. She came and sat for silent reflection all by herself. But she could not sit for too long. Finally she called the girls and began to chat about Dinesh's coming. To her dismay she also found that the girls were equally restless. 'I don't know why that bloody asslicker came here without getting your permission. People don't even know when they should come and when they should simply mind their business. That bloody son of a bitch has the audacity to come and offer his friendship. Who in the first place wanted any relationship with him?' Kala was seething with anger.

"Why are you abusing his mother Kala, to take out your anger against the MLA? If you have anything against him you abuse him and not his mother." Manjula said without looking at Kala. She had rushed there as soon as she heard that Dinesh had visited Poojamma. She was disappointed that he had already left the place when she arrived.

"Madam, now is real danger lurking at our own door. A known enemy is much better. This fellow is a poisonous snake. Now he wants us to put him in our bed. You don't know when this snake will bite us. Let us be very careful with him, madam." Nagaraj gave a grand advice.

Without saying anything Poojamma just walked out in silence. She wanted to be left alone without being distracted even by her close confidante. She ruminated over the way she had put up a hard struggle against this unnecessary intruder in her life. She had a very exhilarating engagement with the poor of the area. Eeranna and Dinesh made life hell for her. No work is ever rewarded without its share of pain. But if only they had realized the need for cooperation things would have been much better for them, for her and for the people. The political ego of the two stood before Poojamma as a big giant challenging her serene personality. Her people were with her always in support but facing life and its struggles alone without a companion at her side did haunt her every now and then and now more than ever.

Who could she share her confusion with? It was something deep. Only someone whom she let to sojourn deep in the inner recesses of her being would be able to stand with her. Nina had asked her a few times if she did not think of marrying someone and have a family with children. Poojamma would look askance at her and say that she had all girls in villages as her daughters. The next moment she wore a comforting look to ease Nina's tension. She was not against the idea of marriage. However, she was not madly in search of a companion. She did not feel compelled to have a man as her companion. There were times when feelings of loneliness used to overtake her. Thousands of admiring followers could not fill the vacuum created inside by the absence of that intimate one. She cast away such lonely feelings by getting alone to herself and occasionally even by masturbating. But these were quite rare as there was not much traits of compulsive behavior in her. She was so composed that often she did not have to compensate her unrecognized need through sex. There were many other ways of compensation that she discovered for herself.

One was her reading habit. She was an avaricious reader of books. And yet there were times when the body spoke its own inalienable language.

Of late however, with advancement of age and with the increase of problems from unexpected political quarters she found it difficult to manage herself. She could not socialize just as other women did because of the status heaped on her by the society in which she lived. No one would allow her to take a walk with freedom that a woman deserved. As she ventured out occasionally to be on her own many heads would pop up even from a distance and people would rush to her to pour out their problems. She had become an icon for them. An icon had no personality of its own. People who needed the icon fabricated its personality. Many on the road only saw her as the owner of a bundle of money from another country. Poojamma felt often violated by the people whom she loved and by the people who loved her immensely. This was a paradox with which she had to live.

One of them was Kala who had no boundaries of time in her interaction with Poojamma. She took the liberty to intrude into her personal space any time she wanted. That day was not different. Poojamma did not notice that Kala was quietly walking behind her like a cat. It was indeed a catwalk that she was doing. She could realize that she was being shadowed and turned to Kala and smiled. She held Kala's hand and both of them began to walk the talk.

"Why did you choose this difficult life Poojamma? All of us want to have an easy life and settle down in life at the earliest. You are not married. You do not mingle much with your relatives. All your life is spent for the poor and that too with so many difficulties. Many of us do not understand why you are doing all this for us.' Kala had a solid rock of courage laid by Poojamma and she used it liberally with her mentor.

Poojamma began to open up slowly to her own prodigy. "I grew up in a different environment that focused on individual freedom. It was not the same as you grow up here in the village. You know well that I grew up in Bangalore city. I was from a family that could be bracketed in the upper part of the lower middle class. My parents brought me up as a pet child and so I enjoyed much more freedom than children of my age and surroundings. Being the eldest daughter in my family I also grew up as a very responsible child helping my mother in taking care of my father whenever he came home. After me there were a few other children in the family. You have met all of them. I was in a way compelled to take part in their upbringing. My father had dedicated himself to the service of the nation in the army. Perhaps I imbibed his sense of patriotism. Whenever anyone said that patriotism was the last refuge of scoundrels I felt that my father was directly insulted and so never hesitated to take up a fight with such people without caring a bit about consequences. My mother would scold me umpteen numbers of time for being bold and for fighting . . ."

". . . Amma had a traditional concept of how to bring up a girl child. It was the same way that your mother brought you up. Her girl child had to be protected, as a mother hen would gather her chicks under her wings. I was known only as Pooja in my younger days. I would come out of the wings of mother hen at the first available opportunity and would design my independent path. Amma would chide me for not being dependent on her. In her view a girl child had to be dependent all her life. My best self-defense was that fighting was the profession of my father and so I had every right to fight against anyone who violated the dignity of my family members or the rights of my neighbors. Complaints galore would follow whenever my father came for holidays from the military. But he would always support me . . ."

'Oh, it is the same for me in my family. My mother also is like your mother. But my father did not go to military. He is only a village farmer. He would join my mother unlike your father.' Kala began to draw parallel lines.

"At every stage of life Amma would put a hurdle on my studies. She would question the validity of the rationale for educating girl children in the family. After all her own parents did not send her to school. Girl children in her mind were to be married and had a role only to beget children and cook for husband and children. But my father, like all ordinary fathers expected a male child and when that did not work, he wanted to bring up his first girl child as he would bring up a son. He was keen on educating me unlike any other child in his entire family and wanted to take revenge on his own family that failed to educate him beyond high school."

Kala had nothing in reply now. She did not want to go to school and she remembered that her father never liked her, as she was the second girl child in the family. All neighbors and his own peers teased him for having begotten a girl child the second time also. They jocularly told him to keep trying every night. She became silent. Holding her hands Poojamma recollected in silence.

Pooja grew up as a rare combination of rebellion and discipline. Plus there was a heavy mixture of a conservative culture that came from the rest of the family. Whenever she did something rebellious and radical the blame would vocally go to her father as to how he dared to bring up a girl child like a boy. He cared a hoot for any such criticism, as when he was young and loved his future wife his family looked down upon love itself and he could not understand it by any imaginable stretch of his imagination. He rebelled against the well-established traditions of his family. He married the girl of his liking though she hailed from a different caste than his. Big people! His parents did not like any violation of the family traditions. Now when his daughter did the same thing he did not want to have double standards. He was proud in a way that his daughter rebelled against the traditions of the society. He encouraged her to the hilt. Pooja went up the scales in her educational qualifications and excelled in her studies.

Soon she began to traverse the boundaries of the nation in an apparent mission to revolutionize the entire set up in the country. While her father protected the borders of the nation she began to stir a hornet's nest within the boundaries. Patriotism began to play its role also in her life in a different way. Who ever cared about her father? In military every soldier had an identity that was never recognized. Number was his identity. The only time a soldier was recognized by his name was when he was shot dead by the enemy. Otherwise he had to die often an ignominious death. Government had its welfare schemes in place. But her father never cared for them. And therefore, he did not have patience to continue his services till the end of his career. He loved his wife more than he loved the country. The boundaries of the country were too vast, impersonal and unrecognizable. The boundaries of his wife's love were often invisible but there was a joy in that invisibility. He could not bargain that with his patriotism. All his companions called him a naïve patriot.

Pooja chose a line of patriotism that would simultaneously give her a lot of recognition of what she did. As a student she did everything that would be within the marks of rebellion. Therefore, when she came to know that there were some outfits in her school that were looking out for fish that would swim against the current she stood in frontline. A frontline soldier was born. Her mentors were made of different stuff. Unlike the ideology of patriotism, they had ideology that took her to the throes of the pains and pangs of the poor. This was much more challenging than shining of shoes and oiling of guns that her father had described to her as his routine work in the army. There was time of peace and a time of war in the army. But for her it was always a time of war, the war against poverty, and war against the rich who were exploiting livelihood opportunities of the poor. This war was a borderless one. Her love was for all the poor living in any part of the world. Protecting borders of the nation made very little sense in this war against poverty and indignity. She wore battle gear at a very young age without realizing how far it would take her in life. Such was the idealism that her mentors instilled in her. She drank the nectar of revolution that she thought would come in her lifetime. She had to bring that near the doorstep of every poor family in the country so that their children would have a brighter future than they had.

It was engineered well with ideology as a cover and strategy as weapon. She was never alone. It was an army of students. All types of them were there. Young boys and girls were ready to battle it out together on behalf of the poor with an unblemished idealism that could belong only to their age. A savior psyche permeated all their nerves and cells in the body. Pooja stood out among many students of her school. She excelled in her studies and also took up extra curricular activities in a student movement. Her teachers encouraged her to do all the work that she did for the society. Fortunately for her she had a headmistress in school that was very committed to the poor and encouraged Pooja to do whatever she wanted to do. This gave her enough courage and freedom to go to different States of India and use her skills in communication. She trained bigwigs in different educational institutions and became popular.

"In your life have you not met any men at all Poojamma. You are always alone. Were you ever married or are you always like this? Will you not marry?" Kala started abruptly in an attempt to break the overbearing silence between her and Poojamma. She was taken aback at such serious question coming from a girl who could be her daughter.

"Why do you ask, Kala? I have not married anyone. But that does not mean that I do not have men as my friends. In fact I have more men as friends than women. You are surprised, no? During my high school days and later in my colleges I used to mingle freely with boys because of my involvement with social issues. There were many of us who were specially trained to become leaders. Our trainers used to mix boys and girls, as they believed that such mixing made us more mature to deal with problems. I even used to live in the same house where young men lived. But they were such decent guys that they would never disturb us. They were very free with us and that gave us a lot of confidence to move closely with them without being abused by them." Poojamma knew that she was confiding in a small little girl details of her personal life. But the maturity of Kala also gave her that extra confidence of opening up her personal life.

"How about your parents Poojamma? Did they allow you to mix with boys? Were they not afraid? I don't know how it is in the city. But in our village we cannot even talk to boys in the presence of others. We have to only stealthily talk to boys.' Kala now began to reveal some details about her.

"Where do you meet boys stealthily in the village? Every place is open." Poojamma provoked her with a question for which she knew the answer before even the question was asked.

"That is not a big problem Poojamma. Best time for us to meet is late in the evening. You know that we do not have toilets at home and we cannot go to nature during day, as we are very shy of exposing ourselves. All of us girls go to answer call of nature only when it is dark. Some of us manage to do it during daytime. We pretend as if we are going for answering call of nature but actually our boys would be waiting for us half way. It is not at all difficult to shout loud and convey the message as if we are talking to one of our friends in the neighborhood and our boys will know that we have started. Occasionally our rivals catch us and there will be furor at home. It is on such occasions that we develop skills for telling lies to our parents in such a way that they will believe in us. That is an art that many of us girls in the village master." Kala was lucid in her explanation and Poojamma was smiling within herself.

"I did not have to do all that you do in the village. Boys used to come to my house whenever I had holidays or even school days. I had beautiful parents who would look after anyone who came to my house. My younger sisters and my mother were extremely happy to cook for everyone who came. My father was a very generous man. He would run to the market as soon as my friends came and they would have good meal along with long chats. My parents had exemplary trust in me. They never doubted me about my relationship with any boys. The behavior of boys used to be very decent too." Poojamma was letting loose her truths hidden till then from the rest of the world.

"If you had so many friends, you should have married at least one of them, Poojamma. Why did you not marry any of them? I think every woman should have a man as her companion. I cannot imagine my life without a husband. Not only that, in the village if we are not married tongues would begin to wag in different directions without any control. Our parents would not be able digest the type of gossip that would roll in the village." Kala now began to take a sort of liberty with Poojamma that she did not ever do with her till then. Poojamma enjoyed that type of liberty that village dames manifested when they began to like a person. Often it was a no holds barred type of communication.

"Yes, there were many men who also wanted to marry me. But somehow I did not feel inclined to marry anyone. My relatives came home asking my parents to get me married off to one of their wards. I declined every such offer though my parents were mildly inclined towards some of them. My father strictly told them that nothing could be done unless I agreed to it. My mother was keen on marrying me off. Just as you say she also believed that the ultimate objective of every woman is to get married and give birth to many children. I have now thousands of children in villages. Just imagine that I had my own children. I always thought that it would be very difficult to love all children equally if I had a family of my own. You know the way I love Pramila more than all other children. You are talking like an old woman, Kala. Let us stop it here and go back." Poojamma released Kala's hand in order to turn back. Both of them walked back without uttering a word to each other. Kala was filled with happiness and pride that she was very close to Poojamma unlike all other dames of her age in the village.

—◦◦❁◦◦—

"So you were that close to Poojamma? I cannot imagine how such a big woman like Poojamma could share such deeply personal matters with you. These are things that normally we share only with close friends." Nina intercepted Kala.

'What do you mean? Am I not a friend of Poojamma? I may look small and young in my age. That is because I have not had as much food as you had at my age. But I have grown up with Poojamma taking part in all her struggles of life and mission. I have stood with her in all her troubles like no one else in this area did. Why would she not confide her personal secret in me? I think I am the one she loved most next to Pramila." Kala retorted back in her style. Nina was truly jealous of her special position in Poojamma's personal world.

—◦◦❁◦◦—

Kala resumed the chain of narration. 'From a distance we could see a group of people waiting for Poojamma. Usually I would easily identify at least some persons in the group at that distance. But it was a totally new group. I could not identify any of them even when they were near. As soon as they approached the house the small group of men and women venerated Poojamma with tears in their eyes welling up and it took no time for the stream to come down.

"They have killed our police inspector Poojamma. We do not know what to do except to come to you. Nasser was such a good police officer. He helped all the poor and was never corrupt. If this is the fate of such a good officer what will happen to ordinary people like us, Poojamma? We are living in 'kaliyuga' (an evil era)." One of them lamented loudly. Women took sand and threw it in the wind cursing all those evil men who killed a very bold and upright police officer. It was their way of invoking the curse of Mother Earth.

'Poojamma asked them in total shock, "What?!! Have they killed Nasser? Why did they do this? Who killed him? Oh, what a good man!!" 'Later she shared with me that at that moment it flashed on her memory like lightning the first encounter she had with him. He was known as a very upright man under the management of the SP who had appointed him to our police station in order that no one may harass Poojamma. However, her first encounter with him was not the best of relationships. Eeranna had made one of his cronies to complain to the inspector about Poojamma as soon as he took charge. With the written complaint in his hand he went straight to her and walked in as if a dog would enter an open house. Poojamma was surprised at the way he entered her house without even knocking at the door. She invited him to sit down and served tea in a cup and saucer. He was surprised that he was treated like a guest in such humane manner. She gave him a few cookies that he liked. She was not at all perturbed when he informed her that he had come to enquire a few things vis-à-vis the complaint. Poojamma replied to all his questions with a composure that he had not seen in any woman whom he had enquired till then. The first goal belonged to Poojamma. Nasser was highly impressed at her demeanor.'

'It was only then that he began to speak openly to Poojamma and enquired about the background to the complaint. She explained to him the situation in the area and the massive suffering that poor people had to undergo in the hands of Eeranna and his master Dinesh. He was convinced. He got up with deep respect and promised to help her whenever she needed help. He kept up his words and became a regular visitor.'

'In one of those visits Poojamma asked him how he managed to be so honest in a government that smacked of corruption at every stage and level.'

He replied with a great sense of pride. "I have obtained this job on my merit and not by the recommendation of any politician. They are the worst type of bandicoots that I have seen in my life. To listen to their dictates would be equivalent to freely selling my dignity. Why should I sacrifice my dignity for the sake of these uncivilized bandicoots? Moreover, I am ready to work anywhere in India, Madam. What can a MLA do at the most? He can transfer me to a dry region where we don't get water. But there are people still living there. If people can live in a region in the most pathetic conditions I too love to live in such a region. I have none to fear. I am a man of my own, Madam." He said with some legitimate pride.

'Poojamma was highly impressed and liked him very much. Such a man had been hacked to death by criminals. Impossible even to imagine! She did not know that the SP had been transferred only one week before that. Just as she came out of the initial shock, Chikkanna and Nagaraj landed there saying aloud to Poojamma that Nasser had been killed by a mob violence.'

"A mob violence? Why was there mob violence? Why did the mob kill a good officer? Were there not other policemen to protect him? Did not the government know of this earlier through their intelligence services? A mob violence would not take place all of a sudden. The police should have rushed their forces when they sensed that there was going to be a mob violence." Nina took Kala by the collar with her volley of questions. She was then completely shocked at the news she heard from Kala.

'It was a huge protest that Dinesh and a few other politicians in the district organized against the rise in prices of seeds. These were farmers. Two other politicians had huge followers of farmers, as they always took up issues of farmers and fought for their rights. Farmers went in procession in the city shouting many slogans against government's procurement policies and price of seeds. Their plan was to picket the office of the Collector and not allow him to go out of his office till he agreed to their demands.'

'When the procession ended at the Collector's office there were more than 5000 farmers altogether. The SP realized that situation would get out of control any time. The few inspectors who were commissioned on security arrangements asked the SP for reinforcement of police forces. They demanded that the Rapid Action Force of the police department be requested to come immediately. But the SP abused them in all sorts of invectives and challenged them on their capacity at crowd control. He asked them to prove themselves to be men. He particularly looked at Nasser and spoke in very harsh voice on the manly powers of his own staff.'

'That was enough to provoke Nasser. He called all other officers and said that they should manage the situation and prove to the SP and to the Government that they were capable of handling any situation. Others agreed and took position along with policemen from their respective stations.'

'MLAs gave their long political speeches. There were vituperative attacks on the policies of the government . . .'

"But why did the MLAs attack the government? They belonged to the government, no?" Nina let slip her hold over her sharp thinking.

'Not all MLAs belong to the government. Some of them belong to the opposition. MLAs who belong to the opposition consider it their duty to attack the government on all fronts. Farmers were highly provoked. They asked the Collector to come out of his office and face them. But the SP who was sitting with him refused to allow the Collector to go and meet the farmers. He cited security reasons for preventing the Collector. There were a few policemen with the SP and he even threatened the Collector of serious consequences if he went out to meet the farmers. The Collector fell in line with his colleague. Since the Collector was not coming out for a long time some farmers started pelting stones on the glass panes of the windows of his office. When stones kissed windowpanes the SP ordered through his wireless sets caning of farmers.'

'As soon as police started caning, farmers became agitated and they started attacking the police. The entire police force was only about 100. When the inspectors present there informed the SP over wireless that situation was going out of control he asked them rather rashly to take control of the situation and gave orders for shooting. But soon it was pandemonium all over. Policemen were too few to control a violent crowd of 5000. They had come prepared with a good stock of stones to throw indiscriminately on policemen. Some of the policemen started running for cover and hid themselves in some of the rooms of the big office. Some began to shoot in the air and later also on the farmers. This further infuriated them. "Hey, let them exhaust the bullets in their guns. Let us see what they will do after that. They have only a few rounds of bullets. Let us catch them and smash their heads." One of the leaders in the crowed shouted aloud.'

'Some of the policemen exhausted the bullets in their guns and ran out of stock. There was no other policeman to bring them more bullets. They began to run towards the road. Farmers were in hot pursuit of the fleeing policemen. The inspectors resisted a bit more and fired at the crowd, as a warning to the farmers. But unfortunately the SP did not send any additional forces in support of the inspectors.'

'Nasser was like a brave soldier leading his force from the front. After some resistance the companions of Nasser also took to their heels and ran helter-skelter. The crowed also got splintered in the direction of each police inspector, running behind them like hungry lions trying to capture hapless deers for a festive meal. Nasser was left alone. Many farmers saw him raising his gun to shoot in the air in a hapless attempt to threaten them. But farmers knew that he could do precious little against their mighty strength. Nasser realized pathetically that his gun was empty. Finally the courage of Nasser began to melt. He looked all around and found none of his companions anywhere near. He also took to heels. He was a good runner in his early days. But it was not the same at the age of 45. He ran a distance of nearly a kilometer in the main roads of the town. There were hundreds of people who stood on the sidewalks of the roads and were watching the chasing of a champion. Most of them knew Nasser. None went to his rescue. The SP got the message of Nasser's plight over his wireless set. But he turned a deaf ear. Now it became evident why he was brought to the district only a week earlier. Nasser turned back a little to see how many people were in hot pursuit of him. It was horrible. Most of the crowd was behind him.'

'In his desire to live he turned to one of the lanes. But the fatigue took him over. As he turned his legs withered and he fell down on the road. In the crowd that surrounded him now he could see many whom he had earlier put in jail. There was no time to even wonder as to how they came out of the jail that day. He realized as a flash that his murder was pre-planned as he saw a dreaded criminal jailed by him leading the crowd that pursued him. Before he could revive his thinking function one big boulder hit his head and he reeled in pain. Not only his companions, not only his subordinates but even his consciousness began to desert him. He writhed in unbearable pain. He stood up to challenge the crowd even in that chaotic situation. As he stood up with blood oozing all over his body from his head and put his hands on his empty revolver another boulder flew across his head hitting him harder in the bargain.'

'Nasser fell down much faster than the stone that struck him. In their maddening frenzy the crowd collected big boulders that were heaped on the side for building construction and vied with one another to throw them on the head of the fallen hero. Their madness blinded them. Animals that passed by were looking at human beings with derision.

"How can they be so human?" they seemed to say among themselves. It only took a few minutes for Nasser to bid a farewell to his lurking spirit. Just before that last moment Nasser pathetically thought of his wife and two children. He was awed at what would happen to them if he were not alive. Just at that moment his very last breath departed from him.'

'Oh, how sad! Crowds can be very blind and violent. I have seen it several times in my career as a journalist. But to listen to the fate of Nasser touches some cords in my heart. It was such a brutal attack. What animals these human beings are?" Nina was silent for some time. Kala did not want to disturb her conscience. But when she resumed the first thing she said mildly was "Please do not insult the animals. They are much more civilized than human beings." Both of them sipped their coffee in dead silence, Nina in particular pondering over the heavy thought of Kala about animals as being more civilized than human beings. "How true!" She thought in that dreaded silence.

'Poojamma did not take it light. The wife of Nasser visited her and informed her of many discriminatory practices within the police department. Initially Poojamma took it as lamentations of a wife who had only recently lost her husband to the madness of violence. But as the narration got deeper she began to see greater conspiracy somewhere. She listened carefully to every word the woman had to say and did a serious analysis after she left. She came to the conclusion that there was something more than what met the eye. She sensed a connection between the sudden transfer of the SP and the events that followed. She called up the Director General of Police for an appointment. She met him and apprised him of her suspicions about the incident and requested him to probe into the matter seriously. She gave a written representation that the death of Nasser could easily be construed as planned murder and that the murderers should be identified and brought to books.'

'The DGP took her version seriously and ordered for an enquiry by the Corps of Detectives. CoD is a government agency controlled by the State government. Though Poojamma was apprehensive of its neutrality it was the best that could happen at that moment. The government was not happy with the DGP for the steps he took to bring the truth out. She also kept up the pressure on the DGP by calling him up over phone every now and then.'

"What happened to the enquiry? Could they find out who really killed Nasser? Or did the government hush up the investigation?" Nina was showering questions to Kala as usual.

'Wait in patience Nina!' Kala had by now begun to take the liberty of a friend with Nina. 'No investigation would end as fast as you imagine. When the results are out I shall let you know.' Kala kept her friend in a bit of suspense.

Assuming that the investigation was not yet over, Nina kept her mouth shut.

That night as they were lying together on bed Nina once again raised the issue of the death of Nasser. Kala knew that Nina would not allow her to sleep unless she concluded the narration. She made it known that though the investigations clearly pointed out to Dinesh as the main culprit the entire episode was hushed up by the government as a farmers riot and a mob violence letting the true culprit a free bird.

ChAPTER TWELVE

'It was early morning one day. Poojamma returned home late in the evening of the previous day from a village. She was very tired and slept a little longer than usual. There was a big commotion outside her house. She looked through the window of her bedroom and could see over a hundred men and some women talking loud among themselves. They were dressed well. She could make out that it was not a crowd from one of her villages. It seemed very different. As she was trying to guess what the crowd could be she could spot Dinesh. She wondered why this politician was in her place again with such a large group of followers. Many of them were in their political attire of white kurta and pyjamma.'

'Poojamma called me up in a hurry and asked me to tidy up the hall quickly. There was no room in the hall for all the people. But she said that some would not come in. We were unable to provide tea for all his followers. He did not hesitate to take the cup of tea offered to him and asked a few other followers of his to share tea. Some hesitated but some others asserted a sort of unknown authority in our place and grabbed a cup of tea. A few others politely refused to accept tea saying that they did not drink tea as a habit. It was often a way of not accepting anything from a Dalit home.'

'The second coming of Dinesh had a lot of free air and flair. He informed Poojamma that there would be a declaration of elections in the next week. He had applied for a ticket to contest as a Member of Parliament and his party had assured him of a ticket. "Amma, if you support me in the next election I shall become a member of the Parliament. This is my best chance in politics. If you do not want me to contest in the election I shall withdraw. You can support whomever you want to win. But I plead with all my followers here that you should support me. If I win I shall bring a lot of development schemes for this area. You can implement all of them for beneficiaries of your choice. I shall not at all interfere in that. I am your servant hereafter, Amma. I hope you will not keep in mind the past and look to the future." Dinesh got up to touch the feet of Poojamma in order to get her blessings.

"This is a bit too much of our leader to fall at the feet of a woman. Is he already drunk so early in the morning?" I could hear his followers murmuring among themselves as I kept serving drinking water to them. I laughed but controlled my tendency to laugh out loud.'

'Dinesh not only touched Poojamma's feet but also prostrated before her. His full body was flat on the floor. It was a sight to watch. I could not control my laughter and ran to kitchen to laugh my heart out.' Nina laughed loud hearing Kala narrating the entire event with peels of laughter.

"Please get up. What is this that you are doing? It may be okay for you politicians to fall at the feet of Chief Ministers. I am not your party leader. I am a humble servant of people. Please do not do such things in this place. You are my equal. In fact all of us are equal. If only you and your party people can treat me as an equal human being, it will be a big honor to me." Poojamma reproved him with care and concern.

"We shall not leave your place unless I get an assurance from you that you will ask your followers to vote for me in the coming election." Dinesh now started a tacit blackmailing of Poojamma. But she was very generous. She was not a person to go by silly calculations of ego. The priority in her mind that morning was to get rid of the entire gang of politicians. Somehow there was an emotional uneasiness in her about politicians. She said that she would support him and make him win. After getting her assurance he took leave of her and the entire gang left the place. Poojamma heaved a sigh of relief.

'Later in the day there was a very serious discussion among the followers of Poojamma about her promised support to Dinesh. In the meantime they had gathered news that for the MLA seat it was Eeranna who had applied to the party High Command. They sarcastically communicated the message to Poojamma. Poojamma was highly disturbed and felt betrayed by Dinesh by what she heard from her followers. That both of them were still in league was evident from the news she heard.'

'Chikkanna was vociferous in his opposition to any support to Dinesh. He argued that supporting Dinesh was a virtual surrender to Eeranna. In people's mind there was no distinction between Dinesh and Eeranna. One cannot support only one of them. Supporting Dinesh was equivalent to putting a leech in the cradle of a baby and singing lullaby to it. However good you are the leech will suck blood from the baby.'

'Nagaraj was a bit more sympathetic to the predicament of Poojamma and adapted a middle path. Chikkanna rebuked him and advised him not to be like a two-headed cobra. He was of the strong view that supporting Dinesh was suicidal. His anger was directed more to Eeranna and less towards Dinesh. Poojamma understood this clearly and asked him to list out the qualities of Dinesh that would deter their organization from marching forward. Much of what he said in reply was centered on a polemic of Eeranna. From his own dialogue Poojamma picked up her argument.'

'People were somewhat convinced that they had no other option but to support Dinesh. A careful analysis clearly showed that he was much better than all other candidates in the fray. He had an inimical past. But he seemed to be converted to good ways. They had to choose between the devil and the deep sea. Since Dinesh had offered an olive branch they were inclined to take it. Poojamma was basically a woman of good heart and not a diehard politician by any standards. Moreover she was also convinced and convinced others that Dinesh was a naïve person and was a better bet than the cleverer ones among them. Finally it was formally decided that the group would support Dinesh but oppose Eeranna tooth and nail.'

'When Chikkanna communicated this officially to Dinesh he agreed to the decision and thanked him and Poojamma for having decided to support him. "Leave out that idiot Eeranna. He is a very bad fellow. He has spoiled my name everywhere. I told our party leaders not to give him ticket to contest elections on behalf of our party. But he paid a heavy bribe to our party leaders and got the ticket. It is good that you decided not to support him. Please tell Poojamma that I shall also work against Eeranna and work for his defeat in the forthcoming election. Thank her for the support extended to me. She is a wonderful woman. When I win I shall speak in the Parliament and extend my full cooperation to your movement." Dinesh almost sealed an agreement with Poojamma's followers.'

'News reached all villages and when results were declared Dinesh was the winner and for the first time he became a Member of the Parliament of India. Everyone in Poojamma's camp expected him to come first to her and extend his gratitude to her. But he was not to be seen anywhere near. Holding on to his paraphernalia Eeranna also gained considerable number of votes but fell short of winning the seat. There were celebrations in the camp of Poojamma mixed with a heavy feeling that Dinesh was such an ungrateful politician.'

"How sad that Poojamma had to suffer such humiliation because of her goodness!" Nina sympathized with her late friend.

'But that was not the way Poojamma saw things. She only said that having been elected as a member of parliament he might be too busy and would come to thank her at a later time. She also rationalized that it was her duty to meet the elected member of the parliament and was preposterous on her part to expect him to come to her. She never lost this simplicity till the end of her life and perhaps that was what sealed her fate.'

'In her utter simplicity she sent Chikkanna and Nagaraj with a bouquet of flowers and a letter of congratulations for having won the seat and become a member of the parliament of India. Both of them entered the house of Dinesh with an authority on their face. After all it was because of their support that he won the seat. Much to their chagrin they were stopped at the door by the security. They revealed their identity and asked the policeman to inform Dinesh that both of them had come from Poojamma. The security went inside, came out and asked them to wait. They waited for a very long time looking at each other's face. They exchanged their looks without words but there was a mutual message that Dinesh was what they suspected him to be.'

'After a long time Dinesh came out with many eminent followers and was about to walk out of the house to the waiting car. Both Chikkanna and Nagaraj ran behind him and called him out. He just turned back touching the door of the car with one hand and adjusting his dress with the other. "Yes, tell me. What can I do for you?" He had assumed the tone and tenor of an elected MP rather too soon and behaved as if he saw both of them for the first time. Both of them swallowed their pride and informed him that Poojamma had sent her greetings to him and handed over the bouquet to him. He did not care to receive it. Instead he asked his Personal Assistant to take it. The PA handed it over to the security at the door. Dinesh simply said that he would see them later and got into the car. As the doors of the car slammed they felt that the world had become a bit darker than it should actually be. They thought of the goodness of Poojamma and its consequences in the world of politics.'

'They were furious when they reached back but did not narrate every detail to Poojamma for fear of hurting her finely tuned sentiments. They knew instantly that Poojamma understood that they were hiding some truths form her. All of them were distracted by the commotion outside the house. This time it was a group of village people, obviously with some problems.

It was a group of men and women from a new village in the constituency of Dinesh. Quite a few events unfolded themselves one by one. One of them got up with a few sheets of papers in his hands. Holding them he started narrating that they were all Dalits from the village of Ramapura.'

"Please come and sit first. I guess that you may have a serious problem. But let us sit together and talk. Have some water first and later tea will come." Poojamma was very inviting in her disposition to the poor. Tension on their faces began to disappear a bit and they started to smile a little now. Men and women sat together and had water. "I was very happy to serve them tea" Kala said to Nina and continued her narration.'

'The same man stood up once again with papers in his hands and started a long story. "Amma, we are Dalits from Ramapura. Now we are in a serious problem. We have heard that you help a lot of people to recover their lost land." Murthy started in all seriousness. He took position of leadership for all who had come with him.'

"Where did you hear about me? Who told you about me?" Poojamma put up a look of surprise on her face. She was a master artist in such dealings with the poor. She knew the answer. But she wanted the poor to talk to her freely without much awe. Therefore, she asked questions at regular intervals and elicited a lot of response from people. It was her easy way of getting all people involved in whatever was happening in her place.'

"I was in the office of the Tahsildar some days ago . . ." Murthy started and was stopped immediately by Kariyajji. "Tahsidar's office is his second home Amma. He spends more time there than he spends time with his wife. Ask her, she is sitting there." His wife was all smiles that her identity was established that fast. All had a hearty laughter and Poojamma smiled at their sense of humor. She was used to and hailed from such a culture. More than three thousand years of unmitigated oppression and exploitation did not steal away the smile from the faces of these 'less than human' beings. Untouchability, atrocity, rape of women, deprivation of basic right even to live, robbery of their land, etc. nothing had deterred them from being happy and smiling. Unprecedented resilience!'

Nina was gaping open mouthed at the philosopher of sorts that was sitting in front of her. Kala took different shades at different times. The narrator was now a heady mixture of philosophy, psychology and spirituality. But her bigger strength seemed to be politics. Kala more or less guessed the meaning of the 'hard to come' smile on the face of Nina. With a sense of greater pride she continued her narration uninhibited.

'Murthy smiled a bit looking around at all the people gathered there and continued. There was an obvious pride in his smile. "Someone asked me why I was found very frequently in the Tahsildar's office. I told him a little about the story of our struggle for land in our village. He stopped me half way through and said that I should meet you first. You are the best person to deal with any issue related to land. He said that when you put your hand on an issue you would not stop till you succeeded. After seeing you I am convinced that what he said is true. There is an inner comfort in us that we shall achieve anything in the world if you are with us. Now we are all happy that we have found you, Amma". He was a bit emotional as he said this.'

'In order not to deviate the main focus of the struggle, Poojamma asked him to come to the point of their struggle for land. He continued. "In the year 1952 the then Revenue Minister came to our village and distributed 835 acres of land at the rate of 2 acres per family." Poojamma had a big question here. "Were you so many families in your village? Where are they now? I see only some of you."

"Ours was a big village, Amma. What could people do with only two acres of land? Many of our people sold their land and went away from our village looking for other means of making a living. Moreover, land was not distributed only to our village. It was given to all families in the surrounding villages too." Murthy clarified. He seemed to have answers for all types of questions at his fingertips.

"In the year 1978 the government came again to our village and redistributed the same land at the rate of four acres per family leaving out all those families that had emigrated to other areas in the meantime. A total of 720 acres were given to Dalits and 115 acres were given to caste people. The government made it into a formal grant in the year 1979. We were unable to cultivate all the land that was granted to us, as some caste people threatened us with violence. We have all necessary documents about the ownership of land. But actual possession of land has eluded us all this while as nobody is supporting us." His tone was almost like the lamentations of Jeremiah.'

"Oh, you know about Jeremiah too. How did you know of him?" Nina was taken aback with surprise at the way Kala had shaped in knowledge of all kinds. That she was able to draw out a parallel from the Old Testament of the Bible was almost shocking. The simili that she took was very appropriate.

'Oh, what do you think of me, Nina? I have been educated in the school of Poojamma. Every possible example is the subject matter of her teaching. An amazing woman and a true mother! I miss her very much.'

198

Saying this Kala broke down uncontrollably. Tears were flowing on her cheeks without any interruption. She started missing Poojamma at her young age. Nina rushed to her, grabbed her in her arms and held her tight to her chest. Two chests were prevented from meeting each other by four breasts.

"Why, did you not get support? We have many Dalit organizations here and did you not approach any of them for help?" Once again Poojamma asked a question for which she had the answer.

"Oh, they came, all of them came to our houses. They demanded that we made chicken curry for them. We also had to provide them with many bottles. That is all. They said that we had nothing to fear. They would take up our case and be with us till we got our land back. When the spirit gave way they forgot what they said to us. After they left us they were never to be seen anywhere. We lost the little money that we had as a heavy price for the trust we reposed on our leaders. Leave them alone Amma. We do not even want to speak of them any more. You are our only hope left. If you also do not help us we shall take poison together and die. We have no other option at the moment. Where shall we go to live, Amma?" Kariyajji wiped the tears off her eyes.

'There was a little silence for some time. Poojamma broke it in style. "Now tell me clearly what your problem is. I need to understand it clearly in order to arrive at a solution that will help you in the long run." She meant business. What she said instilled confidence in Murthy and he began to narrate the entire story with more hope.

"In the meantime caste people also have sold the land to many other landlords and they have managed to create false documents on the land that belong to us. Some caste people have even created false caste certificates that show them as Dalits and they have got land approved for them from the quota that belongs to us." Poojamma was furious when she heard this. She was biting her teeth and I could see her doing it. It was very unusual of her.'

"Did you inform the Tahsildar about the false caste certificates? He is the one to give caste certificates. How did his predecessors do that?" Poojamma asked in all her simplicity.

"Ha, ask that. He is the one who gives false caste certificates and how can we ask him?" Kariyajji intercepted.

"It is not easy any more Amma. In the meantime our land had gone into many hands and finally it has come to the hands of our MP, Dinesh. He is very powerful. We heard that you supported him in the last elections and he won only because of you. Now he has ordered all officers not to take up the question of our land seriously. No officer is willing to burn his fingers in this affair. Kariyajji blamed our Dalit leaders. But what can they do against a Member of Parliament? When they come to know the truth they back out of the struggle. They do not have courage to tell us that they cannot succeed in this case. They want us to believe that they are the alpha and omega of all solutions to Dalit problems. This is the situation Amma. We also heard that you do not care about any power when it comes to the question of justice. We have a firm hope that only you can resolve this issue in our favor." Murthy ended his introduction with a serious note of hope.'

'Poojamma had one full look on all the faces present there and noticed the residues of hope that Murthy splattered. She smiled at all of them. "This is a matter of serious concern. How much is the land that you need to recover from Dinesh?" She still had to come to grips with all intricacies of the issue.'

"The land that was given to Dalits in other villages are in safe hands. No one really tried to grab that land. Only in our village this has happened. Altogether we have to get back 406 acres of land. This is the land that was given to us in the re-grant in 1978 but we could not take possession of our land." Murthy placed before Poojamma the enormity of the issue. 406 acres of land in one village was the magic figure that she had to manage to recover.'

'Poojamma was in total shock that she supported a rascal like Dinesh in elections and made him win. She regretted her decision to support him. But she did not get bogged down with the thought that she made a mistake. Her determination to take serious action against Dinesh was unmistakable. She enquired of them further and discovered that he had even managed to make the government serve eviction notice to Dalit titleholders of the granted land.'

—∞❉∞—

'Murthy narrated further of what happened in previous years. When monsoon arrived three years ago one of our Dalit farmers went to plough his land. Immediately one of the caste fellows rushed towards him and began to beat him up. He made a big noise and his brother rushed to his help. Both of them were clobbered with big clubs that the caste women brought from their homes. Then the third brother rushed to the help of his brothers and was cut in all parts of his body with sickles and knives. Hearing their cries of pain the entire village of Dalits rushed to their help and that brought all the caste neighbors on the opposite side. Dalits are generally not prepared for physical warfare. Their big capital is their mouth. They speak a lot and challenge every power on earth. But when it comes to engaging the caste people in physical fight we always get back and begin to compromise. All of them gave up the fight and began to take stock of the situation in order to send their 'broken' brothers to the hospital for treatment.'

'News from the hospital was bad, really bad. Two of the brothers had died in the hospital. One of them died after a few days. Three lives lost among Dalits for the sake of claiming their legitimate right over their own land.'

"But did you not complain to police immediately. We never heard of such murders in newspapers, nor did anyone tell us anything about it. Three of you murdered! What did the police do?" Poojamma raised her fist of fury. But she could punch only in hot air, as did many Dalits she knew.'

"We went to the police to register an official complaint against the landlord's family. When we went to the police station we saw a person called Eeranna. Later we came to know that he is from this village. It seems that he and MP Dinesh are inseparable friends. The MP had sent him to the police station to support the caste people and the police refused to accept our complaint. They got a false doctor's certificate saying that our brothers died out of heart attack and blood pressure. We had no one to go for succor. We did not know you at that time." Poojamma was surprised that none of them cried, including wives of the three dead men while Murthy narrated the incident of murder. But later she guessed it correct that they had lost their ability to be emotional about such things that took place in their lives. If they became emotional it would be like the churning of an ocean. One required some supernatural strength to deal with consequences of such emotional churning. Having suffered so much in life their emotional cells in body had become completely numb. But it disturbed Poojamma a bit too much. The one thing that she could never tolerate in her life was people without any emotions.'

"Kala, are you also a psychologist? How did you learn all this? You seem to have a firm grip over things that you describe. I am so proud of you my girl." Nina was beside herself with positive energy.

'Whatever I have are the gifts of Poojamma. She has left a big inheritance for me. That is the level of knowledge that she has created in an ordinary girl like me. I should have become a child-producing machine by now. But Poojamma has given a purpose in my life that no ordinary human being can do.' Kala manifested her maturity once again.

"This is an issue that I shall die for. You have come to me trusting in me. Generally I do not promise the moon to anyone. Not because you have trusted in me but because this is a case of clear treachery and injustice. This is part of what has happened to our people from time immemorial. Land is the source of your sustenance in life. I shall stand with you in this struggle till you get back your land. Just as I promise to be with you, all of you also should promise to me that you would always stand together till you take your land back. Don't be overawed by the power of people who have grabbed your land." Poojamma made all of them to stand together in a circle, extend their hands towards Mother Earth and solemnly promise that they would stick together till the end of their struggle. She had another purpose for doing this. Since she found that they were low on emotions she created emotional situations so that they would slowly come back to their world of emotions.' Once again the psychologist in Kala stood up with legitimate pride.

'Next day there was a phone call from Eeranna to Poojamma. She was totally surprised to have received a call from him for the first time. He did not even wish her and started his business straightaway. "Hello, I heard from your own people that you are going to take up the land issue in Ramapura. This is unnecessary on your part to interfere in land issues of this district. We are the sons of soil here and we shall determine about our land. You do not belong to our State and you have nothing to decide on our land issues. It is the land of our leader Dinesh and we shall not allow a woman like you to interfere in his affairs. Be careful." Eeranna gave a stern warning to Poojamma and hung the phone without waiting for her to say anything. She had seen him several times walking in the streets of the village. But she could never talk to him, as he would always walk away from the direction she moved. She was grossly disappointed that she was unable to instill some sense in him. But he had a political sense the extent of which Poojamma could not grasp at all.'

CHAPTER THIRTEEN

Dinesh flew down from Delhi to Bangalore the next day as soon as he heard from Eeranna that the issue of land in Ramapura seemed to be unfolding in a totally unexpected direction. The decision of Poojamma to step into the struggle could spell a possible doom for the political duo. Something had to be done on a war scale. As soon as he landed in Bangalore he called up Eeranna to meet him in his residence. He also called up the Tahsildar and the police inspector for dinner at the Inspection Bungalow. This is the place where Dinesh used to have all his political subterfuge. He did not want his wife and children to know of what he was planning in politics. If they came to know, he was afraid that they might be the first ones to spit on his face.

At the Bangalore airport he carefully packed some liquor bottles in his luggage and headed to the Inspection Bungalow. He called up his wife to inform her that he would be home only to sleep with her that night. The four of them had a few rounds of drinks and sumptuous meal brought from nearby restaurant by the police inspector. Dinesh informed all others of the impending danger to his land. But more dangerous was the reputation he would suffer if Poojamma were to take up the issue. If she were involved, the issue would get media attention. Just when he had become MP for the first time he did not want too much of a negative publicity on land scams. Eeranna said he was furious when he heard of the meeting people of Ramapura had with Poojamma and was boasting that he had abused her over phone. To his utter dismay Dinesh chastised him rather salaciously. Being bad mouthed to a respectable woman like her was not in the best interest of a MP. Tomorrow if people heard of it they would only lose their respect for him. He advised him that he should know how to deal with every individual and not apply universal principles of abuse and vilification on all. "There are some people who should not even be allowed to guess on what is in our mind." He told Eeranna rather seriously.

'Early morning of the next day there was a call from Dinesh to Poojamma. He mentioned to her that the case of land in Ramapura had nothing to do with him. "But you own the land in Ramapura and these were originally given to Dalits. You should give the land back to the people to whom the land was originally granted by the government." Poojamma was strong in her interjection.

"Yes Madam! Do you think I am such a stupid man as to grab the land of Dalit people? I own only 10 acres of land in that area, Madam. All other land belong to different other people. If anyone has grabbed land from Dalit people I shall join hands with you to fight the case. You take care Madam. The fellows in that area are not good. If you need any support please let me know Madam." Dinesh proved that it was not for nothing that he became a Member of the Parliament. Poojamma did not loose the message of threat that he stuffed in his very outgoing support.

"No, this is not true. You are the owner of all the land that has been grabbed from poor Dalits of that village. You may have only ten acres registered in your name. But all other land in that area are yours with proxy owners. As an elected member it is your duty to return the land that you have grabbed from them illegally. Already these people are landless in this country. 90% of them in this country are landless people. To further deprive them of the little land that they own is very uncivilized on your part. Please give back the land to my people." Poojamma was not a politician. She knew only one way of speaking and that was straight.'

'Now Dinesh changed his tone of speech. He spoke from his deep throat. "Madam, you are making many unfounded allegations against me. You should check records before throwing all sorts of accusations against me. This is also not the way you speak to an elected member of the Parliament. You dare to call me uncivilized. Please keep your respect for elected members. I shall come and meet you Madam, and explain everything to you. Till then please do not rush into any action. I have to say this in your own best interest Madam." It was very difficult to make out if he was speaking kindly, or if he was giving a stern warning to Poojamma. She said 'bye' to him and terminated the conversation.'

⋯∘❉∘⋯

'Chikkanna called out to Poojamma from the door. He used to enter the house without waiting for her permission. But since he heard Poojamma talking over phone he was a bit cautious and called out only when he was sure that the conversation was over. His voice sounded like an alarm bell. Poojamma rushed out to see what had happened to him. He was perspiring and panting and informed her that Murthy had been badly beaten up by some thugs and that he was fighting for his life in the government hospital. Poojamma did not expect this turn of things this fast. She took him into the house and offered him water and tea. She called Nagaraj and explained the situation to him. Nagaraj almost flew into the house in no time.' Kala could dramatize her narration of events beautifully well.

"Oh, things went this far. I did not know anything of this." Nina was completely flabbergasted at what seemed to have transpired.

'There is much more than this to our struggle. Just wait till I complete without getting shocked. Our politicians are rare breeds of animals. I am sure it is the same in your country. I don't think political class is different from country to country. But our politicians are supermen and no other country can match ours.' Kala now manifested another character trait in her. She also was adept at explaining the intricacies of politics and politicians.

'As soon as Nagaraj arrived Poojamma started off to the hospital to see the situation of Murthy. She took the other two along with her. When Poojamma reached the hospital some of the nurses came out and greeted her. They took her to the ward where Murthy was admitted. They knew instinctively whom she had come to see. By then Murthy had become the talk of the hospital. When Poojamma reached the ward the police inspector was questioning Murthy left and right. He was a different inspector whose jurisdiction was different from her area. However, as soon as he saw her he stood up and saluted her.'

"Why don't you leave him alone for some time? He has been wounded badly and needs a lot of rest. Did not doctors tell you that he should not be disturbed? Please come after he recovers fully and make your enquiries." Poojamma touched Murthy with all affection that welled up in her heart and that was much soothing to him.'

"Madam, I am just doing my duty. I am a government servant and you are only a private person. You cannot interfere in my performance of duty. Please check with the doctor if Murthy is able to answer my questions or not. I cannot be accountable to every person who comes to the hospital. I have to take legal action against all culprits. I hope you understand basic principles of the functioning of police department." 'The inspector started with an inexplicable anger and concluded with a sarcasm that hovered with bureaucratic arrogance.'

'Gangaiah became furious beyond his control at the way the inspector spoke to Poojamma with disrespect. He protested spontaneously without any hesitation. He asked him to respect her at least for her age and speak to her.'

"You, bloody assholes, who are you to tell me how I should speak and behave. You motherfuckers, do you know how to respect a police inspector. First you asslickers learn that and then come and tell me what I should do. You have no bloody business to tell me how I should behave. If you cross your limits I shall have to arrest you fellows and put you behind bars." The inspector was firing on all cylinders. The way he used his words without discretion in front of a woman invited the wrath of Poojamma.

"Mind your words, inspector. Yes, we are no one to tell you how you should speak and behave. But you should know what type of words you should use in front of a woman. Don't let your tongue swirl much unnecessarily. Let me see how you will arrest them." She turned to Gangaiah and said with perceivable anger: "Gangaiah, you go to the office of the Deputy Superintendent of Police and file a complaint against this inspector under the SC/ST Prevention of Atrocities Act of 1989. Chikkanna and Nagaraj, both of you are the witness that this inspector made verbal abuse of a Dalit person against the law of the land. Remember all the abusive words that he used and give a written complaint. After filing the complaint you call me and I shall speak to the SP."

The inspector was literally sweating in his ass and they could see both his legs shivering more near his ass. He realized the serious mistake he made by using a foul language against Dalits. Indian law did not allow this and he also realized his underestimation of the sharp wits of Poojamma. Liquor and money provided by Dinesh had blinded his normal sense. He thought that women had only limited intelligence and now he was face to face with a highly superior intelligence that worked faster than all his police training and arrogance put together. In an attempt to redeem himself, he apologized profusely to Poojamma for his mistake and requested her to forgive him promising simultaneously that he would not repeat the mistake any more. By then Chikkanna and Nagaraj had rushed fast to the door of the ward. The inspector knew instantly that Poojamma meant business. As soon as he apologized she recalled both of them and asked Gangaiah to forgive him. "He is still a young mare and is jumping all over the place. He will become wiser soon. Let us have some patience and forgiveness." Poojamma took back her own anger and became her usual self. She also winked her eyes to them and communicated adroitly that the inspector was only a pawn in the hands of Dinesh. One more sculpture rubbed on all edges and chiselled into a beautiful shape!

———◦◦◦❏◦◦◦———

'Murthy watched the entire drama in a state of daze and pleasant surprise. He did not know that Poojamma could get angry. Before that he did not anticipate such a big woman to pay him a personal visit as soon as she heard of what happened to him. Many of his brothers and sisters were ill treated and beaten up several times earlier. He had seen the worst in his life. There would be no one to say a soothing word to victims of injustice. They had to languish all alone till they were discharged from hospitals. Dalit leaders came when everything was almost over and would promise the heavens. Rhetoric, the bane of Dalit liberation! Here was a person who met him only once before and there she was to console him and be a solid rock of support to him and his people. He remembered that Poojamma had promised to remain with them till the end of the struggle and she started paving the way with beautiful rose petals. He began to stroll in that path.'

'He had no business to work so hard for the recovery of land for his people. All his paths were strewn with thorns and sharpened stones that pierced every step of his. Now for the first time in his life he saw himself walking the path of rose petals. He worked hard for all his people without due returns but he himself did not have a piece of land. None of his relatives ever bothered about giving him a part of their land. There was nothing much that they could part with. There were times when Murthy used to let tears flow from his eyes secretly. He did not want any of his people to know his inner tribulation. Some of them used to go to his house when he was alone and abuse him for being slow in getting their land back. The worst among them even suspected him to be in league with Dinesh and Eeranna. No amount of his explanations about difficulties involved would convince them. All that they could think of was their land and nothing else. If they did not have a little bit of land their horizon would become completely dark. There was no meaning in their life without land. Much worse! There were times when they used to accuse him of joining hands with dominant castes for the sake of getting some money and food from them. The ultimate humiliation that he suffered in his life! He never let any of these to dampen his spirit. He knew for sure that if he let his spirit down that would spell the ultimate doom for his people. He was that lonely log of wood that was floating in a big flood and storm. All his people were almost drowning and were looking out for that one piece of wood that could save them from the fury of nature. He knew he was that one log of wood to take his people to the shore. Even as the powerful current of waters were taking him away in directions that he could not determine he found himself stuck against the roots of a big tree. He saw the tree standing solid on the banks of the river and did not want any more to be carried away by the flow of water.'

"You are smiling even in the midst of so much of pain?" 'Poojamma asked him as he directed both his eyes in her direction. She did not want to disturb him and therefore, postponed asking for any detail. She asked Chikkanna and Nagaraj to provide Murthy with all his needs and medicines and stationed Nagaraj in the hospital to be with Murthy and his relatives till he was discharged from the hospital. He asked Gangaiah to stay in the hospital even at night and watch if people were still preparing to attack him in the hospital. It took three days for Murthy to recover and be discharged from hospital. In the meantime there was a tangible change in the attitude of the inspector. He had refused to register a complaint in the beginning days. After coming to know the real stuff of Poojamma and her followers he registered a case of attempt to murder and atrocity under the SC/ST Prevention of Atrocity Act of 1989 and handed over investigation to the Deputy SP.'

After three days of dithering the police department came out with the truth that three thugs commissioned by Eeranna had waylaid Murthy and attacked him with lethal weapons. Getting hit seriously on his head he tried to run initially but spotted some of his relatives from neighboring village coming at a distance. He stood back with blood oozing from his head and faced the thugs screaming aloud simultaneously. He also took some stones from the sideways of the road and began to throw them at the thugs. Hearing his loud cry his relatives ran towards him and the thugs took to their heels when they saw a big crowd. One of the relatives caught hold of the slower one and tore his shirt. A piece of the shirt came torn and opted to say in his hand. During the police enquiry by the Deputy SP the piece of cloth was handed over to him. In the meantime the SP had come to know that it was a case taken up by Poojamma and that was the immediate provocation for the attack on Murthy. They had done much harm to him before running away. Murthy had a deep gash below his throat and in his palms as he tried to resist the dagger. The SP gave strict instructions to his Deputy to be completely impartial in his inquiry.

Even as the SP was talking to his Deputy there was a call from Dinesh. He took up the phone and without any greeting Dinesh started blasting off about Poojamma and complained to him that the entire incident of the attack on Murthy was because of Poojamma poking her nose unnecessarily into affairs that had nothing to do with her. She was provoking people and was disturbing peace in the district. It was a stereotype that he indulged in. But he also instructed the SP not to register any case against his followers as none of them was involved in this attack. He requested the SP to just file some namesake report and close the file. The SP told him in plain terms that he would proceed according to law. "I am the legitimately elected member of the Parliament. You should obey my orders and not act on behalf of some private individuals. I say, close the case without proceeding further." He commanded and hung. The SP looked at his Deputy who had a broad smile on his face knowing exactly what was happening there. "Do not worry Sir. I know these scoundrels and their ways. Let us wait and fix them when we have a chance. Till then I shall do what is appropriate" He saluted his superior and left the office.

Chikkanna and Nagaraj spread themselves out into that area in the evening and found themselves in liquor shops in the surrounding villages. They even bought liquor for potential informants with their own money and provoked them into loose talking. As the beans were spilt they collected all of them and put them together in front of Poojamma. The village people were highly defensive of their boys from their villages. It was easy for Poojamma to rule out the involvement of local thugs in the attack on Murthy. All other circumstantial indicators led to her own village. As things began to fall in their places it became evident to all of them that the hiring of thugs was done by none other than Eeranna.

The SP was very happy when followers of Poojamma produced the results of their private investigation to him. He immediately called his deputy to his room and presented all the evidence that were on his table. The Deputy SP agreed that the evidence collected by Poojamma's followers was very true. He informed the SP that he corroborated their version with that of the intelligence report of the department and the piece of cloth that one of the thugs had left behind in the hands of the relative of Murthy. The police went to the shops that sold that type of cloth. It led them to the headquarters of the neighboring Taluk. They further moved carefully to freeze on the tailor who stitched shirts with that type of cloth. Finally they identified the tailor who stitched the shirt and found from his register the name and body measurements of the guy who gave the cloth. Things became much easier from that point of time. They arrested him and asked him to puke out the entire truth. He first refused to tell the truth thus inviting 'police methods' of investigation. He was put on a flight in 'aeroplane' and was treated to a sumptuous journey into unknown destination. When he came to his senses he realized that he had puked out all the truth that he had refused earlier. He was unable to eat his word back.'

'It was too late for Eeranna. The gang of three hired by him was in the firm grip of police. He ran from pillar to post making use of his close association with Dinesh who tried his level best to get Eeranna out of the mess. He called up the SP once again and was told in no unclear terms that only the Home Minister of the State could give any direct command to the SP. It was also made clear that the SP would not budge in to any silly politician against implementation of the law of the land. Dinesh tried to move heaven and earth to prevent Eeranna from going to jail but the SP stood firm like a solid earthly rock. Eeranna cooled his heel in jail for two weeks and Dinesh licked his wound unendingly.'

'People of Ramapura, especially Murthy were extremely happy that they rested their heads on the lap of this mother, Poojamma. The depression that enveloped them for years together and made them totally unemotional to the realities of life now began to melt and they started to celebrate their future with reasonable hope. They rushed to Poojamma's place to pour their gratitude in her presence. Chikkanna and Nagaraj were happy that a sweet revenge was taken and that Poojamma had at last realized the true color of Dinesh. They had been warning her of this but she followed her intuitive wisdom.'

'Poojamma did quite a bit of damage control. She talked to all people and commissioned Chikkanna and Nagaraj to collect all relevant documents. She brought Manjula to support them in documenting systematically what they were able to put their hands on. At every stage of their mission they had to face huge roadblocks. In the office of the Tahsildar everyone had just one word in his mouth, "not available". Some others said, "We don't know where it is." Often they were shunted from one table to another, from one caseworker to another. Frequently they returned empty handed at the end of the day. The trinity of Chikkanna, Nagaraj and Manjula now came up with another problem that looked almost insurmountable.

'The Tahsildar himself was in league with Dinesh and had changed all documents in his office to favor him. They also found out that much of the land owned by Dinesh was registered in the name of proxy owners substantiating the earlier argument of Poojamma's with Dinesh.'

'Now tell me what is land owned by proxy owners? I am sure you know all these details now. You are an amazing girl. There seems to be nothing that you do not know.' Nina asked a question and simultaneously complimented Kala.

'When someone actually owns something but it is registered in the name of someone else, it is called ownership by proxy or benami land. Benami is one who is a virtual owner but knows that he does not actually own the land. This is how most landlords in India own land. In many States of India there are land reform measures that do not allow individuals to own too much of land. Benami ownership is the way landlords hoodwink the system and the government. You will be shocked to know that there is a god in Orissa in the name of Lord Jagannath. He owns 96,000 acres of land. Can you imagine in your country land being registered in the name of Jesus Christ? But in our country this is possible . . .'

Nina interrupted her rather violently. "Do you mean to say that land is actually registered in the name of god? But he does not exist in body. How can a legal system accept a person who does not exist in a body? Do gods also come under human legal system? How is this possible? I cannot stretch my imagination to this level. It just looks like a grand fiction." Her body was almost shivering when she said this.

'In India everything is possible. For all wrong things that we do we always take the easy excuse that India is a very special country different from all other countries in the world. We take pride in the false assertion that India is unique. Even big fellows who get Nobel Prize will camouflage the rottenness within India by writing books on India's inability to eradicate caste discrimination under the assertion that Indians are argumentative. The argument that there is space for argumentation in India is the height of exalted haughtiness. We have had High Court judgments that have officially given land in the name of this Lord Jagannath. There is also one Movement in India that was started to take excess land from the rich as gifts and distribute such land to the poor. But at the end of the day we know that this Movement itself owns 56,000 acres of land just in one state. This is once again in the State of Orissa where poverty is quite high and there are a lot of indigenous peoples who worship Earth as their Mother. This is the irony of India.' Kala now surpassed all adulations of Nina. She not only was in grip with the realities that Poojamma dealt with but was also now highly informed on many data that concerned India. An amazing product of Nina's most admired woman on earth, Poojamma!

—∘∘❁∘∘—

'Now let us come back to our story of Ramapura.' Kala was dot on her task and continued. 'Where did I leave? Ah yes, we started our deviation with benami land. That is also a deviatory path in land ownership. Dinesh had taken recourse to this path, as he was sure that one day or other in future he would have to face this problem. The foresight of a politician was like his memory of defeat. Even on his deathbed a politician would avenge his defeat. This is the way politicians psyche was constructed.'

'I am sure Poojamma invented some way of overcoming this problem too. I don't think there was any roadblock that she was unable to remove from her path. What did she invent in this case?' Nina mildly provoked Kala to continue seriously.

'Poojamma was ingenious, as always. She brought an officer from the government in Bangalore to give training on the Right to Information Act. She did not mention to him anything about the problems that people faced in Ramapura. The officer came only as a resource person for intellectual input on RTI. This was a very powerful tool in the hands of the poor to get to roots of many government documents. Actually land mafia, liquor mafia and mining mafia are terribly horrified by this Act. They have murdered many activists in the field of RTI. Immediately after the training she called the trinity and asked them to make the best use of the Right to Information Act and dig out all the land documents of Ramapura from 1952. It was a landmine in her hands. She knew how to fiddle with that. The trinity was inexplicably happy about their achievement when they finally saw the big bundle of documents that they were able to get hold of.' The multifaceted personality of Kala's now began to spread like the tentacles of a giant octopus and get hold of Nina into its firm grip.

'Armed with all documents in her hands Poojamma called up two eminent lawyers, one from the local court and another from the High Court in Bangalore and entrusted them with the task of filing an unassailable case in the High Court. The lawyers took up the case and as soon as the court admitted the case they also made it a point to give news in the media. That was enough to send emotions of Dinesh to the limbo. His disciple Eeranna had jumped bail in the meantime and was back in the village.

Both of them now had to scurry around the entire world to do a crisis management. Their crisis in the form of Poojamma took the shape of a giant wheel and began to taunt them endlessly.'

'Being in jitters about the admission of the case in High Court, Dinesh wanted to make sure that the land would not leave his hand by a stay order of the court. He knew well that if the court granted a stay order it would say that status quo must be maintained. In order to be on the winning side in the eventuality of the court granting a stay order he gathered his forces and in one night put up barbed wire fence to 40 acres of land. He executed his nefarious design in the thick of night. Early next morning, Murthy literally ran to Poojamma to inform her that within one night Dinesh had erected barbed wire fence around 40 acres of land. She told him not to get disturbed about it. This act of Dinesh was illegal and it would only go against him in the course of time.'

'Before Murthy left her place Poojamma called up Chikkanna and Nagaraj and informed them of the latest development in their struggle. She formed them into a formal team. In order to strike a gender balance she also included Manjula in the team. They evolved a clear strategy to be executed by the four of them. They also decided to speak step by step about their strategy a bit loosely in the villages.'

'The next day, they went as a team to the Collector and informed him that Dinesh had set up barbed wire fence. They made their point clear that it was an illegal measure. He could not do that, as the case was sub-judice. He had no business to put up a fence around any part of land till the High Court handed out its judgment. It was preposterous on his part to take law in his hand. They requested the Collector to either make Dinesh remove the fence or the government should do it. They gave one month's time to the Collector. They also made it crystal clear to the Collector that if he failed to do that in a month's time they would remove the fence. That was almost like a threat. The Collector smiled broadly at them and send them off.'

'They repeated the same with the Superintendent of Police on the morrow. The SP told them clearly that it was not the direct responsibility of police department. It was revenue department that had to do such things. However, if the team managed to get the Collector to do it and needed any protection from police he would be very happy to cooperate. His response was very professional.'

—◦◦❧◦◦—

'It was then that Poojamma set out to prove her true mettle, the stuff that she was made of deep inside. She called up Dinesh and asked him for an appointment to meet him personally. He granted an appointment without asking any question. He knew it was about the land. But he wanted to know the mind of Poojamma in order to design his counter moves. Pretending to be very friendly he had prepared an elaborate tea for her and her accomplices. He knew all of them almost by name and wished them. Only Chikkanna did not respond well to him. He also refused to take his share of the cake and tea that were laid on the table for all. Sipping her tea slowly Poojamma opened up the topic.'

"I do not play ball games with you Poojamma. I have great respect for you and will do with my head what you order with your foot." 'This was a oblique reference to Chikkanna who had earlier challenged him to go to Poojamma's village if he had balls.'

"Mr. Dinesh, why were you in such a hurry to put up barbed wire fence to such a huge stretch of land that legitimately belongs to the people of Ramapura? You have done it in one night so that poor people of the area might not have any chance either to get a stay order from the court or complain to the Collector and stop the work" 'Poojamma's words pierced him like that small tip of a needle that cuts glass. Dinesh knew that Poojamma had already collected all possible documents through RTI and understood the futility of any arguments with her.'

His response was highly calculatedly mild. "I was not here at all, Madam. I was in Delhi. It must have been some of my followers who must have done this work. I myself have not seen the fence till now. I shall ask them as to why they did this. But you people do not worry about anything. If the judgment of the High Court is in your favor I shall remove the fence and give the land back to you. I have no problem with that. But you must understand that I have bought all these land by paying my personal money. Let us in any case wait for the Courts." The seasoned politician in him slowly came out with all its hidden evil power.

"Mr. Dinesh, it is about this that we have come to speak to you. The case is registered in the court and has already come up for hearing. Just at that time you have erected barbed wire fence in order to prevent our people from entering their own land. This is not allowed in law. You cannot do any such activity when the case is sub-judice. Please ask your chamchas (followers) to remove the fence. We give you a period of one month to do this. If you do not remove the fence within a month we shall remove it." 'Dinesh was stung in his ass. He understood that this woman meant serious business and she spoke only business. She meant what she said. There was no compromise on that. There was no point in getting angry with her. He was afraid that he might give out some of his secret plans in a fit of rage.'

"Oh Poojamma, you don't have to be so angry and strict with me. I am your friend . . ."

Before he could complete his sentence Chikkanna interrupted and said, "Yes, yes, you are our great friend. That is why you have not yet acknowledged the fact that you won with the support of our Poojamma. You owe a word of thanks to her for making you win." He stuffed his abrupt intervention with sarcasm.

Dinesh was taken aback but quickly recovered. "There are other followers of mine who have also worked for my victory. It is not only you people. No doubt that you have given your votes to me . . . I shall ask my people to remove the fence within a month as you have told me Madam. Please do not worry. Take my word, Madam." He put his fingers on his tongue and showed it to Poojamma.

"Why did he show his tongue to Poojamma? What was the meaning of that?" Nina could not take anything for granted. She was detail perfectionist.

'You must be happy that he did not show his bloody cock to Poojamma. In India we show our tongue with our fingers pointing out to it to tell people that we respect our words and will not fail once the word has come out from our tongue. This is the value that people attach to word of mouth. It is more important than money and wealth.' Kala, the culture scientist explicated a complicated mechanism of India in her very angry mood. She became a burning furnace especially when she spoke of the evil ways of Dinesh and Eeranna.

"Why are you so angry with Eeranna? I can understand your anger against Dinesh. But Eeranna is from your own village. One day or other will you not feel the need to meet him and talk to him." Nina simply wanted to provoke Kala after she saw her being vehemently angry.

'The fucking bastard is even a distant relative of mine. That is why I am so angry with him. He is such a fucking shame on our entire clan.' Kala became even angrier and Nina enjoyed it much.

CHAPTER FOURTEEN

'One month passed. No movement towards the poor and landless! The fence remained in its place and stared at all Dalits whom it had evicted illegally. Dalits were staring at it with a deep longing that it would uproot itself to another world so that they could have the fruits of their labor in their land. Their future was gaping at them with derision and sarcastic laughter. Poojamma advised patience to all the people of Ramapura.'

"We are a people who cannot be cowed down by threats of exploitation. For more than three thousand years caste forces in this country have perpetuated unmitigated violence on our beautiful self and have constantly deprived us of our dignity and rights. Any other people in the world would have been decimated totally if such a thing happened to them. But we are a strong people who have resilience as our armor. This is the path our Mothers have shown to us. Let us not lose sight of it under any impulse." 'People not only saw sense in what she said but also became more determined to win their battle through peaceful means. They knew in their inner being that they were not made for violence. Being the children of Mother Earth they were naturally peace-loving people. But how could peace be maintained if Dinesh did not remove the fence?'

'The strategy meeting of Poojamma's team had a turbulent discussion. Many wanted to barge into the land, break the fence and occupy their land. Chikkanna and Nagaraj saw sense in the advise of Poojamma that they should wait for one more month. In the meantime they should go and talk to the Collector personally reminding of the need for removing the fence. This was done in right earnest. The Collector only said that he would do it soon with his enigmatic smile. The second month also passed without any eventuality.'

'In the meantime the High Court had adjourned hearing of the case twice and the people were hopeful that it would come for hearing sooner than later. At the end of the second month the same dynamics of furor and patience continued. Poojamma gave only her Delphic look as return for those who advocated strong action. The third month also was about to end without any action being taken from any side. The SP and his deputy had a serious discussion on possible action and consequences. "It is a matter for the revenue department and not at all a matter for our department. If the revenue department asks us to provide our force for any action that they are taking we shall then consider their request on its merit." The SP was firm and professional in his decision though he knew that Poojamma was right in her strategizing. For Poojamma herself, the elliptical silence of the Collector was a loud paradox of sorts.'

'News reached Poojamma's ears that Eeranna was boasting in all villages that she and her cronies could not touch even one pubic hair of Dinesh's. He was a Member of the Parliament and what was Poojamma. After all she was only a female from a different region. He dared her to remove the fence if she had any guts. He even questioned her physical ability to remove one stone pillar in those 40 acres of land.'

'When there was exactly one more day for the end of the deadline of another month, Poojamma invited all leaders of the area and made them discuss appropriate strategy for action. Knowing that she was a very resilient woman and expecting her to advise another month of patience, many of them said that it would be wiser to meet the Collector and ask him for strong action to remove the fence. That almost made Poojamma's blood boil.'

"There is a limit to our patience. We shall maintain patience only till it remains our strength. When we clearly see that our patience is taken as our weakness we must know that it is high time to strike. Peace does not mean that we need to accept a subjugated existence according to the terms and conditions of those who want to dominate over us. Peace would necessarily imply a respect for our dignity and equality. Dominant forces do not gift peace to us. We need to struggle and gain it. Peace has to be gained by us. It has to be negotiated on our terms. We need to establish a negotiated peace. When we stand strong on our dignity and rights and make the best use of the constitution of our country, caste forces are bound to come to negotiating table. If law began to work in our country caste forces would have to run for cover. It is time that we show to all people concerned how strong we are. Be ready for some action packed day." This was the bedrock of Poojamma.

"Wow, wow, what a woman! If only the world had ten women like this it will rid itself of all problems that it faces today. I simply love this woman and I miss her very badly, Kala." Nina began to shed tears. Seeing her, Kala too began to cry aloud and both of them embraced each other.

'Poojamma took Chikkanna, Nagaraj and Manjula aside and instructed them to gather about a hundred people for strong action that evening. Murthy was informed to keep all people of Ramapura in the village that evening. Chikkanna clearly instructed him not to let the cat out of the bag. But Murthy did not have an inkling of the cat in the bag. However, he made a wild guess that there was going to be some collective action in the evening. Chikkanna's caution provoked him to inform some of his trusted friends in the neighboring village to be alert for rapid action that evening.'

'On Poojamma's instruction Nagaraj hired two big vehicles and transported about one hundred people. When they arrived in Ramapura, it was beginning to be dark. To their utter surprise they found another 200 people already waiting for them in the village. Murthy made a casual explanation to Chikkanna that he informed his close friends to come in the evening but they made it a big news and brought all the people for support. All those assembled asked in unison if Poojamma did not come. "We thought Poojamma was coming this evening. That is why all of us came here." They gave a lame excuse.'

'When it was dark enough in the evening all three hundred of them moved to the land adjacent to the village and started removing the fence. Chikkanna and Nagaraj had instructed them that there should be no noise made while doing it. But it was not in complete silence that such a historic operation was executed. Looking at their number people of Ramapura and its surroundings thought that it was unnecessary not to make noise. They arrived at the frame of mind when their mind cared a damn about what would happen. All of them were like starved bulls let loose on a field of fresh grass. They broke the stone pillars of the fence one by one. When all the stone pillars became crumbles of boulders there was a big pile of barbed wires.'

'Chikkanna called up Poojamma and told him with palpable pride that the fence set up by Dinesh was demolished. The operation was completed in breakneck speed. He wanted to find out what he should do with the barbed wires. "Give them to the people of Ramapura and ask them to sell the wires and make some money. It is a way of small compensation for the loss they have suffered till now." He was at a loss to perceive the audacity of Poojamma. "Can a woman be so strong?' the question flashed across his mind.'

—∞∙⦿∙∞—

'News reached Dinesh who was in Delhi on that day. Poojamma had made sure that the operation would take place on a day he was not in the district. Dinesh frantically called Eeranna to find out what really was happening and asked him to also take some people and beat up the bloody villagers. But Eeranna pleaded helplessness as it was already dark and that he would not be able to mobilize necessary number of people to face three hundred frenzied men. The Collector very easily shifted blame on the SP saying that it was his duty to maintain law and order and he as Collector could not do much. The Collector also made it clear that it was his mistake in the first place to have erected the fence when the matter was in court. The SP made it clear that it was a matter that pertained to revenue department and that he would take any action that the Collector asked him to take. Dinesh was furious at their ball game. It was like a strong game of ping-pong. Hardly ever did he know that the Collector and SP had decided to support Poojamma in the event of she taking any direct action. Indifference was a strong support. No legal action was taken. Both of them instructed the Member of the Parliament to approach the courts to resolve the issue.'

'The news that no police action was taken against the breaking of the fence set up by a member of the parliament spread like wild fire to every nook and corner of the district. "Oh, she must be a very powerful

woman. Otherwise how will she dare to do such a thing against a MP?"
When Poojamma heard that this was what people were saying she said,
"My power is my people. I have no influence and I have no other power
except the power that I have derived from you people. If you were not at
my side I would fall like ninepin."

'Dinesh was receiving blow after blow. But he put up a stoic face in
the face of adversities. He called for a press-meet and explained to the
media how innocent he was. The next day newspapers carried news that
Poojamma was creating unnecessary trouble against an elected member.
She was instigating the people who otherwise had great respect for
Dinesh as their leader. However, it was not lost on the people that it was
Poojamma who made him win the elections despite all the trouble he
created for her. Eeranna and Dinesh began to meet more often and have
their fun. "Our Anna Dinesh has such a lot of power and influence in
Delhi. How can this woman win over him on this issue of land? Let us see
finally who wins. If our Anna wants he can destroy that bloody woman in
no time. It is because of his goodness that she still survives." He went
about blurting all over.'

'On the other side of the world the poor were exuberant about the news
that when the fence were dismantled, Poojamma herself led the operation
from front. She did not want any untoward incident to take place. She
knew her people better. In their ebullience they might do anything on the
spur of the moment. There was very little time to think at such times of
success. There had to be someone who could think for all others at such
occasions. If some violence took place Poojamma wanted to be the first
one to receive blows. She was very protective of her people. It came very
naturally to her. She knew the people of Ramapura only in the recent past
but it did not matter at all.'

"Yes, yes. I know Poojamma well on this score. She was very intelligent
and had sharp wits. But when it came to empowering her people she did
not get into any calculation at all. An amazing character she was." Nina
supplemented Kala's narration.

'Dinesh sought assistance from many of his colleagues among elected members. They laughed at him when they heard that he was struggling hard against a woman. They stopped laughing at him only when he informed them that he owed his victory to her in terms of votes. They advised him to circumvent a situation wherein he would be able to gain confidence of the people by stirring up their emotions. "This is the first and foremost mantra of political success." Anand MP roared. "Do not allow voters to think. The biggest risk we run is to have a bunch of thinking voters. In my constituency there are some people who are capable of thinking. I somehow see that they do not come for voting on election days."

"But how do you prevent educated people from coming for voting? If only I knew this mantra I shall be always successful in elections. Pushing ordinary illiterate masses into an emotive situation is not at all difficult for me. But pulling the educated fellows away from polling booths is the most difficult situation. We have to use violence. But then it may work in reverse among educated fellows." Sharma MP was quite serious in his explorations on winning ways.

"You agree that it is all that you know about politics. That is why you are still a teetotaler. What else can you do without smoking and drinking? I am sure you do not touch women other than your wife. This is not the way to play politics man. Do you think that we can win elections by following the principles of that old goon Gandhi? He himself did not contest any elections, you know. He knew well that people loved him much but when it came to obtaining their votes it was a different ball game altogether. The old goose did not want to lose an election." Anand gave it back to Sharma on his own platter.

"Now, stop abusing Gandhi and come to the point. Dinesh is in dire need of some suggestions against this bloody woman. What winning ways will you suggest to him?" Sharma MP challenged him.

"Hey Dinesh, tell me about all the festivals in your area that Dalits are celebrating . . ."

Before Anand could finish his question Sharma interrupted him and asked, "Why Dalits only? Are not other people voters? Do they not celebrate festivals?" he asked.

"This is why you are such a stupid politician. If Dinesh follows your way of thinking he can forget about coming to the Parliament again. We gain power to retain it and not to lose it. Do you know that Dalits are the single largest vote banks in India? We have scattered them so well all over the country that they cannot win any seat on their own but they can make every candidate a winning candidate. Those who do not know how to cash in on Dalit votes are political idiots. Ok now, let us come to Dinesh. Tell me what is the festival that Dalits largely celebrate in your State." The clever MP Anand began to pave a solid way for the future of Dinesh without Poojamma.

"They celebrate the festival of Maramma in Karnataka. Actually this festival is the clever invention of our caste people. They have made it a grand festival of Dalits simultaneously by offering a free buffalo on this occasion. The buffalo is given free to Dalits already in pre-monsoon period. They have to rear it for one year and they can have all the meat for free among themselves. The buffalo is sacrificed in that festival. All Dalits wait for this festival in order to have a sumptuous meal of buffalo meat." Dinesh half explained the significance of the festival to Anand.

"Yes, there you are. Very good festival! Two mangoes in one stone! You have a festival that both the caste people and Dalits celebrate. Call together all your caste agents and instruct them to promote this festival. You offer them the buffalo. Offer a good buffalo. You make your followers print pamphlets and distribute all over the district. Everybody should begin to think that you are a very generous person and Dalits should think that you love them. This should be your focus. They must think that you are giving them buffalo because of your tremendous love for them. You will be able to wean Dalits slowly away from that bloody bitch. What is her name? . . . ya, Poojamma. Make a good pooja for your Poojamma . . ." He laughed loud for a few minutes and all others joined him in the laughter reluctantly.

"Do not say anything bad about that woman. Just ignore her. You only keep on making Dalits emotionally attached to you. They do not care about their long-term benefits. You know it well. Therefore, fill them with short term attractions, especially food." Anand laughed again.

"There is no wonder that you have been elected for three consecutive terms to the Parliament. You are a wonder politician. But tell me now how to get rid of educated voters on the day of elections. They should not come to cast their votes. We shall find other voters to cast proxy votes in their name." Sharma now seemed to drift from his Gandhian way. He did not mind it. Winning in elections was more important than Gandhi.

"That is a long drawn out strategy at the national level. You cannot just do it only in your constituency. You must know that the educated and the elite class in India are in constant communication. They also have faster communication technology. Therefore, you cannot isolate this class in your constituency and evolve a strategy for them. It will be counterproductive if you do that. This is already being done through media at the national level. Just look at the type of news that fills newspapers. Do you think educated persons will be interested in such a thing called election? We created an illusion in them that we are all scoundrels and that nothing good can from our tribe. They are the first fellows to lose faith in democracy if we behave the way we do in Parliament. They are very weak fellows. They get fat salaries and can afford to get disillusioned with democracy and governance. They will not lift a finger to restore democracy and governance in the country. Theirs is a sort of bookworm patriotism. What do they lose if they do not vote? The government and educational institutions ensure their basic security in life. You have to only further plough through their psyche by showing yourself as a jackass and rotten politician. The poor must love you because of generous gifts you dole out to them in their times of need. The rich must get away from you thinking that you are good for nothing and that they are far superior in their intellectual capacity. If your opponents create a good impression about them the elites may as well go and vote for them. Therefore, you should pay the media heavily to create an impression that your opponents are as rotten as you are." Anand could have held a mike and made a public speech at this rate. But he desisted.

—∞ৌ∞—

'Dinesh came back to do exactly as Anand had asked him to do. The festival of Maramma was a common event in Karnataka. But Dinesh and Eeranna started accentuating its significance and began to shower free buffalos in all villages of his constituency. This was a new challenge for Poojamma. She had been already educating people not to indulge in this particular festival and not to sacrifice buffalos given by caste landlords. Now that there was a political design behind, it created a storm within her.' Kala gave her assessment of the situation as it started emerging after Dinesh came back from Delhi.

"I know Poojamma. She would never object to people celebrating their festivals in whatever way they wanted. She was the epitome of personal liberty as far as religion was concerned. I am at a loss to understand as to why she was highly disturbed about this festival." Nina wanted more clarity on the issue and its political significance.

'You are badly mistaken about Poojamma. She had her religious views, which was totally secular. She believed that no one person had any business to interfere in the religious views of another. She herself was not a believer in the divine. You know that she grew up in the Leftist School of thought. But she opposed celebrations of certain festivals in India as they largely reasserted the tacit enslavement of Dalits. She could never tolerate such things in her life.' Kala's analysis of Poojamma stunned Nina. She had been experiencing this convulsion again and again. Her mental picture of Kala had to go through a radical transformation. It was like a larva shaping into a full-grown butterfly inside its own cocoon.

'This particular festival of Maramma is one that establishes the practice of free caste labor firmly in the life of Dalit people. Poojamma could not tolerate anything that told badly upon the dignity and freedom of people, any people for that matter. She managed to liberate many villages from this obnoxious practice in the name of religion. She had the necessary organizing skills for that. But caste people in villages always managed to pay money and liquor to some Dalit families and get them to do this caste labor. They have to do this for the entire year. It would imply that Dalits have to sweep the streets at the time of village festival; they have to clean sewerage, prepare firewood whenever there was a marriage in the houses of caste people, and remove leaves in which caste people ate their food during marriages and festivals. But the more obnoxious ones were practices of removal of dead carcasses of animals. Even if those animals belonged to caste people it was Dalits who had to remove them, as caste people considered touching of dead animals as polluting. And the most horrific free caste labor was a set of jobs that they had to do. Announcing death of caste persons to their near and far relatives in different other villages! They had to play their drums in funeral processions and also dig graves for dead bodies of caste people.' Kala was in a mood to go on and on. In the US she would have passed as a University professor without much ado.

"Is this all true? Are they happening now or are they some ancient practices?" Nina remembered Poojamma telling her of all these. But when Kala described them they looked more real and horrific.

'I am the living witness for all these. They are still being practiced in many villages. They have stopped where the organization of Dalits by us is strong but one has to be constantly following the villages to know exactly when these take palace. Poojamma was so much against this practice of tacit slavery that she decided to go on a campaign in villages as soon as she came to know that Dinesh and Eeranna were making strenuous efforts to establish these more firmly in order to enhance their popularity.'

'She went to village after village with a loud speaker attached to her vehicle and educated people on the need to live with dignity and self-respect. She explained to them the story of Maramma, which depicts the enslavement of Dalits and asked people directly not to celebrate such an enslaving festival. She appealed to caste people to respect Dalits as human beings with rights and dignity. When she went to the caste area of the villages she threatened them that the practice of sacrificing buffalo during this festival was against the law of the land and that necessary legal action would be taken if the festival were celebrated. She educated Dalits that labor was their only capital. They had lost their land, they had no monetary capital, they had no other resources and therefore, it was imperative that they fixed appropriate price for their labor. The law of the land prohibited free labor and free caste labor amounted to the practice of slavery. Her public speeches sent chill in the veins of caste groups. Poojamma's campaign became a hot topic of discussion everywhere.'

'Dinesh and Eeranna countered her campaign by carefully spreading a divine threat that if Maramma's festival were not celebrated there would not be any rain and that all villages would be afflicted with unknown diseases, especially chickenpox. "This woman is not from our religion and therefore, she is decrying our religion among you. Do not listen to her. Maramma will punish her. Wait and see. Poojamma will die with aids. If you people follow her Maramma will also visit you with all sorts of afflictions. Spare yourself and your children from this evil woman who has no respect for our religion. She must be a witch to say that you are not Hindus. Who can accept her Christian theory? This is her preparation to convert you to Christianity." In his enthusiasm to deter people from following Poojamma, Dinesh forgot the caution given by Anand. He had to pay a heavy price for his mistake. Both Dalits and caste people alike began to think seriously about Poojamma in the light of the negative propaganda against her. Many caste people began to feel a sense of shame at the type of slavery to which they subscribed Dalits.' Now it was Kala who was firing on all cylinders without any interruption.

"So who won at the end? I am sure it was Poojamma as usual. But one can never say anything definite in politics. It is like a game of cricket. The best team on the day of the game wins, unless players clandestinely indulge in betting. Well, politics is in fact a big gamble." Nina was just blabbering and Kala did not mind that at all.

'Poojamma had many known and unknown weapons in her armory. She could pull out the most unexpected one at the most unexpected time. She went to Bangalore and met the Home Minister to convince him that what Dinesh and Eeranna were doing in the constituency was unconstitutional and that she needed the solid support of the Home Ministry in legally preventing the celebration of the festival. The Home Minister had already received news of the murky affairs of the political duo. He also understood the political implication of supporting the MP who got elected with the support of Poojamma. He took up the phone to speak to the SP in her presence and instructed him that all possible legal support and protection should be given to Poojamma and her followers in the campaign. He also instructed him to completely stop celebration of the sacrifice of Buffalo in the Maramma festival.'

'When Poojamma met the SP personally he told her that he would have rendered all possible support and that there was no need to go to the Home Minister on this issue. She informed him that she did not want to embarrass him. Dinesh and Eeranna would not hesitate to go to any extent to spoil your reputation if you supported me. He said that stopping the sacrifice of buffalo was not possible only by his police force. He confided in her that many policemen who were from dominant castes would invariably reveal to their caste people in advance of the measures taken by him to prevent the sacrifice. Therefore, he asked for active cooperation of Poojamma and her top guys to keep watch in villages and inform him and local police inspectors. He informed all police inspectors to listen to the staff of Poojamma's organization and rush with them to villages in order to prevent the sacrifice of buffalos.'

It was big news that Poojamma finally managed to stop all sacrifices of buffalos in the entire district. Many caste people found it futile to perpetuate such an infamous festival that would only bring them bad reputation. Finally the district was declared free caste labor free.

———◦❂◦———

'Contrary to expectations of Dinesh and Eeranna the government now initiated procedures to give its very prestigious annual award to Poojamma for her relentless fight for the dignity of Dalit people. Though Poojamma was reluctant to receive any awards, leaders of her Movement insisted that she should receive the award in the best interest of the Movement, as it would bring a lot of reputation to her efforts. The Chief Minister of the State gave away the award to her in a well-organized public function. Followers of Poojamma made a big celebration of the great recognition of their existence by selecting their icon for the award.'

"Yes, Poojamma wrote to me about the award in a very casual manner. I called her up immediately and congratulated her on this achievement. She was very humble. She said that she was just fulfilling her responsibility as a fellow human being. It was simply that the education that she had and her upbringing in the family made her excel in what she was doing. There were hundreds of thousands of people who went about their duty unrecognized by anyone. There was no glory in any public recognition of her work. The only and the biggest award that she expected and had already got were the affection and love of people amidst whom she chose to live. Since she had got that in abundance this award had become redundant for her. I have not seen such humility in people. She sounded to me quite weird." Nina now narrated her experience with her icon.

'Oh, yah what you say is true. To many people she was quite a weird personality because of the innovative methods she designed in her engagement with systems. She was also very firm in her decisions. But most weird was her behavior with supposedly big shots in society. She cared a hoot for their big positions. What mattered to her was their integrity and inclination towards justice. If there were any deficit on that she would stand her ground even to the point of antagonizing her 'friends'. Some of them understood her but there were others who got terribly angry with her. Actually they were the weirdest people to have expected her to feed into their ego. Since Poojamma had no capital of ego she could not feed into anybody's false ego. She lost some of her close friends because of this personality trait." Kala added her multicolored masala into what Nina was grinding.

—∘∘⦂◉⦂∘∘—

'As the crowd was waiting in anticipation of great things to happen Poojamma came out with a radiance on her face that people had not seen normally. They thought that she was very happy about the great recognition that the State had given to her sustained efforts for the development of her people. They greeted her casually, as they had already congratulated her assuming that getting an award for an achievement by itself mattered very little to her. She had argued with them vehemently that it was not her achievement. Rather it was the achievement of those who gave the award. It brought also a lot of recognition to those who gave away the award. She also mentioned to them that giving awards had already become a big business. The simple people who listened to her were overawed at the way she could explain away every small reality in her own big way. She was not following the general interpretation of the society.'

'She had no time to look into the quality of the look on each one's face. She got into her act and called Chikkanna and Nagaraj. She asked both of them to rush immediately to Ramapura and call all people to her place the next day. All of them looked up at Poojamma. Their look had now assumed a fine-tuned expectation. Was there something serious in the air? She understood their anxiety and did not want to procrastinate their agony. She told them with all the happiness that she could muster that the High Court had passed a judgment for the restoration of all land to Dalits. The restoration had to be in accordance with the re-grant of land in 1979 at the rate of four acres of land to each Dalit family. The High Court annulled all purchases of land from Dalits as null and void. Such purchases were against the special legal provision that the government of Karnataka had enacted. It also passed strictures on all future purchase of any land from Dalits to whom the government had granted land. It advised the government not only to grant land to the poor but also to make budgetary allocation for appropriate development of granted land.' Kala could not proceed further with her narration as she choked with emotions of happiness. Nina went near her, patted her at the back and stood there for as long as Kala wanted to remain in that state of happiness.

"She was a humble woman to the core of her being. Look at this. She never informed me of this great achievement of hers. I used to speak to her over phone several times. Not even once did she mention this success story to me. I admire this woman." Nina almost whispered in the ears of Kala as she was still holding her tight in her arms.

'On their way back Chikkanna and Nagaraj stopped at the market and bought garlands, firecrackers and sweets with the little money they had in their pockets. All of us ran out of the house when we heard the sound of firecrackers. By then quite a few leaders had assembled at the residence of Poojamma to celebrate the great and historical victory. All of us joined them in a round of singing and dancing. Poojamma ordered for good food of meat for all those who assembled. Some of them led by Chikkanna had a free go of liquor. The celebration was super.'

"Oh, how I wish I was there for the celebrations." Nina interjected.

In the evening Manjula brought news that police inspectors in both police stations were transferred in one day along with many others in the district. Though it looked like a routine exercise, both replacements indicated the heavy hand of Dinesh. Eeranna's house also saw a bit of celebration with drinks and good meal at the news of the transfer of two inspectors on the same day. "Now we shall see how this bloody woman will play games against our Anna," he swore.

⸻◦◦❮◉❯◦◦⸻

Kala lowered her voice considerably and continued her narration. Nina wondered why she lowered her voice, as there was no one around them during this narration.

'That night Poojamma's behavior was very strange. She sent all leaders away to their homes asking them to come the next day when the people of Ramapura would assemble. The hyper excitement of the area reduced all of a sudden and the place became as calm as a burial ground. Poojamma called me and said in a quiet voice that she was expecting a special guest that late evening and that I should not let anybody inside the house as long as he was with her. "A man late in the evening! All alone with Poojamma! No one to be informed about his visit!" It sent me into a tizzy. "Hey what is going on here? Has Poojamma at last changed her mind about marriage? Was she getting married to someone at this middle age? Or was she having a secret affair with someone?" I could not resist the upsurge of questions in my mind.'

"Who was the guy? Hey tell me soon. Did Poojamma have any plans of marriage?" Nina prodded her to come out with more spicy explanations.

'Wait madam, wait! I shall tell you all secrets one by one. However great a person may be, each one has a weakness. Poojamma had her weakness too as I understood later.' Kala began to unwrap the mystery narration slowly. Now Nina understood why Kala's voice naturally went down when it came to this stage of narration.

'The man came around 11 at night. Poojamma did not have her dinner yet. I scolded her sheepishly for not taking dinner. But I also knew what it meant to wait for the loved one. She waited to have dinner with him. It was an elaborate meal. She herself came to kitchen and joined me in preparing the meal. She did not speak much. I began to smile within myself. I was feeling terribly hungry. She asked me to eat and wait.'

'Finally the moment I had waited for with much anxiety arrived. He was a frail looking man. A perfect match for Poojamma in many respects except for his looks! She was such a beauty of a woman and he was only moderately handsome. I started imagining and genuinely wished both of them living together hundreds of years of married life. I already began to sing lullaby to their child. Poojamma herself rushed to open the door when he knocked at it. She did not allow me to open the door. I could understand. Poojamma asked me to quietly bolt the main door from inside. I did exactly as she said. She asked me to bring all the food to the hall. It was very unusual of her. She never allowed food in the hall. All had to go to the dining hall to eat and there was no compromise on that.'

'I was shocked when Poojamma asked me to close also the door leading to the dining room. This left both of them in the hall all alone even without me being there. I had been with her through thick and thin and I thought there was nothing that Poojamma hid from me. But now that one thing seemed to remain a secret even from me. How and when did she develop this close relationship with this man? My mind started wandering all over the world and started grinding all possible fodder in its gossiping mill, all silently.'

'Oh that is really, really very interesting. I never knew it either. Come on! Don't stop. Proceed further. And tell me when did he leave the place? Did he stay for the entire night with Poojamma? Did they have sex that night?' Nina yielded a little bit to her womanly indulgence of gossip and wanted to go to the core of the matter, the very essence of Poojamma's multiple relationships.

'He stayed for a very long time. I peeped through the gap in the door every now and then. My interest was to see when Poojamma would take him to her bedroom. But they only ate slowly and had a long discussion. They went on discussing. After about one hour Poojamma called me in and asked me to clear the table. She was very apologetic that she could not help me that night in dishwashing. She even suggested that I did the washing next morning. But I was curious to know what would happen between both of them. So I washed all dishes very slowly. From what I heard in between I could understand that it was not about love but only about land. I did not hear anything more than that. He left only around 2 at night.'

'The next morning I could not contain my curiosity. As is my wont I directly asked Poojamma who the man of the previous night was. She evaded a direct answer for quite some time. But I would bring up the topic again and again. Finally Poojamma asked me to promise her not to reveal the secret to anyone. That aroused my suspicion more. "There is something fishy about our venerated Poojamma. She is definitely in love with that man". My fickle mind started repeating to my ears.'

'This is what we used to do in our school. For every small little secret we used to ask our peers for a solemn promise not to tell anyone. We came to know later that this was the best way to ensure guaranteed publicity for something that we did not want others to know. I promised Poojamma secrecy in the best way that I knew. I pulled her palm out and I struck on it with my palm powerfully. The secret that she told me shook the very bottom of my world. I am sure it is going to shake you now.' Kala became a bit dramatic as she narrated this.

"Nothing can shake me at the foundation. I am very strong and I have seen almost the entire world. Come on Kala, be a woman. Have some balls and not mere walls. Tell me anything that you want to say. I like to hear who the guy was." Nina pretended to have strength bigger than she actually possessed.

"He is not my secret lover as you imagine." Poojamma started the revelation with a shock. "How did she know what I was thinking?" My mind started dithering.'

"His name is Yettiramulu. He is from Andhra Pradesh. Have you heard of Naxalites?" I nodded my head in the opposite direction to indicate that I did not know Naxalites. I was also highly embarrassed that she knew my inner thoughts above her supposedly love affair.'

"Like me he also is a Marxian thinker. But unlike me he believes that revolution can come only by taking up to violent methods. So they shoot and kill whenever they think that a landlord has to be finished off. Not only that, often governments behave worse than landlords and persecute them. Therefore, they also fight against the government and kill mainly police."

"But why are they not arrested? If they are killing people police would arrest them and put in jail, no?" I asked in my simplicity.'

"The police cannot arrest them easily as they live mostly in forest and mountain areas. Why do you think he came in darkness at night? It was mainly because he does not want to be caught by police. He came here only after making sure that I would not inform police at all. Even when he was inside our house his assistants were standing outside on the roads to watch if police were near. If they spotted any police nearby they would immediately alert him. Usually they live underground and come out only at night."

"What do they do at night?" I asked Poojamma in my utter naiveté.'

"It is at night that they conduct most of their organizational meetings. In these meetings they study and discuss a lot about their ideology and philosophy. They analyze situations of the poor and state of governance in the country. They also visit village people and have discussions with them. They have to recruit young people as their cadre and train them in warfare. It is a hard life that they lead. We are all living very comfortable life compared to them. They have to go without food and water for several days. They have to hide themselves from police and be on the run often. It is a dog's life out there for them. Yettiramulu is leader of a Naxalite unit bordering on our district." I was stunned at the information that was being dished out.'

"So, did she have regular contact with the people underground? This is what Dinesh and Eeranna had said earlier about Poojamma." Nina proved why she was such a powerful journo. She remembered every little detail that Kala had said earlier.

'I asked Poojamma about that. She said that her first contact with Yettiramulu started with the struggle in Ramapura and not before that. He had heard about the struggle from some Dalits in the remote area where he lived. He sent one of his emissaries to Poojamma and expressed his desire to meet her. When there was big success in Ramapura he made a call through one of his emissaries and wanted to meet her the next day. Poojamma agreed this time, as she was always an admirer of all those who lived underground for their commitment to the cause they espoused. Moreover they shared the same ideology of Marxism.' Kala said casually.

———••◦❋◦••———

'The next morning was a very big celebration with the people of Ramapura and all leaders of the Movement. Each one made a big speech on the need for fighting land cases united. Poojamma made it a point to formally honor Murthy who was the captain of the ship. It was to his credit that he did not allow it to be a sinking ship. Citing his example of sacrifice for his people she urged that all should be as dedicated as he was if the Movement had to make its mark in the life of the poor. She ended her speech without any reference to Yettiramulu. All the people had their sumptuous meal. This was something very special of Poojamma. She always believed in giving good quality food to the poor and never cringed on quality of food.'

CHAPTER FIFTEEN

Back at home Nina was reflecting on all that transpired in India. If attending the funeral procession and burial of Poojamma was one of the best rewarding experiences of her life, listening intently to Kala's narration of the story of Poojamma ever since she left her was more exhilarating. After having come out of jetlag she felt an urge to put down in writing all that she collected from Kala in telegraphic style notes. Since the death of Poojamma occupied most space in her thinking and pushed aside all that she heard from Kala she began to write about the death of Poojamma.

"Poojamma, the indomitable woman power of India" she started her writing in true style. 'When I packed my bag to go for the funeral of this one woman whom I have admired most in my life I never bargained for what was in store for me in India. I could not stomach the fact that Poojamma died in mysterious circumstance. At least this is what I read in police records. Kala came running as soon as she saw me and in her loud lamentations she did not forget to whisper in my ears that Poojamma did not die a natural death. The whisper in my ears was like the blast of one hundred cluster bombs in the hills of Afghanistan. I had read a lot about Americans bombing mindlessly rows of hills in Afghanistan only on suspicion that Osama bin Laden was hiding somewhere in the hills. All those bombs seemed to blast in my ears at a time. I fumbled and stumbled. They brought water for me to drink. But the thirst in me was for many barrels of hard liquor. I wanted to drown myself into many barrels of liquor and get lost to any memory of anything . . . ."

"Blast! Blast!! Blast!! Yes, that is what Poojamma died of. She was done to death at the most unexpected moment of her life. Every poor in India began to look at her as a beacon of hope. She started off in a tiny village but became famous all over the country and was available to anyone who was in need of her help in any part of the world. One of the most active women that I met, a woman who had time for all in the world but no time for herself, a woman who succeeded in her multitasking, a woman who was everywhere, was now lying in state. I stood completely shattered. It was Kala who gathered the scattered pieces and put me together as Nina . . ."

"Thousands of flowers had assembled to pay their last respect to the woman whom they loved most. Only some years back in their life they never heard of her name. She prepared the ground for a grand garden of million flowers. She brought high quality manure to nurture the seedling and the plants as they kept growing. It was an unfathomably arduous task for her. Each plant needed a different kind of manure, a different kind of cultivating. She was tireless. She had high hopes, born out of the promising brightness that she could see in therm. Understanding the character and needs of each plant demanded extraordinary patience. When they started flowering she began to see a million garden behind her. Each garden had millions of flowers in millions of colors. Many of her detractors wanted to see one garden with one kind of flower and in one color. When they did not see their uniformity in her garden they became derisive of her. She thrived in that derision of her detractors. The more the derision the surer she was of the productivity of her work."

"All along the path of nurturing these beautiful gardens she became their household name, a name for every poor household. It was enough to say her name. Many things would get done. That was the power, the womanpower! When she visited villages, children would run as a herd of sheep and flock around her in jubilation. They would dance on the streets as they saw her at a distance. The odd one among them, unable to control his emotion would take handful of sand and throw it in the wind. Elders would leave all their work, wash their hands and legs and rush to meet her, women would run into their houses, apply some face powder and would surround her like beauty queens in a Miss Universe contest, Old people would take their sticks and walk towards her with the broadest smiles on their shrunken faces."

Tallest tree on earth's face
Spread its wings to flutter
Bats batted their eyelids
Nocturnal shame hidden
Beneath her leaves

Brother sun waited in anxiety
For grandmother moon to give way
Piercing through the shadow of night's darkness
He rushed in the morning to touch her feet
To be the first one to look at his sister

Morning dews enveloped with intuition
Ran away from his sight
Lest he decimated them in his onrush
In their flight they left behind
Their misty robes for their Poojamma

Unable to bear the brightness
Reflected through her radiant face
The Clouds ran helter-skelter
Hiding the stars at yonder

Blades of green grass
Holding back the bridal robes
Covering their head, helmets of dew
Lest they melt at his benevolence

Step out! Oh daughter of Mother Earth
The birds screeched to halt their sleep
They went haywire at her sight
They chattered shattering the silence around

The world woke up eyes wide open
To witness the merger, the convergence!

'The mighty Poojamma had become one with Mother Earth. I remember clearly what the Collector spoke in his obituary speech at the funeral.'

—oo◦|◦◦oo—

"Here lies the tallest tree on the face of the earth. She grew straight to face the sky. Those who were crawling on earth envied her unreachable height. They could not perceive her ability to bend from the sky to the earth. Standing tall she was earth bound. Her roots were deep into the womb of the Mother Earth. She thus belonged to two worlds. The world of earthlings and the world of ancestors who are perched in the sky as stars! She was the link, an essential link. When difficulties mounted as insurmountable, she began to shine to her enemies. The radiance on her face at the most hostile situations put her enemies to shame. They began to withdraw into the dark shades of their shells. She was a woman who was in incessant communication with all living beings. I knew her for some time. I am happy that I knew her only for sometime. Had I known her for longer I would not have been able to bear her overflowing goodness. She was exceptional in everything that she took up. The tears that are streaming to inundate her burial ground will soon gather in her lap. They will flow into her womb. Many children will be born in the path that she showed in her life . . . It will be a stream, a stream of life for those to whom the right to live was systemically and structurally denied. The epitome of life, lying in state today will rise in you for eternity . . .' The collector wiped his tears unable to speak more.

'It was then that I noticed for the first time the very well dressed, completely different looking diplomat of a woman. There was an inner urge in me to run to her and hug as she was crying inconsolably but trying hard not to burst out into a scattered emotional bundle. I did not know that it was Pramila, the beloved daughter of Poojamma's. Only when Kala told me later, I could connect her image.'

'There were many others who eulogized her shamelessly. They knew that she would never get up to have a clear look at them. When she was alive they heaped mounds of gossip against her at her back. Now they unleashed unabashed words to capitalize on her popularity. It was very easy for them to eulogize her. They knew that she would never come back to tell them to fuck off and inform the rest of the world how badly they treated her when she was alive.'

241

'The Chief Minister had sent the Home Minister as his emissary to attend the funeral of Poojamma. Many in the crowd murmured that when a leader can command votes she becomes like a honeycomb. The Home Minister came late. Dinesh and Eeranna thought it was a good chance for them to slip through the crowed along with him. There was big surprise among the officers to see Eeranna tagging along the Minister as the acolyte of the MP. Kala rushed to Pramila to whisper in her ears that the two motherfuckers had come with the Home Minister. Pramila did not even care to look at anyone. Eeranna was a man who never dared to meet Poojamma when she was alive and now there he was to pay his tribute after her death. It became clear to me that politicians would do anything to shame themselves if only they could be assured of a few more votes at the time of elections. The anger in me welled up like a spring that had hidden itself from the sight of the people. Accidentally someone throws a stone and it gushes forth with uncontrollable water.'

'The message from Kala only informed me that Poojamma was no more and that funeral would take place after two days. I did not care to ask her how she had died. My next thought was that I should immediately rush to Karnataka to be with her even as she was ready for her final journey. When I landed in Poojamma's place Kala and Manjula started crying along with a few other women who had assembled there. I could see that the wrapping of Poojamma's body was not a normal thing. She looked much fatter than I had known her. Her exposed head was heavily bandaged with white cloth. I turned to Kala and asked her how Poojamma had died. She began to cry aloud uncontrollably. It took sometime for her to recover and shout, "They have killed her". I was numbed for a few seconds and did not know that I existed. The shit in me was ready to splash across anytime on all those who had assembled. I wanted to yell at everyone what the hell he or she was doing when she was killed. I controlled myself, as I was still in the dark on how she was killed and why they killed her. Lowering my voice I asked her if the killers were Dinesh and Eeranna. She said that nothing could be said at the moment. Police are investigating. As a punishment the SP was transferred as soon as message of the brutal assassination of Poojamma was flashed across in the media.'

'After spending considerable time with Poojamma, I cried and cried. After draining my tears and energy out I slowly moved out to the bedroom of Poojamma and was curious to know more about the actual cause of her death. People in the place were not at all in a position to speak on the tragedy that had struck them like an unexpected avalanche. The TVs were full of analysis of the possible causes of the assassination. A few TV channels were of the firm opinion that it was a mere accident and nothing much should be read into the allegation that it was a blast of her car. There was no such case of bomb blast in the history of the district and therefore, they argued that no one had the capacity to indulge in such heinous crime. With the exception of Kala, Manjula, Gangaiah, Chikkanna, Nagaraj and Murthy, all the others began to reconcile themselves to the official version of an accident.

—ooo◉ooo—

Poojamma had completed a grand function of celebration in Ramapura. The poor had given her a warm reception with garlands, band set, loudspeakers and procession through the main village. She addressed a public meeting and asked people to be ready to give their lives for the sake of building a future for their children with dignity and freedom. "It would be better for all of us to die rather than to live in this type of drudgery. An existence without dignity, equality and freedom was not worth living at all." She solemnly promised to the people that if they had to die in the process they should be ready to do so without any fear. If she had to be the first one to die for the sake of the children who were still treated as untouchables, she would be very happy to lay down her life for their liberation.

'When public meeting was over, people insisted that she should step into every house as a mark of divine blessing. As she entered the houses they welcomed her with garlands. Women made her sit on a chair and showered her with rice from her head to feet. Each house offered a blouse piece, a little money, fruits and the traditional betel nuts on a tray. I had seen this in one of my earlier visits when I accompanied Poojamma for a village function. They used to be occasions when even stones would begin to stand up with emotions. On her way back from village, the most accepted version said that her driver lost control of the vehicle at a turning on the highway and smashed the car against a huge wall. Both Poojamma and the driver were killed on the spot with their body parts dismembered and scattered on the side of the road. The car in which she travelled also splintered into many parts. The new SP who took over had ordered an enquiry into the incident as soon as he took charge.'

'I wanted to stand up and shout to Dinesh and Eeranna that they had no right to pay their respects to a woman whom they treated like shit when she was alive. But then I had not heard the entire story from Kala at that time and had only known a little bit about them through the sharing of Poojamma. She was not in the habit of sharing her difficulties and much less of speaking about other people behind their back. I bowed down and waited for political leaders to leave the place. When everything was calm and gloomy Chikkanna shouted from the crowd. "Catch these bloody motherfuckers. They have killed our Mother Poojamma. Catch them and kill them before they touch our Mother." Before anyone could realize what was happening a few slippers flew in the direction of the duo. Dinesh ducked. Eeranna was hit on his face. It looked that Dinesh had groomed him to receive blows on his behalf. Police rushed to cover both of them from further attack. Then I saw Pramila being immediately surrounded by black uniformed policemen. I did not realize that the big woman was the diplomat daughter of another big woman who was lying in state. One policewoman rushed to Chikkanna and asked him not to become emotional. She stood by his side in order to prevent any further havoc. Kala and Manjula rushed to Chikkanna and the angry crowd. They admonished them to have patience in order to pay tribute to their Mother Poojamma. They went to each and every protesting follower and asked him to be calm and restore the dignity of the occasion. Anger was legitimate. But people should know how to take it out. The police took away the villains protecting them from any possible further attacks. As the police were taking away both of them Eeranna spotted in the crowd Pramila guarded well by Black Cats of the Indian Government. For a moment he could not believe his eyes. But his eyes made sure that it was the same girl who hoodwinked him into sexual behavior with him and constructed his waterloo. He turned again and again and looked at her with increased anger. Even in that moment of shame he thought how good it would have been if he had joined the gang of Poojamma instead of the idiotic politician Dinesh. He thought he could have been in exalted places if he had befriended her, as he was repeatedly looking at Pramila. Only later policemen informed him that she was the Ambassador in German Government. The SP took the mike and pleaded for calm. Pramila was watching the entire scene with stony silence and melting eyes.'

'On one of my previous visits to India I had witnessed something horrible in TV. A very famous actor of Karnataka had died and people all over the state were mourning his death. TVs were full of melancholic music and were reeling out his life history. In the evening was the funeral of the actor and hundreds of thousands of people assembled in the city of Bangalore to pay their last respect to their departed hero. Most of the streets of the city were full of his fans. As the funeral procession neared an end some miscreants started trouble by burning car tyres and also by setting fire to some parked vehicles near the venue of the funeral. When police intervened to restore peace they started attacking police violently. In some places police had to take recourse to caning, known in India as "lathicharge".

'In a far off place something else was happening. There was a police vehicle on an important road. The crowed had thinned out as this road was very far from the location of the funeral. Many policemen were still inside the large vehicle cooling their heels. Suddenly there appeared a group of hooligans who started pelting stones on the vehicle and attacking the policemen inside. The policemen did not have necessary mandate to fire back at the crowd and they took to their heels. One young and innocent looking policeman was caught inside the vehicle before he could run away. They threw boulders at him and beat him up blue and pulp with the clubs in their hands. I watched in absolute horror the way they killed him little by little and TVs were showing these horrible scenes repeatedly. It was a cold-blooded murder in full sight. How could human beings be so cruel to another human being? Even animals do not do this to hapless creatures.'

'I was afraid that something similar might happen in the funeral of Poojamma given the extent of her popularity and the level of hardships that the duo of Dinesh and Eeranna had created for her. But fortunately people who had assembled in thousands respected the words of Kala and things became calm. I could not believe my eyes when Kala took up the mike in front of many thousands of people and began to appeal for calm. I could only imagine Poojamma standing there in the shape of Kala. The new SP who had come to give security to the Home Minister heaved a real sigh of relief that a young woman was able to hold sway over a big emotional crowd. He had an extensive survey of her towering personality. He ordered his policemen to whisk away the duo from the funeral arena.

They quietly packed them off to their homes. Much before Poojamma was buried, their ego went into limbo, unable to stand up to the power of the people. Their popularity nosedived into the netherworld from where it could never come back.'

—∘∘❂∘∘—

'The Home Minister made an unusually moving speech though he knew her only from records. However, it was evident from the way he made his speech that the Chief Minister had personally informed him of the greatness of Poojamma.'

"My heartfelt condolences to all of you, admirers and followers of Poojamma on this very unfortunate moment in the history of our State. She was just an individual who changed the course of history of the people of the state by her determination and commitment. She chose an issue that many would not even dare to look at, namely, the issue of dignity, equality and liberty to untouchable people. Unlike many others who have fought against untouchability by their vituperative attacks on others she took into confidence caste people. There have been many in the country that took up the question of untouchability. But they were not untouchable themselves. Poojamma hailed from the same community that she tried to liberate. We, in the government realize that this is an onerous task by any standards. She has established a niche for herself in this noble endeavor . . .

"As you all know, she was a woman and therefore, many thought that it was their bounden duty not to allow her to succeed in her mission. A successful Dalit woman is an indigestible phenomenon in this country. Poojamma is a great woman because she stood firmly in her commitment to her people. In this commitment she manifested her unquestionable loyalty to the nation. Her equation of Dalit development and progress of the nation struck the imagination of many of us in government . . .

"Poojamma chose a very rare path of establishing a collaborative relationship with government machinery in her enterprises. I like to inform you all that it was not easy for her as well as for the government. It was not easy for her because the government always looks at private individuals of this kind with suspicion and is very slow to open doors of cooperation. Poojamma spoke with firmness and stood very tall in her integrity. It was difficult for us because she never hesitated to challenge the assumptions and styles of functioning of the government. She minced no words and she tolerated no nonsense. Hers was a critical collaboration with the government. But she carefully avoided rhetoric of a destructive order. She was angry but she never unloaded any load of anger on wrong targets. We, in the government liked her democratic dissent, as she was very constructive and creative in her critical assessment. What marked her as different from others was her focus on alternatives. We learned a lot from her. You would all agree that she was an amazing teacher . . .

"We have taken cognizance of the fact that Poojamma has died in suspicious circumstances. We shall leave no stone unturned to investigate the matter and find out the truth of the circumstances that led to her death. We promise you that justice will be done at all costs. Till then, I request you to remain calm . . .

"We are proud that this state has given birth to such a noble daughter who dedicated her life for the progress of the most downtrodden people. In doing this she has done the state proud. The chief Minister of Karnataka has specially requested me to convey to you that the State Government will soon set up a formal award of Rs. 100,000/—in her honor to be given annually to an outstanding contributor to the development of poor. We are sure this will be a fitting response of the government in recognition of the limitless service that Poojamma has rendered to the poor."

'There was only a mild clap of hands, as people generally avoided any gesture of celebration at such solemn occasion. For me there was another shock in waiting. As soon as the Home Minister completed his speech the Master of Ceremonies invited me to speak a few things about Poojamma. I was in the least prepared for such an eventuality. I am a writer and now they asked me to speak. I protested but only mildly. Kala and Manjula looked at me reprovingly for protesting. I got up slowly from where I was seated and walked towards the podium to hold the mike and speak.'

"I am sorry to confess that I have not come from the US to make a speech on Poojamma. I am too overwhelmed with sorrow at the sad demise of our beloved mother and friend. It is an untimely end to say the least. I have been a personal witness to the love and affection that you people and

Poojamma had for each other. I know that you have lost a strong pillar of support in your journey of building a bright future for your children. But I am also sure that Poojamma has not left you in the lurch. There are many among you whom she has prepared well to carry forward all responsibilities that she handled . . .

"What attracted me most to Poojamma is that she was like a glass through which you can see the other side of the world. There was nothing behind her that you could not see. She was straight in her response and never related herself to anyone with hidden agenda. The quantum of trust that she generated in interpersonal relationship was huge. She was an international personality but was deeply rooted in her culture and had no reason at all to feel bad or low about what she was. As a leader she stood tall in her unassuming nature. Hardly did I see any sort of rhetoric in her assertion of future liberation. She only said what could be achieved and did not create any illusion among her followers neither about herself nor about themselves . . .

"History has taught us that success is achieved only through a lot of perspiration. Poojamma was the epitome of hard work. She was not against marriage. There were times when she thought of marriage. But her commitment to you and your children did not allow her time to think much of her own personal needs. She sacrificed everything for you. She capitalized her personal energy and life for building a future for your children and did not capitalize on your ignorance or innocence to design a future for herself. She focused on developing women leaders but she was never against men leaders . . .

"It is not you any more who are losers. It is not the state of Karnataka. It is not even India. It is the world that has lost her physical presence."

'Kala was highly sensitive. She made it a point to ask Chikkanna and Nagaraj to bring Gowdajja for the funeral and gave him a place of honor among all the VIPs who had come. She was deeply aware of the very personal affection Poojamma had for this great man who had the entire humanity in his big heart. He had no caste, no religion, no ideology, no party etc. and yet contained all ideology in his simple vision of life. People who had put on images of greatness were not equal to the dust in his feet. Poojamma made it a point always to touch his feet and get his blessings.

He walked in the funeral procession as an unassuming human being. He had to be supported to walk all the way. Many people tried to talk to him and keep him in good cheers. But he remained as hard as a stonewall. He would only look at those who tried to capture his attention but would not say anything to anybody. He was aghast that she had left him speechless. He remembered the many times he had told her that she should live long in the service of her people. He admonished her to preserve her energy for many generations to come. When she bent to touch his feet he would bless her always with long life. Now he had constructed a wall of stone around his emotions. He did not want to make a show of the pain that he was suffering deep inside at the departure of the one who loved him most in his life. He had many children. But none had loved him with such selflessness, as did Poojamma. Her death touched a few chords in his body. Two days after I returned from India, Kala called me to inform that Gowdajja had followed Poojamma. What an age to follow someone much younger than he was! Gowdajja the great! Two great people merging into one in the lap of Mother Earth!'

'Kala did not lose her sensitivity even in such a deeply emotional moment. She called up Chikkanna to speak a few words on what Poojamma meant to him. He touched the mike to say something. The water that had filled up his eyes began to flow like a falls. He could not say anything. He could not speak when he cried. His emotive functions and rational functions did not synchronize well enough. Kala touched his back as Poojamma used to do and indicated that he should go. Nagaraj came and repeated the scene exactly as Chikkanna did. Even in that moment of sadness I could clearly see that men are the weaklings in terms of dealing with their emotions and they have floated a paradigm that intellectual functioning is better than emotional functioning. They should simply acknowledge the fact that women are much better in synergizing their emotive and rational functions.'

'Kala had organized a grand meal for all the thousands of people who had assembled for the funeral of Poojamma. There were plenty of contributors. Kala contacted all of them and organized the meal. All the poor and VIPs who came, left without the slightest dissatisfaction. Kala did not want to leave anyone unhappy on that day. She was highly disturbed at the way Chikkanna created a scene at the arrival of Dinesh and Eeranna. Later she argued that Poojamma would have welcomed them and served them tea if they had come when she was alive. She was never guided by what others did to her. She always guided her life by what she was deep in her inner being. Chikkanna and Nagaraj could not fully understand what Kala was trying to communicate about Poojamma's core essence of life.'

'The Home Minister made it a point to step down and meet me and Kala along with all others who were close to us and console us in that hour of loss. "She had the great ability to bring out the 'human' even in hardcore bureaucrats and ministers." He said this to us as he departed. As he left he pushed an envelop into the hands of Kala in our presence and said that it was his personal contribution towards the funeral expenses of Poojamma. Kala opened it immediately after he departed in our presence and it was a cheque for one hundred thousand rupees. I wondered why he would make that type of a personal contribution, especially when he was a politician and a minister in the government. But the accompanying note in a small paper said everything about him. He had written: "My small contribution to a towering human being. I am a Dalit." There were a few extra drops of tears in all those who were around Kala at that time.'

••◦◦|◘|◦◦••

'I spent three full days listening to all that Kala had to narrate to me about Poojamma. On the fourth day there was a formal meeting of all leaders who were associated with Poojamma in her engagements. Kala welcomed all of them and thanked them profusely for all the spontaneous initiatives they took to make it possible to give a fitting send off to Poojamma. Manjula greatly appreciated the outburst of Chikkanna and his success in sending out the duo of Dinesh and Eeranna. They had no right to come for the funeral and it was only right that they were forced to leave the venue. Many others who assembled joined her in this chorus. I could understand their pain and sorrow as well as their anger. But I failed to understand why they were in such rage of taking revenge. It was not politically expedient for them. They seemed to be overestimating their own strength. There was still a big gap between the way they dealt with life and the way Poojamma used to deal with life situations. Kala was a great exception in that group. She even reproved Manjula for her appreciation of the way Chikkanna created that commotion during funeral. She asked all of them to reflect on what would have happened if one or other of the crowed also reacted the same way. There would have been mayhem. Was that the best way to give a fitting funeral to the mother? They saw Kala's point of view and agreed that such an angry reaction should have been reserved for another occasion. Chikkanna apologized to everyone present in the meeting.'

'They had a long discussion about the circumstances that led to the death of Poojamma. The predominant question in everyone's mind was whether the death of Poojamma and the driver was an accident or a well-planned murder. The story that police initially put out was that there was a cyclist who crossed the road all of a sudden. The driver was in high speed and swerved the car out of the road. He was unable to control speed and hit a tree in high speed. But Chikkanna and Nagaraj who rushed to the spot of the accident differed with that view. They asserted in unison that it was a planned accident. A man in bicycle could not have come in that part of road unless it was planned. There was no possibility of a break failure in the car as it was a well-maintained car. There was also not the possibility of over speeding as police said. Poojamma would never allow the driver to drive fast. She never hesitated to tell the driver not to be rash. They swore that they would find out the truth of the entire plot and come out soon with their findings. It was decided in that meeting that Kala would continue to look after the place and all those who visited it. The existing leaders would carry the mission of Poojamma's forward without interruption. Kala slipped into Poojamma's shoes rather smoothly. I was happy that the transition was smoother than what normally takes place, especially given the type of popularity and power that Poojamma enjoyed.'

—◦◦❯◉❮◦◦—

'On my way back I could not help remembering the many conversations I had with Poojamma when she was alive. There were many times when I used to tell her that she should take care of her personal safety, as politicians could prove very unpredictable. They acted weird if they were defeated. On all those occasions Poojamma would retort nonchalantly that even those who surrounded themselves with tight security died with a heart attack at the most unexpected time. She recollected how her own security guards felled Indira Gandhi. She would ask what guarantee was there that she would not die the next day for one or other reason. There was no point in being afraid of dying. It should come any time and one should be always prepared to welcome death. I would then tell her that there were thousands of people who were in need of her and if she was killed or kicked the bucket what would happen to all of them. Poojamma would laugh and say that she was not born to be the guardian of anybody's future. She engaged herself with the liberation of her people simply because she loved and enjoyed it and not because she thought that she was indispensable for people. They had lived much before she was born and they would continue to live much after she was gone. Millions of people were born and died in the world and nothing much changed. The cosmos had a movement and change of her own and it was only our duty to become part of this movement and change of the cosmos.'

'There was this particular occasion when I asked her the reason for her success. On different occasions she gave me different reasons. She never allowed stereotyping of her self. But once she told me that she lived with gusto mainly because she was always ready to die. She was not afraid of anything or anybody simply because she was not afraid of dying.'

'There were times when I used to question her just for the heck of it and she would not mind that at all. Instead she would take time and explain every detail of the reply that she wanted to give. She had deep respect for people who volleyed questions at her. One of the questions that elicited striking response from her was what she considered to be her singular achievement in life. I also asked her if she had anything that she considered as her singular achievement. "Yes, there is something. Many people bring up the economic development programmes that I have done as a big achievement in my life. There are others who point out to the total reduction of untouchability practices as a marvelous success in this area. In the same vein they will also point out to the stopping of atrocity in this area as a miracle. They would say that it is impossible for everyone to do this type of work. Almost everyone who comes here will proclaim that the enormous land recovery that we have done for the poor is just phenomenal. Every small thing that is achieved in the lives of the poor is great. I am definitely happy about all these. However, there is something that very naturally makes me happy without thinking even for a fraction of a second. That is the level of psychological change that has taken place among the people in this area. I have worked consistently to bring about this change. I consider that unless there is a psychological change among oppressed people there will be no sustainability of the transformation that is wrought among them. Please do not think that I have grand psychological plans to bring about changes. I worked on building a strong positive psyche among the poor picking up lessons from them, especially from women in these communities. What I found in them was an inexhaustible resource of internal strength that sustained them in the face of unmitigated exploitation and oppression. I thought that if these resources were made the foundation of building them up it would be wonderful. I began to insist on their strength more and more and that naturally reduced my talk with them of what others were doing to them. It also removed a lot of repetitive focus on their weaknesses."

'I could not comprehend what she was talking about. In my understanding the society had been intermittently reeling out a barrage of negative ascriptions on the untouchable people and had been consistently oppressing them leading them almost to slavery. How could there be any liberation of Dalits without talking of their weaknesses. They were a weak people and that is why they were unable to fight against caste forces. I asked her to give me an example of how she built on the strength of people. Poojamma was ever ready for any sort of explanation that I demanded on any damn thing. She continued.'

"There are many examples as my work is filled with such strength of the poor. But I shall give you one of the most recent ones. There was a visit of a group of big shots from one of the organizations that supported us from the Netherlands. Their Director, their President of the Board, and five others had come to visit our villages in order to extend their support to our work. They visited our villages and as it was our custom we had called our leaders together to meet them on the last day of their visit . . .

"Many of our leaders were women. Even in their visits to villages they found this as a striking feature. When they saw more women in the group and less men there was visible surprise on their faces. Our women were vociferous already when they started introducing themselves to the visitors. I think that created a bit of uneasiness in them. When it was their turn to introduce themselves the Director started saying that they also focused on equality of women in their organization. Immediately one of our illiterate women retorted in a very casual but sarcastic manner, "Oh, that is why there are six men among you and only one woman."

There was a peel of laughter in the hall mixed disproportionately with embarrassment . . .

"This was the strength that my people manifested at every stage of their development journey. I did not have to tell them that they should only speak of their strength. It was sort of spontaneous and therefore, it had tremendous credibility. I did not have to later reflect with them that this was what was expected of them. When they did this very naturally there was no need for me to teach them that they were right. That they were right was what mattered most and I had to learn that from them . . .

—◦◦◦🔷◦◦◦—

'Just before I left India there was another meeting among the followers of Poojamma. Chikkanna insisted that he would prove that the death of their mother Poojamma was a cold-blooded murder and not an accidental death. Kala began to see the strength of his argumentation and did not want to construct any roadblocks. Later she told me that everyone in the group had a right to an opinion and that had to be respected even if we have a different point view. The group decided that they should submit an official memorandum to Home Minister asking for a thorough investigation that would not be in the hands of state police. It seems there was a central government investigation agency with independent authority. They said it was difficult to get them investigate the death of Poojamma. However, given the stature she enjoyed while alive it would not be a big problem. The group sat together and prepared the text of the memorandum demanding investigation by the Central Agency.'

'To my great shock and to the surprise of all followers of Poojamma newspapers carried a story on her death that none of them anticipated. Dinesh and Eeranna had called for a press conference and made a statement that the death of Poojamma was not natural and that it was a calculated and brutal murder. They issued a statement that the murder suspects were none other than the Naxalite friends of Poojamma's. They floated the story that a Naxalite leader visited Poojamma stealthily several times and demanded money from her. They suspected that she had a lot of money through her connections with other countries and wanted her to part with part of that money on a regular basis. They also agreed that they would protect her from all her political enemies and would also help the poor to regain more land than all that she could do. However, Poojamma was a very good woman of high integrity and therefore, she refused to give them any money. Instead she told them that they were always welcome to meet her and discuss ideological and strategic issues but not money.'

'The story continued further to assert that Naxalites became very angry with Poojamma and stopped meeting her. They began to follow all her movements and found out that she was visiting the village people of Ramapura frequently. They set up an agent to observe every movement of hers and inform them. They also set up another informer near the residence of Poojamma's and made it a strict point that their agent should inform them of all the people who visited her. From the frequency of each one's visit they would draw their own inferences. They found that government officers visited her more often and she had a very cordial relationship with the SP of the district. This aroused their suspicion more. The SP was after them to stop their 'criminal' activities. He had taken some young cadre of Naxalites to Bangalore city and killed them in encounters there. This angered them a lot. In his personal discussions with Poojamma the Naxalite leader found out that Poojamma was fully aware of such encounter killings and expressed her inability to stop police from doing what they planned to do.'

'Since Poojamma also frequented the same villages from where they had recruited many of their cadres and such young people were killed in encounters their suspicion that she was a police informer grew rapidly and they decided to put an end to the life and mission of Poojamma. Now it was left to police to find out how they hatched the plot to murder Poojamma.'

'It was quite unfortunate that many in the public consumed these stories put out by the duo of Dinesh and Eeranna. They were gullible public who tended to consume what suited their taste most. The story looked quite convincing. The SP immediately called for a meeting of all his officers and demanded that they look into this angle of the story in a serious manner. He also told them that it would add to the credibility of State Police if they came out with exact truths of the murder before the Central government decided to order the Central Agency to do a thorough investigation.'

CHAPTER SIXTEEN

'Two days after I reached the US Kala wrote to me to inform that the postmortem report of Poojamma had arrived.

"Dear Nina

We have been going through a period of turmoil ever since you left us. It was very difficult for me to even think that you would not be with me in this period of extreme difficulty. Thank you for coming for the funeral of our Amma and for spending those precious extra days with us. Your presence helped all members of our team and we miss you.

Coming to brass-tacks, let me inform you that the postmortem report of Poojamma's has arrived. It very clearly says that Poojamma had already died a few minutes before the supposed car crash. Shrapnel other than wreckage of the car had pierced her body. Though there was not a big gap between her death and car crash it is a significant indicator that she did not die out of any car crash as we were made to believe till now. There seems to be a truth in what Chikkanna and Nagaraj have been saying.

The other report of the post mortem of the driver's body also corroborates this report. It clearly says that the driver was not rash in his driving. He had first died and then the car crashed. His body too was pierced by similar shrapnel that were very similar to those in the body of Poojamma.

Going by these reports it becomes imperative to conclude that Poojamma and the driver were done to death by a bomb blast in the car. Police are of the opinion that someone had planted a bomb in Poojamma's car when she was in the village function.

Police are still supporting the story floated by Dinesh and Eeranna that it was the Naxalites who blasted the car. However, the top guy among Naxalites has given a press statement that Naxals had nothing to do with bombing of Poojamma. They have even asserted that they admire the great and noble work done by her and that such work deserved much international adulation and it was unfortunate that such a good work had been rewarded with murder. You must know that if Naxalites are the real killers they usually own it up claiming public responsibility for killing of someone. Unlike politicians they do not deny their responsibility.

All of us are inclined to believe that the killers are still at large and that a professional investigation should be conducted to find out real culprits. In the meantime many of us have been devastated by the fact that our beloved Amma has been felled. We refuse to buy the theory that bombs of the Naxalites assassinated her. The present Naxalite leader is a very good person. He eliminates only those who have become eternal pests in society.

Missing you much

Yours
Kala"

'I was in a state of shock for a few days after hearing this news of assassination. What a way to face death by a saint. She knew no guile in her heart and nurtured no grudge against anyone. Yet there were people who wanted to kill her and succeeded in their fiendish design. Why would anyone want to kill a person as innocent as Poojamma was? It was not because Poojamma did any harm to them on her volition. It was simply because her goodness was dispelling the evil that was the bedrock of operation of many evil men. If they became good their existence would reach its nadir. They were afraid of the end of their evil existence. They enjoyed it to the full and whoever took upon herself the mission of minimizing evil on earth will have to go through the process of gradual elimination. In Poojamma's case, since she was the epitome of goodness there was no possibility of any gradual elimination. She had to be done away with in toto. Before I could reconcile myself to the idea of the brutal murder of Poojamma there was another letter from Kala. It was a very depressing one.'

"Dear Nina

Thank you for such a sweet reply to my previous mail. All of us were happy to read some consoling words from you. However, there is much worse news from our side. You may not have expected this. I had been several times to meet the Home Minister of the state. In the beginning he welcomed me well but as days passed by I could see a casual indifference in him towards the investigation of the murder of Poojamma. Indifference turned into irritation. I was aghast at the callousness of bureaucrats when they realized that the Home Minister was refusing to meet me in person. Now we are officially informed that the Home Ministry of the state has refused to request central government for an official enquiry by the independent Central Agency. This is a big blow to our efforts to get to the roots of truth.

Chikkanna and Nagaraj are bent on going into streets to demand an official enquiry by the Central Agency. If this does not happen, they are threatening us that they would murder Dinesh and Eeranna. I think Chikkanna has developed a personal animosity towards Eeranna and he somehow wants to take revenge on him. They make use of their love and affection for Poojamma as an easy excuse to let their negative steam out. This is very rewarding for them, as people begin to appreciate their anger as unquestionable loyalty to Poojamma. For me it is very difficult to argue with them. They have as much right to manifest their affection and love for her in a way they deem fit as I have. It will be too arrogant on my part to expect them to behave in a uniform way. However, I wish that they distinguished between the personal and the professional.

Now that the state government has decided not to hand over investigation to the Central Agency the question of establishing justice vis-à-vis Poojamma's murder becomes highly questionable. We have had such wonderful relationship with bureaucrats of government and now all that nurturing that Poojamma did seems to go into the drain. The state government has also decided to entrust the task of investigation with its own state agencies. This adds to the already existing level of doubts in the minds of our followers that ultimately justice may not only be delayed but also it may be denied. It is unfathomable for me why the state government is taking such rigid stand and blocks a free and fair investigation.

It is a time when all of us feel quite helpless in the absence of Poojamma. I am afraid that the more the government delays the process the more will be the level of frustration that will set in the followers and that may lead to totally unanticipated consequences. What is very disturbing to all of us here is the propaganda by Dinesh and Eeranna that the bombs of Naxalites felled Poojamma. Their intentions are very clear. They want to implicate Poojamma with Naxalites and violence. This was something that she shunned. Even when she was alive they tried to do this to her. Now they know that she can never come back to challenge them. They are emboldened to do it with more vigor. I think she had once explained to you her position vis-à-vis Naxalites in one of our previous struggles.

I do not know how to end this mail. I am utterly confused. I shall close this here.

Yours confused
Kala"

—∞•●•∞—

'Kala's letter reminded me of an earlier incident in the life of Poojamma. I had failed to understand the intricacies of politics at the time she explained it to me. But after her death when Kala explained what transpired in her life, this became clear. Much before Poojamma came in direct contact with the Naxalite leader there was the murder of a caste man in Kempanahalli. It was a village with more than 100 houses of dominant caste people and only 40 houses of Dalits. The biggest landlord in the village was Krishnappa. He had more than 100 acres of land and was still in the habit of grabbing land from Dalits. Every year during monsoon he would enter lands of Dalits and begin to plough them unannounced. If Dalits resisted he would physically lay his hands on them. Police would not go to the help of Dalits, as Krishnappa was a very powerful landlord in the region. Moreover he had his caste identity as his greatest support.'

'The 'dalam', which means the local unit of Naxalites met together and decided to give a serious warning to Krishnappa about his wayward ways. They sent repeated warning to him asking him to stop his headstrong ways. But he would not bother about them at all. He thought that he was above the law of the land and was emboldened by the fact that Naxalites would never come out in the open to take legal action against him. He went on unchallenged for quite some time. Then he began to lay his hands on women of the Dalit community. Dalits were unable to resist his forays into the personal life of their women. Initially he started assaulting women in the darkness of evening. It was the time when women went into the fields to answer call of nature. He used to capture them in pitch darkness and force them to have sex with him. Later he began to frequent houses of Dalits at night and had sex with women and girls in families. He would somehow force husbands to sleep in the houses of neighbors and would spend the entire night with their wives. Dalit men were frightened of the big sickle that he carried with him. Little did they understand that it was because Krishnappa was frightened that he carried a weapon always with him. Later it became a habit with him to go to one Dalit house every night. Occasionally he would stay back home to also play with his wife. During the day he would meet his victim of the day and make sure that she did not have her periods. There were frequent quarrels in his house in the beginning stages of this anomaly. But he would invariably beat up his wife and threaten to kill her. She gradually got reconciled to the fact that she had a bad husband and that it was her fate to live with such a son of a bitch.'

'Men took up this issue once again with Naxalite dalam. They used to meet Yettiramulu at night. Police were in hot pursuit of Naxalites and Dalits became Naxalite informers. When police approached the village they would send signals to Naxalites to escape from the region. After many warnings and much patience the dalam decided to put an end to the woes of Dalit men and women by exterminating Krishnappa. Recruitment of young people of the village became inevitable in order to execute the operation. Yettiramulu drew a map of the village and explained the strategy to the young people. He asked them to carefully study all movements of Krishnappa at night. Starting from his house his movements to different places had to be carefully observed. He would not follow the same route every day. There would be occasions, even if they were rare, when he changed his route. They needed to be carefully studied. Timings of his movements had to be watched. The speed that he took at different streets needed observation. When he entered a particular Dalit house his own caution about not being seen needed to be observed. Behavior of other caste men and women was significant to watch. Yettiramulu educated them on all these intricacies and slowly unfolded to them his blueprint to extricate their community from all such intricacies weaved by Krishnappa.'

'Yettiramulu himself had to be careful with his ward. Not all of them were equally committed nor were they equally capable. He had to distribute responsibilities to each one according to each one's aptitude. There was the queer case of a very strong and robust young man who was also equally committed to the liberation of his people. However, he was given easily to excessive drinking. While all comrades appreciated his commitment and thought that he was their frontline leader, Yettiramulu dismissed him from the dalam itself saying that he would hardly be able to put his trust on anyone who was given to compulsive drinking. He could turn out to be a betrayer at any time. He could blurt out any secret planning of the dalam in a drunken mood. He could easily lead police to their hideout without knowing that police were following him.'

'There were two streets in the area where Dalits lived. The entrance and exit to each street had to be covered by two men. When the first attack took place Krishnappa would naturally run in a direction, which he saw closer in order to hide himself. Or he could also run in the direction of the main village of the caste area so that he would get support from his relatives and caste friends. Therefore, entrance to the caste area had to be carefully covered so that he did not even go anywhere near his area. All had to keep silent in all places and only concentrate on following him for short distances. He should not be allowed to run far. There were two gaps between houses in each street. These gaps were identified as the most likely route of his escape. Boys had to be placed in those places to hack him and kill him instantly without giving him much of a chance to move into the next main street. If he was not felled in the first strike and started running for cover those who stood at the entrance and at the exit of the streets should converge on him in such a way that he would be led to the gaps in between houses at the center of the streets. That was the most likely place to finish him off.'

'The final phase of planning was very intensive and was done in camera. No one from the village was allowed anywhere near the meeting. Yettiramulu gave good food to the cadre. Alcoholic drinks were strictly prohibited. The type of dress they had to wear, the type of weapons each one should possess and the final signal for the end of the mission etc. were finalized. Yettiramulu also instructed them on the routes each one should take to arrive at a particular place in the neighboring hillock after successful completion of the operation.'

—⚬✳⚬—

'And finally the 'D' day arrived. The 'executioners' moved about casually as did all villagers. They did not show any sign of being on a special mission. Each one ate in his house and took up his assigned position. No one in respective homes could suspect anything amiss. As usual Krishnappa went into the house of one Dalit. After a long time two of them went behind that house and began to speak a little loud. That aroused the suspicion of Krishnappa that he would be caught red-handed in the house with the woman. Therefore, he covered his face with his towel and began to make a quick exit. He was wearing only a half trouser. He had to rush with his usual job. His body sang its own song even in that situation. He did not want let go of the opportunity. In a terrible hurry, of course! All that he needed was a little orgasm. He had a compulsive need for sex. Therefore, he used to have two or three in a night depending on the attractive bodies of Dalit women.'

'The two men anticipated this and were waiting at the side of the door of the house. As he came out he could not see them. His face was covered with towel. The two men rushed to force their weapons at his throat. But they did not anticipate the fast reflexes of Krishnappa. He intuitively knew the presence of men near him and ducked instinctively. Attempt number one failed miserably. Krishnappa shouted: "they are killing me. I am finished. Oh god save me" and began to run for cover. As soon as he bellowed from his deep throat men from both sides of the street converged on him and as they planned he ran to the gap in the middle of the row of houses in order to escape to the next street. They speeded up his fate and even as he entered the gap the two men standing there in fine anticipation thrust the sharp edges of their sickle across his throat. Krishnappa fell in two pieces. The end of a man and his evil deeds!'

'Early next morning there was a big wailing all over the village. It started in the Dalit area with women shouting in utter fear and shock of seeing a dead body in their area. They did not even recognize that it was their worst enemy who was lying in two pieces signifying the end of their indignity and exploitation. The entire family of Krishnappa and his caste group took no time to rush there and to take away his corpse to their area. Krishnappa's wife was happy but pretended to be shocked and wailed loud not to raise anybody's suspicion. His sister however, ran helter-skelter and shouted her life out crying for revenge. She sent her brothers to near and far villages where her relatives lived and in a few hours set fire to all the houses of Dalits. One man killed! Forty houses burned to ashes! Collective punishment for individual crime! A three thousand years old pattern repeated religiously!'

'News spread far and wide, both of the killing and of the burning of houses. Two in one! The media made a big hype about the killing. Human rights outfits made a hue and cry about burning of houses. All vied with one another to be big statement makers. There was not a single individual who went alone to Kempanahalli for fear of being attacked either by Naxalites or by caste forces. They made it a point to visit the village only in groups. They were very busy giving press statements.'

'The first one to rush to Kempanahalli was Poojamma. She cared a damn about caste fellows and their anger. Seeing a large contingent of police Krishnappa's relatives took to their heels and pitched their tent in unknown places. Top police officers that rushed to Kempanahalli saw Poojamma there and greeted her in the midst of tensions. One of them went to Poojamma and walked with her for some time. The officer then picked up courage to tell her the truth that he had buried in his heart for some time. "I have been in many places in such crisis situations. Generally NGO leaders flee from villages when such major disasters visit people among whom they work. They return only after making sure that there would be no physical danger to them. But you, Madam, you are the first one to be in such places. It is an extraordinary courage. No wonder that people love you so much." Poojamma was not much excited about such adulations at that moment of difficulty for her people. She only mumbled to the officer: "It does not need extraordinary courage to be with my people when they are in such difficult situation." And she kept walking.'

'Poojamma pitched her tent in Kempanahalli for two weeks. She mobilized her leaders as well as contributions from different generous hearts to erect temporary sheds, to buy clothes, utensils, provisions, grains etc. so that Dalits whose houses were razed to ground could live in the village and eat, so that children could be looked after well in such turbulent time. She had nothing to hide and no one to fear. The state government gave as much relief as was legally possible and was also out to catch the culprits. Contributions from private individuals poured in. Poojamma saw the spring deep inside a hard rock. She never lost hope about anything. After settling the people of Kempanahalli to meet their basic needs Poojamma got to work on permanent solutions to their problems.'

'Many of their sons were arrested by police for the murder of Krishnappa. More than lack of food, parents were highly worried about the future of their children. Many of them were innocent and had nothing to do with the murder itself. All of them liked Yettiramulu. But that was no reason for police to castigate them, as if they were from an alien land. Almost all young boys above the age of 20 were arrested and put in jail. The new SP seemed to have gone through some mechanical training without bothering about execution of justice.'

'Poojamma contacted some conscientious lawyers and organized them to fight for bail for the young people. Lawyers too were mechanical. They only wanted their fees and cared a damn about who was guilty and who was not. They had a highly stereotyped paradigm. Everyone had a right to be defended. This was their paradigm. There was no possibility of effecting a shift in this paradigm. Beneath the paradigm was the huge fee that they collected from real culprits. When they knew that someone was a real culprit they put up their price. Some of them even threatened the culprits that they would expose them if they refused to cough out the money that they demanded. It was difficult to make out who was a worse criminal between the defender and the defended.'

'Poojamma was different. They shuddered to play their 'lawyer 'game with her. She identified three among them who were ready to argue for bail to all the young people without taking any fee. That was a big measure of her success among people.'

'To her great surprise and to the shock of the town, the judge granted bail to all young people at one go despite the hardest efforts by state government to oppose bail to 'Naxalites'. Poojamma did not want to condemn young people to hell already when they were alive by branding them as Naxalites. The city wore a very gloomy look. The sister of Krishnappa was spitting venom at the legal system of the country. She swore that she was ready to do anything to avenge the death of her brother. Police cared a hoot about her threats. They felt she had a legitimacy to spit venom. There was anticipated celebration in Kempanahalli as well as in Poojamma's place. She tried to downplay celebrations as much as she could. But it was beyond her control.'

'It was also beyond her emotional and rational control when it came to the question of where the young people released on bail should go. Poojamma insisted that they should have festive meal in her place and spend the entire night with her before they went home to meet their parents. Little did she realize that the boys had already decided that home mattered very little to them in the face of what she had done to them and to their people during their dwelling in jail. Both jelled well. The young peopled headed straight to Poojamma's place where they were given a royal welcome with drum beating, garlanding and dancing. They were treated to a very sumptuous meal. Poojamma was keen that they should spend a lot of time with her explaining to her their life in jail.'

'Anand kick started the sharing in his very deep voice.' "We thought jail was a place for punishment in order to correct criminals. We thought that jails are meant for preventing crime. But we found that many criminals enjoyed life in jail. We also understood that jails are virtual breeding ground of crime. If criminals had the right type of money and influence with jailers they could have anything they wanted except women within the walls of jails. But even that was not denied to them. The more influential among them escaped for selected nights from jails and came back in the morning. The next day it would be a common talk among many about their sexapades. We were beaten up in the first two days. But when jailers came to know that we were in a big group and were suspected of being Naxalites their respect for us increased manifold."

Kiran intervened to say: "It was not respect for any of us. It was simply fear that overpowered them when they came to know that if we informed our leaders they would be done to death. They were ready to give us anything that we wanted. They were shocked to know that we were very disciplined without drinking and womanizing. Their idea of Naxalites went through a total transformation. They could not make out who among us was a real Naxalite and who was a mere supporter. At times they thought that we were all murderers and at times they thought that we were all implicated by police to save their own skins."

Ramesh chipped in: "Some times ministers visited the jail and had secret meetings with several criminals. There were many gangs of criminals within jail and there were frequent quarrels among them. They were conducting their business of supari killing staying safe in jail. Their enemy gangs would have butchered them ruthlessly if they were out in the world. Sometimes ministers fabricated criminal cases against them only to protect them from murderous attacks on them by their rival gangs. Jail is a world of its own. It is not a correction center of crime. Instead it is often the breeding center of criminals. Thank you Poojamma for having liberated us from that filthy world of criminals. We are now ready to lay down our lives for the sake of our people. We are more determined to work for the liberation of our people. We have seen the worst of life now and are now more determined to pursue the cause that our leader Yettiramulu taught us."

"We do not want you to get into any sort of trouble because of us. You are legally safe now because we have obtained bail. But you can never trust the police. They could arrest you anytime for having supported us. Be safe Madam. You are very precious to our people. What we do in hiding you can do in the open. That makes a world of difference and this difference is very important for our women and children." This was Anand once again.

'Poojamma was visibly moved by the manifestation of their commitment. She wished her leaders in the Movement could be half as committed as they were. India could be transformed into a nation of justice for the poor. But alas such committed young people were often criminalized and had to languish in isolated existence. She let them go to sleep as she carefully observed their faces longing for the much neglected sleep. She was a bundle of conflicting emotions in her bed. While the rest of the world was sleeping she was fully awake thinking of problems it faced. She regretted that she did not make a choice to be one like them. The corrupt systems in her country demanded radical transformation in favor of the poor. She legitimized her choice to herself and got convinced that not all could be doing the same thing with the same approach. Naxalites were extraordinary beings. But the element of compulsive drive could be very disastrous to even well-meaning people.'

'Early next morning, the youngsters were full of ebullient life. They had a mobile talk with their leader Yettiramulu who told them that they were in the right place. He praised Poojamma in the superlative. All of them touched her feet and got her motherly blessings even as they were bidding farewell to them. None of them realized at that time that soon after that each one of them would be caught by police individually, taken to Bangalore and shot dead one by one in the name of encounter. Flushing the society so that the rich may be liberal in their exploitation of the poor!'

—◦◦◦|◦|◦◦◦—

'Dinesh and Eeranna knew this well. Even the SP knew this. But he considered that Poojamma was within her legal limits and appreciated her highly for the work she did in Kempanahalli. On the one side was the execution of law and on the other side was Krishnappa who cared a hoot about any law. What he made was law in that village and no one could dare to question him including the implementers of law. His own men clandestinely took the side of Krishnappa for the crumps that he threw under the table. The SP knew that Poojamma would not do anything against law and above all against her own conscience, which was a refined and cultured one. When he heard from Poojamma that Yettiramulu was willing to surrender his happiness knew no bounds. He did not want to kill him in any encounter nor did he want to put him in jail for the rest of his life. He knew that if that happened the courts might hand him over a death sentence. That would be an unjust reward for a great man who fought for justice all his life. He transferred the inspector who sacrificed the lives many young lives in the altar of 'encounter'. That was all that he could do. Nor could he wipe out the tears of Poojamma when she heard that her pet boy Anand was also murdered by police.'

'Kala translated and quoted to me from the dairy of Yettiramulu, written in Telugu. "My eyes are shedding tears of blood today. One by one all my boys have been done away with. I have never seen such cruelty even in people like Krishnappa. My boys killed only one man who was taking law into his hands. This was something that the State had to do. When they failed to protect law we took the responsibility of administering justice and taught the infidel bastard a fitting lesson. But police have demonstrated that they are a law unto themselves. I am at loss to understand where in the Constitution 'encounter' is approved. Having lost all my boys, being unable to come out in the open and being fragile in my failing health I have no other option in my life but to surrender to police and accept whatever law decides as my fate. Tonight I have a strong feeling in my inner being that I am taking the right decision and I shall approach Poojamma to negotiate my surrender to police. Who else can be a more fitting person than Poojamma herself to negotiate my formal integration into the larger society?"

'Poojamma explained everything to the SP and got his permission to welcome him in her place secretly and work out terms and conditions of his surrender. The SP was extremely happy. Visits of Yettiramulu to

Poojamma's place became more frequent. 'Pot breaking while the milk is boiling!' Just when everything was going according to plan Poojamma was violently taken away. Five days after I left India Kala informed me that there was news in media that Yettiramulu had surrendered in presence of the SP. But the truth was that a special squad of police arrested Yettiramulu when he had gone stealthily to the funeral of Poojamma. The SP knew that he would go for the funeral by all means. Therefore, he had prepared a trusted squad to arrest him equally stealthily. He was whisked away to a secret place and another plan was hatched with him for his surrender in public. The SP got an immediate promotion in his ranks.'

—∞◦Ю◦∞—

I wrote a second letter to Kala in the following manner. "Dear Kala, Thank you for all the news that you have given. Many missing links are now falling in place. I am sad to know that the state government has turned down your appeal for recommending investigation by a central government agency. Now I have decided to take up issues from my end here. I shall do all that I can to bring the truth out and bring the guilty to books. Justice should be established in the case of Poojamma. On your part please keep me informed of all developments there."

'After writing this letter to Kala I went to the Indian Embassy in New York and asked them if they could help me to get in touch with the right bureaucrat in India who could order an investigation into the murder of Poojamma. They excused themselves saying that the issue did not come under their roles and responsibilities and that I should get in touch with the government of India directly. As I left the Indian Embassy a bit depressed one of the officers in the embassy met me outside and took me aside. He was not a high-ranking officer. He informed me that he was a Dalit working in the Embassy and knew Poojamma well through media. He was a secret admirer of such great woman. He said what the embassy officials told me was correct. They would not be able to do much in this case as the murder took place in India. He suggested that I met the Secretary of State in the US and discussed with her the entire story of Poojamma's murder. He also suggested that I met her with a written request to take up the question of formal investigation by a central government Agency in India through diplomatic channels. He also revealed to me with a glee that an official visit of the Secretary of State was scheduled within the next one month and that I should really rush to meet her. A new hope was born in me. My depression vanished like the early morning due that lived to welcome the sun but opts to disappear as soon as he arrives. I walked back to my apartment ruefully.'

'Meeting the Secretary of State of the US was a Himalayan task. I knew the difficulty well, as I was a journalist. Unless I plotted something to do that it would never become a reality. In one of my casual conversations with Jenny who also had met Poojamma once earlier I expressed my difficulty to her. Jenny was the General Editor of the 'Daily News' in the US. It was a very famous newspaper in the US both for its hard copy as well as Internet editions. It commanded great respect among American citizens as well as among politicians. Jenny blamed me for not having informed her of the death of Poojamma for this long. I apologized profusely saying that I was devastated myself and was in need of comfort zones and spaces to overcome my difficulty. When I told Jenny that Poojamma was actually massacred she could not believe her ears and took a few minutes to recover from her state of shock. From the Embassy I headed straight to her office. She took me out of the office immediately to give me a cup of coffee and talk things over. I explained to her the entire scenario lucidly and she was seriously concerned about bringing out the truth of the murder of Poojamma.'

'More than being General Editor Jenny was a schemer. She had to scheme many things to scoop stories from people of different kinds. She had developed an expertise in designing plots and executing them without giving the least suspicion that she was up to some genuine ruse. We were very close friends and I knew for sure that she would never turn down my request at any time in her life. An additional advantage for me was that she knew well my relationship with Poojamma and was fully empathetic. She kenw well that I was not just a journalist for Poojamma. My emotional vibes with Poojamma transgressed many beaten boundaries of journalisting ethics. In one of my trips to India she also maneuvered an official trip to India and met Poojamma. She returned to India as a great fan of Poojamma's. Since she was busy with her career she did not carry her fan following too far into the territory of Poojamma's. However, whenever I met Poojamma the first things she would enquire was about Jenny and it always happened also with Jenny.'

'She talked to her boss in the newspaper office and made it look authentic that she wanted to interview the Secretary of State for the paper on the struggle in the Indian Parliament about Foreign Direct Investment in India. Opposition parties in India wanted to pin down the ruling party on this issue and topple the government by asking for a discussion in the Parliament with voting. The ruling party fumbled with its knee jerk reaction and made many decisions without taking into confidence even leaders in its government. Jenny found this issue as a very important one for an interview with the Secretary of State. She called up the office and fixed up an appointment. She also made it a point to make the appointment for her assistant, who was myself.'

The interview took place as planned. The Secretary of State was surprised that there were only a few questions on the issue of Foreign Direct Investment in the Indian Parliament. It was such an important issue for the US government. Jenny was quick enough to inform her that there was another issue related to India and asked me to explain the entire situation with the murder of Poojamma and the reluctance of the State government to probe into it professionally. I had very carefully packed with visuals and written documents that I handed over to Jenny. She in turn gave them to the Secretary of State. At the very first perusal the Secretary of State was quite impressed at what she saw and read. She called her secretary and asked her to give a brief of the documents and visuals that evening. She assured Jenny that she would ask the US Ambassador in Delhi to speak to the concerned authorities in India and do something.'

'The Secretary of State took aside Jenny and sprang a surprise on her. "This is for your private consumption. Do not write in the papers what I am going to say to you now. I am going to India at the insistence of the German government and not exactly to assist the Indian government on FDI. Pramila, the daughter of Poojamma has worked overtime with the German Chancellor and convinced her that adequate pressure should be applied on the Prime Minister of India to take up enquiry into the death of Poojamma very seriously at the top most levels. The German Chancellor spoke to the President of the US and he has asked me to speak to the Indian Prime Minister personally. This is the secret of my visit to India this time. Therefore, do not worry about the investigation. The Indian Prime Minister will do everything possible to please the President of the US. You do not have to apply any more pressure on any one. Tell your assistant to be calm about this case. Please do not let the cat out of the bag prematurely."

'I did not inform Kala of what happened between both of us and the Secretary of State lest Kala spoke about it in India. That could spoil our chances of an impartial probe. I also asked Kala not to precipitate matters for the time being by taking up to streets in protest. Chikkanna and Nagaraj were very keen on doing that. Jenny informed me of the private conversation she had with the Secretary of State only much later when an official investigation was ordered. Jenny was pleasantly shocked to know that Poojamma had a daughter who was the German Ambassador. I admired the diplomatic skills of Pramila. There was no doubt in my mind that she was a genius. Kala replied back to say that Chikkanna and Nagaraj were convinced of the need to be silent for sometime leaving matters to me. Anything foreign was more powerful in the mindset of Indians. They were not alone in this. In my visit to other places in India I found this true in most people I met. Most Indians operated from an inferiority complex with regard to White people. Such a complex came out often as arrogant manifestations of innate inadequacy.'

'The visit of the Secretary of State to India was a much hyped event especially in view of the approval the Indian government got for FDI. Authorities in the US thought that the government was on the verge of a fall. That did not happen. They were very happy. A day after she left for the US there was news in Indian media that the Central government had ordered for an impartial investigation by its own Agency that would work independently of both the State and the Central government. TVs and Newspapers flashed the news across the country, as the assassination of Poojamma had shaken many sections of Indian society. Most editorials of national dailies welcomed the decision of the Indian government. Both Jenny and I knew that the Secretary of State had done her job quietly without making a fuss. Jenny called up her office and thanked her profusely for this extraordinary gesture.'

'Kala chose to ring me up this time instead of writing to me emails. There was hyper excitement in her voice. The euphoria of success had pervaded every word of hers. I had to hide my excitement carefully. I did not want anyone to know that I was behind all this. I also did not want the name of Pramila to float in the air unnecessarily. I promised to Kala that I would soon be with them to celebrate the victory. Many things took place in India after this to comply with jurisprudence. I shall now go to sleep with the satisfaction of having achieved what I could in the best interest of justice along with the strenuous efforts of Poojamma's worthy daughter Pramila.'

CHAPTER SEVENTEEN

The state government was completely in a state of stupor about the sudden turn of events. They could not do anything about it. Their credibility would suffer much if they chose to oppose the move of the Central government for an impartial investigation. Intellectuals and academicians began to write many articles about the investigation as the need of the hour. According to most of them it was a good precedent to be set for future governments. Chikkanna and Nagaraj were literally dancing on the streets. Kala was very happy that there was a ray of hope to dispel doubts in the minds of many people. They were still confused whether the murder was by Naxalites, as put out by Dinesh and Eeranna or if it was an accident, as the police made it out first.

The Central Agency was given strict orders that they were dealing with a rather high profile case and that they should complete the job of investigation within 6 months. But they took only four months to submit their report. Kala got a copy of the report and sent a long mail to me.

Before getting hold of the copy of the report, Kala had sent me many mails about the different steps that the Central Agency was taking. The first thing they did was to go to the place of Poojamma and speak to Kala, Chikkanna, Manjula and Nagaraj together as a group and then to each one of them individually. They asked them to narrate what actually took place on the day of assassination.

Poojamma started off as usual. She got ready and got into the car without any difference in her behavior. She was alone to go to the village. Chikkanna and Nagaraj had gone to the village the previous evening and made preparations for Poojamma's visit. This was their routine. The Agency asked to recall all the people who were present in the meeting. Manjula clearly recollected two young people who had come in a motorbike. They even met Poojamma at the end of the meeting. When Poojamma asked them from where they had come they said casually that they had heard a lot about her and wanted to listen to her. Therefore, they came from the city all the way for the function. For Poojamma this was a very ordinary happening. In every village that she visited there used to be always young people of all hue and cry.

It was then that the officers asked Manjula to identify the young people from her memory and she fumbled totally. She herself got frightened and was scurrying for words. But she mentioned that she had seen both of them on previous occasions too in villages when Poojamma made her speeches. Kala remembered all of a sudden that Kiran had taken photos of the function that day and had handed over the camera to her. Since Poojamma was assassinated on her way back no one ever cared to look at the photos. The officers pounced on this treasure trove. They asked Kala to hand over the camera to them. Since it was a digital cameral they went through the pictures again and again. They confiscated the camera and took it away.

Photos of the two young men were flashed across the country to all police stations. It was only a question of time before both the young people were arrested from Kolkata and were taken to Delhi for further investigation. It became evident that both of them were hired for the assassination of Poojamma. When everyone was busy with the function in the village the driver had locked the car and went to the public meeting where Poojamma was addressing village people. The duo opened the car with false keys and locked themselves up in the car. Since it had tinted glasses no one could make out what was happening inside. When Poojamma's speech reached a crescendo they went beneath the car and planted a bomb that would blast when it hit something or other. They had carefully chosen the spot for the accident to take place. It had to be open on the sides of the road so that if there was a need to escape it should be easily possible.

It was a big network and all arrangements were made through secret codes and telephone calls. They came a few months early and had conducted dry runs in village meetings of Poojamma's. They also picked up some broken Kannada in order to communicate with locals. Now it became evident that the villager who crossed the road suddenly did not do it by accident but by design. He had done that once again later and was killed on the spot by a truck. Local police passed it off as an accidental death and wrote the case off with out of court settlements with the owner of the truck. The two young people revealed that the man was paid heavily to cross the road when Poojamma's car came. But in order to wipe out evidences he was killed in the same spot under same circumstances. When the vehicle swerved and hit a tree the bomb blasted and killed both Poojamma and the driver on the spot. The post mortem report was cooked up to misguide investigators and show that the bomb had blasted off much before the car hit the tree so that it became easy for local police to blame Naxalites.

It was a very strenuous effort on the part of Police to establish true identity of persons who helped Dinesh and Eeranna to hire services of killers who were professional and meticulous in their operations. They reframed the story from what was spilt by actual killers. But it was only partial till the arrest of the kingpin.

"Sir, we have a daunting task on our hands. All evidences we have gathered point out to a big mafia lord in Karnataka who has multiple operations." The chief of the investigation team appraised the Central Agency's Chief de Affairs.

"Arrest him. Do not look at faces. Whoever is instrumental in killing is a criminal in the face of law. No sympathies please!" The chief was not a mean person. He meant serious business.

"No sir. There are problems. The kingpin of the mafia is a big politician-cum-businessman in Karnataka and we need permission of the Governor to arrest him. He is a minister in the government of Karnataka. This has to be done very carefully. Even if he gets a small clue he will use all this political clout and power to destroy evidences that will lead to him. He has done that several times earlier." The lower level officer had pragmatic wisdom.

"Oh, you are right. I shall do everything possible to obtain permission from the Governor without bringing your investigation into picture at all. Just wait for some time. I shall get an appointment from the Governor. In the meantime, do not reveal this to anyone even in your own team." The serious warning was taken with all seriousness.

"Here you are. You have permission from the Governor of Karnataka to arrest the bastard minister." The Chief de Affairs called the chief of the investigation team and handed over written permission.

"Sir, how did you manage this in two days? It is a letter on the letterhead of the Governor with his original signature." The Chief de Affairs proved why he was sitting in that position.

"No questions please! Certain truths have to be imprisoned for eternity. This is one of them. Go and do your job well, as you have done till now." He sent off his junior with a smile that was extremely difficult to fabricate by anyone else.

Dinesh and Eeranna were together when police of the Central Agency went to arrest them. It was a rude shock to all local politicians that both of them had hired killers to finish off one of the finest flowers of human race. But then, this was not totally unanticipated. Dinesh had to immediately resign his MP seat after his arrest. Both of them were taken for police interrogation for a week.

"Senior Minister in Karnataka Government arrested on abetting murder!" The newspapers blew up the sensational news. Chikkanna and Nagaraj rushed to the nearest tollgate in their bicycles to get the newspapers. The news spread like wildfire. Followers of Poojamma were bundles of happiness, confusion and unknown fear as to what would happen next.

The Minister was having his usual evening party of political and business friends with heavy drinks. He was joking loudly about the 'two idiots who could not even plan an execution properly and got arrested. When police entered his den he was inebriated beyond his control. He began to shout his usual abuses at policemen asking them how they dared to enter his den without his permission. The officer slapped him in return and handed over the arrest warrant. All other politician stood up to protest his arrest and began to call up the Chief Minister. The CM was in total shock at the news. He had no clue on what was happening. He was however, happy about the arrest of the Minister but was unhappy that he was not informed earlier about the arrest. Even as they dragged the Minister out of his den the politician and businessmen friends blocked the way of police. The policemen took out their guns and shouted at them that they were armed with shooting orders if anyone stood on the way of taking the Minister to court. As soon as they saw the gun their spirits gave way. The Minister was taken in a car directly to a High Court judge in his residence. The judge remanded him to judicial custody and informed police that they should apply for police custody when the matter came up for hearing next day in the court. In his inebriated condition the Minister shouted abuses also at the judge and the police added an additional clause in their FIR later.

Police brought the threesome together for a rendezvous. Many truths began to tumble out of their cupboard without much resistance.

It was Mining Minister Venkatesh who sarcastically asked Dinesh one day in the residence of the Chief Minister. "What Bhaiya, you cannot even control the menace of an individual woman in your constituency? How do you plan to climb up the political ladder in such a situation? A private woman is creating so much of problem for you. What a bloody shame!"

"Anna, do not underestimate her power. She is not an individual. She is a world of her own. She has people with her. She is also very influential among bureaucrats and ministers. I am just helpless." Dinesh tried to measure Venkatesh before opening up fully.

"What yar, I have seen both people and bureaucrats. We are ministers in the government. You are an elected member of the parliament and you are still hesitant to tackle a bitch in your constituency. Tell me what you want to do with her. It can be done easily." Venkatesh invited him to have a look at his internal world. Dinesh grew in confidence of the strength of Venky, as many in political circles called him.

"What will you advise me to do in this situation? As long as she lives she will continue to be a major threat to my political career." Dinesh was still hesitant to come out fully into the open but opened the door more than half.

"See man, it is not my business to advice people. You should tell me what I should do to safeguard you in politics and my followers will do that. Tell me clearly without any hesitation what you want to do with her. If you are not bold enough even to tell me what you want to do with her then you forget about an upswing in your political career. You can as well go home and take refuge in the lap of your wife or give bath to your children." He was cutting like a sharp edged sword. Dinesh got up before he was felled and opened the door fully.

"I have no big options, Anna. She should be eliminated. I tried to send her away from my constituency. But she only got entrenched in the place. Now there is no other way except eliminating her physically. I do not know how to do it. If I am caught then that will also be the end of my career. Please show me some way." Dinesh tried to register Venky's sympathy.

"You go home peacefully man. Your Madam will not exist for more than two months. Do not ask for any details. It is my job. You pay me 5 million rupees when the job is accomplished. Bring 2.5 million rupees tomorrow if you trust me. If you do not bring money tomorrow you can just find your way. Forget about me after that. I do not need this money. You know it well. I can dig out money from my mines. I am the king under the earth. I sit on a golden chair and eat only on silver plates. Your money is equal to my shit. But there are many other things that are involved and I do not want to spend my money for a shit that you want me to remove."

Next day Dinesh was at the door of the house of Venky with a suitcase. It changed hands. Venky measured the amount of cash inside just by measuring its weight with his hand. He was so used to it. Within two months Venky executed his plans to perfection. But there was no way of hoodwinking the Central Agency. Venky gave a description of his underground links with illegal arms producing gangs in Kolkata and in Delhi. He could procure any arms from them at any time that he needed.

Once a particular operation was over they were ready to take back the weapon for a price that they fixed. Among them were some sharp shooters who could be contracted for killing any person. The killers did not mind whom they killed. Their rates differed from person to person depending on the weightage potential victims had in society. Besides sharp shooters they also had people who could plant bombs and destroy either eminent persons or many persons together.

In order to smuggle arms to different places Venky had invented an ingenious method. He would dismantle long weapons into three parts and pack all of them in large bags filled with chilly power. He would place the dismantled parts in such a way that no police dog would be able to sniff the metal inside the suitcase in which the bag of chilly powder was placed. The general mode of transportation was train where police would often come with their sniffer dogs. When the dogs could not smell the metal police would walk away without applying their metal detectors. Depending on the destination they would also transport by speedboats from the sea in Kolkata. All bags and boxes passed as finer quality of Indian spices. In case they were caught the bargain for bribe would be heavy through middlemen known to officers in all such cases and they would not care to know who the ultimate culprit was. It was enough that their fixed rates for different weapons as bribery reached either their table or their bank accounts or that suitcases were exchanged in bars. Generally they avoided bank transfers, as officers would not like to share their bank details unless the 'customer' was fool proof.

—◦◦◦🜚◦◦◦—

The criminal trinity was put in different jails and awaited trial in the court. Their repeated attempts to come out on bail failed. During the trial it had become evident that both of them would be hanged according to Indian laws. There was a large gathering in the court hall on the Day of Judgment after conviction. The judge had convicted the three of them and the next day would be the pronouncement of sentence. Just before adjourning the court the judge asked both lawyers if they had anything more to say. The defense lawyer stood up to say that he had nothing more to say. But the prosecution lawyer arguing on behalf of Poojamma's followers stood up to say that the judge should not hand over death sentence to the culprits though it was the rarest of rare cases. He argued that Poojamma stood against death sentence and was for the change of Indian law. She argued that no one had the right to take away the life of another person. Awarding death sentence to those who killed her would be travesty. It would be an ultimate insult to the 'rarest of rare' person in human history. The judge obliged the next day and handed them over imprisonment till the end of their lives.

A few lawyers and others surrounded the prosecution lawyer after the verdict and the court was adjourned for the day. They questioned him left and right as to who gave him the authority to plead for the deference of death sentence to the bastard killers of one of the noblest of human beings. The lawyer turned to Kala standing nearby and pointed to her. All of them looked at her with suspicion. She smiled at them and repeated Poojamma's words. "Taking away the life of another person is no one's right. If this right is given to human beings as a legal provision there will be no morality in society. The duty of the State is to protect the right to life of citizens and not to take it way. If some persons in society are beyond correction they can be isolated for life from the rest of society. But no one, including the State, can appropriate the right to kill another human being."

Kala then made her statement. "Come what may, it is my duty to fulfill the dreams of my mother Poojamma. We are here to perpetuate her mission and not to sabotage it. Our conscience is clear that we have done exactly what Poojamma would have done if she were alive." Saying this she walked away quietly to the car that was waiting to take her.

Dinesh and Eeranna marked the end of a chapter in dirty and revenge politics. They targeted an innocent woman because she was a woman, she was a Dalit, she was from a different region and they suspected that she was from a different religion. Their families were in tears when police whisked them away to jail never to return to the world. Kala turned back from the car and reversed her steps. She went near the family members of the three and consoled them. The wife of Eeranna hugged Kala repeatedly and showered her with kisses. "Thank you Kala for saving the life of my husband. I know he deserves death sentence according to our law. But you have spared his life just as our mother Poojamma would have done. Now I am happy that at least I can go and meet him in jail and live with the thought that he is living. Thank you for not making me a widow in this life. Thank you for not making my child an orphan. Many people think that in the death of Poojamma they have lost a treasure of life. But I think that in her death too Poojamma has left a much bigger treasure. You are our treasure that the great Poojamma has left for us. As if to compensate for all the evil that my husband has done to the poor of our area in the company of that motherfucker Dinesh, I have decided to join you in serving the poor. Please call me whenever you need me. I shall also come to your place and meet you. I am sure you are an exact replica of Poojamma. In leaving us Poojamma has not left behind a vacuum. Instead she has left for all of us a big treasure. That is you, my beloved Kala."

'Before I went to sleep I got a call from Kala informing me of all the developments and I appreciated her deeply for her persistence in upholding the values that she learned from Poojamma. I wrote to Kala immediately, greatly appreciating her for the strong stand that she took vis-a vis the death sentence of the culprits. All of us knew Poojamma and it would be a contradiction of spirits if someone were to be killed in her name.'

'It took a full year for the investigation and judgement to arrive. I was following closly the chain of events from the US. After I returned from the first anniversary of the death of Poojamma I decided to write the entire life and relationship with Poojamma and inform the rest of the world about such a great woman in human history. I need to now pack up for my next visit to India and join Kala to accord a grand welcome to Pramila who is on leave to spend a few weeks in Poojamma's place. I am sorry. Did I say Poojamma's place? Old habits seldom die. It is now Kala's place to carry forward the legacy of Poojamma.'